The Cliff Road Chronicles

Praise for Anne Fraser's Gideon Redoak

"...this impressive dark fantasy debut...introduces a stirring classic vampire...Fraser keeps the pages turning with brisk pacing and a thoughtful, sensitive portrayal of Gideon's struggles with Corbeau and his inner puritanical demons."
Starred Review

Publishers Weekly

"...an epic tale that few books accomplish...reminiscent of Anne Rice's vampire novels in that the story is gothic in nature and the timeline is vast. The romance in this book is very sweet and the sexual encounter described lovingly without explicit detail, which may appeal to a wide variety of readers...I recommend this book, especially for lovers of "old school" vampire novels."

Katie Seely, ParaNormalRomance.org

"*Gideon Redoak* may be the story of a vampire, but at its deepest level it is a story about the very human search for meaning and independence. Baron Gideon Redoak is a significant addition to the pantheon of literary vampires."

Elizabeth Miller, author of *Dracula: Sense and Nonsense*

The Cliff Road Chronicles

Tales of the Brotherhood of Darkness

Anne Fraser

Edited and with an Introduction by
Inanna Arthen

By Light Unseen Media
Pepperell, Massachusetts

The Cliff Road Chronicles
Tales of the Brotherhood of Darkness

Cover and interior design by Vyrdolak, By Light Unseen Media.

Hardcover Edition

ISBN-10: 1-935303-26-0
ISBN-13: 978-1-935303-26-8
LCCN: 2011929357

Published by
By Light Unseen Media
PO Box 1233
Pepperell, Massachusetts 01463-3233

Our Mission:
By Light Unseen Media presents the best of quality fiction and non-fiction on the theme of vampires and vampirism. We offer fictional works with original imagination and style, as well as non-fiction of academic calibre.

For additional information, visit:
http://bylightunseenmedia.com/

Printed in the United States of America

0 9 8 7 6 5 4 3 2 1

Contents

Gideon and Joshua: A Love Story

The Adventures of the Brotherhood of Darkness

Introduction

I first got to know Anne Fraser when I joined the Vampyres email list at the end of 1994. At that time, Vampyres List, whose original host at guvm.edu Anne immortalized in her story, "Vampire Conventions," was populated by dozens of avid amateur writers. They wrote and posted fiction of every length, from very short stories—what are now called "flash fiction"—to entire serialized novels. None of this was fanfic. Everyone invented their own characters and fictional universes, which varied in depth, complexity and derivation, but were original to the author. The list even voted on an annual "Golden Fang Award" for the best fiction posted during the year.

Anne was the shining star of the Vampyres List writers, by far the most prolific. She had several sets of established characters, and she was constantly posting stories ranging in length from two pages to novellas. *Gideon Redoak* was her only full novel, posted to the list in so many parts that it earned the nickname, "The Endless Saga." Anne exemplified the answer to that eternal question posed to writers: "where do you get your ideas?" Her stories often featured her characters riffing on news of the day or some discussion topic on the list. Almost anything could inspire her to dash off a piece featuring some of her "cast of dozens." She was fond of silly humor, outrageous puns, and ridiculous situations.

But writing was not simply a solitary pursuit for Anne. It was also one of her favorite social activities, and one to which she devoted enormous energy. A great deal of the fiction posted to Vampyres List was co-written, and no one coordinated and wrote more collaborative stories than Anne. She would write intensively with one partner at a time, or plot out a multi-author story with contributions by as many writers who wanted to join in. Everyone wanted to write with Anne, and she was somewhat choosy about her writing partners. I was one of the few who never co-wrote anything with her, not even as part of a group effort, although I made several proposals. I used to tease Anne that I always knew who her current online best friend was, because it would be whoever she was co-writing with most actively, particularly when certain of Anne's characters were involved. For the record, I'll note that Anne always vehemently denied this allegation.

Co-writing, on Vampyres List, reached its peak in the v-party (for "virtual party"). The premise was simple. The party host—and listmembers competed to hold these parties—set up a fictional party location, and usually a set of special conditions or situations to give the party writers something to work with. Since everyone was writing supernatural characters with all kinds of magical powers, the parties almost always had various magical gimmicks and traps. For three to seven days, twenty-four hours per day, party writers wrote and posted chapters describing events at the party—and just about *anything* could happen. A big party going full blast generated hundreds of e-mail posts. To participate fully, let alone host one, you had to be reading all those posts, keep track of the wildly careening plots, invent your own twists and reactions, and be able to write and post very fast. The biggest and best parties were mind-blowing. It was pure brainstorming, at top speed, non-stop, for days on end. For anyone who was really into writing, improvisational story-telling and bouncing ideas off other people, a v-party was, as I used to say, the most fun you could possibly have with both hands on a keyboard. One of the first v-parties that I participated in was hosted by Anne.

Unfortunately, v-parties were dependent on a large quorum of people who were all good writers and played well with others, and after a few years, Vampyres List ceased to have such a quorum. I actually hosted the last of the really big v-parties, in December 1996, and after that, they were much smaller and slower and gradually faded away. Not everyone was as sorry to see them go as Anne and I were. Vampyres List members also enjoyed extensive discussions of vampire-related topics and occasional sessions of a vampire trivia round-robin called Visceral Pursuit, and the list established rules limiting the duration and frequency of v-parties. As v-parties and fiction posting in general declined on the list, Anne joined several other email lists, such as Nightstalkers, Ghostletters, and Quillings, where she and other writers continued their collaborations.

Anne's characters tended to shift and change depending on who she was co-writing with at a given time. Sometimes she had second thoughts about changes she'd started to make in a character's canon and would go back and revise previously posted stories to eliminate them. In other cases, Anne rewrote earlier tales to make them consistent with fresh directions she was taking with new co-writers. But continuity, especially when it came to v-party plotlines, took second priority for Anne after accommodating her fellow writers and their ideas.

Anne inspired my writing more than any other direct influence I could name. Several of the characters and plot threads now critical to my own series of novels were invented for v-parties and fiction on Vampyres List, although they've changed a great deal from their initial form. I owe a huge debt to Anne's boundless enthusiasm for the sheer joy of creating stories and characters and sharing them freely.

As I edited Anne's stories, I kept in mind what I knew—because we'd had extensive discussions as we worked together on *Gideon Redoak*—about where she intended her characters and plotlines to be going, even if she hadn't had time to make those updates herself. Ray Griffin, for instance, had been evolving in a way that Anne decided to change, and I made some alterations in his stories in accordance with this. I deeply regret that I could not use much of Anne's more recent fiction, because it was co-written so tightly with other authors. I had the same problem with some of the fiction that covered major events in Gideon and Joshua's relationship. Their engagement party, wedding and reception were all multi-author productions, as was Joshua's "buying trip" in London alluded to several times in the stories in this volume.

Had Anne not passed away in 2008, the first section of this collection would most likely have become a novel in its own right and a sequel to *Gideon Redoak*. Anne would have been able to rework storylines from co-written fiction and fill in gaps that I simply could not. With Anne's help, the second section of stories could likely have been integrated into a cohesive frame, as well. But each piece was originally written as a stand-alone tale. I hope that Anne would be pleased with the way they're presented here.

Inanna Arthen
May 9, 2011

Gideon and Joshua
A Love Story

Club Undead
(1995)

Mail call!" Mitch came breezily into Oakwoods, holding a batch of envelopes out of the reach of Pumpkin, who was leaping up trying to grab those enticing items. "Get down, dog! There's no mail for you!"

Evan emerged from the kitchen and Joshua came downstairs from his office. Both looked expectantly at Mitch.

He grinned and began sorting the mail, after dumping his winter coat and boots sloppily on the hall floor. "Let's see...bill, bill, mail for the boss, mail for the boss, mail for me! Here's one for you, Josh. Your weightlifting mag, Ev. Bill, mail for the boss, another one for Josh, one for Evan...scented!" He waved the letter under Evan's nose and then sniffed it elaborately. "Gardenias? Lilacs? Deadly nightshade?"

"Give me that!" Evan grabbed for the letter and a scuffle ensued in which the remainder of the mail fell on the floor.

Pumpkin pounced, picking up a flashy brochure which had caught her eye. Warg gave her a wolfishly disgusted look.

Joshua gave Pumpkin a light swat on the tail section and rescued the brochure. "Children, stop it." He wiped doggie drool off the shiny pages that Pumpkin had coveted and looked at them curiously. "What on earth is this?"

Evan stopped whacking Mitch with the weightlifting magazine and came over to peer at the glossy paper in Joshua's hand.

"Advertising," the protector grunted. "Some travel agency."

"But it's addressed to Gideon."

"Some travel agency that doesn't know he's a vampire. Gideon's on quite a few upscale mailing lists, you know."

"I don't know, Evan. Look—most of these photos are night

scenes."

Mitch joined them, wanting to have a look, too. "Get a load of this!" He pointed to the inside front cover. "Club Undead!"

"What?" Joshua flipped the pages back. "That's what it says," he affirmed incredulously. "Club Undead. A unique vacation package catering to the special needs of the supernatural client. We offer a full line of services and facilities to suit your unlife-style. Club Undead gives you the vacation you need; whether a weekend getaway for some night skiing in the mountains, or a luxurious week of being pampered on our private Caribbean island. Our trained travel agents will assist you in booking to suit your special needs, so you can relax and not worry about the full moon catching you unawares. We offer a full range of activities, archery excluded."

Evan chuckled. "Wouldn't want to accidentally skewer one of their clients, now, would you?"

"A travel agency for vampires." Mitch shook his head. "And werewolves, too, I guess. That line about the full moon is aimed at us."

"A week of being pampered on a Caribbean island sounds pretty good." Joshua mused. "Gideon's so tense that it frightens me. We've been through a lot lately. I'm going to study this brochure more closely." He took it and his mail up to his office on the second floor.

Soon he was immersed in the section describing the Caribbean island. The services offered included massage, "special dietary needs fulfilled"—which Joshua interpreted, correctly, to mean they served blood—and complete security and privacy guaranteed. A wide range of activities was available, from a swimming pool and golf course through tennis, horseback riding, waterskiing and surfing. The brochure promised that no one would force you to participate in anything you didn't want to do. If your aim was to lie on the beach and vegetate for the duration of your stay, that was fine. Since all persuasions of supernatural critters were catered to, there was a large restaurant as well as snack counters and bars on the island. The main dining room offered music and dancing as well as food and drink.

Joshua threw caution to the wind and dialled the toll-free number.

"Travel agency, may I help you?" A woman's voice, with a soft Irish accent, answered.

"Ah, yes." Joshua coughed, wondering how to proceed. "I've been studying your brochure, and I have a couple of questions."

He could almost hear the woman on the other end sit up. "Which brochure would that be, sir?"

"The one for 'special needs' clientele."

"Very good, sir. Are you on a private line?"

"Yes, I am, and in an office where I can't be overheard."

"Excellent. Your name, sir?"

"Joshua Trevallion. The brochure was sent to my...good friend, Gideon Redoak. We...share a house."

"And what questions do you have about Club Undead, Mr. Trevallion? You may speak freely, we guarantee discretion. My name is Reagan. And Mr. Trevallion...sexual orientation is of no consequence to the Club. When we say discretion, we mean it."

"Thank you, that's good to know. I'm very tempted by your island in the Caribbean. Both Gideon and I have been through a very trying time lately, and I think a week on your island sounds like what we both need."

"The island is an excellent antidote for tension, Mr. Trevallion. Now, my file on Mr. Redoak shows that he is a vampire, which is how he got on our mailing list. No need to worry, sir, our files are absolutely confidential. But I have no information on you, Mr. Trevallion."

"That was what I needed to ask. I'm, well, at the moment, I'm still human. A breather. Is that a problem?"

"None at all, sir," she laughed. "Many of our clients travel with human companions. Your safety is guaranteed, your needs will be seen to by our trained staff, and there's a restaurant on the island that serves a variety of dishes. Should you wish companionship during the daylight hours, any of our staff will be delighted to be at your command—whether for tennis, golf, chess or just talking. I'm certain there will be other diurnal guests on the island at the time of your visit as well."

"It sounds wonderful. I'll have to talk Gideon into it, but I don't think that will be a problem. Thank you, Reagan. I shall definitely be calling back."

"Thank *you*, Mr. Trevallion, and we look forward to hearing from you."

Gideon woke up as the sun dropped slowly out of sight in the west. He sighed as he felt the tension tug on his back muscles, the ever-present headache grinding behind his eyes. The recent crises with Genevieve's serious illness, Joshua's grief and exhaustion after a buying trip to London with tragic consequences, the piling up of several corporate problems—all had taken their toll on the Baron. His temper was frayed. If he had been human, he likely would have been heading for a heart attack or a nervous breakdown. He felt like he was fairly close to the latter, anyway.

Not even his ritual evening bath had the power to relax him, nor did the cup of herbal tea Michael had recommended. Gideon knew that his friends were all concerned about him—more than one of the Brotherhood had lately dropped a hint about taking a vacation. His tension had caused problems in the bedroom, as well. Joshua had been spending a few nights on the cot in his office rather than share a bed with a bad-tempered vampire. Gideon couldn't blame him. He didn't even want to keep himself company.

He rose from the bath, towelled himself dry, and dressed slowly. A pile of work waited for him in his study. He wanted to chuck it all and go out with Joshua, try to recapture some of the charm of their early romance. Perhaps they could go back to that Italian restaurant...

The stern Puritan in Gideon (which sounded remarkably like the voice of his father) made him go into the study, pour himself a glass of his special stock, and go to work.

He was on the phone with his stockbroker when the study door opened and Joshua came in. Gideon briefly looked up, wondering what the glossy catalogue in his lover's hand was for, then went back to arguing with his broker. Joshua sat down in an empty chair, and used his feet to propel it and himself up against Gideon's desk. While Gideon was still talking about bulls and bears, Joshua slowly reached over and depressed the little button on the phone, effectively cutting off the conversation.

"I trust you have an explanation?" Gideon's eyes sparked dangerously, but Joshua didn't flinch.

Joshua leaned back in his chair. "Can this marriage be saved?" He put the Club Undead brochure on the desk in front of Gideon. "You. Me. An island. One week."

The phone rang just as Gideon reached for the brochure. Joshua managed to grab the receiver first.

"I'm sorry," Josh said sweetly to the puzzled stockbroker. "But Mr. Redoak has been called away on a household emergency. His assistant will call you back shortly."

Gidcon frowned at Joshua, but opened the brochure. "Club Undead?" he said incredulously.

"Keep reading."

Pursing his lips and biting back sarcasm, Gideon read the introductory blurb. He turned to the pages describing the island.

The telephone rang again, jarring his headache. He let Joshua answer it as he scanned the description of the island and its facilities. "Massage" caught his attention.

He looked up at Joshua, taking note of the anxiety mixed with determination in the other's demeanour. He had not been given a choice, but an ultimatum. "It sounds wonderful. But..."

"No buts," Joshua warned. "Mitch and Evan can run the business for a week. Nothing is pressing in the Brotherhood. It's another month until the wedding. I have no clients who need me immediately."

"I was only going to ask, what about you? Are they set up to accept breathers? Will you be safe there?"

"Guaranteed safe. I called the 800 number and talked to a lovely lady named Reagan, whom you are going to call right now to book reservations."

Gideon reached for the telephone. "I don't own any bathing trunks."

"We'll get you some. With polka dots."

The Club's small jet touched down on the landing strip at the private airport on the secluded island. Gideon nudged his dozing seat companion.

"We're here."

Joshua yawned and grinned. "Why do I feel like we're going to be greeted by Ricardo Montalban and a tuxedoed dwarf?" he quipped, then sighed at Gideon's blank look. "Never mind. I keep forgetting that you don't watch prime-time TV."

There were only three other passengers: a beautiful African-American vampiress in a white silk poet's shirt, purple suede pants and killer stilletto heels; a forlorn-looking stocky man with a heavy beard, dressed in a safari jacket, worn chinos and Birkenstock sandals; and a delicate-looking, greenish-tinged young woman whose lime-coloured dress only contributed to her appearance of severe motion-sickness. Joshua felt quite concerned about this girl, but perhaps she belonged to some exotic species. The fact that even her hair had an emerald cast to it bore this theory out.

The duo from Maine were casually dressed, although Gideon's idea of casual was a light grey business suit with a pale blue shirt and a striped tie. Joshua had not bothered to argue, since it was something of a miracle that Gideon was on the plane at all. His own outfit, tan Dockers and a purple short-sleeved sports shirt, was more practical for a vacation. As the blinking passengers emerged from the plane, they were greeted by Club Undead employees. Neither Ricardo nor a dwarf was in evidence—rather, two young men with dark complexions and very white teeth whisked them into a mini-van.

The island offered "guest cabins," which sounded more rustic than the quite lovely little private cottages that were available. The windows were shuttered and provided with curtains that effectively blocked the sun. Excellent and subtle lighting made the interiors cheerful. The cabin reserved for Gideon and Joshua had a roomy bedroom with a large, modern bed, several chairs, a dresser, bright pictures on the walls, a striped bedspread, an en-suite bathroom nearly as large as the bedroom, and a living-sitting room with comfy chairs, a big sofa, and more colourful art pieces.

The smiling young people left them to adjust to their surroundings. Joshua slipped off his shoes and measured out his length on the bed, testing it for comfort. He picked up the booklet from the bedside table and flipped through it idly. Several of the services were offered on a "home visit" basis. He could order in dinner, drinks, a massage...

Gideon paced. Now that he was here, he wondered if it had been such a good idea. It seemed ridiculous on the face of it—a resort island catering to the supernatural? He prowled into the living room, snorting at the furniture. Where was his favourite chair, at a comfortable distance from the fireside, a glass of brandy at hand, a wolf curled up at his feet? Where were his favourite pictures, his treasured knick-knacks, all the comforts he had accumulated over the years? How on earth was he supposed to relax and enjoy himself in this strange place?

There was a soft knock on the door. Gideon turned, startled. He frowned. Had they not been promised they would not be disturbed? He moved towards the door, ready to angrily dismiss the intruder, but Joshua beat him to it. He admitted an efficient-looking, muscular young woman in white, who was carrying a bag.

"There," Joshua said, flipping a hand at Gideon.

"Oh, yes," the young woman nodded. "I see what you mean." She studied Gideon closely, especially his shoulders and his eyes. "This *is* urgent."

"What?" Gideon said.

"I'll need you to take off those clothes, sir," said the woman briskly, "and lie down, on your stomach, on the bed. We'll get some towels down first, so no oil gets on the bed."

"I'll do that," Joshua volunteered, then turned to his dumbfounded lover. "You heard the lady, Gideon. Get your clothes off."

Dazed, Gideon followed Joshua into the bedroom. "I will not undress in front of some unknown female!" he protested, watching Joshua spread towels over the bed.

"For pity's sake, Gideon, she's not in here now. Get undressed and lie down, and I'll cover you with a towel. You can't expect to get a massage with your clothes on. You need one—you could slice bread with your shoulder muscles."

Gideon sighed and undressed, neatly hanging up the business suit. He left his underwear on. Glaring at Joshua, he stretched out on the towels that covered the bed. Joshua shook his head and placed a towel discreetly over the underwear.

"Okay, miss," Josh called.

She came in and ran practised hands over the Baron's back, probing the musculature. "This will take more than one session," she warned. "You've pushed yourself beyond your own healing abilities. I should have you on the table, but your friend thought you wouldn't come willingly the first time, especially if you knew my gender. Let's see if I can't loosen these muscles up, just a little."

Gideon felt warm oil being poured on his back, then her strong fingers and hands at work. It hurt as she massaged, especially his too-taut shoulders. She spent a long time on those shoulders, and the pain began to ease. She worked her way down his back, stopping just short of the towel. Despite himself, Gideon felt much more relaxed when she was through.

"The massage clinic is up in the main building," she said, drying her hands on a towel. "Come and see me tomorrow night if you can."

"Thank you, Miss...?" Gideon turned his head enquiringly.

She smiled. "Arden. Just Arden. You have very tense muscles, Mr. Redoak, you really need to relax."

"I'll try," he smiled back as she departed.

"We'd best get those towels off the bed," Joshua said. He handed Gideon his pajamas. "Here, put these on. Next time, you won't be able to leave your underwear on."

Gideon stood up and threw the bundle of rumpled, slightly oil-stained towels at him. It seemed the only viable response. Joshua laughed and disengaged himself from a tangle of terrycloth.

"You're obviously already feeling better," he said as he shed his own clothes.

As they slid under the covers together, Gideon turned to

Joshua.

"I've been rather impossible to live with lately, haven't I?"

"You've had your reasons, though." Joshua's fingers brushed Gideon's thick, dark hair.

"Not reason enough to drive you away. Forgive me."

"There's nothing to forgive. Now, shush. Let's just snuggle together and listen to the night."

His muscles loosened by Arden's fingers, his eyes and temples not pounding for the first time in weeks, Gideon cuddled next to the person he loved more than anything. Eyes shut, he let the sounds of the night lull him—Joshua's steady breathing and familiar heartbeat, the soft wind that ruffled the palm trees, the ocean waves spilling onto the beach...slowly his head dropped further and further down on Joshua's shoulder and he slept. Not the death-like coma that took him in the daylight, but actual sleep.

Joshua very softly kissed the top of Gideon's forehead, breathed a soft thanks for this seeming miracle, and drifted off to sleep himself.

When Josh woke, he was temporarily disoriented, then recalled where he was. He looked at Gideon. The vampire was out for the count, so it had to be daytime. Josh turned on the bedside lamp and consulted his watch. Ten a.m. His stomach grumbled a complaint, so he rolled out of bed, tucked Gideon in, and headed for the palatial bathroom.

Fifteen minutes later, spiffily attired in a blue polo shirt, gray walking shorts, and boat shoes, he made his way into the restaurant. A smiling island employee in, yes, a polo shirt and shorts, met him and showed him to a table, passing the breakfast buffet en route. Joshua's stomach growled again. He told his cholesterol count that he was on vacation, and went to the buffet for scrambled eggs, bacon, sausage, pancakes and baked ham. *Salad for lunch,* he told himself sternly, or more likely no lunch at all. If he ate like this every day of his sojourn, he'd by leaving the island by air ambulance.

His smiling waitress brought him fresh-squeezed orange juice and the most excellent coffee he'd ever tasted.

"I'm moving here permanently," he told her after sipping the coffee.

"Oh, you'd get tired of it after a while."

"Doubtful," Joshua murmured, accepting a refill.

He looked around the dining room, noting that the largish,

hairy man who'd been on the plane was steadily attacking his own breakfast. There were less than half a dozen others eating, most by themselves.

"Breakfast isn't our most popular meal," the waitress said.

"Understandable," Joshua laughed. He noted the servitor's dark complexion, and all those white teeth, and it hit him who she, and all the other staff, reminded him of—Evan. Of course. She was a Nameless One, the perfect solution to the service problems on the island. They had enough staff to solve the cycle problem, the race was used to serving vampires, and none of the guests would dare make unwelcome advances to staff who could break them into little pieces.

Finally replete, Joshua sat sipping coffee and watching the ocean for a while. Then he left the restaurant and set out to explore the island. There was just the right balance of civilization and wilderness, and the civilization had been planned with the wilderness in mind. As little damage to the island's ecosystem as possible had been rendered. Even the golf course and airstrip had been ecologically designed. The native wildlife had been left in peace.

Having walked off some of that large breakfast, Joshua went back to his shared quarters and had a nap. Then he put on his bathing suit and headed for the pool.

Gideon stirred and woke at sunset, as always. Had he actually fallen *asleep* last night? He felt refreshed and his headache was gone. A slight tension gripped his shoulders as he arose, but it was not nearly as bad as it had been. He rose, showered and dressed in the clothes Joshua had left out for him—a dark blue short-sleeved shirt and tan cotton slacks. It would take more than one night of relaxing to get Gideon into a pair of shorts.

Dressed and restless, the vampire went in search of Joshua. He found the tennis courts first, where the lovely black vampiress was playing against an Asian woman, non-vampiric, who had not been on the plane.

"Evening!" called out the ebony-skinned woman. "Do you play?

"Gideon shook his head. "No," he admitted. "Have you seen my friend? I believe he plays tennis, perhaps he will give you a game later."

"No, hon, I haven't seen him, but like you, I just got up." Her teeth flashed in a grin. "You don't play tennis?"

The Baron raised his hands and shrugged his shoulders in

mute apology.

"What do you play?" asked the Asian woman, coming up and leaning on the net. "Ping pong?" She looked hopeful.

Another shake of the Baronial head. "Billiards," he offered, and both women sighed. "Chess?" Two more sighs. "My apologies, ladies." He bowed. "Gideon Redoak, obviously not very much at your service."

"Leanna Darwood," said the black woman.

"Yvonne Huang," offered the other. "Is this your first time at Club Undead?"

"Yes, it is. I have not had much of a chance to form an impression, as yet."

"You'll like it here," Yvonne assured him. "Whoever bought this island and turned it into a resort for us is now very rich."

"I'm certain of it," Gideon smiled. "If you ladies will excuse me, I really must go find my companion." He bowed again and departed.

When he was safely out of earshot, Leanna turned to Yvonne with a heavy sigh. "Shee-it, why *are* all the cute guys gay?"

Gideon, unaware of this remark, continued his search. He encountered the swimming pool next, with a small contingent of guests and staff. The fragile-looking girl from the plane was here, comporting in a green bathing suit and obviously in her element. Two male vampires of the European ladykiller mold were lying on beach chairs, making desultory passes at this and all other females. Three of the dark-skinned staff, whose race Gideon correctly guessed, were doing laps in the pool while another coached them from the side. A towel-wrapped couple were cozying up to each other at the poolside bar, but Gideon could not quite decipher just what type of creature they might be.

No Joshua. Gideon wondered if Josh had returned to the cabin and was wondering where *he* was. He asked the bartender for the use of the phone, and called. No answer. He frowned.

"Hey," said the bartender, "Don't worry. Nothing can have happened to your friend. The island is completely safe. Try the restaurant."

"Thank you," Gideon murmured, dialling the number.

Joshua was not there, either. In desperation, Gideon asked for the massage clinic and requested to speak to Arden.

"Yes, he's here," the masseuse laughed, greatly to Gideon's relief. "We figured you would deduce it sooner or later. He's keeping the massage table warm for you."

"I'll be right there," Gideon promised. He left the bartender a tip for letting him use the phone, and was at the door of the massage clinic almost before she finished saying, "That's not necessary, sir."

In a few more minutes, he was on the table (and without even his underwear, as Joshua had predicted), Arden's skilled hands finding the kinks and tension spots still remaining. Joshua sat and watched, managing not to laugh when Arden whipped away the concealing towel and worked on those muscles, much to Gideon's discomfiture.

"Muscles are muscles," the massage therapist said, giving the muscles in question a friendly pat. "You've got tension lines going all the way to your toes." She worked her way down, replacing the towel so that her client wouldn't feel so embarrassed—or em-bare-assed, as the case might be. In her line of work, Arden had seen many bodies, living and undead. All had passed beneath her experienced hands, some so badly abused and scarred that they had stirred her sympathy. This current client had some very old, faint scars on his backside. She had been around long enough to know them for the legacy of a birch rod. He had been a breather in the days when they still whipped children. There was another, newer scar in the small of his back, and she recognized the puckered seam left by silver poisoning. That made her shudder. Someone had tried to give this vampire the true death.

"Done for now, Mr. Redoak," she told him cheerfully. One never, ever, mentioned the clients' scars to them.

"Thank you, Arden." He smiled at her, and she retreated so he could get dressed.

"Sorry if I frightened you," Joshua told him. "I should have left you a message, but the massage she gave you last night looked so good that I wanted one, too."

"It's all right. I was just a little concerned, not frightened. Have you had dinner?"

Joshua shook his head. "I had a huge breakfast," he grinned. "I'm just starting to get hungry now."

"Shall we, then?" Gideon offered his arm.

The dining lounge was much busier for dinner than it had been for breakfast. All three of their fellow plane passengers were there, as well as most of the others both Joshua and Gideon had met. The Baron nodded his head to Leanna and Yvonne, who were sharing a table with the two playboys who'd been at the pool.

"Found a new girlfriend already?" Josh teased.

"Well, with you neglecting me, what else was I to do?"

"Feel like doing anything tonight?" Joshua asked him as they took their places at their table. "I know you too well to ask for a tennis match."

"Ask my girlfriend for that," Gideon smiled, his eyes indicating Leanna. "No, I don't think I feel like any activities tonight. We still have plenty of time for those. I need to get a feel for relaxing, first." He flexed his now loosened shoulders, a wondering expression on his face. "Amazing. Arden has a deft touch."

"You look happy," Joshua said. "I haven't seen that for far too long."

Gideon's hand enclosed his. "I am happy. Thank you."

Joshua flushed and studied his menu. "I'd better not have any more cholesterol. Steamed fish sounds about right, after that breakfast."

"Are you feeling all right?" Gideon asked anxiously.

"I'm fine, don't fuss."

"What did you do all day?"

"I explored the island, went for a swim, baked in the sun, then had a massage. I'm taking it easy."

Gideon nodded, thinking that Joshua no longer looked quite so pale and drawn. The sheer exhaustion that had flattened his lover after that buying trip had passed. Joshua seemed healthy.

The waitress came by to take their order. Joshua requested the fish and white wine. Gideon, a hint of a twinkle in his eyes, asked for a glass of the special house red. She nodded and departed. The order was filled quickly and efficiently. No fuss was made about Gideon's order, and other vampires could be seen sampling the house red. It was served in the finest crystal, as was Joshua's more ordinary white wine.

Josh, well-used to vampiric drinking habits by now, didn't even make a face as he watched Gideon delicately sip the contents of his glass. He blithely attacked his own excellent, low-fat dinner as if he was not sitting across from someone drinking blood.

"Trifle high in cholesterol, perhaps." Gideon set down his glass, a smile twitching at his lips.

"You," Joshua waved a forkful of rice at him, "are asking for it."

Gideon giggled. Yes, giggled.

Joshua shook his head. "We should have thought of this ages ago."

"We didn't know this place existed."

"Sure, be that way. Use logic."

After dinner, they took a leisurely stroll down the beach, plunking themselves onto bar stools and sipping whiskey and soda while watching the more active guests play in the water. Leanna and one of the playboy vampires rode past on horseback. Joshua felt Gideon stir and watch with interest.

"I haven't been on a horse in decades," the Baron sighed. In the grip of a sad, sweet nostalgia, he watched the equestrians until they were out of sight.

"Do you want to go riding?"

Gideon relaxed and took a swallow of his drink. "Not tonight. I'm still unwinding." He reached out and touched Joshua's cheek gently. "I'm still getting reacquainted with what's really important."

As the night thickened, all but the hardiest of the water babies came ashore, got drinks, and sat watching the waves roll in. The half-moon, surrounded by a glittering court of stars, reigned loftily in the velvet sky. A few torches had been lit on the beach, and some light came spilling out of the buildings, but not enough to spoil the general effect.

Couples began drifting away from the bar, lured by the music from the main building where the dining lounge had become a dance floor, or walking entwined in each other's arms towards their cabins. Joshua tugged on Gideon's hand, meeting no resistance.

Holding their shoes in their hands, they walked along the shoreline, laughing as the waves slapped over their bare feet. The cuffs of Gideon's pants were soaked by the time they drew close to their cabin, but he barely noticed. He stopped, idly disinterring an empty shell from its sandy grave, in front of the path to their rooms.

Joshua realized he was walking alone, and turned. He saw Gideon standing in the water, a slight breeze playing in that short dark hair, moonlight reflected in those equally dark eyes.

"What?" Joshua asked.

"I love you so much," Gideon said simply.

Joshua walked back to him, leaving footprints that vanished smoothly as the next wave washed in. His arms went around Gideon and their lips met. They broke apart when a larger than normal wave swept over their knees. Gideon laughed, surveying his sopping pants.

"Perhaps there is a reason to wear shorts," he said ruefully.

"Come on," Joshua said, placing the palm of his hand in the small of Gideon's back, "We'd best get you out of those wet clothes."

The idea that a vampire could catch cold—or that anyone could, given the tropical temperature—was mildly absurd, but Gideon voiced no disagreement. He and Joshua walked to their cabin arm-in-arm. A trail of wet sand and discarded clothing marked their progress through the interior. A hot shower dispersed the remainder of the sand. The normally fastidious Baron did not even "tsk" at the mess they'd left for the cleaning staff.

Lips and arms locked, the lovers fell onto the bed. They made love with an urgent abandon that had not been in their relationship for some time. When the first wave of passion had passed, they lay together, touching and kissing more gently.

Gideon kissed Joshua's neck, his tongue tracing the pulse along the vein. The taste of sandalwood soap mixed with sweat lingered on his tongue. He could smell the hot metallic blood under Joshua's skin, the scent mingling headily with those of the soap, the tropical flowers and plants on the island, and the salty ocean only a few yards away. Joshua moaned, his "yessss" coming between his teeth like escaping steam. Gideon's teeth gently raked the skin, his fangs sliding out as he pierced Joshua's neck. The act made him so attuned with Joshua's thoughts and emotions that he felt the same thrill of pleasure and pain that his lover did at the bite. The sweet savour of his lover's blood exploded in Gideon's mouth, intensifying his pleasure and the intimacy of the moment. As Gideon drank, his body moved in a rhythm that matched Joshua's heartbeat and the hypnotic sound of the waves on the nearby shore. The pace increased as Joshua's breathing grew harsher and the sounds and scents of the island became a blur, the pleasure building until they both cried out.

Later, in a tangle of limbs and damp sheets, they listened to the island sounds. Gideon gently wiped away the last trickle of blood from the already healing wounds on Joshua's neck.

"Don't ever leave me," he murmured to the half-asleep breather.

"Never," Joshua promised drowsily.

The next day, Joshua ate a more sensible breakfast and took himself to the tennis courts in search of a partner. He found the stocky, hairy man playing against the frail, green-tinged young lady. This slip of a girl was beating the pants off of her robust opponent.

"I'll play the loser," Joshua offered, having observed the verdant one's murderous backhand.

The big man grinned and wiped sweat from his forehead. "Good call," he grunted. "She's vicious."

"I am not!" declared the victorious femme with a toss of her greenish-blonde hair. "I'm Ladriel, a nixie."

"Colin," offered the hairy one. "Lycanthrope, as you can probably tell." He laughed, fingering his heavy beard. "Beaten by an elf!"

"Joshua. Human."

"Really?" Colin extended a paw—er, hand. "Not too often one of your sort turns up here."

"I'm on vacation with someone who fulfills the requirements." Joshua shook hands with Ladriel, too.

"Your friend on the plane," she nodded. "He's a vampire."

"Just let me get a drink, and I'll give you a game," Colin said, and proceeded to quaff half a gallon of Gatorade. "Vile stuff," he spat. "Okay, Joshua, you're on."

The werewolf won, 6-4, 3-6, 6-1. By this time, a few others had turned up at the courts and Joshua was asked to play a few other games, both singles and doubles. At length, weary and sweating, the players called it quits and headed for the pool.

The early twilight fell gently over the island and Joshua made his way back to the cabin to shower and change for dinner. When Gideon woke up and saw his lover peeling off a wet swim suit, they were a trifle late for dinner.

The guest on the island were beginning to loosen up and get to know each other, and there was a certain amount of table-hopping at dinner that night. Arrangements were made for a game of beach football, with even Gideon dragooned into playing. Since he had never played football in his life, and thought it meant soccer to boot, he stood blinking rather stupidly at the plastic oval in his hand that Colin had thrown to him.

"Run with it!" yelled one of the other vampires, whose name Gideon had not yet learned.

"Toss it here!" Joshua called out.

"Throw it to me!" insisted Ladriel.

Leanna took matters into her own hands, and tackled him from behind, knocking him down into the shallow surf. "Gotchya!" she laughed, pinched his butt, and stole the ball.

Much to his surprise, Gideon found himself laughing. He scrambled to his feet and set off in pursuit.

Eventually, everyone had been tackled and dunked at least once, and the football had been lost at sea. The fact that no one had immediately noticed this loss could be attributed to the frequent drink breaks the players had taken.

It was Joshua who needed the massage the next day, but even though stiff from slightly overdoing it, he was feeling very happy. This vacation had been what *he* had needed, too. The haunting spectres of that buying trip—the bearded mage, poor Alexandra, the blood magic—had finally been laid to rest. He felt less tired and ill. He was getting a tan, not to mention plenty of rest and exercise, and his relationship with Gideon had improved immeasureably.

His musings came to a rude halt when Arden whacked him—very, very gently—on the back of the head with the edge of a towel.

"That's for overdoing it," the masseuse said sternly. "You're here to rest as much as your friend is, after all. You'd better not let me catch you waterskiing."

"Not much chance of that," Joshua laughed. "I'll be careful, Arden, I promise. But I thought you weren't supposed to boss the guests around."

"I only do it to the ones I like. Why don't you go have a nice game of golf?"

He made a face. "I *hate* playing golf."

"Well, tennis, then, but not more than two games."

He twisted around and saluted her smartly. "*Ja wohl, Fraulein Doktor!*"

She whacked him with the towel again.

Josh ended up spending most of the day lying on a raft in the pool while Ladriel described life as a water nixie to a fascinated audience of Colin, Yvonne, two anonymous guests, Joshua and the pool staff. Josh suspected that the hirsute werewolf was falling for the little faerie. Yvonne, it turned out, was a mage. A good mage, she hastened to add, seeing Joshua shudder. He explained about his recent brush with the other kind, and the Asian sorceress nodded.

"Heard of him," she grunted. "A bad lot." She sighed. "I'll be sorry to leave this place tomorrow."

"You're not going?" Ladriel squealed in distress.

"Sorry, children, but my week is up."

"You know," Colin remarked, ever-so-casually draping a long, hairy arm around Ladriel's shoulders, "that's something weird about this place. They only allow you to stay a week."

"Too long in Paradise and the taste sours," said Yvonne, a bit cryptically. "Leanna won't be happy, those two Eurotrash playboys came on the same plane as I did."

"I've noticed that the number of guests here at any one time is pretty low," Joshua remarked. Besides the ones who had been on the plane and those he'd met otherwise, there were perhaps a dozen guests on the island.

"They don't want to flood the island."

"Makes sense," said Colin.

"Sort of," added Ladriel, who didn't seem to be objecting to Colin's advances.

Yvonne rolled her eyes and gave Joshua a conspiratorial grin. "Now *there's* a strange pairing," she whispered. "Werewolf and nixie. Can you imagine the kids? Little green water-loving puppies."

Joshua laughed.

Since he had promised Arden he would take it easy, Joshua did not suggest either horseback riding or joining in the beach football game that night. Instead, they once more sat in companionable silence, sipping drinks and watching the water. The sounds of music and laughter spilled like audible shadows over the beach.

"Do you think our masseuse would permit us to go dancing?" Gideon enquired.

Joshua almost fell off his bar stool. "Yes, I think she might."

Gideon smiled and finished his drink. The music had been calling to him for some time. He wanted to dance with his lover, and the reactions of the others be damned.

But no one reacted, other than to smile in a friendly way, when the two men entered the dance floor. Gideon thought he'd never been happier in his life than here, with a soft sweet song playing in the background, his lover held closely in his arms, and the gentle tropical night folding open like a chrysanthemum, many-petaled and smelling vaguely like cinnamon.

Somehow, that same quiet music seemed to be playing in the privacy of their bedroom as they performed another sort of dance entirely.

Still later, Gideon found himself humming that tune as he walked in solitude down the beach, hands in his pockets. Joshua was peacefully asleep back in the cabin, and there were still hours until dawn.

"Hey!" called out a voice. "C'm 'n' join us!"

He turned to behold a rather inebriated Leanna sitting at the beach bar with the two vampire gigolos.

"Theesh two are leavin' t'morra'," Leanna hiccupped, and

Gideon wondered what she'd been drinking. It took a *lot* to get a vampire in that state. "I'm havin' a sho-long party."

Gideon shook his head. He sought quieter company. "No, thank you. Enjoy yourselves." He walked on.

There seemed to be a dark mound in the sand, a writhing dark mound at that. As he drew closer, Gideon's vampiric night vision allowed him to make out two people who were, er, making out.

"Heh, come here, you little nixie."

"Oh, Colin!"

Suppressing a mental vision of green aquatic puppies, for Joshua had shared that joke, Gideon continued his peregrination. He came to a small cluster of guest cottages. Most of them were unoccupied, or otherwise quiet for the night. But one person was sitting on the wooden porch swing in front of her cabin, gazing up at the waning moon.

"Ah, the man who doesn't play tennis," Yvonne chuckled. "Good evening, Gideon."

"Good evening, Yvonne." He nodded to her. "I understand that you are leaving tomorrow."

"Yes, and I'll miss this place." She patted the swing. "Come and sit with me, keep an old mage company."

"You're not old!" he exclaimed, obeying her summons.

"You, of all people, should know that appearance isn't everything. What's the idea of going around looking nearly forty when you're not even twenty?"

He smiled wryly, momentarily dropping his obviously useless illusion. "And how many people take an eighteen-year-old seriously?"

"Eighteen." She shook her head. "Ancient Chinese proverb say eighteen too young to be vampire."

"Is there really an ancient Chinese proverb that says that?"

She shrugged. "Maybe it was a fortune cookie." She reached over and patted his knee. "You listen to an old lady, my boy. There is magic on this island. In it, maybc. I don't know if it's in the air, the sand, what. Healing magic, very subtle. That's why no one can stay more than a week, except the staff. That lot is immune to magic. But for everyone else, it would be too much of a good thing." She reached under the swing and produced a bottle of brandy and two snifters that hadn't been there a moment ago. She showed the bottle to Gideon. "Your brand, I think?" At his murmur, she poured them both a measure and stowed the bottle...somewhere.

"The people who come here are the weary, the heartsick, the troubled in mind, or body, or spirit. I mean most of the people. Some are here just for vacation, but the Club has a way of finding who needs time here and sending them brochures. Don't ask me how they know. But generally, if you come to the island you're in need of more than a massage and beach football. By the time your week is up, you will have been restored, healed, refreshed—whatever word you like. You've felt it already, I think."

Gideon nodded. "Yes. It's quite remarkable. More than my health and temper have been restored to me."

Yvonne's sharp eyes flicked towards him. "You look after that breather of yours. He has a beautiful soul. And he loves you."

"I love him," Gideon said to his brandy.

There was a long silence as the Chinese mage examined this statement. "Yes," she said finally. "You do."

"And I'd best get back to him." Gideon stood up, returning the brandy glass. "Thank you, Yvonne. Have a pleasant journey home, and I hope the healing influence of this place stays with you." *What an odd thing for me to say,* he thought.

"Thank you, dear." She touched his cheek. "Put your illusion back on, unless you want your boyfriend to start asking you to wear military school uniforms. I think we shall meet again someday, Baron Gideon Redoak."

"I trust that will be so." Something moved him to give her a full formal court bow before he departed into the night.

The remainder of the week passed too quickly. Gideon often thought of Yvonne's words. No amount of money was too high to pay for the peace he had found here—he could never, ever, repay the Club for giving him back not only Joshua, but himself. As he thundered down the beach on horseback for the first time in decades, danced with his lover under the moonlight, dunked Ladriel in the ocean during a football skirmish, or joined with Joshua in the ancient rhythm of love, Gideon knew that he had been singularly blessed. He knew, too, that he would do everything in his power to keep the magic. Only once before had he been so wholly healed.

On their last night, Gideon and Joshua kidnapped Arden from the massage clinic and took her out for a drink to thank her for her help. After they released her, with many hugs, they went shopping. They wandered into the "trading post" to buy Mitch a souvenir, because he'd be crushed if they didn't. They made a few purchases for other friends as well.

Having paid for their souvenirs, the pair returned to their quarters and began the arduous task of packing. Somehow, the pajamas got packed first, so they didn't bother to dig them out again.

After one last dinner the next evening, the five guests who were leaving were taken to the airstrip and put on the plane. Somehow, leaving wasn't as difficult as they'd expected. One week on the island was exactly enough. The plane taxied and took off over the Caribbean, dipping its wings to give its passengers one last look at Paradise.

"That's the last time I throw out junk mail without reading it," Joshua murmured, resting his head on Gideon's shoulder as the island slid out of sight below them.

Return to Redoak Hall
(1995)

Joshua and I arrived at Heathrow without fuss or fanfare; just two more Americans stumbling wearily off the plane. We'd had to leave Maine dangerously early for me, drawing puzzled stares at my dark sunglasses and the collar of my coat pulled high around my face. The reward for this risk was landing in London with hours of the gentle English night still left to share with my companion.

As the taxi I had hired pulled up in front of my house in London, I paid the driver and glanced around the neighbourhood. When I had bought the sturdy Tudor-framed house, its second story jutting out over the first in a balance that looked precarious, it had practically been in the country. My main concern then, as now, had been privacy. Despite intense political, economic and social pressures, I had refused to sell the land on either side of the house, so that it now stood in lonely splendour in an otherwise busy suburb. The dark wood and white daub contrasted with the eclectic architecture of the rest of the street—here a stretch of Georgian row houses, there a tower of modern flats.

Often I had been tempted to sell the house, as I could have commanded the top price on the market. Certainly it was conspicuous, and caused much gossip about the eccentric Yank (a description that made me smile) who clung to the property. However, if this was attention, it was an innocuous sort. The neighbours already thought I was mad, so any unusual behaviour or occurrences in my house would be regarded merely as further proof.

A small group of youngsters were kicking a ball around in

the street in front of the row houses. They stopped in order to watch us, their curiosity plain even in the dusk, as we emerged from the taxi. Joshua waved to them, and they returned hastily to their game, ashamed to have been caught looking. A quick glance down the street showed me more than one curtain twitching in a window. I had phoned ahead to the couple who looked after the house in my absence, so everything had been cleaned, aired and made ready for us. A note from Mrs. Anderson, left in the kitchen, assured me that there had been no problems with the house, that there was food and drink amply laid in, and that dinner was being kept hot for us in the oven.

The kitchen had long since been updated from the flagstone-floored scullery with a broad open fireplace that it had once been. Not a trace now remained of that crude room. A very modern refrigerator hummed to itself, accompanied by a gas stove that made me slightly nervous, a deep freeze, pine cupboards, a double sink, and even a dishwasher. All the modern conveniences, I thought, wondering what my original servants would have thought of such appliances. There was a breakfast nook with a white-topped pine table and matching chairs off on one side of the room. This was neatly set for two, even down to fresh flowers in a vase in the centre.

"It's as if we never left," commented Joshua. "Spooky."

In truth, we had not been together in this house in over a year. Blinking away those memories, I checked the refrigerator. A bottle of wine was cooling on a shelf inside. I took it out, opened it, and poured it into the waiting glasses. Joshua helped himself to a serving of the casserole in the oven.

With an effort, I focused back on what Joshua had said about house looking as if we had never left it.

"So you didn't come in while you were here on that buying trip?" I asked, references to that venture now safe to make.

He shook his head. "No. I figured I might as well stay in a hotel and let Mrs. Sims-Jones pay. I didn't want to trouble the Andersons to open the house for only a couple of days." He sat down at the kitchen table and took the wine glass I handed him. "And anyway, I hate staying in this house alone."

I smiled as I sat down at the table across from him. I had to look through a screen of multicoloured daisies, carnations and ferns to see him, rather like peering through a tame jungle.

"I feel the same way, but hotels are such a risk." My eyebrows rose of their own accord as a different interpretation of what he said occurred to me. "Or are you implying that the house is haunted?"

He looked surprised and ran a hand through his hair. One sandy lock flopped down over his eyes. Unable to resist, I reached precariously through the floral undergrowth and brushed the stray swatch of hair back into place for him.

"Haunted?" he echoed. "No, I've never felt a presence here. Who would haunt it, anyway?" He stabbed a chunk of meat from the dinner on his plate and held it up. "Long-departed stews?"

The notion of disembodied chickens and ghostly diced potatoes was quite diverting, and I said so. The conversation degenerated rapidly after that, with references to undead cups of tea, spectral roast beef sandwiches, and ectoplasmic sausages rattling their links. By the time Joshua, laughing so hard that tears were forming in his eyes, proposed a toast to the Ghost of Christmas Fruitcake Past, neither of us remembered what had started the silliness to begin with.

I settled back in my chair, sipping my wine while Joshua finished his meal. The jokes had been triggered by my suggestion that this house was haunted, I recalled. Now what had ever made me think of that? No restless spirit stalked the remodeled halls of this home, although the Long Gallery upstairs seemed to cry out for the shade of beruffed Elizabethan gentleman, or a mournful headless lady in a pearl-studded gown. For me, this house would always be haunted by memories, rather than by any ghost.

Memories were why we had come to England—older memories than the ones in this house. Joshua had expressed curiosity about my birthplace. Enough time had passed, I felt, for me to return home without causing myself pain. Three hundred and fifty-four years is enough time to heal almost any wound.

Tomorrow night we would head north, towards the Welsh border, and spend the day in a discreet hotel in Shrewsbury. It was owned by a Nameless One, and the staff were well-trained not to disturb certain guests during the day. From there we could easily reach Redoak Hall, my ancestral estate, in time to take part in the last public tour of the day. That was one held after dusk, as it was felt that the tourists considered this suitably spooky.

It amused rather than distressed me that my modern day heirs had been forced to open Redoak Hall to the public. How my father would have hated that!

I tried to imagine the changes that had been wrought over three and a half centuries. Electricity, indoor plumbing, central heating, the cessation of agriculture, the selling off of land...I doubted if I would recognize the estate when I saw it.

Joshua finished his dinner and washed the few dishes he'd dirtied while I examined the brochure the National Trust had produced about Redoak Hall. There was the usual blurb about historic baronial halls, and how unusual it was that this one had been preserved from Cromwell's cannons. There was no mention that this preservation had been because of the family's Puritanism. Cromwell had attacked those estates whose owners maintained loyalty to the king, but any noble who had taken up the Puritan faith was spared.

I chuckled when I read about Ambrose, the first Baron, for the writers of the pamphlet made the time-honoured mistake of assuming that his nickname of "The Monk" had been given him for his sober and pious habits. I knew that the sobriquet of "The Monk" had been bestowed ironically—to say the least.

"You're smiling," Joshua said. "What's so funny?"

"Propaganda about dear old Ambrose," I replied. "How many times I heard his name quoted to me as a standard I failed to live up to! I was told that I could never hope to be remembered as reverently as The Monk. When I dared to mention that his habits could not have been too monastic or he could not have produced children, I received the worst beating of my life." I poured more wine into my glass, distressed to see that my hand was shaking so badly that I slopped it over the table "Which is saying something."

"This will be hard for you, won't it?" Joshua asked softly, taking hold of my hands. "So many bad memories...if you'd rather not go, I'll understand. We can just have a nice time together here."

I gained control over my emotions again. "No. I promised you this. I've been repressing those memories too long. I have to do this. I have to go home again." I looked up as Joshua began to massage my tense shoulders. "If you are with me, I can bear it."

He leaned over and kissed me, his lips hard against mine. "I'll be there for you," he promised when he let go.

Then, somehow, we were upstairs in bcd, and his weight and warmth blanketed me, giving comfort. I think I wept, and he held me tightly. This return home would be hard. But Joshua's love and support, which he was manifesting enthusiastically, would be the key to seeing me through. Just then, what he was doing blanked all other thoughts from my mind.

"*Did you read* the whole brochure?"

"Hm?" I asked as Joshua entered the bathroom. I was still in the tub, getting ready for the drive to Shrewsbury.

"Did you finish reading that brochure?" he asked again, picking up the back brush and proceeding to scrub my back for me.

"No, I was, ah, interrupted. And very nicely, too."

"You're mentioned in it."

"I am?" I stopped washing my legs to stare at him in surprise. "Good heavens, what for? I did nothing remarkable."

"Except try to solve the murder of your tenants, die under highly mysterious circumstances at eighteen, and have your body completely disappear from the family vault."

"Oh. I hadn't thought of that."

"...and here is the only portrait of the young Baron..."

With all the others in the group, I looked up, and saw myself at eighteen.

I remembered posing for that portrait. The artist had come shortly after my father's death, an enterprising soul who knew that the new Baron would need an official painting of himself. He'd been a little shocked at the lack of mourning in my demeanour.

He had put me in a typical pose, standing near my desk to show that I was industrious, with my hand on the head of a large wolfhound to show that I was masterful. The wolfhound, I recalled, had growled steadily throughout the procedure. It had been my father's dog.

The boy in the painting was short and stocky. His hair was straight and dark, an unidentifiable shade between black and brown. It was cut short in the Puritan fashion, parted in the middle and falling to either side of the face, to about halfway down the ears.

His face was somewhat square, but in no sense too broad or unattractive. His forehead, under the silly-looking bangs, was as yet unmarked by care. There were no lines at the corners of those fine eyes. The eyes, under thick brown eyebrows, were easily his best feature. Their colour was again difficult to determine—hazel, perhaps. They were a perfect almond shape, and he had longish lashes. I heard more than one person in the tour murmur about what pretty eyes he had. I smiled at these remarks, and Joshua elbowed me slightly.

The artist had captured an expression in those eyes, half-wistful, half-apprehensive, that seemed to forebode this boy's untimely end.

The rest of his features showed a compromise between the aristocrat and the farm boy; he had good cheekbones, somewhat obscured by their width. His nose was not too long or too square, but belonged on that quiet face. The mouth was straight, the lips thinly compressed. It was a mouth that did not look as if it had smiled much. He had a straight jaw, just saved from severity by a slight curve.

It was a good face, not outrageously handsome, but by no means ugly. It topped a body that was, perhaps, a little too solid to meet modern standards of beauty. Not that the boy was, by any means, fat—there was no extra weight on him.

I felt no particular worry that someone would look from the portrait to myself and make the connection. People are simply not that observant, for one thing. For another, the boy was in black Puritan plain clothes with a white lace collar, and I was wearing a light gray business suit. There was also the fact that I had aged my appearance by twenty years. There were lines on my forehead now, and some at the corners of my eyes. My hair was cut in a modern business man's conservative style, and I had willed the hint of grey into it here and there to enhance the illusion.

My height and build remained the same, since there was nothing I could do about those. The shape of my face, my eyes and ears—all were the same as in the portrait.

No one noticed, except Joshua, of course.

Still smiling from the reaction to seeing my own portrait, Joshua and I hung back a little from the rest of the tour group.

"How are you doing?" he asked, slipping his hand into mine.

"I'm all right," I replied. "This really hasn't been that bad—yet."

Indeed, it had not. The Hall still looked much as I remembered it, from the outside at least. A massive fortified house from the fifteenth century, it had suffered few indignities over the centuries. Now that it was being run by the National Trust, it was untouchable—if one could overlook the tea shop and rows of tour buses on the grounds. Some of the other buildings were long gone—the tenant farmsteads, for example. The stables were still there, converted into garages. But the dower house was missing—burned down a century ago. It grieved me to see it gone, the house where Jamie and Prudence had been so happy. The Hall itself endured.

Inside, it was a slightly different story. It did not, as I believe is often reported in such cases, look any smaller to me. It was altered internally, but not by very much. The National Trust experts had been at work here, restoring the Hall to a close approximation of how it had looked when I had been a child. Some things were not quite right, or my memory had dimmed, so that I was spared an overwhelming sense of déjà vu.

"It's lovely," Joshua murmured, eyeing the Jacobean furniture. "It's all in excellent taste."

"Well, I'm glad to hear that, at least. Good to know my modern-day cousin isn't a total disgrace to the illustrious family name."

The portrait gallery was well along the tour, and up until then I had been able to disassociate myself from any of my memories of this house. At no point did I turn a corner or open a door and think, *I grew up here,* or *In this room, did such and such happen.* Not even seeing my own portrait and hearing the story of my mysterious death and the subsequent disappearance of my body opened the floodgates of memory.

No, that shock waited until the guide led us into the study.

This, alone of any other room we had seen, remained completely unaltered from the day of my death. The desk, the black carved oak chair, the carpet on the floor, the plain silver candle stand, even the quill pen and ink bottle...all had been left in exactly the position they had been in when I had abandoned them to take to my sick bed. I knew that if I was allowed to approach the desk, I should see my own handwriting in the ledger that was open upon it. This was the desk in the portrait. I half-expected old Nimrod, the wolfhound, to come growling to his shaggy feet at my ingress.

"As you can see," said the tour guide, oblivious to the fact that one of her flock had started to shake badly, "this room has been left unaltered since 1641. This was at the decree of the young Baron Gideon's sister Prudence, who wished this study left as a monument to her lost brother. She was a most devoted sister. The ledger is a fascinating study of the day to day running of a typical baronial estate..."

"Gideon?" Joshua's eyes were peering concernedly at me as the guide's voice faded into the fog that was forming in my brain. "Gideon, speak to me." His arm went around me, uncaring of the crowd and their reaction. "Love, you're shaking. I've got to get you out of here."

I let him guide me from that room. A hunter armed with stakes and silver could have given me the True Death right then and I would not have resisted. I was too numb, too lost in the grips of painful memory. Joshua led me outside and got a passing tourist to fetch me a glass of water from the tea shop.

"He's got dust allergies," Joshua told the concerned tea shop lady, who brought not only the glass of water but a first aid kit. "They hit him like this sometimes. I've given him an antihistamine, he just needs to rest until it kicks in."

I drank the water. It could have been poison. Joshua kept up a steady stream of nonsense to the Good Samaritan until she finally went away and left us. Then he pinched me, hard.

"Gideon!" he said urgently. "Snap out of it!"

I blinked, and eventually stopped shaking. Slowly, the present came back into focus. I found myself sitting on a picnic table bench, clutching a paper cup full of tepid water, with Joshua gazing worriedly at me.

"I'm sorry," I said, rather lamely. "But imagine walking into your past, unchanged like that after three hundred and fifty four years...she kept it for me," I added, as the initial shock wore off.

How had Prudence managed to preserve that room? Why had she? It was a strange tribute to my memory. I had not had time to impress my own personality on that room. There was nothing in it of mine, other than my handwriting in the ledger.

It had been my father's study in my time, and my memories of it were chiefly of being beaten there. I had been bent over that carved black oak chair far more times than I had sat on it.

The pain of my dismal childhood came rushing back to me as I thought of that chair. I clenched the paper cup in my hand so tightly that it was crushed, the contents fountaining up and spraying my clothing. I didn't even notice.

"Gideon?" Joshua's arm was around me at once. He drew me close, and I instinctively turned to him for comfort, resting my head on his shoulder.

"What is it? What's wrong?" He held me tightly.

The words of pain were jammed up behind a dam of years of repression, but Joshua's support was weakening this once-formidable wall.

"He never hugged me," I finally said, feeling the hot red tears form in my eyes. Luckily, Joshua was wearing dark clothes and the crimson stain would not be obvious. "There was never a hug, never a kiss or a kind word."

Once started, the flow of pain and words could not be stopped. "I did everything to please him. I tried so hard to be good, to be the son he wanted. Not once did he ever notice that effort, see that I was trying. It was never enough. I wasn't smart enough, well-behaved enough, Godly enough to be his son! He might have been happy with an angel, but I doubt it. There was always fault to find, always an excuse to bring out the rod."

I lifted my head from Joshua's shoulder, and saw the love in his eyes, felt the comfort of his arm around me. "I wanted to love him, to be loved by him. But I couldn't love him. The Puritan God was one of hellfire, not love, and my father served that God. 'Spare the rod and spoil the child!' As if a child could be spoiled by affection. Even now, I see a father hug his son, or play with him, or even just smile at him, and I think 'my father never did that.' I was so cold as a child. I needed my father to warm me."

Joshua said nothing, but his silence was born of sympathy and warmth, not disinterest. He knew I needed to talk, to purge that repressed hurt. The flow was almost over, though, and I was feeling much better. If it was this cathartic to speak of my feelings for my father, then perhaps someday I could bring myself to talk about Corbeau. Not now, though. One catharsis was enough for an evening.

"You okay now?" Joshua whispered.

"Getting there." I managed to smile at him. "I love you."

"I love you, too."

"Why couldn't my father say that to me?"

"Consider this, Gideon: he was a product of his time. Children died young, it was too hard on the parents to get attached to a child that would most likely die."

"That's not entirely true," I contradicted him. "Ben Jonson wrote a very touching tribute to his son who died at three."

"I suppose your father must have been one of the ones who believed it wrong to show affection, then. Very likely your father's father treated him the same way. They say that often people who were abused as children grow up to be abusive in their turn."

"Do you mean that I would have become like my father if I'd had children?" It was an appalling thought.

"No, I don't think so. Your psychology isn't wired that way. Your father was too fanatic about the new Puritan religion, and you suffered the consequences."

"Did your father beat you?"

Joshua sighed a little as the question intruded on *his* personal hurt. "No. At least, not the way you're thinking. I got the occasional spanking, sent to bed without dinner, that sort of thing. My father was pleased to have a son. I was supposed to reaffirm his masculinity, or some macho myth like that."

We held hands tightly, commiserating with each other in our grief.

"Are you all right?"

I looked up to see a man his twenties peering concernedly at us from the top of a small rise on the lawn. He strolled casually down towards our bench, hands in the pockets of his corduroy trousers. He had on a faded blue sweater, wellingtons, and a rather grimy tweed cap, his whole appearance suggesting that he was perhaps a gardener or some other outdoor employee of the estate. His bearing, however, marked him as a member of the aristocracy. More than that, his dark hair and fine, dark eyes betrayed him for a Redoak.

"I heard that somebody on the tour became ill," he said, peering sharply at me. "You aren't going to faint, are you, sir? You look frightfully pale. It was that wretched preserved study that gave you a bad turn, was it not?"

"How do you know that?" I asked, fearful that somehow this man had divined my secret. He was, after all, by way of being a relative. I had no doubt at all that I was addressing the current Baron, although these days he would be addressed by his title only on legal documents. More properly, he was Lord Redoak.

"Why, the tour guide told me," he replied guilelessly. "It takes people like that, sometimes. Though it's usually silly girls who come over all faint about the romanticism of it all."

"In our case, it was allergies," Joshua said. I could tell that he was trying hard not to keep looking from the lord to myself, and thus draw attention to the resemblance between us. "All that preserved dust got to him."

"Sorry to hear that. Why not let me make it up to you? Come and have a drink with me, since you missed most of the tour."

"If you're sure that his Lordship won't mind..." Joshua began dubiously.

Our new acquaintance grinned. "He won't mind. I'm him. Percival Ambrose Redoak, Lord Redoak, umpty-umpth Baron, at your service. No, don't rise," he chuckled as Joshua tried to stand. "It's not necessary. That's why the mufti." He pulled at his sweater. "So that the daytrippers think I'm the undergardener. If you go all formal on me, next thing I know, I'll be surrounded by children asking to see my crown, and little old ladies wondering if I've taken tea with the Queen."

"Have you?" Joshua asked before he could stop himself.

The current Lord Redoak laughed. "Yes." He looked at me and said, "You're a quiet one. Bad allergies?" He cocked his head to one side. "You look awfully familiar..."

My brain was obviously still not working properly, for I did nothing to distract him from this dangerous thought. I was caught in a spiral of memories that would not release me, not even to cope with a present threat.

Joshua, seeing that I was struggling with my own internal

problems, did his best to distract Lord Redoak.

"Milord..." he began.

"Percival. Ghastly name, but there you have it. I'm Percival to my friends, and to stray Americans who take a bad turn in my ancestor's study. Come and have that drink with me. Please," he added.

They both looked at me, and I was able to free myself from my mental prison long enough to accept.

Lord Redoak led us into the private apartments he had kept for himself in the house. These had been some of the guest quarters, but they were now modernized.

"Let the N.T. have the bloody antiques," said Percival cheerily, seeing Joshua eye the Danish teak couch. "Now, then, are you going to introduce yourselves?"

Joshua flushed. "Sorry. I'm Joshua Trevallion."

Percival looked at me. It was on the tip of my tongue to give him an alias, but something made me change my mind.

"Gideon Redoak."

The lord's brow cleared, as if a puzzle he'd been trying to solve fell into place. He slapped his knee. "Thought so!" He turned to a well-equipped liquor supply. "Let's have a drink first, and sit down, then we'll have a chat...cousin." He grinned. "I even have ice for you barbarians."

We were soon settled with drinks and a box of biscuits. Joshua looked apprehensive, and I must confess that I felt more than a little anxious myself. How much had my "cousin" guessed? Likely not that I was a vampire, but I wondered how he thought I was related.

"Now, then," said Percival, examining his own whiskey with satisfaction and leaning forward in his chair. "I suppose you're wondering why I gave the family manse to the Trust."

"Death duties, I'd assumed," I replied, knowing that these taxes were still exorbitantly high.

"You're right," he sighed. "I didn't expect to inherit. You've likely got as much claim to the title as I do."

"I doubt if the law would see it that way."

"So, then, is what I've always suspected true?"

"And just what have you always suspected?" I heard more than an echo of danger for this amiable aristocrat in my voice.

"The family mystery, the one the tour guides love to show off. Your namesake, the 12th or whatever Baron. The one whose body vanished from the crypt." Percival nodded more or less in the direction of this structure. "He didn't actually die, you see."

"Didn't he?"

"Not then. Of course he did die, but not when everybody thinks he did."

"Really."

"See, I can read between the lines of that ledger. The steward was either dismissed or left at the same time as the poor little Baron allegedly died. I think that somehow our Gideon faked his death and he and the steward went off together."

Joshua coughed, and had to pretend it was a piece of biscuit caught in his throat. I would have given much to be able to see the expression on my own face at that moment.

"Whatever gives you that idea?" I managed to ask after swallowing a gulp of the brandy in my glass.

Percival smiled. "Oh, just a fancy of mine. I wouldn't blame the poor boy. He must have felt awfully trapped. I'm pretty sure he was gay, or leaning that way, and the steward was a handsome devil by all accounts. An amazing number of the family are that way inclined, you know." He winked at me "But he must have been bi, or you wouldn't be here. Maybe he just experimented."

"Could be," I said cautiously, not really knowing how to respond. "I never could get anyone to tell me the family history. I've always been curious, and when I heard the house was open to the public..."

"You came over to have a recon. Only natural. Welcome—cousin!"

"So how did you come to inherit?" Joshua asked.

"Well, when Gideon supposedly died, the title went to his sister Prudence. It was an old title, and so could be passed to the female line. They weathered out the civil war because old Cromwell thought they were on his side, and they survived the restoration because Old Rowley thought the same thing. Canny girl, that Prudence. Her husband got his name changed by deed poll so that the name as well as the title stayed Redoak. I suppose that "Carter" wasn't nob enough. They had four children who survived, got married, and proceeded to have more children, and so on down the line. I'm actually descended from their third child, Paul. They didn't keep the Puritan nomenclature, luckily, or my ancestor could have been Sword-of-the-Lord. We're a short-lived clan, for some reason: or the title's unlucky. They had do some scrambling to find the heir when the last Lord Redoak died. He didn't leave any offspring. Or much money." He sighed. "I'm surprised they didn't try America for relations."

"I suppose they would have, if they hadn't found you," I said.

"Do you plan to marry?"

"I suppose it's my duty." He sighed again. "I don't mind, really. I like women. I don't have that particular family trait, no offense. But I'm not fond of children. Suppose I'd better have some, though. I doubt if you'd be too happy suddenly finding yourself Baron Redoak." His intense look conveyed that perhaps he knew more than he was telling, that he'd penetrated at least part of my secret.

"No," I said, softly. "No, I wouldn't."

Percival nodded.

"Well, we should be going," Joshua said. "Thank you so much for the drink and the family history, Percival."

"You will drop in again next time you're in England, won't you?" He looked wistful, and I wondered if he was lonely. "I don't get guests that I can gossip about the Redoaks to very often."

"Yes, of course we will," I assured him on impulse.

"Um, do you mind if I use your bathroom?" Joshua asked him, looking embarrassed.

"Not at all. Just to the right, three doors down."

Joshua departed, and Percival turned to me.

"You know, I like him," he said. "I hope I haven't offended you by talking about gays in the family."

"Not at all. I'm aware that it is something of a Redoak trait."

He nodded again. "At least we don't have any axe-murderers or mad rapists...that I know of, anyway." He grinned. "Unless you...?"

I laughed and shook my head. "I have never murdered an axe in my life."

Percival roared. "I like you, too!" he declared.

I heard Joshua's footsteps in the hallway, returning from his mission.

"I really must be going," I said. "I do thank you so much, and we will visit again." I offered my hand.

He shook it with great emotion. "It's been my pleasure, cousin." Then, just before I exited to join Joshua in the hallway, he added, "Gideon?"

I turned my head. "Yes, Percival?"

"It was the steward, wasn't it?"

Threnody
(1995)

Dedication: To absent friends. You are missed.
And to Sara K., whose idea this was.

Threnody: (n) A song of lamentation; a dirge. (Webster's)

Joshua looked up from his client files as Mitch entered his private study, a mug of coffee and a plate of cookies in his hand.

"Coffee break," said the young werewolf firmly. "You've been working too hard."

"I thought I was the parent substitute," Joshua kidded.

"You look tired," Mitch flopped down on the cot Joshua kept in this room for emergencies. "You're putting too much energy into the wedding plans. And you're planning another road trip. I hope it's not like the last one."

Recalling his somewhat nightmarish expedition to satisfy Mrs. Sims-Jones, Joshua agreed. "Yes, I seemed to be a long time from home. It'll be awhile before I go off on that kind of trip again. But this is an important client and I can't refuse him. It's nothing like that buying trip for Mrs. S-J, don't worry."

"I wish you wouldn't go," Mitch said in a low voice.

The older man looked at him gently, his eyes radiating warm sympathy. "There'll be a day when I won't be on the road any longer. But it's my career, and I love it."

"Just don't overdo it, and get sick, or anything. Remember, we need you healthy and alert for the wedding! And the party! How will it look if I have to push you down the aisle on a stretcher? You'd better take it easy." Mitch left the room with a sniff.

Joshua smiled after him, warmed by the concern and affection. If he had had a son...he'd rather not have that son be a werewolf, thank you! He chuckled at the thought, and went back to his records. Mrs. Sims-Jones had paid all his expenses without a quibble, even though he'd back-tracked on himself and hopped back and forth between cities and countries with no rhyme nor reason. He really hoped all those haunted antiques didn't turn on her or worse. The client he had now was in the market for some perfectly ordinary, non-haunted, non-magical furniture, and Joshua felt he could handle this request. He'd been turning a few down lately because he hadn't been feeling quite up to par.

The coffee and cookies came as welcome respite, and Joshua was feeling a bit more energetic when the telephone rang. This was his private line, so it had to be a client or one of the few friends who knew the number.

"Trevallion."

"Joshua!" exclaimed a female voice with a British accent.

It took Joshua a moment to place his caller. "Tamara?" He had not heard from the English doctor for several years.

"Joshua, I…I…how are you?"

"Fine. Are you all right, Tamara? You sound upset." Her voice had been uncharacteristically quavery. She didn't usually fumble for words, either.

"You remember your appendectomy?"

"Vividly. Or at least," he chuckled, "I remember the parts leading up to it and after it. I don't seem to recall the operation itself. Why?"

"It was in August of '85, wasn't it?"

"You know it was. What's this all about, Tamara?"

"My God, I don't know how to tell you. Someone else who had an operation at the same time just sued us. Joshua, you know that screening wasn't really stringent until October of that year…"

"What do you mean, 'screening wasn't stringent?' Why did this person sue, Tamara?"

"The blood we used was HIV tainted. You have to get yourself tested."

"Christ." Joshua didn't swear often, but he thought this situation warranted it. "Tamara, how did this happen? How in God's name did HIV-tainted blood end up in the operating room?"

She started to cry. "It was before we screened, I told you that."

She had, but Joshua hadn't taken it in. He knew that his operation had been done during a high-risk period, before stringent screening, but it had been ten years ago and he had thought anything would have shown up by now.

God, had it? Did that explain the fatigue, the dry cough…?

"Tamara, don't. Don't cry. It was an accident." But he had to grip the side of his desk to keep from passing out. He started coughing.

"It's horrible, Joshua. If...I can't even say it. I will never forgive myself. Are you coughing?" She sounded terrified.

"Tamara, it wasn't your fault." Joshua's natural soothing abilities were on automatic pilot. So were the rest of his functions. HIV tainted blood from the hospital. The irony was just too much. He was in such a high risk category that he was banned from donating blood, and he'd been exposed to the virus by having his appendix taken out.

At least he couldn't infect Gideon. He hoped.

"Get yourself tested, Joshua," Tamara insisted again. "I'll be praying for you."

Joshua had never bothered to find a personal physician in Fletcherville. Until recently, he'd always been fairly healthy, and he was living on the same road as a Druid healer and a registered nurse. He trusted Michael and Mary over any doctor. The only major surgery he'd ever had was his appendectomy, and he'd had that in England.

Before they'd started proper blood screening.

And he, who campaigned for AIDS awareness, for funds for research, for the rights of AIDS patients, who had seen friends die of AIDS, had never given that operation another thought. Not even though he knew of cases of bad transfusions. Those happened to straights or hemophiliacs. Gay men got AIDS from unprotected sex, or sharing needles, right?

He'd thought he was safe. He'd had only two lovers in his lifetime, one of them during university days and the other one now. He was in a monogamous relationship with a vampire who could neither give nor get AIDS, so he'd thought he was safe.

And he was going to get married in a couple of weeks...

He had to get tested. As the dry cough wracked his body again, he already knew the results. The healing ceremony for Genevieve and the week at Club Undead had both eased his symptoms, but the effects had been temporary. Already whatever mysterious mechanism it was that turned HIV into AIDS was at work within his body. Joshua knew the symptoms. He'd just been ignoring them in himself. Ignoring...or denying?

His legs shook as he rose from his desk. Josh knew he was never going to be able to drive into town in this condition. Mitch. Mitch would drive him. No. He'd have to tell him why, and the boy would fall apart on him.

"Evan." Joshua whispered. "I'll get Evan."

About five seconds later, there was a knock on his door and the auburn-haired muscular bodyguard came in.

"What's up?" he asked softly. "Are you okay?"

"No." Joshua blinked. He didn't think he'd spoken loudly enough for Evan to hear him.

"I come when I'm called. What do you need?"

"You to drive me into town," Joshua replied shakily, dismayed to find himself so unsteady. "To the clinic at the hospital."

"Hey." Evan frowned. "Wouldn't you rather see Michael or Mary?"

"I can't. Not for this. I'll explain later, okay?"

"Okay."

Evan managed to get Josh downstairs without looking like he was helping him. They both agreed it was better not to upset Mitch.

"Josh needs to go down to the village," Evan told the werewolf when Mitch popped up to see what was happening, "and I'm going to drive him because I need a few things, too. You can keep an eye on Oakwoods till Gideon gets up, can't you?"

"Sure!" Mitch said, pleased at being in charge.

"Anything you need or want from town?"

Mitch started to shake his head, but Pumpkin chose that moment to paw at his knee and look adorable. "Doggie treats," Mitch sighed, patting her and then Warg.

"What flavour would you like?" Evan asked, but his heart wasn't in the teasing.

Catching this lack of fun, Mitch studied Evan and then Josh. "Something's going on. Come on, I'm not a kid, I can handle it. I can't handle not knowing."

"I promise I'll tell you both later," Joshua said, smiling at Mitch. "I just don't want to have to repeat myself three times, so I'll tell everyone once Gideon is up."

"I'm holding you to that promise, Joshua."

"I'll make good on it, Gaylord." He turned to Evan. "Let's go while I can still make it."

The trip to the village was made mostly in silence. Evan knew this was no time for joking, and Joshua was too preoccupied to chat. However, Evan's solid presence and manifest concern, his friendship and support, buoyed Josh up considerably. By the time they reached the walk-in clinic attached to Fletcherville Hospital, Josh was able to get out of the car and stand without any assistance. A faint feeling of unreality had crept into his brain, as well as the remarkable capacity many humans have to deal with crises in a calm and rational manner. He was determined not to fall apart.

He held onto the thought that he was getting married at Christmastime, held that like a lifeline...

The clinic was busy, with the usual clutter of people coughing, sneezing, moaning and generally spreading diseases. There were mothers with screaming babies or crying toddlers, a sulky, bruised teenage boy accompanied by his grim-looking father, a young woman in a huge leg cast who was quietly reading horse magazines—a typical cross-section of the occupants of all walk-in clinics everywhere.

"Oi," said Evan critically. "I'm glad I don't get sick."

"Welcome to a good look at what it is to be human," Joshua answered with a wry smile.

A woman in a nurse's uniform appeared from the depths of the clinic. "Joshua!"

"Mary?" Joshua stared. "Whatever are you doing here?" She was, after all, the head nurse at the hospital.

"They're shorthanded, as usual, so I offered to help out. What are *you* doing here?"

"I need to see a doctor."

Mary's gaze quickly checked for visible wounds, signs of fever, or other urgent needs. "Not in this zoo, you don't," she said quietly. "Come with me. I've got some pull."

She led them through the clinic. After treading the maze here for a short distance, Mary knocked on a door marked, "Dr. G. Tenfeathers, Gnrl Prctnr."

"Yo," said an answering voice.

"Need a favour, Gill," Mary said after opening the door and ushering Josh and Evan into the examining room with her.

The middle-aged American Indian woman standing at the overcrowded counter grinned. "Shoot, kimosabe. Anything in my power to give you, except my truck." She looked at Evan, her grin widening in appreciation, then at Joshua. Her expression visibly changed gears to strictly professional. "Mary, as usual, has forgotten about introductions. I'm Gillian Tenfeathers."

"Joshua Trevallion."

"Evan Jones."

"Josh here wants to see a doctor," Mary told Gillian. "I don't know why, but he's a good friend and my neighbour, and I didn't want him to have to wait in that plague-pit. I knew you were free."

"This is highly unorthodox, Nurse." Gillian chuckled. "I like it. I take it you don't have a family doctor, Mr. Trevallion?"

"No. And I haven't filled out any paperwork..."

The doctor dismissed the paperwork with a wave. "We'll worry about that later. Now, you other two, shoo. Don't go too far, Mary, I might need you."

"Evan and I will do the paperwork," Mary said. "You know Josh's medical insurance info, don't you, Evan?"

"Hm, yeah," replied Evan, a little startled as Mary pulled his sleeve to get him out of the examining room.

When Mary and Evan had gone, Gillian got out of her chair and came over to Joshua.

"You're not doing too well, are you?" she asked softly.

"No, I'm afraid not," he admitted.

"Is it okay if I call you Joshua?"

"Sure."

"Okay, then, Joshua, I'm Gill. I think you need to be honest with me, okay? I'm going to ask you questions I'm not supposed to, but this whole scene isn't legal, anyway."

"Fire away."

"Are you a sexually active homosexual?"

"Yes."

"Are you HIV positive?"

"That's what I came to find out." Joshua looked up at her. "I had an appendectomy in England in August of 1985. They started screening blood in October. Other people who had transfusions around the same time are infected. If I'm positive, it came from that transfusion, not my lifestyle." His tone was defiant, almost aggressive.

"But you can spread it to your partner or partners."

"Partner. I'm in a monogamous relationship with someone I love very much. I hope to God I haven't infected him." *I'm going to marry him...* he added silently. It had become his mantra.

"Are you having any symptoms?"

"Fatigue. A dry cough. That's it so far."

"Right. Those aren't conclusive, you know. Only the blood test will tell us for sure. But let's have a look at you before we take blood. Drop the Dockers, sweetie, I've seen it all."

"I see why Mary sought you out," Joshua chuckled, undressing. "You do things your way."

"Listen, my friend, I'm a Native American and a woman and a doctor. Anytime you want to trade oppressed minority stories, I'm ready for you." She patted her examining table. "Plunk those cute buns that I'm sure your lover admires right here."

She proceeded to give him a very thorough physical. Afterwards, she called in Mary and they took blood samples to be sent to the lab in Bangor. Mary looked grave when she was told that the samples were to be sent under a number code only to the HIV testing facility. She gave Gill the paperwork for Joshua, then turned to the patient.

"Does Gideon know?" she asked, putting a hand on Joshua's shoulder.

"Not yet," he replied.

"Josh, if you need to talk, Michael and I are available any time."

"Thanks, Mary."

"You're actually still fairly healthy," Gill said when Mary had left with the blood in vials. "You've been treating the symptoms somehow, haven't you? What are you taking?"

"Herbal tea, actually," Joshua confessed.

The doctor raised an eyebrow. "Good. Keep it up. Better than antibiotics at this stage. There's a healer in the Cliff Road Crowd?"

"Yes. And Mary."

"Talk to them. I'd like to, but I know how that lot guard themselves against the medical profession. And talk to your lover. Let him know his risks, and what you're going through. The tests may not be positive, Joshua. You could just as easily have Yuppie 'flu, you know."

He smiled. "Thanks, Gill. Guess I'd better go home now, though."

"I'll be in touch the second I get the results. You'll have to come in for them, you know. Bring a friend. The redhead with muscles is nice." She grinned, and Joshua returned it briefly. "Take care of yourself, Joshua, and don't let this prey on your mind during the next few days."

"Thanks again," he said, and departed.

Gideon sensed the tension in the household almost as soon as he woke up. No one was there to greet him, for one thing. While not entirely unusual, this was something to give him pause. He hurried through his bath and dressed quickly, wondering what was wrong. He went downstairs in his shirtsleeves and with his hair still damp.

The other members of the household were gathered in the drawing room, the coziest room on the main floor. Although there wasn't a real need for one, it being a mild winter day, a cheerful fire burned in the grate. Mitch was stroking Warg's head, which the wolf had thrust into his master's lap. Pumpkin was curled up in Joshua's arms and he was cuddling her absently. Evan was playing with the logs in the fireplace, poking at them to stir up sparks.

"I got a phone call today," Joshua began, talking to Pumpkin.

Gideon went over to him and touched his shoulder. "Yes?" he encouraged, wishing he could read minds. There was a lot of emotion in the room, but he couldn't decipher exactly what it meant.

"From Tamara. Remember her?"

"Very well. Your doctor friend, in London. What did she have to say?" Gideon sat down across from Joshua, his eyes urging his lover to speak.

"She talked about my appendectomy."

Evan stirred the fire again, and a log fell. Everyone jumped, including the animals.

"I thought that was a long time ago," Mitch said, obviously wondering what the rest of the story was.

"Ten years," Joshua said. "August of 1985. They didn't start screening blood for HIV until October of 1985."

Three separate pairs of eyes locked on him: blue, hazel, and an indefinable dark brown-black.

"That's why Tamara called," Josh went on, feeling the weight of those gazes. "Because tainted blood did get into the operating room at the time I had that appendectomy. She advised me to get a blood test. So I had Evan drive me down to the clinic. Mary was there and arranged for me to see a doctor. The blood's on its way to the lab in Bangor, and I'll know in about a week."

Silence, except for Pumpkin's soft whimper and Warg's asthmatic breathing. Mitch looked at his wolf, and realized that Warg was getting old. Evan stopped toying with the fire and sat down near Joshua.

"And this test will mean what, precisely?" Gideon asked.

"If it's negative, then I don't have HIV." Joshua coughed quietly.

"And if it's positive?" The Baron's gaze was intense.

Joshua turned his head, unable to meet that unblinking vampiric stare. Unable to meet the worry.

"Some people live a long time with HIV," he said. "Sometimes it doesn't become AIDS, you know. It could be ARC. It doesn't have to mean death."

The fire crackled and popped. The mantle clock ticked loudly, like a deathwatch beetle.

"What can we do to help?" Mitch asked finally. Although his voice wavered a bit, it was a man's question, not a boy's.

Joshua swallowed hard. "Try to act normal. Don't treat me

as if I'm fragile or dying. Don't be afraid of me. You can't get HIV from casual contact." His eyes finally met Gideon's. "Assuming any of you are at risk in the first place."

"I haven't heard of any of my people getting it," Evan said. "Which doesn't mean it's not possible. But I'm not going to take up wearing surgical gloves." He grinned at Joshua, who took his offered hand. "Hang in there."

"I'm not worried!" Mitch asserted, shifting Warg's head off his lap. He got up and hugged Joshua, Pumpkin and all. "Josh," he said, emotion throbbing in his voice.

"Thanks, Mitch."

Gideon said nothing, but it was an eloquent silence. At last he smiled faintly.

"You needn't think I'm worried," he said. "Although our contact has been far more than casual. Joshua—I love you. Nothing changes that. We will wait this out together. I will do my best to behave in a normal manner, as I am sure will both Mitch and Evan."

They both nodded. Joshua managed a smile, warmed by the feeling of togetherness, of...family. "Good. What's for dinner?"

Mitch looked blank. "Dinner?" he whacked himself on the head. "It was my turn! I forgot!"

"You forgot?" Evan glared at him. "Lucky for you, I'm not in high cycle! You march out to that kitchen right now and make something, or I'll baste you!"

The familiar sound of bickering did more than anything else could have to restore the atmosphere of the house to normal. Mitch and Evan both headed for the kitchen, the animals trailing hopefully.

"What doctor did you see?" Gideon asked Joshua.

"A woman, Gillian Tenfeathers."

"An Indian?"

"A Native American, yes. I'm not sure if you'd like her. She's a little...unorthodox." Joshua grinned. "She told me that I have cute buns and thinks you must admire them."

Gideon choked and fought to keep a straight face. "Hardly professional medical conduct," he said dryly.

"Not really, no," Joshua chuckled.

"But she's right."

The days came and went in as normal a routine as possible. Other than a tendency on everyone's part to jump whenever the phone rang, the Oakwoods household managed to deal with the tension and uncertainty. By mutual agreement, nothing was mentioned to the rest of the Brotherhood. There was no point until the results were known.

The wedding preparations went forward as planned, although consultations with the pastor and various friends taking important roles were a bit tricky as nothing could be said about the possibility of one of the wedding couple being seriously ill. Joshua was hoping that by holding the wedding on Club Undead, the magic in the island would help him get through the ceremony.

Then at last the phone call came. Gill was brisk and professional.

"Please come down to the clinic for the results of your test."

Once again, Evan drove Joshua into town. The clinic waiting room was still crowded—in fact, Joshua could have sworn it contained exactly the same people as it had a week ago. Mary was there and again let Joshua jump the queue and go directly back to Gill's office/examining room. She wouldn't let Evan go in.

"I think you'd better sit down, Joshua," Gillian said. There wasn't any joking today.

"It's bad news, isn't it?" he asked, sinking into the hard metal chair.

"I'm sorry. There's no way to say it gently. The tests came back positive."

He put his head in his hands.

He was a long time in Gill's office, as the doctor and Mary spoke to him, held him, let him come to the realization of the truth at his own speed. It was nearly dark by the time Mary came out to ask Evan to drive Joshua home.

The car pulled into the driveway at Oakwoods, and Joshua thanked God that he was home. He needed to see Gideon, to be held by him, talk to him, maybe cry a little on his shoulder. He went slowly into the house.

Gideon was in his favourite chair in the living room. Evan and Mitch had made themselves scarce, knowing that Joshua would want to speak to Gideon alone. Wondering why Gideon didn't get up and come to greet him, Joshua stopped in the doorway.

"I got the results of the test." No reaction. "I'm HIV positive." There was still no reaction. "Did you hear me?" he asked, suddenly angry.

"Yes." Gideon looked up, his expression unreadable. "You tested HIV positive."

"Doesn't that bother you? Worry you just a little? Do you know what it means?" Joshua felt anger and fear in equal measures. Why was Gideon taking it so calmly? "It's a terminal illness, Gideon, if it develops into AIDS. Doesn't that mean anything to you?"

"Of course it does," Gideon replied calmly. "Come upstairs, and I will turn you, then we don't have to worry about it."

Joshua turned white. "Just like that?" he whispered. "Without even consulting me about it? Is that your solution? Turn me into a vampire?"

"Yes. Really, I do not see what the problem is."

Rocking on his heels, Joshua clenched the door frame for support. "You don't see what the problem is?" he shouted. Controlling himself, he went on more quietly, "I wonder what it is you think you love about me. You are proposing to take away my humanity, to *kill* me, damn it, and you don't see what the problem is. Damn you." He turned and walked out.

Upstairs, Joshua threw some clothes into a suitcase without even really looking at them, and went back down. He avoided the room where Gideon sat, stormed out of the house, and got into his car.

Gideon sat, staring at the doorway in total incomprehension. He had proposed a solution to the problem, why was Joshua so angry? What had they just fought about? He heard the car go down the driveway. Joshua often went for a drive when he was angry, to the village for a drink or to one of the Cliff Road Crowd to complain. He'd likely gone to Mary or Michael for comfort. He would be back soon, having come to the realization that Gideon's solution was the only one.

The hours passed, and Joshua did not return. Gideon continued to sit and stare, reworking the conversation over in his head. No other solution offered itself, and no explanation for Joshua's reaction appeared to him. Something had happened that the Baron simply did not understand.

He held onto his feelings with his usual tight control. The stress was what had made him answer Joshua so unemotionally. It was his way of dealing with intense strain...go cold and quiet and not let his feelings show. Inside, he was hurt and terrified, but he would rather face the True Death than let anyone know...

Dawn found Gideon still in his chair, and the sleep of the undead came upon him by surprise for the first time in a very long while. Evan had to carry the Baron's unconscious form upstairs and put him to bed.

Gideon woke slightly disoriented. He recalled sitting and brooding in his chair, and now he was lying in bed. The morning must have caught him by surprise. How embarrassing, having to be put to bed like a child. He rose, confident that Joshua would have come home and would be waiting downstairs for him.

He would have to apologize, he knew that. He had reacted badly—or rather, not reacted at all.

He found Mitch in hysterical tears, and Evan patting the werewolf on the shoulder. The bodyguard looked up grimly when he heard Gideon approach.

"Joshua didn't come home," Evan said.

The Baron stopped in his tracks at those words. Panic flooded his dark eyes. "He didn't come home?" He repeated the words as they pierced him to the heart. "Did he call?"

"Not a word. Gideon, I've checked with the hospitals, the police—he's not hurt or been in an accident. I think he just went somewhere to think."

Gideon sank into a chair. "He left me," he said, stunned.

"It's your fault!" The hurt, angry words hurled out of Mitch.

"Mitch..." Evan growled.

"No, he's right." Gideon put his head in his hands. "He's right. It's my fault, I drove him away." He gave a long, shuddering sigh. "I have to find him."

"Maybe he doesn't want to be found!" said Mitch tearfully. "He'd have called...someone would have called us."

The phone rang, as if those words had been a portent. Gideon moved faster than the other two.

"Oakwoods," he said cautiously, not daring to hope to hear Joshua's voice.

"Gideon..." the voice was shaky and tired, but undeniably Joshua's.

"Joshua! Where are you? Are you all right? I am so—"

"I'm at Fairlawn. Please come. We can talk here. Bring a car, I'm in no shape to drive myself home, okay?"

"Of course, whatever you want." Gideon shook his head at the questioning looks from the other two. He felt his whole being soar at the words "drive myself home," which meant that Josh wanted to come home. But of course they had to talk. "We'll be there as soon as we can."

He hung up and turned to Evan and Mitch. "He's at Fairlawn, with Michael and Mary. He wants me to bring a car."

"I'll drive!" two voices chorused.

Evan ended up behind the wheel of the Caddy—mostly because he wouldn't let Mitch drive it in such a highly emotional state. When they arrived at Fairlawn, though, only Gideon got out. Evan and Mitch stayed in the car, not wanting to interfere.

"Hi," Joshua said softly.

Gideon leaned against the door of the Fairlawns' living room and studied him. Josh looked tired and a bit tremulous, as if on the verge of tears. Love welled up in the Baron's heart, overriding the old pain and guilt.

"Hi," he replied.

He moved into the room and sat down near Joshua, not quite touching him. The cat in his lover's lap yawned and stretched, purring, eyes opening to scan the new arrival. "I am so sorry," Gideon said.

"Don't say anymore," Josh smiled. "That's all you need to say. I'm sorry, too."

"I love you." Gideon hesitantly reached out and scratched the cat behind the ears. The animal's purr rumbled beneath his fingers. "You look good with a cat in your lap."

"Careful—it's been said we need one around Oakwoods." Joshua grinned. His hand curled around Gideon's. "I'm glad you came. I know this is hard for you to deal with, Gideon. I know that you panicked. We're going to have to work this out together, love."

"I shouldn't have said what I did, not the way I did." Gideon turned his head. "To turn someone like that...it's rape. I should know."

"Gideon..." Joshua sighed, and set the cat down gently on the floor. She looked indignant, as only a rebuffed feline can, and stalked off in high dudgeon. Joshua stood up, unconsciously brushing off the cat hair. "Gideon, I am not going to die tonight, tomorrow, or even next month. It could be years. It depends how fast the AIDS accelerates, and Michael's sure that we can keep it from doing so for a long time. I...I have to believe him, but it's not easy for me. It won't be easy for either of us, I know. But please... don't act as if I'm going to drop dead any minute."

"I don't want you to die. Ever." Gideon swallowed, but the icy lump in his throat did not dissolve. He was seeing himself, one hundred and eighty years before, walking across a room full of flowers to the side of a coffin.

"I'm mortal, Gideon. You knew that when we started out together."

"I had always hoped..." He sighed, seeing the look on Joshua's face. "We have never discussed this." He was still seeing the past, recalling another conversation. "'...I can't be what you are. How you find the strength to go on with such a life, I don't know...I don't wish to be a vampire,'" he quoted softly. "Oh, Joshua, are you making the same choice Jonathan did?"

"I don't know," Joshua replied. "I don't know what motivated Jonathan. I do know that I would make a lousy vampire." He went over and held Gideon's hand again. "You are my heart, my soul, my home, my very life. I love you, and it hurts to be dying, hurts to think of leaving you alone again. But I am mortal, Gideon. I am human. I...I'm not sure that I want to lose that humanity. Don't say that you haven't lost your humanity. You've lost touch with what it is to know that death awaits you."

"Yes, I have. Whatever it is that you decide, Joshua, I will love you. I will try to support your decision, but I can't pretend that it's easy for me. I am so scared at the thought of losing you..."

"I know. I know." Joshua hugged him, and somehow their lips met.

"Well," said Mary's voice, somewhat amused, "I guess you've made up."

They separated, grinning. Mary had come in, followed by Mitch and Evan, who'd been getting cold in the car. She'd offered them the fire and hot tea, and they'd accepted.

"I'm going home," Joshua said, snuggling up to his lover. "We still have things to work out, but somehow, I think it'll be okay."

Reinstalled in Oakwoods, Joshua was very happy to be home. It would not be so bad, he thought, to die in such surroundings. He loved Gideon very much—the argument and its consequences hadn't changed that. Oddly enough, rather, that flare-up had made him love the Baron even more intensely—that Gideon had been so heart sick at the thought of losing him made their relationship even more special. Now that they understood each other more clearly, things were well between the lovers again.

It was Gideon who raised the inevitable question, the night after Joshua came home. They were sitting in the parlour, enjoying the fire and a glass of brandy. Pumpkin and Warg were both asleep in front of the hearth, dreaming of rabbits.

"Are we still going through with the wedding?" Gideon asked suddenly.

"Shouldn't we?" Joshua looked up in surprise. "I'm not letting you off the hook that easily, my friend."

"Then...you still want to marry me?"

"Oh, Gideon, of course I do." Joshua bit his lip. "Or don't you want to marry me, now that I'm..."

"Nothing changes the fact that I love you." Gideon stirred and looked away. "I just wonder if...well, frankly, are you well enough to go through the ceremony and the party afterwards?"

"I'm not that sick yet. We'll just have to hope it's a good day."

"Yes, I suppose." He didn't speak the obvious—that if Joshua would allow himself to be turned, they wouldn't have to hope for a good day.

"Besides," Joshua continued, "everyone's been invited, they've probably already bought gifts...we can't cancel, our friends would kill us. If we were lucky." His smile faded. "We need to tell the Brotherhood. They deserve to know—they're our friends."

"Yes, I agree," Gideon nodded. "If you're sure..."

"I am." The answer was firm. "At least they won't condemn me." Joshua thought bitterly about what the world in general would think. His parents, in particular, would tell him that AIDS was God's judgment on homosexuals.

It was much the same gathering as had celebrated the news of the engagement. Genevieve and Jean had flown in for the wedding a day ago, joining Alexander, Janine, Ray, Francis, Druids Maggie and Nicholas and the Fairlawns in the parlour at Oakwoods. But tonight the atmosphere was totally different. There were no flowers, no champagne and no music. Instead, the Brotherhood sat or stood in little groups, their attention focused on the big wing chair in front of the fire. Joshua was ensconced in this chair. Gideon stood behind him, hands on his lover's shoulders.

"Friends," Joshua said quietly, "Gideon and I have asked you all back here because we have something to tell you." He saw them stir, saw questioning looks and one or two faces go pale. "No, we're not calling off the wedding," he assured them, with an almost-chuckle. "In fact, it's become more important than ever that we go through with it. No, what I have to tell you..." he faltered, and Gideon's grasp on his shoulders tightened. "What I have to tell you," Joshua went on more steadily, "is that I am HIV positive." He heard gasps of dismay. "It may already be AIDS. I received infected blood during an operation!" he almost shouted, then calmed under Gideon's touch. "It's not because of my 'lifestyle.' But I am sick. Michael is going to do everything in his power to keep me alive and healthy for as long as he can. That may be longer than conventional medicine could. I am not going to use such medicine—I won't go on AZT or anything like that." He paused. "And before anyone asks, yes, Gideon offered to turn me. I refused." He paused again, uncertain how to interpret the absolute stillness in the room. "Well, we thought you should know."

Joshua closed his eyes as the silence became almost unbearable. He relaxed as a slow murmur of somber conversation began, full of sympathy, not condemnation. Francis was the first to approach, probably because he was closest. He wrung Joshua's hand, hard, and suddenly grabbed him in an awkward hug.

Maggie took his place. "Hey," said the flame-haired Druidess, giving Joshua's knee a squeeze. "Cheer up. It could be worse."

"It could?" Joshua cocked an eyebrow at her.

"Yeah—you could be pregnant."

He laughed and shook his head. "Mags, you're a nut."

"Seriously, though—listen, I'm really upset about this. Are you going to sue the hospital?"

Joshua looked shocked. "I haven't even thought about it."

"You should. Damn. Wish I'd studied law. But if you ever need me for anything...I'm not a healer, but I can help—I'll feed Michael some of my energy so that he can keep you going."

"Thank you, Maggie."

"Damn," she said again, and kissed him. She stood up, marched over to Gideon, and kissed him, too—and for once he didn't object.

"Maggie," he said.

"Hang in there, Baron." She gripped his upper arm. "Don't you come apart at the seams, you hear me?"

"I'll try," he smiled.

It was getting thicker around them now—Janine was hugging Joshua, Alex and Genevieve were both talking to Gideon, Jean was bouncing up and down with anxiety and helplessness. Michael, Mary, Maggie and Ray were all conferring. It was an unusual group—two Druids, a nurse, and a mage, but their concern for their friends drew them together. The conversation was about healing magic, herbal tea, energy levels, side effects, and treating the symptoms.

It was several hours later when the last of the Brotherhood left for home. Genevieve and Jean had gone to their guest room, respecting the privacy of the soon-to-be wedding couple. Though he was weary to the core, Joshua was deeply touched and heartened by the unwavering support of their friends.

He met Gideon's questioning eyes and grinned suddenly, no cloud over his head for the moment. "Remember how much better the island made us both feel?" He leaned forward. "Why don't we go there in advance, and let it work its magic on me, so that we can be sure it's a good day when the solstice comes around? Evan wants to go ahead to set up security—we can go with him, and have a little privacy before the wedding. We're sure not going to have any afterwards."

"That is an excellent idea. Why don't you call Reagan in the morning and arrange it with her?"

"I could call her now..."

"Oh, no. I have other plans."

"Really?"

"Mmm-hmm. Come to bed and you'll see what those are."

Joshua laughed and put his hand in Gideon's outstretched one.

Afterword

AIDS is now the number one cause of death of men aged 19-35. The number of women infected rises daily. Children are being born with it. The arts community has been decimated by it. No one is "safe." —Anne Fraser

Immortal Addictions
(1996)

"Good evening, Mary, is Michael in?" I offered her a smile, and she returned it.

"Yes, Gideon, he's in the library. Is anything wrong?" Her concern showed in her eyes.

"Everything's fine," I assured her, knowing that she was thinking of Joshua. "I'd have telephoned if it was anything serious, I just thought I'd drop in for a moment."

"Go ahead, then, I think he'll welcome the distraction." She stood aside to let me into the house.

"Thank you. How are the children?"

"Just fine, thanks."

I nodded again and made my way towards Michael's library. It was amusing how many of us had his own personal "lair" in our own house, an inner sanctum that was all our own. Mine was my second floor office, the secluded den outside my bedroom where even Joshua had to knock to gain admittance. Alexander had his study, with its leather sofas and huge fireplace where he liked to pose. Michael had his library, book-lined, fully supplied with a bar and other necessities, a thoroughly masculine room.

"Come in, Gideon," he said, without looking up from the papers on his desk.

Something seemed to be missing from that desk—a handsome carved teak and mahogany antique that he prized highly and that Joshua coveted. But as usual it was piled high with papers, books, pens, a globe, various artifacts and even a small skull, so it was hard for me to place what wasn't there.

"Anyone I knew?" I inquired, picking up the skull.

He grunted. "Not unless you were personally acquainted with

my barn cat."

"Ah. Alas, poor Frisky..." I set the cat skull back down on the desk. Michael frowned and patted his pockets, then sighed and looked up at me.

"What can I do for you this evening, my dear Baron?"

"Nothing, really. I just needed to get out for a bit."

"Everything well at home?" he asked sharply.

"Fine, everything's fine. I was starting to feel too domestic, in fact."

He grinned, and once again reached into his jacket pocket. He was wearing the disreputable old tweed that Mary had tried many times to jettison. "I know what you mean, Gideon. Whatever happened to the old days when adventures galore awaited us? The Brotherhood is all settling down, getting soft in its old age." He toyed with the skull, then with the globe, then patted his pockets again. "Oh, bother," he said under his breath.

Then I realized what was gone from the desk—Michael's pipe rack and smoking paraphernalia. He was patting his pockets in search of his tobacco pouch and matches. The penny dropped.

"You've given up smoking!"

The Archdruid gave me a wry grin. "Aye," he said with another sigh. "Well, Gideon, between Mary, Joshua and the kids nagging me, what choice did I have?" He stopped himself from searching his pockets again. "I'll admit it's a terrible habit, but I miss it already. Gave me something to do with my hands." Realizing he was once again fiddling with the cat skull, he promptly sat on said hands to keep them out of mischief. Since I had seen what else he could do with those magically skilled fingers, I was glad he was stilling them.

"There is the danger of second hand smoke, after all," I pointed out.

"I know, and that's why I gave it up. Distract me, old friend. Let's talk of something else."

We passed an hour or so amicably, talking of doings in the village, of the Brotherhood and our wider circle of supernatural friends, of how passive our lives seemed to have become.

"Not that I'd go through another White Lion or fight with the likes of Corbeau," Michael noted. "But a little spice might be a nice change to keep us from getting too soft."

"You just want something to take your mind off of nicotine withdrawal."

"Just as you want something to distract you from worrying about Joshua all the time," he shot right back.

I freely admitted as much. We drank a last tot of his excellent brandy, and then I departed to make my way back home. On the way, I pondered his words. It was true—I would welcome danger, trouble and the possibility of meeting the true death just to shake me out of a domestic slump. Hadn't there been enough of that in the past? Hadn't we all had our fill of the dangerous times? Wasn't it incredibly stupid to wish for such diversion?

Who was it who said "be careful what you wish for?"

A Gay Old Time
(1997)

Dr. Gillian Tenfeathers looked over her patient's record carefully. For a man to whom she had given a death sentence two years ago, Joshua Trevallion was doing extraordinarily well. The virus in his system had apparently been...contained, was the only word she could think of. He showed no sign of sliding into full-blown AIDS. Although he tended to fatigue easily, he was otherwise almost as healthy as a person without HIV. He still tested positive, but he wasn't any worse off than he'd been when she'd first seen him. In fact, he was better—he'd lost the persistent cough.

"What the hell is your secret?" the doctor demanded. "Your platelets...t-cells...how do you do it?"

Josh smiled. "If I say alternative medicine, will you hurt me?"

"Of course not. I'm not one of those medicos who swear by the book, you know. If you've found something that works that isn't strictly by the AMA, more power to you. Just for the record, though, what *are* you doing?"

"Would you believe me if I said magic?"

"No. Although it depends on the magic. You did say there was a healer...a witch?"

"I think that depends on your definition of the term," Josh grinned, anticipating Michael's reaction to that particular label. "But it is largely herbal treatment, and a little of the power of positive thinking."

"Hm." Gillian kept her reservations to herself. She'd seen "the power of positive thinking" fail all too often, and had had to deal with patients who felt guilty that they'd been unable to think themselves well. But if it was working for Josh...she'd seen stranger things. Things that could only be called miracles. Maybe, just maybe, this time...

"And I'm watching my diet," Josh added.

"Don't obsess," Gillian warned him. "You can't afford to lose weight."

"Not in that sense," Josh assured her. "I'm just eating healthier, keeping up my strength."

"Lots of protein?"

"Yes."

"Good. Okay, whatever you're doing, keep it up. I don't see any reason to change."

"Right, chief," Josh saluted, glad she hadn't mentioned drug therapy. Not even Gillian wanted him on the possibly debilitating AZT "cocktail" of drugs that was having results with some AIDS patients. Josh didn't have AIDS, not yet, and the treatment had some pretty severe side effects.

"I'm not a chief, I'm a shaman," the Native American chuckled. "Okay, get those cute buns of yours out of here, see you next month."

He saluted her with a grin and departed.

When he arrived back at Oakwoods, Josh looked through the mail that Mitch had stacked on his desk. A few letters from friends, a few advertising circulars, two requests from steady clients, an invitation...

He read the invitation over twice. One of his friends from the antique world was having a party to celebrate his acquisition of a rare sculpture, would Joshua and his partner care to come?

Since he had moved in with Gideon, Joshua had circulated a lot less among his old friends. He couldn't envision explaining to them that his new lover was a vampire; nor imperil them by introducing them to the Brotherhood. He still visited and called, but they often wondered why he never invited any of them to his new home. None of his old circle had ever met Gideon. He knew that speculation about "Josh's husband" was rife.

Well. Time and past to at least partially remedy that. He wrote an acceptance to the invitation, then ripped up the letter and called his friend, giving a verbal RSVP and ending up having a great conversation.

Too long without his circle, he thought; too long cooped up in this house or going to parties where the punch bowl and ladle had to be chained down and you were likely to wind up in a different dimension. He *was* still human, and sometimes he missed human company.

Gideon, he reflected, was not going to be happy. Too darned bad.

There was the inescapable fact that most of the people at the party were going to be gay, and flagrantly so, and that alone would make the retiring vampire upset. Gideon didn't flaunt his preference, but did his best to downplay it. Being thrust into a party full of raging queens was going to give him fits. This should prove interesting...

That evening, as Josh and Gideon played a friendly game of billiards in the basement games room, the antiques expert carefully introduced the subject of the party. He braced himself for Gideon's anger—or worse, sarcasm—when he stated that he'd already accepted. He was caught off-guard when the dark-haired vampire nodded.

"You're right, of course," Gideon said, sighting along his cue.

"I am?" Josh replied incredulously.

"Yes." The Baron made his shot, gave a sharp nod of satisfaction, and moved around the table for his next attempt. "It is not fair that it is always I who takes you to parties. Of course I should meet your friends. Long overdue, in fact. I thought you might be afraid to introduce me to them, or I would have suggested it years ago."

The balls clacked across the baize again, and once more Gideon followed their progress. He had a devastatingly keen eye and steady hand at this game. Josh had never beaten him.

Joshua managed not to gape. "My friends..." he said, groping for words, "they're not...I mean, they..."

"Are human?" Gideon looked up, laughter dancing in his dark eyes. "I rather expected that, you know." He sent the balls off on their appointed rounds again.

"They're gay."

Another sharp glance from those eyes. "And the problem with this is...?"

The breather threw up his hands. "Nothing, of course. But remember how you felt about Jeffy..."

The cue missed, nearly tearing the green cloth. "Oh," sighed Gideon. "You mean they're *gay.*"

Another problem never really resolved between the two of them was Gideon's intense dislike of those who trumpeted their homosexuality to the world. He eyed public outings with horror, feeling (and Josh found it hard to argue with this) that one's sexual preference was a private matter. This caused him to avoid any activities or mannerisms that would label him "gay," except of course living with a male lover.

But Gideon could not only pass for straight, he could graduate with top honours. He loathed the more flamboyant members of the gay community.

Joshua was much more comfortable and easy with his homosexuality than Gideon would ever be. He'd known this from the beginning, of course. It had taken him months to break down that icy reserve, to find the warm and loving man under it. He knew he'd never get Gideon in a Gay Pride Day parade, or anything along those lines. "If you don't want to go," Josh said, "I'll call Trev back and tell him I'm coming alone."

Gideon pulled himself to his full height of five foot six, and looked Joshua in the eyes. "You will not."

Josh knew that tone, Gideon's Lord Of The Manor voice. Usually he tried to get his lover back down to normal when he talked like that.

But in this case, whatever worked...

"Fine. I'm glad. You might surprise yourself and have fun."

"I doubt that sincerely," was the dry response. "Your shot, I believe."

They arrived on the doorstep of Trevor's house in a suburb of New York shortly after dark on the day of the party. Gideon was as relaxed as the average bowstring at Agincourt. Joshua had given up trying to get him to calm down. He glanced at his husband to make sure that Gideon wasn't going to bolt, and rang the doorbell.

The strains of Sondheim rolled out into the street as the door opened, along with a cloud of "Oscar" cologne. A thin man with short hair and a mustache in nondescript brown opened his arms and grabbed Josh in an effusive hug.

"Joshie, darling, it's been *ages!*" he exclaimed, kissing his guest on the cheek and leaving a trace of lipstick.

"Hello, Trev," said Joshua, who hated being called Joshie.

"Oh, you came! You darling! And is this the new husband? Oh, he's shy, isn't that cute? Come on and let Trev see you, darling, I won't bite."

Struggling with himself as he swallowed the reply that readily came to mind, Gideon stepped into the light that streamed out onto the porch. He was dressed in a burgundy sweater, white shirt and dark blue pants, at Josh's insistence. A suit would have been horribly out of place at this party. He felt ridiculous, even though the clothing was conservative by anyone's standards.

Compared to Trevor's "Bette Midler is a goddess!" t-shirt and tight jeans, Gideon's clothing looked downright formal. Joshua was wearing a multicoloured sweater and casual black pants.

Trevor took a couple of steps back. "Oh, goodness, Josh, you never said you'd found such a treasure! No wonder you've been keeping him to yourself! So *you're* Gideon. You're delicious! You must come in and meet the girls, they'll be salivating with jealousy!"

His expression speaking volumes, at least to the one who loved him, Gideon followed Trevor and Joshua into the house. "Into the Woods" swirled around them as they were ushered into the living room and a sea of sound. The mostly male assemblage were draped around like so many manikins, talking, sipping drinks, or listening to the music. A few women were scattered here and there for variety, and a couple of the men were looking self-conscious or nervous.

Straights, thought Josh with sympathy, *Or ones like Gideon, who hate all this affectation and wish this stereotype would die out...*It was a stereotype, he realized. He himself fell into it from time to time, although never when Gideon was with him.

Trevor clapped his hands for silence. "Girls! Girls!" he called out. "And boys, for the few of you who are." Giggles. "Look who's here! It's our long-lost Joshie and his husband! This is the Gideon of whom we've heard so much! Isn't he precious?"

Feeling decidedly less than precious, unless that was an apt description of a deer caught in the headlights, Gideon felt every pair of eyes in the party focus on him. He was unused to being the center of attention, and he didn't like it. Every instinct shrieked at him to get out of here, to fade into the woodwork, to be safe...

"Where *did* you find him, Josh?" asked one of the "girls," a pretty young man leaning on an older male who was rubbing his hand up and down his companion's jeans.

"In an antique store," Joshua replied. "He was right next to the old Victrola and had a sign saying "Will you give this bear a good home?" around him."

They all laughed, and even Gideon managed a tremulous smile, and the ice was broken. Trevor fetched drinks for the newcomers, spots were found for them amongst the mounds of humanity, and the party began in earnest.

The Sondheim was cranked up, people were dancing, a couple were passing around a joint that Josh and Gideon both refused. Josh was drawn into shop talk by several of his friends from the antique world, and he entertained them with stories of triumphs on the auction floor.

Although Joshua threw himself into the spirit of the party, he couldn't help but notice that Gideon remained uptight and unhappy. He wasn't the only one who spotted that, either. Trevor drew the guest of honour away on the pretense of looking at the statue that was the ostensible reason for the occasion while Gideon was trying to listen politely to a conversation about the relative merits of knee pads. He was managing not to look horrified.

The host pulled Joshua into a nook lit with a yellow spot focused on a bronze statue of a naked boy strumming a lute.

"Cellini," said Trevor off-handedly as Joshua admired the bronze. He sounded like he bought Cellinis every day. "Joshie, darling..."

"Trevor, I adore you, but don't call me that."

"Sorry. Habit, you know. Josh, then, if you must be macho about it. What is it with that husband of yours?"

"What do you mean?"

"Why does he have such a poker up his ass?"

"Gideon's a very private person. He's not an outie."

"Not one of the girls? Pity. He'd look darling in Chanel."

"Don't even think it, Trev. He's having a lot of trouble dealing with this, don't push him."

"Wouldn't dream of it, sweetie. But I can't speak for the girls."

The "girls" were indeed circling Gideon once he'd lost the protective colouring of his husband. The pretty young man who'd spoken earlier came and leaned against the vampire.

"Want to dance?" he cooed. "Rafe, be an angel and put on some ABBA."

Rafe complied, and disco music began smothering the room with the unmistakable beat of the Australian group. "Come and dance," urged the young man, pulling on Gideon's hand.

"No, thank you," replied the Baron coldly. He cast his eyes around furtively for help, but everyone was waiting for him to dance with his new acquaintance. Gideon, close to panic, couldn't even remember the boy's name.

"Not even to ABBA?" asked the boy, whose name was Robbie.

All eyes were on him again, Gideon realized. Was he failing some kind of test? What was an ABBA?

"To whom?" he asked, and knew it was a mistake.

Jaws dropped. Even the women looked shocked. Someone stopped the tape right in the middle of "Dancing Queen" and the silence that filled the room was terrible. Joshua and Trevor re-entered, too late to save Gideon.

"Whom?" several voices squeaked. Then the inquisition began.

"Do you like flowers?"

"Are you a friend of Dorothy's?"

"How do you feel about Bette Midler?"

"Have you ever seen Kiss of the Spider Woman?"

"What's the title of Barbra Streisand's fifth album?"

All of which Gideon could not answer.

"Josh, honey," Trevor turned to his guest. "Are you *sure* he's gay?"

The couple fled to their hotel shortly afterwards. Gideon was nearly speechless, but Joshua couldn't bring himself to apologize. He didn't have anything to apologize for. Trevor and the "girls" were his friends. On the other hand, the years at Oakwoods, in Gideon's company, had changed Joshua's perspective on the gay life. One didn't have to be quite so outrageously out of the closet, he knew. It was partially an act. But Trevor, at least, had been playing the role so long that it had become his personality.

Yet there was more to being gay than wearing make-up, having limp wrists and calling people "darling." You could be gay without being a stereotype. Josh had been hoping to bring Gideon a little out of his discomfort at his own sexuality, but now he was afraid he'd gone too far in the opposite direction. Such an immersion had hardly been gentle, and Gideon needed gentle treatment. Was nothing in this relationship ever easy? Joshua sighed. Maybe he had made a mistake. Gideon's reserve was an integral part of him, and if he loved Gideon, he should love that aspect, too. Just as Gideon needed to come to terms with Josh's mortality and illness, Josh needed to come to terms with Gideon's hangups. They'd worked through a lot of things in the years they'd been together, but there was still a lot of ground to cover.

"You aren't like that." They were the first words Gideon had spoken since leaving Trevor's place.

"No," Joshua said, not having to ask what he meant. "I can be, if I want, but usually it's too much work. Sometimes I'm bad, though. Some people bring it out in me."

"But not all the time," Gideon went on. "Is that all...necessary? To be a 'real' homosexual, do I have to learn to like Barbara Sondheim and Stephen Streisand?"

Josh managed, with a valiant effort, not to either laugh or

correct his lover. "No, of course not. You don't have to give a damn about either of them, or about interior decorating, hair dressing, Bette Midler or *Kiss of the Spider Woman*. They have no right to define you by their standards."

"Just as I have no right to define them by mine?" Gideon said softly. "Of course you are right, and I am as guilty of being judgmental as they are."

"Definitions are always difficult," Josh said. "The very word 'gay' has undergone a radical transformation. It used to mean 'happy.' Just as 'queer' meant 'odd' and 'faggot' meant 'bundle of wood.' The last two are considered pejoratives if used by outsiders, yet gays use them to take the sting from the words. Much like some blacks now use the word 'nigger.'"

"And the point of this lecture, Professor?" Gideon asked mildly.

His husband threw a slipper in his general direction, missing by a foot. "The point is that what's important is how you define yourself, and if you're comfortable with that definition. Do you define yourself as gay?"

Gideon thought about it, then shook his head. "No. I don't. I am a person who just happens to be a homosexual vampire. I don't make either one my ultimate definition, they're facets of who I am, not what I am."

"Oh, well said." Josh applauded.

"All the same, even though it was something of a disaster, I am glad we went tonight. It opened my eyes somewhat."

"Mine, too," Joshua replied, putting his arms around his husband. "I realized again how much I really do love you."

"Will you give this bear a good home?" Gideon asked, eyes dancing.

"Without a second of hesitation." Josh ruffled the dark hair within his reach. "But...are *you* sure you're gay?"

"Would you care for a demonstration?"

Reprise
(1999)

Dedicated to the memory of Marcus R. Blake, 1960-1996, who wanted the dragon. Mark, I never knew you, but you were a friend. Rest in peace.

Dry, dead leaves danced over the driveway, a crinkly papery noise marking their progress. A fresh gust of late fall wind sent them swirling up into the grey sky, as if they were trying to fly back to the tall oak trees from which they had fallen.

"'Like the dry leaves that before the wild hurricane fly, when they meet with an obstacle, mount to the sky,'" quoted Joshua Trevallion, one of two men standing below the oaks, watching the leaves tumble down as the breeze deserted them.

"'Up to the rooftop, his coursers they came,'" gamely replied the other man, Evan Jones, "'And he whistled and shouted and called them by name.' It's still a few weeks till Christmas, Josh."

"I know." Josh drew his cloak more tightly around him. It was a beautiful cloak, patterned with brown, gold and crimson oak leaves, and it had been a wedding gift from...well, a god. A woodland deity. The Green Man, The Oak King.

Oak leaves, somewhat stylized, also decorated the white gold wedding band the cloaked man bore on his left hand. He himself had oak-like colouring; hair the colour of golden fall leaves, eyes the colour of those same leaves as they died.

Evan had nothing of the oak in his appearance, except perhaps as a general impression of solidity. He was auburn-haired, tallish, well-muscled, and had the quiet alertness of the professional bodyguard.

"Winter's coming in, though," Evan observed. "We'll have to get Mitch to chop some firewood."

"And make sure the snowblower and generator are in working order," agreed Joshua with a smile. "And stock the pantry and the freezer..."

Evan nodded seriously. "And rake up the leaves, fix that loose shingle on the roof, clean out the eavestroughs, round up the cattle..."

Josh's mouth twitched. "We don't have cattle."

They both broke out laughing. Of course most of the work mentioned would have to be done before the snow flew, but nobody expected the youngest member of the Oakwoods household to do it all by himself. Evan would most likely do the lion's share of it.

"Well, round up the livestock, then," Evan said when he could stop laughing.

Josh looked down the Cliff Road, where three of the "livestock" were out taking Mitch for a walk. A large gray panther, a small brown and white spaniel, and an aging timber wolf...only a jet black horse with red eyes was missing from the inventory.

"If we ever get an elephant, we can open a zoo," Josh said.

The wind picked up again, sending more dead leaves scurrying. Josh's cloak flapped, oak-patterned wings. He sighed as he gathered it close again.

"It's not too cold for you, is it?" Evan asked, instantly solicitous.

"No," Josh assured him. "It's just windy. And the changing of seasons always makes me think. Especially when it's fall turning to winter; it's a bit depressing." He shook his head. "Listen to me!" he exclaimed. "I think I had better go inside."

He turned back towards the house. Evan automatically turned to go with him, but Josh shook his head. "If you don't mind," he said softly, "I'd rather be alone for a bit. Don't worry, okay?"

"Okay," Evan promised, but his dark eyes were veiled as he watched his friend walk towards Oakwoods.

Inside the warm house, Josh carefully hung up the oak leaf cloak. He walked into the kitchen and made a pot of coffee—both Evan and Mitch would want it when they came in, and he could do with some as well. He opened a package of cookies and put some on a plate, then sat down at the breakfast nook.

The turning of the seasons, fall to winter; the death of the land. Before long it would be the winter solstice, the shortest day of the year. A time when once sacrifices had been made to the gods or goddesses; bright blood shed and bright fires lit to ensure the return of the sun and the rebirth of the land. Many traditional, innocent-seeming Christmas decorations still echoed these older sacrifices: the red holly berries, the Yule log, candles, mistletoe...

The weight of his own mortality seemed to bear down on

Joshua's shoulders these days. The coming of winter was a dangerous season for him; despite the excellent attention he was receiving from his assorted healers and caregivers, he could easily catch pneumonia and it would be straight downhill from there. But his health and the HIV/AIDS threat that lurked in his blood weren't his major concern.

There were gray hairs in his comb, new laugh wrinkles around his eyes.

Joshua Daniel Trevallion would be forty-five on his next birthday. His husband, his lover, his friend and dearest companion, Gideon Redoak, would be three hundred and seventy five on his next birthday.

On the night they had become lovers, more than seven years ago, Gideon had explained that he was a vampire. But Joshua had been in love—still was, for that matter—and he had also long suspected there was something a trifle unusual about Gideon.

Life with Gideon had never been dull, and things had certainly been extremely interesting since the two of them had gotten involved with the global subculture of supernatural beings—a loose, always fluctuating collection of assorted vampires, werecreatures, merfolk, mages, witches, and some who defied easy categorization. Almost a very large, unofficial extension of the Brotherhood of Darkness, although without the Brotherhood's underlying purpose, this secret underground culture had provided friendship and support for the Oakwoods residents through the most difficult period in their lives, and had helped them celebrate their wedding.

Joshua now understood far more about vampires and other such beings than he had ever thought possible. He knew about the bloodlines, that different turnsires meant different abilities in their get. Gideon's bloodline was an old one; the vampires of his line had many of the stereotype abilities and limitations. But there were vampires with reflections, or who could withstand sunlight, who had no aversion to silver, even those who did not need to drink human blood.

Josh had had compassionate offers, not just from Gideon. He had refused them all.

That had been three years ago.

He had seen Gideon, sometimes, watching him as if he were a soap bubble or an impossibly fragile piece of porcelain. He had seen the look in Gideon's eyes whenever HIV or AIDS made the news. The household tiptoed around the issue.

Three years ago, the prospect of turning had filled Joshua

with horror. The fall-out had been awful; he and Gideon had nearly split up over it. Gideon had not handled the question diplomatically; in fact, he had not even asked, he had simply stated his intention to turn Joshua. Nothing had been quite the same since. Three years of silence was a long time to a mortal who didn't have the time to spare. Gideon had made it very plain that he did not wish to discuss it. Maybe it was high time Joshua broke down that barrier.

But then Smoke and Pumpkin were racing into the kitchen, bringing the smell of autumn with them, closely followed by Mitch, Evan and Warg. The men were in search of hot coffee, the animals of treats. The noise and laughter brought Joshua out of his funk and made him temporarily forget his dark musings.

The fall seemed unduly stretched out. Not even the coast of Maine was being hit by the usual heavy snowfalls and cold winds. Since a terrible winter had been predicted, the mild weather was regarded as a joke. On December 1st, it was sixty degrees in downtown Fletcherville. Local wags suggested putting up the Independence Day bunting instead of the Christmas decorations. The stores lamented that the unseasonable weather was hurting Christmas sales; the owners of ski resorts looked grim.

Where had the time gone? Joshua found himself wondering about this as he handed evergreen boughs and red bows up to Mitch. The young werewolf was perched atop a stepladder decking Oakwoods' halls. A careless move on Mitch's part made a substantial branch fall, almost decking the lord of the manor.

Gideon blinked and picked up the branch of pine. "A little more care, please, Mitch," he said dryly, handing the offending branch up to the blushing lycanthrope. "I would prefer not to have a forest dropped on me in my own home."

"Sorry, boss," Mitch grinned.

Gideon looked at his husband. Josh felt a wave of familiar emotions and once more gave thanks that he had somehow ended up paired with this man.

This vampire.

"Our decorator seems to have forgotten something," Gideon observed, glancing around at the wonders Mitch had wrought in the living room.

Josh looked around in some confusion. A twelve foot Douglas fir had sacrificed its life to the Christmas cause and stood in its pot of water in one corner, waiting to be decorated. They always waited for Gideon to get up before they did the tree. But the fireplace mantel, the doorways, and several other surfaces bore evergreen boughs festooned with red bows. Two handsome wreaths adorned the front doors. Holly, candles, the beautiful antique St. Nicholas that Josh had given Mitch last year...all were in attendance. Eight stockings hung by the chimney; one for each person and one for each animal.

"What could possibly be missing?" Josh asked.

"Mistletoe," Gideon replied with a smile.

"So, who needs it?" Josh asked, drawing the shorter man into an embrace. His death would mean that Gideon would lose him. The thought, flickering across his subconscious, even as Gideon's lips met his, startled Joshua. Something of his confusion must have been conveyed to his partner, for Gideon stepped back.

"What is it?" the vampire asked softly. Seven years of intimacy had taught him to read Josh's moods. "Is something wrong?"

"No," Josh reassured him. "Just...not in front of the kids." He indicated the ladder with Mitch grinning down at them.

"Pfui," said Gideon. "He's seen us kiss, we're hardly shocking him." But his eyes were troubled; he knew Josh was lying.

The intimacy of the moment was lost, and Joshua cursed himself. He gave his lover a chaste peck on the cheek. "That's my IOU for when we get mistletoe," he said, and walked away.

The month of December was a whirl of snow, a gust of wind, a scent of pine and gingerbread. With Gideon's birthday, their wedding anniversary, Christmas itself, New Year's Eve...

"So, what are your resolutions?" Joshua asked Gideon.

It was perhaps two hours into the new year. After watching the ball drop on Times Square with Evan and Mitch, Gideon and Joshua had retired to ring in 1999 their own way.

"The end of the millennium," Josh mused.

His lover, who had seen the end of three previous centuries, shrugged. "I don't see what the fuss is all about."

Josh propped himself up on one elbow and stared at Gideon. "No, you really don't, do you?"

"2000 is just a number," said Gideon, a trifle smugly.

"It's a little different from my perspective."

"Explain it to me."

Josh leaned back on the pillow. "The end of a millennium is always time for a certain amount of hysteria. People are convinced the world will end. There's an increased religious fervour; a swelling of belief in angels and miracles...surely you've noticed how popular angels are suddenly? There's also a rise of belief in the occult and the supernatural. Coincidentally, vampires become very popular."

"We don't have anything to do with ends of millennia," Gideon protested.

"I didn't say any of this was logical. But we mere mortals don't always use logic. You're forgetting the herd mentality. If enough people tell us that the year 2000 will be the end of the world, then a lot of us are going to believe it. And this time around, there's also the millennium bug."

Gideon nodded. He read newspapers. He knew that the millennium bug wasn't an insect. "All the computers in the world will fry their circuits at one second past midnight, January first, 2000. Is that it?"

"More or less," Joshua agreed. "It's throwing people into a panic. We've come to rely on computers for everything. There are those who believe that all the electricity will fail, so they've bought wood stoves and Coleman lanterns. People are scared, Gideon."

His husband's right arm encircled his shoulders. "You're not afraid, are you?" Gideon asked softly.

"I am, a little," Joshua confessed.

"You asked me what my resolutions are. My first one...my only one...is to be right here for you. Always. End of millennia, end of the world, bug or no bug. Always."

But it wouldn't be always, Joshua thought sadly as Gideon kissed him. I don't have always.

Unless.

Gideon's kiss was deepening, his fingers were exploring Josh's erogenous zones, and all thoughts of mortality fled.

January was a bleak, cold month. The winds off the Atlantic were daggers of ice. Joshua didn't get out of the house very often; there were few auctions in January, and to go out for pleasure was too big a risk to his health.

He had lots of time of contemplate his upcoming birthday, his future, and the fact of his mortality. As of yet, he kept these thoughts to himself, not wanting to upset Gideon.

One day, when the winds were calm and the sun shone, he picked up the phone and asked Mary Fairlawn to come and visit.

They were nearly of an age, he and Mary. They both had married men who were immortal. He'd always felt he could talk to her without feeling the unspoken pressure of talking to any of the Brotherhood. She had been the third person to know he was HIV positive, after his doctor and himself.

They ate lunch together in the Oakwoods kitchen. Mitch was off in town, Evan doing chores around the house. Over coffee, sleeves of his sweater rolled up, Josh looked at his friend.

The years were telling on her, too. Child-bearing unexpectedly late in life had left her a bit plump. Her reddish-brown hair had grey in it, and she wore contact lenses.

"Just a pair of middle-aged biddies," he sighed out loud.

Mary's eyes sparked. "Who are you calling a biddy?"

Josh grinned. "Okay, middle-aged wives, then."

She swatted his hand. "Stop that. I'm a wife. You aren't."

"Huh." He sipped coffee. "That's what you think."

Mary frowned. "Is anything wrong between you and Gideon?"

"No, no, that's not what I meant. Everything's fine. Except, of course, for the Great Unmentionable."

"Ah." She settled back in her chair. "Yes, the Great Unmentionable. I can only imagine how difficult this is for you and Gideon both."

"Mary...can I get really personal?"

"Of course, Josh."

"Do you and Michael...do you ever talk about it, that you're going to die while he goes on living?" He shook his head. "That was blunt."

She smiled. "It's okay. I've come to terms with it. Yes, we talk about it. Not obsessively, but we don't try to pretend it's not going to happen. Michael and I both accept it."

"Nobody's offered to turn you into a vampire," said Josh, a trifle bitterly.

"Well, no. Oddly enough, Josh, it was Gideon who was the first to mention the problem to Michael, that he was immortal and I was not. That was long before Gideon met you; he was thinking of Jonathan."

"And what did Michael say?"

"That we never know how long we will have to share with a loved one. It could be five years, or fifteen, or fifty...it is the loving that counts, not the amount of time. It's not entirely impossible that Michael could die before I do. I nearly lost him once. Gideon could be killed before you die."

Joshua's surprised look told her that he'd never considered the possibility. "That's true," he conceded. "Something else I have to take into account."

Mary reached out and took hold of his hands in hers. "Joshua, the only things that you have to take into account are your own needs and wishes, and those of Gideon. You can't go through life waiting for the other shoe to drop, wondering what's going to happen or which of you is going to die first. You've had three years to come to grips with being HIV positive and the backlash of that; you've had almost forty-five years to come to grips with being mortal and human."

"Time to fish or cut bait?" Josh asked, but he was smiling.

She shook her head. "There seems to be someone missing from this conversation. I can't tell you what to do. Michael can't, either, wise as he may be. Our situation is a little different, though there are some similarities. Gideon," and her voice softened, "is not Michael. I know that when the inevitable happens, Michael will miss me and grieve for me, but he will get on with his life because that is what he has to do. I do not begrudge him that. I love him very much, and I long since reconciled myself to the fact that I come second to his Goddess." She grinned and Josh couldn't help grinning back. He knew that Michael was much more firmly grounded than that, Mary came first—by a very narrow margin. "But we aren't talking about Michael," Mary went on, still gently. "We are talking about Baron Gideon Redoak."

Joshua pulled back his hands, ostensibly to take a sip of his now cold coffee. "Talking about him is one thing," he sighed. "Talking *to* him is another."

Mary looked at him steadily, the look of a head nurse who didn't take any guff from patients or underlings, the look of a mother who had raised an adopted daughter and natural twins and didn't take any guff from them, either. "Have you *tried?*"

"I..."

"Lately?"

"But..."

"Joshua, you're beginning to rethink the situation after three years. Don't deny it, it's been preying on your mind. You're thinking about your mortality, and dying, and you've been thinking about becoming a vampire."

She watched the white of shock wash over his face. "How did you know?"

"What would be the point of this conversation otherwise?" Mary's tone softened again. "It's obvious that that's what you've been thinking, Josh. This is not something you should keep to yourself. Don't exclude Gideon from a decision-making process that affects you both."

"You're right, but it won't be easy."

"Nothing important is ever easy." Mary stood up, and so did

he. She reached across the breakfast nook to hug him. "There are worse fates than being a vampire," she whispered.

Roses, Joshua thought as he watched Gideon move amongst the plants in the conservatory, *play far too large a role in love.* A dozen long-stemmed beauties doesn't signify love, it just signifies that the giver couldn't think of anything else. The number of poems, literary quotes, songs and stories about roses was staggering. A rose lay at the heart of many a fairy tale. Their scent, in the close confincs of thc glass walls, was almost oppressive.

He watched Gideon. The Baron, dressed in his oldest clothes and protected by a thick, tough cloth gardening apron and gardening gloves, would have killed himself if anyone had walked in to observe him. He only grudgingly allowed his housemates to observe him at work in his conservatory. As he pruned and deadheaded and shifted compost, his face was utterly peaceful. A happy man, working with his beloved plants. When he was relaxed, like this, he tended to forget about maintaining his dignity and illusion of middle-age. He was a young man, a young, good-looking man, playing in the dirt.

Joshua fought a grin. *Behold, the dreaded vampire,* he thought. He broke off, disturbed.

He had never, ever thought of Gideon as a monster. It was impossible to do so now, with Gideon's dark head bowed over a clump of old floribundas, as he inhaled their scent and tenderly touched their velvet petals. *Anyone who loves roses as much as he does can't be that terrible.*

Gideon looked up at his husband's laugh, a smile playing at his own lips. "What's funny?"

"Beauty and the Beast."

"And which one are you?" Gideon teased.

"I'll get you for that," Josh promised. "But...it's always struck me as a slightly unsatisfactory story."

His interest piqued, Gideon stopped what he was doing and came and sat by Joshua. He peeled off his thick gloves, revealing his pale, manicured aristocrat's hands. But he kept his unappealing gardening apron on, its numerous stains and rips testifying to hard use in the cause of the roses. A most unlikely Beast, this quiet little man with the serious dark eyes.

"Beauty," Joshua began, feeling odd to be telling Gideon a bedtime story, "eventually fell in love with the Beast, did she not?"

"So I've always understood."

"The whole point of the story is that she fall in love with the

Beast. With a monster, or a man in the semblance of a monster. She is terrified of him at first, then comes to pity him, value his company, and eventually to love him."

"Yes..." Gideon was looking dubious now, wondering where this was going.

"Roses," Joshua reached out to touch the nearest one, a pale yellow rose that bobbed above Gideon's head, "play a very important part in the story of Beauty and the Beast. When she wants to go back to her family, he gives her a rose, and tells her she must return before it dies, or he will die with it. For he has come to love her. It is not until the rose dies that she realizes that she loves him, and returns to him in a panic, thinking that he is dead. She finds him barely alive, and promises at last to marry him."

"I have heard the story, you know," Gideon said, bemused and amused. "When she agrees to marry him, he turns back into a handsome prince and the spell is broken."

"That is the unsatisfactory part," Joshua said. "He turns into a handsome prince, a total stranger to Beauty. It is the Beast that she fell in love with, not a handsome prince."

Gideon thought about this for a long time. The sound of the heaters and the air circulation system in the conservatory were loud in Joshua's ears, the beating of his heart seemed to be in time to the growing of the roses.

"So," the Baron said, stirring and frowning as he thought it out, "the Beast should have remained a Beast?"

"It is he that Beauty loved."

"Interesting," Gideon observed. "I'd never thought of it that way." He thought a little longer. "I wonder if the Beast wanted to be turned back into a handsome prince...or if he would have chosen to remain a Beast."

"If it meant keeping Beauty's love?" Joshua kept his eyes level, fighting the urge to look anywhere but at Gideon. "What if he could have made her a Beast?"

In the utter silence, a rose petal could have been heard falling.

"Perhaps the Beast offered," said Gideon just when Joshua was sure he was going to get up and walk out. "And Beauty said no."

"Beauty said no when he asked her to marry him," Joshua reminded him. "Yet she changed her mind."

Gideon stood up, but he did not walk away. He shrugged out of the stained apron, and neatly folded it up. He stood, holding it awkwardly, not quite sure what to do with it or how to continue this conversation.

"I cannot ask 'Beauty will you marry me,'" he finally said. "We are already married, and neither of us has turned into a handsome prince as a result. But I know, my Beauty, that when this rose," he touched Joshua's shoulder, "dies, I too will die."

Joshua stood up, too, and hugged Gideon. He breathed in the rose and compost scent of his husband, felt the absolute stillness of the vampire body pressed against his. No heartbeat, no breath, no stomach gurglings or other signs of busy mortal life. A Beast. A Beast who loved roses, who never allowed his emotions to rule him. A Beast who loved him.

"It's my birthday soon," Joshua said.

"I know. But are you really asking for that kind of a gift?"

"I still don't know, Gideon. Things...have been weighing on me. The turning of the seasons. Growing older. The millennium. But..."

Gideon nodded. "But," he said, gently, "it's still not something you think you want."

He stood there oddly vulnerable in his old clothes. He looked, Joshua thought with the beginnings of more laughter twitching at his lips, more like the undergardener than the Lord of the Manor...just like Percy had, when they had first met him.

If this was being a vampire, then maybe it wasn't really so bad.

"I just don't know," Joshua bit his lip to keep from laughing. It would have hurt Gideon's feelings. "But for both our sakes, Gideon, let's try to be more communicative on the subject, okay? It's been three years. More."

Gideon nodded. "I don't ever want you to run away again."

Joshua woke shortly after dawn. He knew the time simply by the fact that the man lying beside him was literally dead to the world.

This was one of the many problems of being a vampire. No sunlight, no daylight. A literal death each dawn, a literal resurrection each nightfall. No more being able to watch the play of sunlight on leaves, watch the shadows change, see the sunset set the sky on fire. Of course, it also meant not getting any sun in your eyes as you were driving...Josh had to fight a sudden grin.

Sure, look for the up side.

Gideon claimed not to miss sunlight. Josh supposed that, after almost four centuries without it, Gideon had simply forgotten it. You could get used to anything in time. But no more food? No eating, no joy of cooking gourmet meals, no more chocolate cake or Pad Thai or chicken Della robia or grilled cheese sandwiches? Josh, a gourmet to the bone, wasn't sure he could ever get used to that.

The alternative was also never eating again, only more so. At least vampires got that liquid protein diet. If he thought of it that way, it wasn't so utterly terrible. Gideon made do with bottled animal blood, black-marketed by the Nameless Ones from slaughterhouses. Josh suspected that Gideon didn't actually like it very much, but he did it in order to lead as "normal" a life as possible. He didn't want to prey on human beings for their blood if he could help it.

Were those the actions of a monster, an undead fiend, a predator? No.

They'd managed to have a long talk tonight, in the conservatory and after. Gideon had talked about being a vampire. He seemed to have come to terms with it, though he never thought of himself in terms of being just a vampire, anymore than he thought of himself in terms of being gay or being short.

Joshua lived with a vampire, and dealt with others every night of his life. They were his friends, his confidants. He had lost his fear and horror of vampires, and had come to realize that most of them were not monsters.

But it was one thing to accept them, to befriend them, to sympathize with their plight. It was another thing entirely to contemplate becoming one.

How would he ever adjust? What sort of vampire would he become? Could he ever learn to live in the nighttime, to shun sunlight, to...drink blood?

Mary had told him to include Gideon in on the decision-making process, to ask his opinions, not to shut him out. It hadn't been easy, for either of them, but a lot of progress had been made tonight. Gideon was finally willing to listen and advise rather than merely command; and Joshua had had plenty of time to assimilate his emotions and his responses to the threat to his health and life. They'd had three years to deal with this separately, now it was time to deal with it together.

Joshua stared in horror at the Kaposi's Sarcoma lesions.

Trevor had gone downhill fast. He had looked fine at that party of his just a few months ago, Josh recalled. Smiling and laughing, and teasing Josh about Gideon. Josh hadn't even known Trev was positive, and here he was, dying of AIDS.

It could happen that fast, to go from being HIV positive to

being in the last stages of cancer or pneumonia or any of the several ways AIDS patients could die. AIDS itself didn't kill you, opportunistic infections or cancer did. Sometimes within months, sometimes it took years. But Trevor...

"Joshie," Trevor said, struggling to sit up.

Josh helped him, plumped Trevor's pillows, and said nothing about being called "Joshie."

"I'm glad you came," Trevor extended a trembling hand. "Look at me. Remember the old times, eh, Josh? I used to campaign for AIDS research. Wore so many red ribbons I looked like a damn Maypole."

"How long did you have HIV?" Josh asked, fearful of the answer. He'd had it fifteen years, or very nearly.

"Five years, six..." Trevor shrugged. "Don't even remember where I got it. A glory hole somewhere. Rough trade." He grinned skeletally up at Joshua. "Bad blood."

"That's not funny, Trev." Josh didn't really have the heart to scold.

This antiseptic room was getting to him, enclosing him like a sterile coffin. He shuddered. "I told you I was positive, why didn't you tell me?"

"Didn't feel like it," Trevor replied. "You've been too out of touch since you moved in with your boyfriend. He keeps you locked up in that mansion."

"He doesn't." The protest was automatic, but Josh felt the sting of the rebuke. He had been circulating less amongst his friends since moving in with Gideon. Introducing his lover as "This is my husband, the vampire," just caused too many questions. He had introduced Gideon to Trevor and assorted hangers-on; the evening had been nearly a disaster.

"You know now," Trevor pointed out. "Joshie, darling, I adore you, but why add to your burden with mine? I'm dying, I know it."

Looking down at the wasted man, half a corpse already, Josh couldn't argue. Despite the antiseptic overtones, the room smelled of illness and decay.

"Thanks for the roses, darling," Trevor said, gazing at the beauties Josh had brought in.

"Gideon grows them."

"Does he really? Maybe he's not such an old bear, after all. I'm sorry I said that about a poker up his butt."

"Well..." Josh grinned. "He can have, that's the funny thing."

Trevor's laugh turned into a cough that made his wasted

body twist in torment. He coughed up blood. Josh pretended not to see.

"I hope he's taking good care of you," said Trevor, when he could talk. "I've had too many one-night stands, Joshie, too many gropes in bushes in parks, and stranger's pricks sticking through a hole...you have something better, you hang on to it. But even with the rough trade, and being a stupid queen who didn't stop screwing around even when I knew the danger...I wish I wasn't dying."

Joshua looked down at him again. God, it was a terrible way to die. It wasn't the first AIDS death Josh had seen, but this was the first really close friend he'd lost. It was hurting, hurting on levels that Josh wasn't ready to explore.

"I know, Trev," he said, squeezing the paper-thin hand he held.

"Life's a funny old bitch," Trevor mused, "but I'm sorry to be leaving her. No choice, though, Joshie. No choice."

No, Joshua thought, *Trevor had no choice.* But he, Joshua Daniel Trevallion, had a choice. This was a brutal way to die. Robbed of strength, of dignity, of the things that made you human.

He stayed with Trevor until the dying man fell into an uneasy sleep.

Life was a funny old bitch.

It hurt to lose a friend, to watch a friend die by inches, see the KS lesions erupt on his skin, hear the cough, the overworking lungs and underworking heart. It hurt not to be able to offer Trevor the option he himself, Joshua, had once refused and was now contemplating. Trevor, he knew, would have taken it without question or hesitation. A chance to spit death in the eye, to truly defeat the awful specter of AIDS.

A Beast who loved roses, who was always gentle and considerate with his "victims;" a Beast who usually tried to drink bottled and stored animal blood to avoid having to hurt human beings...that kind of a Beast?

Joshua stayed in a hotel near Trevor's hospital, and called home to Oakwoods at least twice a night. He missed Gideon, missed that cool calm presence, missed the shared laughter, the minor squabbles of the household. He missed the animals, and Mitch and Evan, and even the sounds of Mitch's computer as the young man played yet another game that seemed bloodthirstier than an entire clan of vampires combined.

How much more would he miss all that if he were dying, not

just away on a trip to sit deathwatch on a friend?

He went to sit with Trevor every day. Other friends came and they rotated the watch. Joshua spent most of his time either in the hotel or in the hospital; he did make a side trip to a couple of antique stores and one auction. He was greeted at the latter as the prodigal son and got taken out for an early birthday treat.

The next day, Josh took Trevor some leftover birthday cake, but realized that Trevor would be unable to eat it. He was hooked up to life support, only fluids entering and leaving his emaciated body.

"He's gone very fast," the doctor whispered to Josh out in the hall. "Some do, you know, we still know so little about AIDS. It's a shame, he's got such a will to live."

Joshua's own will to live, with some bolstering from mages and healers, was keeping his HIV from turning into AIDS. Trevor would have loved that, basked in the gift of extended life.

He would have chosen to become a vampire.

Josh sat with Trevor, while his friend was still conscious. "Trev," he said, "if you had the chance to live forever, would you take it?"

Trevor, too exhausted to speak, nodded and blinked his eyes. *Damn straight,* his expression seemed to say. Although *straight* and *Trevor* didn't tend to be words that mixed well.

Trevor died later that afternoon. His poor, shriveled body simply had no more reserves left to feed his will. Josh sat and cried as the monitors flatlined. Eventually a doctor gave him something.

Another good friend buried, another light snuffed forever.

Gideon was sympathetic when Josh returned to Oakwoods, grieving for Trevor. He had seen friends die, after all, far too many of them. He and Joshua convened to the privacy of the master bedroom to talk.

"The downside to being immortal," Gideon commented as he handed Joshua a handkerchief to wipe suddenly-brimful eyes, "is that so few others are."

"So you get to live forever, but watch everyone else die?" Josh sniffed. He pulled the white bedspread up closer to his body.

"There are prices," Gideon said, gazing off somewhere where Josh's eyesight couldn't follow. "That's one of them."

Joshua leaned against him, both offering and seeking comfort. "It doesn't have to be," he said softly.

The shoulder he was leaning on turned to stone. "What do you mean?"

"Trevor died hard, Gideon. It was a horrible death, by inches, all his dignity gone. He told me he hated leaving life, that he would have done anything not to die. He had no choice. I do."

Gideon's head turned so slowly that his neck creaked. "It is not an easy choice."

"I know." A bitter laugh punctuated this short reply. "God, do you think I don't know? I've been...looking around, my love. Asking questions. Finding things out. I've done my homework, never fear. I know what it is to be a vampire. I don't want to have to drink human blood in order to keep living, the thought still horrifies me. But I don't want to leave you. I don't want to die."

"I don't want you to die. Joshua...to be turned against your will is a terrible fate. Death is kinder."

"It wouldn't be against my will. I don't think I would enjoy it, but if the alternative is to go like Trevor, to leave you alone to mourn me..."

"You would do this for me?"

"Gideon, I would snatch the sun out of the sky and make it stop shining for you if I could. I love you, you idiot."

The Baron snorted, in a very refined and genteel way, of course. "I love you too, you idiot," he retorted. "What made you change your mind? Watching Trevor die?"

"That was simply the culminating factor," Joshua said. "I've had more than three years to think about this, to come to grips with having a terminal illness, to observe other vampires and see how they cope, to realize that it is not really so terrible a thing to be one. Not when you consider the alternative. I don't think there was one particular moment when I really changed my mind... maybe on New Year's Eve, maybe when I watched the leaves fall, I'm not sure. I know this wasn't an easy decision to make, and that it won't be an easy one to deal with. But I'll have lots of time to adjust." His grin was wry. "And you to help me."

A slow nod. "Yes. It requires time, and help." There was a long silence, punctuated by the noises of Oakwoods settling in the winter night. "When?" Gideon finally asked.

"After my birthday. I would like to turn forty-five as a mortal human. After that...Gideon, please, don't take this the wrong way. I don't want you to turn me."

I must be a gorgon, he thought after a minute. I've turned him to stone.

"No," said the Baron distantly. "I can understand. I will not turn you. It would be awkward, to say the least, to have a master/ fledgling relationship. We are equals, Joshua. We must remain so. But if not me...who?"

"I've thought about that, too. A lot. I've seen so many different types of vampires, even some who can stand the sun and eat food...but I think we should keep this in the family."

Gideon was silent again, his mind churning. After all this time, he knew the way Joshua thought. "Family" meant the Brotherhood. There were only two other vampires in the immediate vicinity, but Gideon dismissed them both from serious contemplation. Alexander had proven his unsuitability as a vampiric sire, and Francis was far too young and feckless. He could not imagine Joshua choosing Janine. Look to France, perhaps?

"Genevieve is coming for your birthday," Gideon finally said.

"She's a good turnsire. Turndam? All these terms are so sexist. Master, sire...no room for the ladies." Josh smiled. "I've talked to some of her 'get,' especially to Jean. They all adore her, and she makes no demands on them. Those that serve in her, er, neighbourhood watch and ward program, do so of their own free will. She asks nothing of them but that they be good vampiric citizens, and not to turn too many people or kill indiscriminately. She's been around a long time, she's very wise and not at all bitter. She's been seriously ill, so she knows where I'm coming from. If someone has to be a vampire, they could do a lot worse than emulate Genevieve."

Gideon's smile was gentle. "You don't have to sell her to me. I love her, Joshua, and I agree that you could not make a better choice."

"Your approval means a lot to me." Josh yawned, snuggling more securely under the comforter. "I don't know if she will agree. I've never discussed it with her."

"The reason she has so many fledglings is that she finds it difficult to turn someone down when they ask her. I do not think she will refuse you."

"Poor Trevor," said Josh softly. "How he would have loved to have this option."

A large bouquet of Gideon's best roses dominated the center of the dining table. The fine porcelain and bone-handled silverware gleamed in the candlelight. Joshua swallowed as he took his place, smiling at all the friends who had gathered for his birthday.

He hadn't been allowed to help at all in the preparations. Mitch and Evan had made the dinner. Gideon, naturally, had provided the flowers. Michael and Mary had brought the birthday cake. Maggie had brought the booze; Nicholas had his guitar ready; Alex had provided the appetizers. Genevieve and Jean had set the table. Percy, Ray and Francis had been left with nothing to bring and no service to provide, but were told not to let it worry them.

Joshua savoured every bite of his dinner, every sip of wine, every laugh, every candle flame. Afterwards, he wasn't even certain what he had eaten; it had been good, he was sure, but the details of that birthday dinner blurred into the memory only of happiness.

The cake caused much laughter, and was truly memorable. Gideon and Michael, bearing it to the table between them, were both in danger of dropping it because their shoulders were shaking. It was a large rectangle, the icing coloured and designed to look like a hardwood floor. As decorations, doll furniture had been arranged on the "floor" to look like a conventional room setting.

It was a great joke. Joshua was laughing so hard that he couldn't blow out the nine candles (four plus five) on the cake.

"What did you wish, *cheri?*" Genevieve asked him, blue eyes twinkling, when he finally achieved flame cessation.

He looked at her and smiled back. "I can't tell you."

"Oh, of course!" she exclaimed. "Forgive me."

He smiled again, and cut the cake, distributing pieces of furniture and thick, moist chocolate amongst those who could eat it.

"Thank you, Mary," he said, plucking an armoire off his own piece of cake.

"You're welcome," the creatrix of the wonderful dessert replied.

The diners slowly migrated from the dining table to the comfortable parlour. Nicholas produced his guitar and sang the mandatory song, plus a few of Joshua's favourites. Gifts were given, unwrapped, exclaimed over. Joshua was tempted to tell them all his decision; but it was too private, too new. There were a few he would have to share it with. Genevieve, of course; Mitch and Evan, Michael...the ones he was closest to. He knew, by rights, that Evan and Mitch should be the first to know—after Genevieve. If she agreed. If Genevieve refused him, then he wouldn't need to tell anyone.

The party wound down around midnight. The women all had to have a hug and a kiss from the birthday boy; the men all shook his hand. He thanked them all for coming, and for the gifts. Joshua was tired by the time the last guests had gone;

he sagged in his chair while Gideon rubbed his shoulders from behind.

A faint clatter of dishes betrayed the fact that Mitch and Evan had begun the clearing away. Joshua smiled; he was left in the restful presence of two vampires and three animals. Remnants of the logs in the fireplace popped and crackled, nearly down to coals.

"Enough, enough," Joshua told his impromptu masseur. "Pour yourself a brandy and come and sit."

Gideon obeyed, sitting on the chair next to his husband.

"Perhaps I should leave you two alone, no?" Genevieve asked, not wanting to intrude.

"No," Joshua replied firmly. "Don't go just yet. I want to talk to you."

"Very well." She had half-risen, now she settled back in her chair. "I am listening."

"I'm forty-five years old today, Genevieve," Joshua began. "That's quite an advanced age for someone with HIV. I know I've been very lucky, but my luck may not keep holding. I may not even have one good year left, despite Michael's efforts. I've had three years given to me, an amazing gift."

Genevieve patiently wondered where this was going, but was too polite to ask.

"Three years ago, Genevieve, I was handed a death sentence," Joshua went on. "Or so I thought. Neither Gideon nor I reacted well to the news of my illness; but we've both had time since. Time to come to terms with it. Time," his voice dropped, "to consider the alternative."

The beautiful Frenchwoman nodded. "And have you?" she asked. "Considered it?"

"Very much so. I know that vampires aren't just stereotypical monsters, Genevieve. I still feel that I myself won't be very happy as a vampire. But I can feel my mortality closing in on me, and I'm scared." He squeezed Gideon's hand. "And I don't want to leave Gideon."

"Becoming a vampire is no easy choice, Joshua," Genevieve warned.

"I know. I'm totally aware of the consequences, Genevieve. I'm also aware of the consequences of not becoming a vampire."

She studied him for a few moments. The fire settled to glowing ash. Smoke yawned and turned her head to the other side of her paws.

"Joshua," Genevieve finally said, "Tell me you do not want to become a vampire because it is...what is that expression?...cool."

His jaw dropped. He looked at Gideon, sitting ramrod straight in his Saville Row suit and tie, probably the least "cool" vampire on the planet.

Josh started to laugh. He couldn't help it. In a minute, Genevieve and Gideon were laughing, too, and Smoke rose and padded indignantly out of the parlour in search of quieter company.

"Ah, *dieu,"* Genevieve gasped, wiping her eyes, "that was not meant as a joke."

"I want," Joshua said, sobering at once, "to be with Gideon. I don't want him to be alone again. Not when I can do something about it."

She nodded. "And you wish me to be the one to change you, or you would not be discussing this with me, am I not right?"

"It can't be Gideon," Josh said, once more squeezing the Baron's hand. "We've talked about it."

Aware that he had contributed nothing so far to this discussion, Gideon stirred. "I will not be a turnsire to my own husband," he said flatly.

"I agree, that would be most unwise," Genevieve said. She looked at Joshua. "Why me?"

His butterscotch eyes twinkled. "You come highly recommended."

That delighted her. "I adore flattery," she admitted, making Gideon laugh. "But I hope you have given this some serious thought."

"I have. I want someone in the family, so to speak; and none of the immediate Brotherhood are appropriate. I have been asking questions, feeling out the territory. I want you." He spread his hands out; Gideon touched him softly on the shoulder. "Genevieve, will you turn me?"

"You knew the answer before you asked, Joshua," Genevieve replied, all seriousness now. "Yes, I will. For both your sakes."

Joshua stood up, smiling in reply to the questioning look Gideon shot at him. He crossed the floor to Genevieve's chair; never before had the parlour seemed so large.

"Merci," he said, kissing her on the cheek.

"You are welcome," she replied. "But not tonight. We are all too emotional and you are too tired."

"Not tonight," Josh agreed. "There are people I have to talk to in the next couple of days. I'm going to bed now." He winked at Gideon. "Alone. You two have a good time talking about me behind my back. Good morning." He left the parlour.

The silence that filled the parlour after Joshua's exit was an old, comfortable one. Only Pumpkin, moaning her sleep, little spaniel legs churning, punctuated the quiet.

"She must be dreaming," Genevieve remarked, observing the twitching dog.

"Chasing Smoke," Gideon said.

The silence settled in again, but wasn't allowed to get comfortable.

"So," Genevieve said, "the moment has finally come."

"Yes. It has."

"How do you feel, *cheri?*"

"Torn," he said frankly. "Oh, Genevieve, of course I don't want to lose him! I love him so much. But I thought...I thought he would never agree to be turned. I don't know how to feel. He will lose...so much."

"Yes, he will. But he will also gain so much, will he not?"

Gideon shook his head. He could see only loss. "Daylight," he listed, "gourmet food, easy travelling, humanity..."

"That," said Gen severely, "is nonsense. You have not lost your humanity, nor have I; nor have any of the Brotherhood or the others we know."

"But the rest..."

"We have all lost those things, Gideon," she reminded him. "Daylight? To us, the night has a hundred colours and smells and shapes; it is our daylight. If you survive long enough in this life, then you can tolerate small amounts of daylight. As for food... there are other compensations, *non?*"

Gideon flushed. Her meaning was transparent. The feeding could be highly sexually charged.

"He will not have to give up his work," Genevieve continued. "There are evening auctions, computer auctions, the telephone; his clients will not mind his new hours. Travel is far more reliable these days; I believe you have a fully accredited young pilot in your own household. And," she reached over to touch the knee of her beloved "son," smiling, "he will have you, and you will have him, and there will not be the specter of AIDS over this house any longer."

"He will not be happy as a vampire."

"That is entirely up to him."

Mitch took the news much better than Joshua had expected.

He had told Evan and Mitch at lunch. Evan, in low cycle,

was picking at his sandwich, intent on stabbing the innocent cold cuts to death. Mitch, appetite whetted by having walked the animals, cheerfully masticated his way through two grinders. Joshua chewed more slowly, enjoying the textures of the multi-grain bread and lean chicken.

"So," Evan said, having shredded his sliced ham and bread, "feel any different than yesterday?"

"I've got a hangover I didn't have yesterday," Josh said. "And I seem to have acquired a number of very nice gifts. Otherwise..." he shrugged.

"So there's still life at forty-five?" Mitch asked, hoovering the last of the cole slaw.

Joshua looked at the young werewolf. His mind's eye still saw a gangly, smart-mouthed nineteen-year-old; but his real eyes saw a surprisingly mature man of twenty-six. When had Mitch grown up? "I hope so, Mitch. In fact, I hope there's still life at a hundred and forty-five."

Mitch looked puzzled. Evan betrayed no expression at all.

"Um," said the werewolf. "How?"

Josh could have been flippant and said something like, "By not dying," but this was serious and so was he. "By becoming a vampire."

Mitch blinked and put the remains of his second sandwich down on his plate. "A...vampire?" he repeated.

"Yes, you know, like the man who pays you an exorbitant salary to do not much of anything." Evan's voice was a dry drawl; it changed when he turned to Joshua. "I know this wasn't an easy decision for you to make. You have my support."

"Thank you, Evan," Joshua said. He'd been worried that the protector would look askance on another vampire in the house.

"Mine, too," said Mitch. His voice wasn't completely steady, but he smiled at Joshua. "I'm really glad, Josh. I don't want you to die."

Touched, Josh returned the smile. "Technically, I still will," he said, his own voice shaky.

"Well, yeah," Mitch said. "But you get to come back."

"Sort of a round-trip ticket, in fact," Evan added.

Joshua looked at Evan. The solidly-built bodyguard had a perfectly straight face. Mitch's mouth seemed suspiciously twitchy; he might have been struggling against laughter, tears, or both.

"A round trip ticket," Josh mused. "That's a new way of looking at it."

"Just don't pick up any souvenirs," Evan warned.

Mitch snorted. "Souvenirs! You mean, like 'been dead, done that, didn't get the t-shirt?'"

That made them all laugh. Mitch came over and hugged Joshua. "I'm really glad you're not going away," the young man said, sniffling a little.

"I'm glad too, Mitch." Josh returned the hug.

Mitch turned and hugged Evan. "Josh is gonna be a vampire!"

Evan pushed him away, face twisting in disgust. "Hug me again, and you're the one who will be getting a one-way ticket." He looked at Joshua. "I suspect there's a reason why Genevieve asked me to change her flight reservation back to France. She's an excellent choice, Josh."

"Genevieve?" Mitch stared. "I thought..."

"Of course it can't be Gideon, Mitch," Joshua said. "Gideon and I want a relationship as equals. He can't be my turnsire—he wouldn't be."

"Oh." Mitch's face fell, then brightened. "Genevieve's okay."

"I think she's more than okay," Josh said. "I think she's perfect."

"I think we need to have a private talk, you and I," Genevieve said to Joshua.

He nodded, ignoring the anxious look Gideon sent him, and rose from his chair. "Let's go to my office," he suggested.

Genevieve stood up as well, gesturing at Gideon to remain seated. She and Joshua went up the stairs together in silence. He ushered her into his office and shut the door. She settled into an antique chair, not bothering to wait for him to offer it, and regarded him solemnly.

"Okay," Josh said, perching on the edge of the cot, "is this the big 'this is what it means to be a vampire' speech?"

"Would you like one?" Genevieve asked without a trace of her usual affectations or idiosyncrasies of speech. "No one can tell you what it means to be a vampire, Joshua. Not Gideon, not Alexander, not Francis, not I. No. You are the one who must decide what it means to *you*. But that is not what I wish to talk about."

Josh studied her for some clue to her intentions, but there were none. "I'm listening, Genevieve. I am your pupil."

That evoked a smile. "I hope you will prove a somewhat more apt one than your older brother, Jean," she said, but the smile belied her harsh words. "Joshua, we must discuss the turning."

His own smile faded. "Yes," he sighed, "I suppose we must."

"It is never easy," she said, hooking her heels on the stretcher between the chair legs and drawing her knees up higher. She clasped her hands around her knees, hugging them to her, and for a moment Joshua saw the carefree young girl she once must have been.

"There hasn't been one minute of this that has been easy, Gen. Why should it start now?"

"Things...happen in the turning, Joshua," she warned, ignoring his sarcasm. "There is a chance it will go wrong. A slight one, yes, but still...that chance."

"And if it does?" He thought he knew, but he wanted her to answer.

"You die." The flat, undeniable answer made him blink. "That is the most preferable of the possibilities. You die, and you do not turn, and we bury you. Or the turning does not fully take, and you become a...freak, a half-vampire living in the twilight like that young man in Toronto. There is even the chance that you will become as Elrich and Jared, my little cousins; poor half-wit ghouls living on carrion meat and my guilt."

Joshua shuddered. "You did not make them."

"No. But they are mine, all the same." She released her knees, setting her feet back down to the floor. "Joshua, I chose to become a vampire. So did the majority of my children. Their reasons are their own, and I am not at liberty to discuss them with you; but I know that you have spoken with a few of my flock. They are not, on the whole, unhappy with their choice."

"Are *you?"* Joshua challenged her.

She took it in good humour. "No. I cannot say that I have *never* been unhappy with it, but we all have those times. When I was...ill," she couldn't quite repress a shiver, "I was extremely unhappy. But it passed, and I was the stronger for it. I chose this existence, Joshua. You will become one of a small but growing number of vampires who *did* choose. And to do so, as I did, for love..." Genevieve's voice trailed off.

"You must have loved him very much," Josh said softly.

Her eyes met his. "I gave him my life. And it was not enough. There are no guarantees, Joshua. None."

He reached out and took her hand, turning it palm-up so that the small scar from the hilt of a magical silver dagger was revealed. "No," he agreed, "there are no guarantees. But even though you lost Claude, you still carry on his cause. *That* is love, Genevieve. I know that my turning won't necessarily mean that Gideon and I will be together always. But I'd like to give it a shot."

She nodded. "A shot you shall have." Then she relentlessly steered the conversation back to where she wanted it to go. "About the turning itself, my pupil, have you no questions to ask?"

"Will it hurt?"

"Yes."

Gideon had wanted to watch, and Joshua had wanted him there. Genevieve was not used to having an audience for this process, but she had made no objection. So the three of them had assembled in the Willow Room, one of the inner, windowless guest bedrooms in Oakwoods. Joshua had vetoed being turned in the master bedroom and the other two had agreed. That room's associations were too intimate; the bed Josh and Gideon shared was not an appropriate venue for the turning.

Joshua lay upon the bed, looking up at the ceiling. An old sheet had been spread under him to protect the expensive bedspread; a conceit he might have found funny on some other occasion. Tonight, he didn't feel like laughing. Only the perfect love in Gideon's eyes kept him from panicking.

He could still call it off at this point. He could get up, say he'd changed his mind. But he knew that, should he do such a thing, that he would never have this chance again. He had gone too far in this process to stop it now, and he found he did not want to. Although the frightened hammering of his heart was loud in his ears, sending his infected blood spiralling through his veins, he did not want to stop.

His life would change tonight, forever.

Genevieve leaned over Joshua's body in order to look him in the eyes. "You are ready?" she asked.

"I am," he affirmed. His hand sought Gideon's and clasped it. "Stay with me," he whispered.

"I'm right here," Gideon promised.

Josh's eyes focused on Genevieve. "Do it now."

Her mouth opened, revealing fangs. "*Tais toi, Gideon,*" she warned, "*N'intercederas pas.*" She bent over Joshua's neck.

What was this place? It seemed familiar, yet strange. He had just arrived, and yet he had always been here. He was blind, deaf, paralyzed. The strangeness held him in unbreakable chains of silence and darkness. On the blank wall of his mind, memories played. He did not know whose memories; they seemed a hopeless jumble of unrelated scenes. Running down a street, thrusting a stick through a picket fence to hear the machine-gun sound it made. Dancing, in improbable layers of lace and velvet, with a man with no face. Cycling through a gray stone city with a college-aged girl over whose head a strange stone pot floated. Holding a toddler in his arms, the weight of an unborn infant distending his belly. Two achingly familiar people, a man and a woman, screaming at him, sending him away, denying him. Two small graves and a larger one, and grief the weight of the earth. A terrace, where a man stood staring down at dancers below, loneliness radiating from him. A severed hand, ring still on one bloodied finger. A ballet, a first kiss in the snow. A black cat, dying in his hands. The cinnamon scent of flowers and the pound of surf in his ears as someone made love to him. Hands, clasping his as he climaxed. Hands.

Hands. Fingers.

His finger twitched. Neural pathways screamed open, real memories washed away the ghostly projections. His finger twitched, and he knew that the strange and sensory-free place where he had been was his own body. Pain roared behind his blind eyes, flashed in his deaf ears. More fingers twitched.

Beneath the twitching fingers, he sensed...a fabric? Questing, his awakening sense of touch conveyed to him the weave, the thread count, the knowledge that this was *cotton;* a *sheet* and that it covered a *bed.*

More doors slammed open, making him wince as the sensations went bouncing off the walls of his mind.

A sheet. A bed. A coppery smell that was most intriguing, but that he was not yet ready to explore. Suddenly he could feel each individual texture; the knitted cables in his sweater and the minute pressure where his own weight bearing down on the mattress drove the thicker knots of wool into his skin. The close weave of his trousers, the way they bunched up behind his knee and fell in folds across his calves. His socks had slipped down and were scrunched up around his ankles. He could even feel the closeness of his knit underwear, the pinch of elastic.

The sheet he lay on smelled beige; a dull bland scent.

He was growing tired of the thick grayness beyond his closed eyelids. As his body began to wake up and obey him, he commanded his eyes to open.

Shapes swirled and sparkled in his vision. The first colour he could identify was blue. Sky?

No, unless the sky had texture. Slowly, painfully, the images stopped their frantic dance and arranged themselves in more seemly fashion.

The blue was a dress.

There was pressure on his hand, now; fingers curled around his own. He returned the pressure wonderingly; and his brain gave him the information that someone had taken his hand and squeezed it.

Waves of sound broke against his ear drums; far too loud, and he tried to pull away. The gentle pressure on his hand stopped him, and the sound slowly, agonizingly, lessened to understandable syllables.

"Jaw-shoo-wya. Jo-shoo-wa. Jo-shu-a. Joshua. Joshua?"

He blinked, to show he understood, and the pressure on his hand returned.

He knew that voice, knew it well, and the memory of that voice suffused him with love and warmth. For the sake of that voice, he had undergone a momentous transformation, he knew. But the memory cheated him of names, of details. He had no voice. There was a dryness in his throat, and behind that, a terrible need.

"We must give him time, Gideon." The blue dress spoke. The voice seemed to come from the very weave of the fabric.

Gideon. He knew that name, the love that spilled over from that name. It had the texture of cashmere, the scent of roses and dog, the taste of brandy, the colour of hot sex. Gideon.

Joshua's hand closed over the fingers again. Gideon. Yes.

The blue, the scent of wine, the sound of France in every word. He knew this, too; shared memories, shared...

Blood.

With that, the vampire awoke.

Horsing Around
(2000)

Calvin's glossy black head peered benignly over his stall door. The stallion's placid expression didn't fool the horse's owner—if anyone could be said to *own* such a beast. He was either a fairy horse or a demon, depending on who you asked.

To the man standing by the loose box, the horse was a large animal of uncertain disposition and a known appetite for stock portfolios, acacia trees and argyle socks. Calvin had been a wedding gift from a Lord of Chaos. Transporting a 17-hand stallion that closely resembled an Andalusian down from a second floor study had been quite a feat, especially since this horse would not tolerate any iron, including a bit or stirrups. Calvin had never been shod or saddled, but did permit the use of a show-jumping hackamore—a bridle with reins but without a bit, only rings that put gentle pressure on the sides of the horse's mouth.

Despite the lack of a saddle, Calvin never permitted his rider to fall off and was as tame as milk when ridden, at least by Joshua. Ridden by anyone else, including his putative owner, it was another story.

Gideon Redoak held out the bridle. "Care for some exercise tonight?" If he felt foolish speaking to an animal, he did not show it.

Calvin was not an ordinary horse.

The stallion bobbed his head in agreement and nudged open its stall door. No iron bolts or hinges impeded him...Evan had had to get strong brass hinges and nails for the stall, and no bolt in the world would keep Calvin where he didn't want to be. Calvin flowed out, muscles moving smoothly under the glossy black coat, allowed the hackamore to be put in place, and knelt at Gideon's feet.

It wasn't subservience. It was so that the Baron, who was only five foot six, could mount the tall horse. Gideon swung a jodphurred leg over the stallion's bare back and took the reins.

"Giddyap," he said.

Calvin trotted, tail swishing, out of the stable of which he was the lone occupant. The unexpected arrival of a horse had necessitated a great deal of hasty renovating of the outbuildings at Oakwoods, and the long-disused stable had been refurbished. Once free of the building, the horse stretched his legs...and ran.

Down the Cliff Road they flew, man and horse; the man leaning low over the horse's neck, riding jacket flapping in the breeze. Although it was night and the road was not artificially lit, Calvin never once misplaced a hoof and no hole threatened to break his fragile legs. His hooves were striking...air. In his excitement to be free and beneath an experienced rider, Calvin had lifted himself up and was running on the ether. His red eyes glowed.

Past Ray Griffin's small house, which showed no lights...the mage must have gone to bed or else was down in his workshop, cut out of the cliff itself. Past Francis's shack, littered with motorcycles. Down the winding, unpopulated part of the Cliff Road. Past the cottage where Percy Redoak lived...

Calvin slowed to nicker a greeting, but the other branch of the Redoak family was likewise not at home. He was in England this month, maintaining the historically crumbling Redoak Hall.

Gideon exerted no pressure on the reins, letting Calvin choose his own course. The wind ruffled his dark hair and he found himself grinning with the illusion of complete freedom. He seldom allowed himself such indulgence. There were too many pressing responsibilities on his head. But for an hour or two, on Calvin's back, he was just a wild boy on a wild horse...a liberty he had never had in his actual youth.

Right down into the quiet streets of Fletcherville went Calvin. Just a red-eyed demon horse with a vampire on board galloping through a small fishing village in Maine. Perfectly normal. A few cautious heads peeked out of windows or doorways, saw the glossy black hide of Calvin go blurring past, and withdrew.

Just one of those damned Cliff Road people. They paid their taxes and kept themselves to themselves, but occasionally you had to put up with a damned silly stunt from one of them. If the Baron broke his neck, there'd be hell to pay. But nobody made a move to try and stop the horse.

Calvin, heedless of the thoughts hurled his way, veered

towards the decorative park tucked into the center of town. Without visible effort, he cleared the low fence around the perimeter of the park and took Widow's Green in four strides, sailing over the fence on the other side with an ease that would have made Hap Hansen's eyes water.

Only when they ran out of town did man and horse slow. A few short blocks past the Green and Fletcherville ceased to exist...there was only ocean, cliff and bog. Calvin pranced in a piaffe that would have won him major dressage medals if he'd only allowed himself to be saddled and then stood still, bending his head to nibble at the beach grass.

It was a calm summer night, Gideon saw now that the scenery was no longer a blur. A few high dark clouds obscured the stars and the quarter-moon but the wind was gentle and barely ruffled the Atlantic. He patted Calvin's neck and requested to be allowed to dismount. He could see Calvin actually thinking about it before the black stallion obligingly knelt.

Gideon swung off the sleek back and stroked Calvin's neck again, as far as he could reach. He watched the ocean for a while, wondering why he felt so restless tonight. He should be perfectly happy. All was right with his world, after all. Joshua was adjusting to being a vampire. There was nothing too overwhelming or alarming with any of Gideon's various financial ventures. Oakwoods ran like a fine watch. The Brotherhood wasn't threatened by anything or anyone. Nobody was ill or injured or in danger.

"Calvin," he murmured to the red-eyed demon horse, "I'm *bored.*"

The stallion's ears pricked up and he whinnied. It sounded quite incredibly like laughter.

The light changed. The full moon beamed down through dark, stormy clouds. The waves crashed onto the shore, sending salt spray over Gideon's riding boots. He grabbed Calvin's reins and drew back, not frightened but aware that something had happened. His foolish words had started something, and he was no longer on the same beach.

Calvin's ears went back, flattened against the skull. The sound of the waves was louder, more insistent. Looking around cautiously, Gideon wasn't terribly surprised to see that the landscape had changed. No lights from Fletcherville could be seen at all. This was a far wilder beach; stonier and somehow older than New England.

"I said I was bored, Calvin," Gideon sighed out loud to his

horse. “I didn’t mean that I wanted an abrupt change of time and location.”

The storm clouds obscured the moon and lightning forked towards the beach. There was nowhere to hide, so the Baron stood his ground though Calvin jerked at the reins. Gideon didn’t let go, and vampire strength won out over demonic horse’s. He reached over and stroked Calvin’s neck.

“Easy,” he soothed. “Easy, easy. We shall meet whatever adventure awaits us. And this is all your fault, anyway.”

The mad red eyes stared at him, plainly retorting *Oh, yeah?*

The clouds roiled, turning darker and seeming to boil over. Shapes began to form in those grey, smoky depths. Sharp hooves, tossing manes, flicking tails, long, fragile legs. Horses. Riders. Gleaming eyes, spears, ragged clothes, a helmet with antlers.

No. Not a helmet. The antlers sprang from the head of a rider, who plunged his cloud steed towards the earth and the now wide-eyed Baron. Gideon bowed low. He knew this rider. “King Herla,” he said. The leader of the Wild Hunt had many names, many aspects, but the dwarf king was the one Gideon knew.

The antlered spectre laughed. “Well met, good Baron!” he said in a voice of thunder. “But you are far from home.” The undead eyes of the leader of the Wild Hunt fastened on Calvin. “Ah. Your steed brought you here.”

“I suspect so, yes,” Gideon said.

“How came you by a Sidhe horse?”

“It was a wedding gift, King Herla.”

The spectral king threw back his head and his laughter split the sky. “I wonder,” said Herla, rubbing his chin, “if the Sidhe have noticed the loss of one of their horses. Still, he is yours now. And since he has brought you here, you must join the Hunt.”

It was not a request. Since Gideon was lost, with no idea of where or when Calvin had brought him, he had few alternatives. He bowed his head and motioned Calvin to kneel. He mounted, and Calvin surged to standing position.

“Ride at my side,” Herla said. “As my guest. You need not Hunt.”

Gideon chucked the reins and Calvin trod up an invisible path to stand beside Herla’s spectral mount.

“Away!” cried the Hunter.

The landscape beneath the Hunt roiled. It made Gideon a bit queasy to look down at the hooves churning in thin air, so he concentrated on watching Herla. The antlered leader of the Hunt was laughing, enjoying the ride and the unexpected company of an old acquaintance.

"And how is Joshua?" Herla asked. He and the Hunt had once more or less kidnapped the Baron's husband, but Joshua had taken his abduction in stride and ended up teaching the Hunters how to play poker.

"He's fine," Gideon replied, inadvertently glancing down and recognizing the landscape. They were over Shrewsbury, not far from Redoak Hall.

"No..." he whispered, fear for Percy tightening in his throat. Then he realized that the countryside was far too dark, and less populated than in the present day. Time meant nothing to the Wild Hunt, after all. No electric lights, no automobiles, no television antennas. In this night, almost nothing stirred.

"But he is one of you now," Herla said. As Gideon turned his head, startled, the king laughed again. Everything amused Herla. "Do you think that we of the Other World do not know when a mortal turns? Especially a cherished mortal, one who has the favour of the Oak King? Joshua has friends in high places, and they are watching him anxiously."

He shook a skeletal finger at Gideon, coursing beside him on red-eyed Calvin. "You are advised to treat Joshua well."

Gideon bowed as best he was able. Although it was giving him vertigo, he watched the landscape, unable to turn away. The Hunt was riding above Redoak Hall, but an earlier Hall than he'd last seen. Nothing stirred on the estate. The tenant farms were still intact, he saw; the land appeared to be cultivated but not with modern farming methods. All was, in fact, the way it had been in his breathing days.

A terrible suspicion formed, and Gideon looked over at Herla. "Please no," he said softly. "I could not bear it."

Herla shook his antlered head. "It would break several rules for me to show you yourself. Fear not. Even I do not wish to invoke the spirit of the one who turned you. That is not what we have come to witness."

The cavalcade in the air rode on past the quiet Hall, moving along the road towards London. It was a long ride from Shrewsbury to the capital as mortals rode, but the Hunt could cover the span in the blink of an eye and Calvin kept pace. Yet they did not travel right to London. Several miles outside of the capital, the road was lonely and wild. Urban sprawl had not yet spread; here it was pitch dark, not a habitation in sight, and dark trees by the roadside could have hidden an army.

A carriage, lanterns at its doors, horses pulling uneasily in the darkness, travelled the road.

Gideon's face tightened. He knew that carriage and team. Knew the driver's voice as he urged the nervous pair onwards in the dark, trying to reach an inn a mile or so further on, softly cursing his stubborn master who had refused to stop for the night earlier.

The Baron glanced at Herla, but the King's face was implacable, comfortless. This was something Gideon was meant to witness. Out of the darkness of the trees, there came a small band of men. Despite their ragtag appearance, they were well-organized. They had pistols and dark lanterns. The horses stamped as the driver of the carriage pulled them to a stop to avoid running down armed men in the road.

"Stand and deliver!" cried out one of the highwaymen. Likely he could not believe his luck—a rich lord travelling almost alone at night.

The driver raised his hands to show he was unarmed. Foolish to be so, and driving after dark, but he obeyed his master. One of the thieves moved to the door of the carriage, studying the arms by lantern light. He shrugged, obviously unfamiliar with the device.

Even without his vampire vision, Gideon could have told him what those arms were. Argent, an oak tree gules, fructed or. A red oak tree with golden acorns.

"M'lud," said the thief at the carriage door, "I suggest you step out of the carriage slowly, and give over your purse and any valuables you happen to have."

"I shall do no such thing," replied a voice that Gideon recognized only too well.

"M'lud," the highwayman smiled unpleasantly, "you shall." He wrenched open the carriage door as two of his fellows came up to help him. Together they dragged out the carriage's lone occupant and threw him down on the road.

"You shall rue this," said the figure on the road, shivering in righteous anger. "The wrath of the Lord shall descend upon you and you shall suffer in eternal damnation."

"We have robbed a preacher!" snorted one of the thieves. He gave the victim a kick that sent the man sprawling head-first in the dirt of the road. Two others surged forward and thoroughly searched the prone figure, coming away with only a small purse.

"So fine a carriage to hide such a poor booty," said the leader of the thieves when the purse was presented to him. "No gold, no jewelry, no finery? Pah." He spat on the struggling lord. "Puritan."

"Aye," said the robbery victim. "And God shall avenge me."

"Tell me, Puritan, have you wife and child?" asked the thief in silken tones. "Dost care for them, if so?"

Gideon tensed for the answer.

"I have," spat the Puritan. "They are my right, my chattels. That is all I care for them."

"Then they will not mourn you," said the thief, and shot his victim cold-bloodedly in the heart.

The carriage driver jumped at this murder of his master, and started to run. One of the other highwaymen shot him in the back, and down he fell. They took the carriage and pair as recompense for their night's work, and left the carrion laying in the road.

The Wild Hunt descended upon the cooling corpses, a pale-faced Gideon beside their leader, and whooped and hollered after the departing souls of the foolish Puritan lord and his driver.

"Why have you shown me this?" Gideon asked Herla when the Hunt tired of the chase and let the souls depart to their ultimate destination.

"You have always wondered, have you not?"

Gideon acknowledged the truth with a bow of his head. He had.

"Hah!" Herla laughed, though Gideon saw no humour in it. "Your father was an unhappy man, Gideon Redoak. A ball in his heart was a swifter end than many."

"In cold blood," Gideon objected.

"Had he acknowledged that he felt some fondness for his wife and children, who knows how that scene might have ended? Let the past go, Gideon. You could never have been the son he wanted, and that is no shame to you. What he wanted was another like himself, a cold preacher with no love in his heart."

The Wild Hunt rode on, crossing the wide Atlantic. They approached the rugged coast of Maine. Now lights could be seen, the cheery yellow lights of electricity in houses, the long-reaching white light of the lighthouses, the flickering blue of television sets, the white headlights and red tailights of passing cars. The night was humming with activity as they followed the coastal highway. Soon they were nearing the outskirts of Fletcherville.

"We leave you here," Herla said as the Hunt came down upon a beach Gideon recognized. "I hope you have learned something tonight."

Gideon bowed again. "Thank you for the lesson, King Herla. I have learned."

Herla threw bony arms around him in a hug from horseback. "Good. See that you remember. *All* that I have shown and told you. Give my regards to Joshua, and tell him that he owes me a poker game."

"I will." Gideon almost smiled at the thought of imparting that news.

Herla lifted a hand, and the Hunt rose again into the air. Calvin whinnied a farewell, and the host was gone into the clouds.

Gideon looked down at the horse he was mounted on.

"Calvin," he said quietly, "if you ever do anything like that to me again, I will make you into fairy horseburgers."

The stallion laid his ears back and rolled his red eyes. He whickered. It sounded like a laugh.

"Let's go home," Gideon said.

The Turning of the Tide
(2000)

It had been a year. A bit over a year, actually; funny how time didn't seem all that different now. He'd thought that time should feel different. Slower, maybe, or less noticeable in its passing. Have a different flavour. Something. But more than a year had passed, and it had been like blinking.

It had not been a good year. Adjusting was much, much rougher than he'd expected. It had been hard to let go of all the trappings of his former life, and there'd been very little to take their place.

Joshua Daniel Trevallion was not a happy vampire.

He knew that his depression over his new state of being had not gone unnoticed. He had more support than the Brooklyn Bridge. Loving concern surrounded him; he knew he could turn and talk to any one of a dozen or more people and have them understand and comfort him. In fact, the aura of concern was almost suffocating. He knew, ultimately, that this was something he was going to have to work through for himself. It helped to know that there were so many people willing to hold his hand through this transition period, but he didn't want his hand held.

Josh didn't know, exactly, what it was he did want. It was worse than futile to want to turn back. Vampirism wasn't something you could just give up, like smoking or a religious cult. He'd thought he'd been ready for all the changes; God knew everyone had talked about them enough. When it got right down to brass tacks, though, he hadn't been prepared for the massive alterations in his lifestyle.

He missed the sun. He missed the taste and texture of food; the silky glory of chocolate, the burn of curry, the subtle blend of flavours in a stir-fry, the crunchiness of fresh carrots. He missed cooking; his one attempt since turning had been a disaster because he could no longer taste what he was preparing. Sipping room-temperature pig's blood just didn't have the same appeal as tucking into veal cordon bleu.

He knew that the changes had affected Gideon, too. To have your lover, your partner, your constant companion go from a living, breathing, warm human being to a cold, undead creature of the night had to be something of a shock. It would be horrible to no longer feel that familiar heartbeat or curl up against skin still warm from the sun. He'd spared Gideon that, at least. But damn, he missed having sex.

Gideon...ah, damn, was he blowing, that, too? Gideon had said it didn't matter, that he understood what Joshua was going through. Gideon could afford to be patient and wait for Josh to find himself, to adapt to being a vampire. He'd been a vampire for over three centuries already. He hadn't once said he was hurt or disappointed or that he wanted Josh back in bed.

Damn him.

Josh knew he was being unfair, and he didn't care. He knew perfectly well that Gideon was treading around him very, very carefully these days, wary of saying or doing anything to further upset him. He knew that Gideon had problems expressing his emotions under the best of circumstances, let alone when there was trouble or an emotional crisis. He knew that he was hurting his husband quite badly. It would at least clear the air if Gideon actually *said* so.

Might as well wish for bat wings and mist while I'm at it, Josh thought wryly.

God, he needed out. Not to run away, exactly, but just to get away. By himself, where nobody could look at him with that worried expression or tell him that they loved him and wanted to help him. Somewhere that the taste of the air didn't have that overtone of furniture polish, roses and the dust of long sleepy afternoons that meant Oakwoods. He felt trapped, under the microscope of the Brotherhood, under the caring but unrelenting eyes of the Cliff Road Crowd. Even the Fairlawn twins looked at him with that expression of wanting to make it all better for him.

At least he could get away from the house and scrutiny for a little while. Gideon and Mitch were conferencing over the stock market and Evan was down in the basement, working out in his weight room. Ancient Warg was asleep on the rug before the cold fireplace, dreaming of younger, less arthritic days. Pumpkin and

Smoke were keeping each other company somewhere, likely in the kitchen at their food bowls. Josh decided to get while the going was good.

He left a note taped to the fireplace mantel and another one on the fridge so that nobody would panic when they found him gone, and fled before anyone could stop him. Out the back door, towards the edge of the cliff, going where his feet propelled him. There were ancient stairs here, cut into the face of the cliff, seldom used and not overly safe. They led down to what was jokingly referred to as the private beach for the Cliff Road Crowd... rocks, a fairly serious bog, a few dead trees and straggly bushes, and more rocks. It was only passable at low tide. Hardly anyone ever went down to it.

Perfect. The sea-smell became more intense each step downwards. Dried seaweed, the cast-off tresses of passing mermaids, straggled across some of the lower steps. He stepped on a fragile shell, heard the crunch under his Dexters, looked down at the shards of nacre on the step. The resident of the shell was long since dead, eaten and its house cast here by some seabird no doubt, but Josh still felt bad.

The half-moon cast a faint glow over the Atlantic at the foot of the cliff. The tide was out and hours from turning, so he had plenty of time to explore or just muse. He was getting dangerously close to reciting John Masefield. He laughed at himself, bitterly, and followed the lines left by the tide in the rocks.

Masefield was right, though. The sea was lonely. The darkness meant that no gulls flew overhead, no whales or porpoises cavorted in the grey waters. The only evidence of the abundant life in the ocean was its carcasses; here a starfish, there another broken shell. Even the smell of the sea came mostly from dying and dead organisms in the tide pools and on the shore.

Everything died, sooner or later. Even vampires. A dead vampire's ashes had been scattered to the waves from this very spot, although Joshua had not witnessed this ritual. Did the lapping waves speak with Corbeau's voice? Now there was a scary fancy and a damned depressing thought. Better to imagine that those ashes had been carried far out to the mid-Atlantic and lost in the hurly-burly of other drowned voices.

This walk wasn't bringing Josh out of himself at all. His thoughts seemed to constantly spin into a vortex of death and depression. The sea only held ghosts, not answers. The creaking of a tree branch became the creaking of a doomed schooner, the soft susurrus of the water sounded like the murmuring of dead sailors. He started to run, to try and get away from the voice of the sea and his own morbid thoughts. Loose stones flew from under his shoes as he ran blindly across the shoreline, pursued by only he knew what demons.

"Whoa!" a voice literally came out of the night air, and two strong arms grabbed him around the waist, effectively halting him in his tracks.

Angry, Josh pried at the confining arms, seeking escape. He might as well have been pushing against a brick wall or steel pipes. Still blind with anger, depression, frustration, his fist lashed out and connected with the abdominal region of the person whose arms had nabbed him. The arms around his waist let go, but only briefly. One strong hand clamped on his left shoulder, the other gave him a hard, star-making back-hand smack upside the head.

"Ow!" Josh protested, vision clearing. He turned, finally, to see who had grabbed and then struck him, and found himself looking into a pair of eyes as grey and lonely as the sea itself. "Alex?" he asked, rubbing his head.

The taller vampire backed off slightly, but did not relax his posture. Alex Goldanias held himself as if he was quite prepared to haul off and smack Josh again if the situation warranted it.

"What did you smack me for?"

"You punched me in the stomach."

"Well, you grabbed me around the waist. You scared me."

"You were about to run headlong into the bog."

Josh blinked, and looked at the path he had been set upon. Ten feet further, and he would indeed have careened into a morass of quicksand, mud, slime and treacherous footing. It was a Cliff Road legend that an entire Viking ship had been eaten by the bog. It was a Brotherhood joke that Michael had watched it happen. Joshua wasn't certain what would happen to a vampire who slipped into a bog and couldn't get out again—you wouldn't die, of course—and he didn't want to find out.

"Do you want to hit me again?" Alex asked, still tensed.

"Will you hit me back again if I do?"

"Damned straight."

"Then no, I don't think so." The fledgling's legs gave way without warning, and he whacked the stone beach, hard, ass-first. There was a sharp pebble under his right buttock, too.

"Josh?" Alex looked down with some alarm. "I didn't hit you that hard, did I?"

"No." Josh's voice was shaky. "I think you probably saved my life, or whatever you want to call it." He shifted so that the pebble cut into a different square inch of his cheek. "What were you doing down here, anyway?"

"I rather think that should be my question," Alex said mildly. He sat down on a weathered rock and drew his gold cigarette case out of a pocket in his cargo pants. "But since you asked first, I often come down here to just sit and reflect."

"And smoke?" Josh asked, watching as the handsome Count took out one of his specially made cigar/cigarette hybrids and lit it.

"That too." Alex grinned around the butt in his mouth and blew out rum-scented smoke. "Now, what were you running from, that you nearly got yourself bogged down literally?"

Josh huddled, drawing his knees up to his chin and wrapping his arms around his legs. "Myself," he muttered.

"Ah." Alex smoked in silence for a minute or two.

Josh was grateful for that silence. Alex didn't try to comfort him, or ask him why he was running, or give him any advice...

Oddly enough, Josh felt compelled to speak. To Alex, of all people; moody, Byronic, self-destructive Alex. Alex was one of the few who had never tried to support Joshua or make him feel loved and helped. Alex was selfish, and slightly homophobic. How he'd ever gotten to be friends with Gideon was a mystery. Josh had never really felt any particular closeness to the Hungarian vampire. But now, in the face of Alex's silence, he talked.

"Everything's different. I'm not *me* anymore, Alex. There've been too many changes, too fast. I don't like being a vampire."

That comment earned him a laugh that sounded self-deprecating, but no answer.

"I know," Josh went on, either not hearing or not heeding the laugh, "I know. I *asked* to be turned. I thought about it for nearly a year. I studied all the vampires I know, I asked for advice, I talked and talked and talked about it. It seemed better than dying of AIDS. And yes, everyone warned me about the changes. It's not like I was turned against my will or without knowing what I was getting into. But I miss being human! I never imagined how badly I would miss seeing the sun, or being able to eat, or feeling my own heartbeat."

Again Alex made no answer, just stubbed out his cigarette on the rock and idly traced a pattern with his finger, following the grains of sand that had long since compressed to make his natural chair.

Josh shifted again, finally getting rid of that sharp stone. He didn't feel at all ridiculous, sitting on the rocky beach with a silent older vampire. At least Alex was listening, or pretending to listen.

"It's...I don't know," Josh went on, making a lame gesture of helplessness. "It's not what I thought. There's no mystery, no power. I didn't get a black cape or a funny accent. And I know that's not what makes a vampire. I know that the Brotherhood has a pact to hunt as little as possible and to drink animal blood. I just thought that maybe being a vampire would be a little less, well, routine."

"You thought you'd own the world," Alex finally spoke. "You thought there'd be power, and mortals cowering at your feet, and orgies of blood. You thought you'd be stronger and meaner, and you're surprised as hell that you're still Joshua. You started off by saying that you aren't *you* anymore, but you sure sound like Joshua to me." He opened his cigarette case again, offered the contents to Josh. "Want one? No?" He took one and lit it. "You aren't human anymore, Joshua," he said through the smoke. "Right now, you're in either denial or grief, I can't quite decide. It's natural."

"Natural?" Josh gaped. "Being a vampire is natural?"

Alex flicked ash. "You know what I mean. You're going through the stages of any major life change. Being turned is about as major as it gets. It's going to take time. More than a year."

"How long did it take you?"

An ironic smile answered him. "I'm still in the last stage. Josh, you're just a fledgling. Your emotions are out of control, you haven't grasped the idea that everything's changed, and you don't know how to deal with it. That's understandable. You have the right to be confused, angry, lost."

"So you went through this?"

"I went through this, Gideon went through this, Francis did, Janine..." he paused and an unhappy emotion crossed his face, then vanished. "Every single vampire you know and all those you don't went through what you're feeling. Think how much worse it is if you got turned involuntarily." He flicked more ash and looked down at Josh. "You know who really helped me in those first few years?"

"Genevieve?" Josh guessed. He knew, hazily, that Alex was somehow related in the same bloodline.

"No. She washed her hands of me, at my request. I'm nobody's grandchild. No, the person who really was a stabilizing influence was the man you call your husband."

"Gideon?" Josh felt sure his mouth was hanging open.

"Unless you're married to someone else I don't know about." Alex treated this cigarette butt in the same fashion as he had the first, and resolutely tucked the gold case back into his pocket, fastening the button. "Gideon's calmness gave me a great example, a goal to try for. He stopped me from killing myself with stupidity, and never failed to treat me with kindness and patience when what I really deserved was a good smack."

"So why did you smack me?" Josh asked, his head still smarting where the blow had fallen.

"Because I'm not Gideon," said Alex with the hint of a twinkle in those deep grey eyes. "When I see someone who's asking for a good backhand across the ear, I damn well give it to them."

"I thought you said I have a right to be angry, confused and lost." Josh was certainly feeling confused.

"You do. But you don't have the right to hurt those you love." Alex stood up, towering over Josh huddled on the beach. "Do you have any idea what it cost me to learn that?" he asked quietly. "I offer you that lesson for free. You are being almost as selfish as I once was. You're thinking only of yourself, Joshua. And if you keep it up, you are going to lose the most wonderful thing you've ever had. And damn it, if you hurt Gideon that badly, I will personally stake you out in the sun."

Josh was shaking when he looked up. "You love him," he said in a voice that barely carried over the sound of the sea.

"In an entirely different way than you do," Alex said. "He is my mentor, my best friend, my guide through this dark-blighted world. You should have seen him when he met you, Joshua. It only showed to his closest friends, those of us who love him, but he was so happy, so hopeful. He'd finally met someone who resonated with him, someone he could trust and love and who would love him. And if you don't get off your butt and go back to him right now and try and work through this thing together, I will kick said butt all the way to Oakwoods."

Despite his words, although the expression on his face indicated he'd meant every one of them, Alex reached down and offered Joshua a hand up.

This time, Joshua accepted the offer of help. He let Alex hold his hand and help him rise from the stony beach. When he was on his feet, he didn't let go but turned the gesture into a hug. After a slight, startled pause, Alex returned the hug. He smelled like cigarettes and seawind.

"You are my mentor," Josh said.

"No, just your little voice of reason," Alex grinned. "Now, git!" He raised his foot meaningfully.

Joshua got. His pace back to the foot of the steps to Oakwoods was much slower than his mad rush the other way had been. The sea smell was stronger, the waves a little more energetic. The tide was turning, though there was still a lot of time before it covered the private beach.

Step by worn step, past the seaweed and broken shells, past the white salt marks and scallop-edged dirt tracks of high tide, past the rocks and brave warped trees clinging for life to the cliff face, upwards he climbed. Soon the beach was far below. He could no longer see Alex at all, and the sound of the waves dimmed in his ears.

At the very top of the cliff, he paused. Here, on a winter's night eight years ago, he and Gideon had shared their first real kiss. The memory warmed him and he walked rapidly toward home.

He let himself into Oakwoods through the back door. Evan was in the kitchen, making himself some coffee. There were no snacks in evidence, so Joshua assumed the protector was in mid-cycle, that calm in between the two extremes.

"Hullo," said Evan. "Have a good walk?"

"Yes," Josh replied. "Where's Gideon?"

"Still hard at it with Mitch. Coffee?"

"No, thanks. I'm going to go interrupt them."

The red-haired Nameless One grinned. "You go, girl," he said, and ducked, laughing.

"Very funny." Josh shook his head and left the kitchen, heading towards the other wing of the house. He walked into the downstairs office without knocking, finding Mitch and Gideon craning their heads together over a computer screen.

"If you press ctrl," Mitch was saying, "you get extra missiles to take out the aliens."

Sounds of rapid gunfire filled the office, some bells rang, and a computer-generated voice intoned "You have reached quadrant ten. You are promoted to the level of Space Commander."

"Hey, level ten, nice shooting, boss!"

"Ahem," Joshua said. "And this is helping out the financial health of Oakwoods, how?"

Gideon looked up guiltily from the computer screen. "Mitch was merely trying to help me improve my computer skills," he said sheepishly.

"You are allowed to have fun, you know," Josh said with a

grin. "But I think you should probably rest on your laurels now, Space Commander."

"Yes, I quite agree." Gideon stood up. "Take the bridge, Ensign," he said, quite seriously, to Mitch.

"Aye, aye, Commander." The werewolf saluted and pressed a couple of keys.

The other two men could hear the computer saying "Quadrant ten is full of space mines and hostile aliens, but there is a treasure planet hidden among the stars. What is your will, Space Commander?"

"So, did you have a difficult evening of blowing up hostile aliens?" Josh asked.

"Those games are excellent for hand-eye coordination," Gideon replied. "What have you been up to?"

"Took a walk along the beach," Josh said. He stopped and turned to look at his husband.

This had not changed. He loved this man. This vampire. For all that pomposity, the so-upper-crust behaviour and accent, the three piece suits even around the house, the always-guarded emotions...he loved Gideon Redoak. This had not changed. Would not change.

"I love you," Joshua said.

The carefully maintained front crumbled. "Oh, Joshua..."

"I'm sorry for the way I've acted this past year, Gideon. Please, forgive me."

"There's nothing to forgive. I love you, Joshua. I've only wanted to help."

"I know. I know, and I'm sorry I've been rejecting your help. Everyone's help. From now on, we go through this together. If it's not too late."

"Never," Gideon assured him, taking his hand.

"Let's go upstairs and make love," Josh whispered in his ear.

Gideon was so surprised that he dropped Joshua's hand. "Are you sure?"

"Oh, yes."

As they took the stairs up to the master bedroom, Gideon looked at his lover. "That must have been quite a walk on the beach. Did something happen?"

Joshua decided not to tell him about Alex. Somehow, that meeting had been special and private. "Not really. But the tide's turning."

A Walk to Remember
(2002)

Oak leaves, crisped brown by the relentless summer and curled up in protest against their early demise, crunched underfoot as two men walked side by side across the lawn of Oakwoods. The smell of their decay mingled with that of the ever-present ocean below the cliff. From far across the lawn came the excited staccato barking of a spaniel.

"Pumpkin probably found a squirrel," remarked the taller of the two men. Lean and handsome, sandy-haired and warm-eyed, Josh Trevallion smiled indulgently as he said this.

Gideon Redoak nodded, although he did not smile. It took more than a spaniel to make this dark-haired vampire with the beautiful eyes smile. "What on earth would she do if she ever caught one?" Pumpkin the spaniel was the terror of the Cliff Road squirrels.

"Faint from the shock, probably," Josh laughed.

Another nod, but it was obvious that Gideon wasn't thinking about squirrels or spaniels. He continued walking, ignoring the antics of the spaniel, deep in thought. Joshua knew his husband well. If he prodded, he'd never find out what was on Gideon's mind. Better to let Gideon be the one to speak.

"There has been an increase of talk from the supernatural community," Gideon said finally. "Once again, a new person has arrived on the scene and asked questions which are difficult to answer."

"Yes, Mockingbird," Josh nodded. "I'm not sure if it's a man or a woman."

"Asking what attracts us about vampires," Gideon continued as if Josh hadn't spoken. "As if most of us had had a choice."

"Ah." That one syllable, almost a sigh, said it all. Most of the supernaturals had *not* had a choice about what they had become. Joshua was a real rarity. He had quite deliberately chosen to become a vampire. He was still so new a one that you could smell it on him, like the sizing on new clothes.

"So, is it the freedom, or the recognition?" Gideon asked.

"The recognition, my dear, of course," Josh answered, in a fairly decent imitation of Adrian Talbot.

The look he got would have flattened mountains.

"Gideon, you know what made me choose. It came down to two things; I could not bear to leave you, and I did not wish to die a slow lingering death by AIDS. Neither freedom nor recognition came into it at all. Being a vampire is not freedom, except to the very young and careless. Simply because you *can* do nearly anything you want without fear of the consequences does not give you the *right* to. As for recognition, who wants to go around shouting that they're a vampire? I chose out of love, not for any other reason. I suppose that makes me nearly unique."

"Your turndam is another who so chose," Gideon said, referring to Genevieve de Monet, his old friend, who had turned Joshua.

"Yes," Josh nodded. "I think that's why she agreed to turn me. That, and because she loves you."

"She loves you, too, you know," Gideon demurred, embarrassed as always by any suggestion that he was in any way special.

Josh shook his head, sighing. "I don't feel as if I have unlimited freedom, or that I want to have mortals bowing to me and obeying my commands. What it means to *me* to be a vampire is simply a slightly changed diet and an inability to tan. Yes, I'm stronger and faster than I was as a human, and those powers may come in handy if we ever have another bad situation with the Brotherhood; but I'm quite content until then to live quietly with the ones I love and just try to get on with my life."

"There are those who would see that as a betrayal of everything a vampire stands for," Gideon warned, although he agreed with Joshua. What was the point of brandishing your power about and behaving like a monster? In the end, it only earned you enemies and an unquiet life.

"Fuck them," said Josh simply. "They can live however they want to, but they've got no right to criticise me for my unlifestyle."

That earned a rare laugh from Gideon. "My dear, I wasn't criticising, your lifestyle is my own, remember?" Something, close to devilment, danced briefly in those pretty dark eyes of the Baron's. "And I certainly don't want to fuck *them.*"

The shock of hearing Gideon swear combined with the promise in those eyes made Joshua laugh again and hold out his hand. "Well, then," he said, "come with me, and we'll go chase our own squirrels."

To Burn In Hell
(2003)

Sometimes, you just have to respond to headlines. The headline that the Pope has declared that our Prime Minister, Jean Chretien, will go to hell if he legalizes gay marriages made me write this. It's not particularily vampiric or occult in nature; and it might possibly offend those of differing opinions than mine. But that's what makes the world go round. Okay, it's actually gravity that makes the world go round, but you know what I mean. At any rate, no doubt there will be some strife and contention over this, but I've never been afraid to open my mouth—and shove my foot quite firmly in it. If this offends anyone of any deeply held religious belief, then I apologize, but I did warn you. —Anne Fraser

Quiet reigned over the living room in Oakwoods. It was a warm, if wet, summer night, so no fire burned; yet Warg and Pumpkin both lay flopped in front of the cold hearth. Smoke was curled up with slightly more dignity at Josh's feet. Josh was reading a newspaper and making "tch" noises softly under his breath. Gideon, making concessions to the seasonal heat by not wearing a suit jacket or tie and hence looking oddly underdressed, was reading the *Financial Post*. Mitch and Evan were bent over a chessboard. It was the sort of calm domestic scene that the master of the house had come to cherish—and to deeply distrust.

Finally, Gideon couldn't take it anymore. He set down the Post and turned to Joshua. "All right," he said, making all three animals and the other two occupants of the room look at him, "what are you reading that's so upsetting?"

Joshua rustled his newspaper in irritation. "The Pope."

Gideon waited for further enlightenment. It did not seem to be immediately forthcoming. "What about him?"

"He's spoken out on the whole gay marriage issue."

They had discussed the gay marriage issue already, at some length. Gideon was satisfied that he and Joshua were, in fact, already married. The ceremony hadn't been legal. No documents had been signed. They could now take a quick jaunt up to Ontario and become legally married, but the union would not be recognized by the State of Maine. Gideon hadn't seen the point. Joshua had had to admit that there wasn't one, really. Besides, going to Toronto would put them smack dab in Adrian Talbot's territory, and neither of them felt like pushing the limits of Gideon's truce with the actor.

"I don't imagine that his Holiness is in favour of the idea," Gideon said.

"He has apparently told the Canadian prime minister that M. Chretien will burn in hell if allows the legislature to legalize gay marriages. It's against the natural moral law, according to the Pope."

"I wasn't aware that there was such a thing as a natural moral law," mused the older vampire. "If anything, I would say that amorality is the natural state."

"But what about his statement to Chretien?" Evan asked. "Do you think that the prime minister of a large country is going to stop legislation out of fear for his soul?"

"It would certainly be the first time a politician ever did anything out of fear for his soul," Gideon replied, but it was automatic nastiness, without any real heat. "I take it that Monsieur Chretien is a Catholic?"

"Oh, yes."

"I do not envy him," the Baron mused. "Imagine his position. Not only does he have to try to pacify an entire country which must be nearly equally divided on a thorny issue, but he also has to deal with the leader of his religion telling him he is damned if he does. He will be feeling enormous pressure from religious fundamentalists of all kinds, not just Catholics."

"An Archbishop has said that homosexual marriages threaten families," Josh read.

Gideon looked around the room; first, at his husband/partner, then at his two employees, then at the three animals. "Pick up the phone and call all the families we know," he suggested. "Ask them if they feel threatened by us."

"I think," Mitch said, fighting a grin at the mental picture this suggested, "that what he means is that gay marriages make a mockery of the holy institution of marriage. Marriage is supposed to be between a man and a woman; for the purposes of making babies."

"Supposing a straight couple chooses not to have children, or cannot," Gideon argued. "Are they then threatening families? Making a mockery of marriage?"

Mitch shrugged. "I don't make the rules, boss."

"Marriage is a pretty patriarchal institution, anyway," Evan put in his oar. "There should be a legal, civil, total equivalent, like say, domestic partnership, that has all the legal, financial, medical, whatever benefits and ramifications of church marriage and that is recognized in a court of law. That way churches can keep their moral high ground and marriage can still be defined as a man and a woman; but anyone who wants to can set up a domestic partnership."

"But what if a gay couple, like us, *wants* to get married in a church? What if we want that patriarchal institution?" Joshua turned on the protector. "I don't want to go around introducing Gideon as my domestic partner; it makes it sound as if we're just housekeeping together."

Evan shrugged. "There are still churches that will marry you."

"But not legally," Gideon pointed out. "Full circle."

"What about the separation of church and state?" Mitch asked. "Chretien shouldn't make a political decision based on what any religious leader or figure tells him."

"True enough in spirit," Evan nodded, "but tricky to hold fast to when it gets down to this level. The voters in Canada are making decisions based on religious grounds."

"It will be interesting to see what develops from this," Gideon said. "Unfortunately, the Pope seems to be operating in another century. Approximately the fourteenth, in fact."

"That's Catholics for you," quipped Josh, who'd been raised Methodist.

"I rather doubt that M. Chretien is worried about burning in hell for legalizing gay marriages," Evan remarked.

"It does seem a bit harsh," nodded Gideon, who had been raised in the Puritan sect and knew something about burning in hell. "Even for a politician."

"There are so many worse things to burn in hell for," Mitch said, "like bombing a hospital in Chechnya, or raping and murdering toddlers. I don't think that Chretien is going to be frontline for the fire."

That seemed to be the final word; everyone went back to their original pursuits. Evan made a move on the chess board. Pumpkin bit her paw. Smoke purred. Warg thumped his tail and went back to sleep. Gideon's head bent once more over the stock reports.

Joshua picked up his paper again, but his eyes didn't focus on it. He was thinking.

"What's wrong?" Gideon asked after a moment, the closeness of his relationship with Josh giving him a certain amount of psychic radar. So to speak.

"So, can we?" Josh asked.

"Can we what?"

"Go up to Ontario and get married?"

"What, and burn in hell?" Gideon replied.

Josh threw a slipper at him.

Lost Boy
(2006)

Due to a chain of circumstances much too convoluted to attempt to explain here, Francis Calvert is now living in Oakwoods, having lost his shack, and has been fully assimilated as one of the Oakwoods Boys.

—Anne Fraser

It was a normal evening in Oakwoods. All five of the Boys were downstairs in the recreation room; there was a movie on that Gideon and Joshua had wanted to watch, and Mitch and Francis were playing billiards. Evan was enjoying just sitting for a change, half-watching the movie and half-watching the billiards game. Since Gideon felt it was practically a sin to just watch a movie, he was opening and reading his mail during commercial breaks.

Amongst the bills and circulars and letters was a small package. The return address had been smudged into illegibility, and Gideon didn't recognize the handwriting. But it had gotten past the wards and Evan's inspection, so he didn't worry about it. Once he'd opened all the regular mail and read it, he picked up the package. While the television droned on about antacids, he removed the brown paper to find a sturdy little cardboard box. During a stern admonition that he should ask his doctor about Levitra, he opened the box. An antique glass jar, like the kind once used by apothecaries, was carefully packed into the box with excelsior to keep it from breaking. He searched through straw-like stuffing as an extremely stupid car ad blared from the set.

"How odd," he said aloud.

Josh blinked, half-hypnotized by the commercials. "Hmm?"

"Look, someone sent me this jar," Gideon held it up, "but no note. No return address, either. I've no idea who sent it."

"Odd," Josh agreed. "Nice little jar. It would look good on your dressing-table." But the movie started again, so he switched his focus back to it.

Gideon stared down at the jar, distracted from the movie

by the mystery of who had sent him this thing, and why. There seemed to be a bit of liquid inside it, distorted by the thick old green glass. Curious, he flipped down the small metal clasps that held the lid in place and then twisted it off. He sniffed at the now-open jar.

"Gideon!" Evan had turned just in time to see his employer slump soundlessly out of his chair to the floor.

Josh was up out of his own chair in a nanosecond, and at his stricken husband's side in another. "Gideon?" he asked, touching the Baron's shoulder.

No response. Gideon lay in an untidy heap, unmoving.

Mitch and Francis abandoned their game and ran towards the fallen head of the household. Joshua lifted Gideon in his arms, peering into his face anxiously. Mitch reached for the fallen glass jar, but Evan, reacting quickly, slapped his arm out of the way, perhaps a bit more forcefully than he needed to.

"Don't touch that!" he said to the startled werewolf. "Get back, Francis, Josh, whatever it is affects vampires, obviously."

Josh nodded, and stepped back, still holding Gideon.

"Call Michael," he urged the others. "Now." He glanced down at the glass jar. "Better get Ray, too."

But someone was already knocking at the door upstairs.

Francis was closest and raced up the stairs, while Mitch went for the phone by the far wall to call Michael. Evan offered to carry Gideon, who was still unresponsive, but Josh held him fiercely. So Evan led the way upstairs more calmly than Francis had gone, to find the blond vampire deep in conversation with Raymond Griffin. Ray looked at the procession coming up from the basement.

"Is Michael coming?" he asked, upon seeing Gideon's still form in Joshua's arms.

"Yes, Mitch is calling him," Josh said.

"Good. He'll take care of Gideon, then. Show me this jar. I could feel the magic the moment it was opened."

"I'll show you," Evan said, and led the way back down to the rec room.

Josh watched them go downstairs, and then carried Gideon up to their bedroom and laid him down on the bed. He was still completely unresponsive, and rather floppy. It was hard undressing him in that state, but Josh managed and got him into pajama pants. The top was out of the question at the moment.

There wasn't a mark on Gideon. But he didn't wake up, or make a noise, or anything. Just lay there as Joshua had arranged him, eyes closed, face neutral. Of course he was pale, he was a vampire. What was in that jar, that it had affected him so? Who had sent it? Gideon had no enemies that Joshua was aware of. The last of Corbeau's bloodline had been beheaded months ago. Well, the last one they knew of, but even if there were other minions of the blood left, would they have access to such powerful magic?

As Joshua stood there, staring down at his beloved, he heard another knock on the front door. Michael had come, commendably quickly. Mitch let him in, and then Josh heard the Druid's footsteps on the stairs as he climbed up to the master bedroom. Josh went and opened the door, and Michael came in.

"Do we know what it was that did this?" he asked.

Josh shook his head. "Not yet. Ray's down looking at the jar."

A nod. "Go down and talk to him, Josh, see if he has any ideas."

The antiques broker opened his mouth as if to protest leaving Gideon, but realized Michael wanted to examine his patient in peace, without a worried spouse hovering nearby. "Okay," he said, and left the room.

Ray did not touch the green glass jar, once he saw it. He sniffed the air, muttering to himself, and made strange passes over the jar. He knelt down near it and looked at it very carefully, and did something that made it glow.

"Evan," he said, "get me a silver box, big enough to put this in, and a pair of tongs."

If he found these instructions perplexing, Evan did not say. He left the rec room, and met Joshua on his way down.

"Best stay out of the way," Evan advised. "I don't think Ray knows what it is, yet. He's trying to neutralize it. Do we have a silver box anywhere?"

"Try my office," Joshua said. "There's one around somewhere." Toxic to vampires, silver was generally kept out of sight, but Josh sometimes had to handle it for clients. He had special gloves for doing so.

"Okay. I have to borrow a pair of tongs, too. They'll probably be useless afterwards."

"Help yourself. I'll go make some coffee."

"Good idea. How about some biscuits or something?" Evan wanted to keep Joshua busy.

"Yeah, okay."

"Josh." Evan gripped his shoulder, briefly. "We'll do our best for him."

"I know."

Michael studied Gideon. In all the years he'd known vampires, he'd never quite worked out how to treat them. Oh, wounds were easy enough, but any kind of malady was usually magical in origin. This was unknown magic.

He lifted up an arm by the wrist and let it flop back down again. No resistance at all. Hm. He tried to pry open an eyelid, then suddenly gave that up and stared down at the limp body on the bed. Slowly, as if not quite believing, testing to be sure he had not just imagined it, he felt for the wrist he had lifted a second ago.

Yes, the skin was warm. There was definite colour in it; pale colour, to be sure, but still a healthier tinge than your average vampire boasted. Michael shifted his fingers around on the wrist and felt.

He dropped the arm again in sheer surprise.

He had felt a pulse.

He looked at Gideon's bare chest. There was no denying the lungs were working. A very faint snore escaped from the Baron.

Michael sat down on the bedside chair. He'd seen a lot of strange things. He'd tended wounds made by silver weapons. He'd helped Genevieve recover from an illness caused by drinking the blood of an alien. He'd been to Hell. He had raised teenagers. Nothing had prepared him for seeing someone who'd been a vampire for over 350 years suddenly becoming...human.

There didn't seem to be any doubt. Just to satisfy his curiosity, he opened the unresisting lips and peered at the teeth. No fangs.

How the hell had this happened?

Down in the recreation room, Raymond Griffin was asking the same question. He'd gotten his silver box and tongs, and put the glass jar in the box, carefully. Silver neutralized some black magic, although Ray couldn't have testified as to the colour of whatever was in that jar. It didn't feel like black magic, but it didn't feel like white, either.

"I should examine the packaging it came in," he said to Evan, who was maintaining a safe distance.

"Should be right there," Evan replied. "Gideon never left that chair."

Ray looked around. There was nothing on the floor but the glass stopper for the jar. He lifted that gingerly with the tongs and placed it in the silver box.

"There's nothing here," he said.

Evan frowned. "There should be brown paper, you know, the kind you mail packages in. And a cardboard box. And that packing stuff, the excelsior."

"See for yourself," said Ray, standing up.

The Nameless One peered around the chair. The floor was clean.

"Weird," he grunted.

"Self destruct spell," Ray said. "I can taste the aftermath. Whoever sent that jar didn't want to be traced. I'm surprised the jar is still here, actually."

"Can you tell what kind of spell was in the jar?"

Ray shook his head. "Only that it was specific to Gideon. If anyone else had opened the jar, nothing would have happened. It was keyed to his karmic signature."

"Who's got it in for the boss?"

A shrug. "Someone powerful. This is not footling magic. I could do it, and one or two others we know. There aren't many mages of that calibre around."

"You don't think it was some kind of joke, maybe?"

Another head shake. "This doesn't feel like a joke. And it doesn't have the scent of anyone we know."

Evan knew Ray wasn't talking about cologne. "I guess you don't recognize the signature."

"No. Too indistinct. Someone was very clever."

"Damn. I hate the clever ones."

Mitch and Francis sat in the kitchen, watching Josh make coffee and whip up a batch of chocolate chip cookies. Nobody was talking, because nobody knew what to say. Every so often a pair of eyes would look up, as if able to penetrate the beams and floorboards and see into the master bedroom.

Michael had made Gideon as comfortable as possible. The psychic shock of suddenly turning mortal again had to be pretty intense. No wonder he was still out, still unable to be wakened. Otherwise, he seemed fine. His colour was better, the pulse was strong and steady, the breathing normal. No fever.

There was nothing more Michael could do at the moment, and he felt the urgent need for some coffee and conversation. He pondered how to break the news as he went downstairs to the kitchen.

Ray and Evan came upstairs at about the same time, Ray handling a silver box very carefully. He left it in the hallway and didn't need to admonish anyone not to touch it.

They all got coffee and the breathers got cookies and sat

sipping and munching for a few minutes.

Then everyone else looked at Michael. He sighed and pushed his coffee mug out of the way.

"I don't really know how to say this, and I can't explain it. First of all, he's essentially in shock. I've made him warm and comfortable, but it would be a good idea to just let him sleep. Best thing for him right now."

Michael waited a bit to see if anyone would twig to the rather large clue he'd just handed them, but everyone was too worried to pick up on it.

"Ray?" Josh turned to the mage. "Did you learn anything at all from that jar?"

"Whoever sent it is powerful magically. Grand mage calibre. It's not easy to hide a magical signature from me." Ray wasn't boasting. He knew he was good. "The packaging disappeared, probably soon after Gideon collapsed. They knew I would try to trace it. And whatever spell was in the jar was tailor-made for Gideon, not for anyone else. Only he could be affected by it. I still wouldn't recommend anyone else handle that jar, mind."

"No fear of that," said Francis, while everyone else nodded.

"So, black magic then?" Mitch asked.

Ray shrugged. "It doesn't quite have that feel. As you know, black magic—or white, for that matter—is a matter of intent, and I can't quite fathom the intent of whoever sent that jar."

"To do Gideon harm, obviously," said Josh, almost angrily.

Ray looked at Michael. "Is Gideon harmed? Beyond being in shock and asleep, that is." Then he thought about what he'd just said...

"Asleep?" echoed at least three voices.

"Yes," said Michael. "Asleep. Breathing. Warm. He has a pulse."

"How..." Josh began, and looked blankly at Ray.

The ex-sorcerer whistled. "That's pretty powerful magic, all right. Is he fully human again? Mortal?"

"As far as I can tell," Michael replied. "I'll know more when he wakes up."

Josh was already heading for the stairs. "I don't believe it."

"Josh, don't you wake him up!" Michael warned, getting up to follow.

Mitch, Francis and Evan looked at each other. Ray was staring at his hands.

"So, if the boss is human again," Mitch said, "what exactly does that mean?"

Evan shrugged. "I will be his protector no matter what. I've sworn an oath."

"If he started living again at the same point he stopped," said Francis thoughtfully, "he'll be my age."

"You'd better not teach him how to drive a motorcycle," said Evan.

"How do we explain this to people? The companies he's on the board of. His stockbroker. Outsiders." Mitch sighed. "It's fine when he can project that mind control to make people think he's older, but he won't have that now."

"Let's worry about that when the time comes," Evan replied. "He does most of his business over the internet and phone anyway." He looked at their mage. "Ray, can you reverse the spell? Or find a way to?"

"I will try," said Ray. "But are you sure Gideon will want me to reverse it?"

"What do you mean?" Mitch said.

"Gideon was turned against his will, by a monster. He had a pretty lousy life even before that. He might not want to be turned back into a vampire."

The other three let that sink in and exchanged dismayed looks.

Upstairs, Joshua took Gideon's hand in his own, feeling the warmth, listening to the pulse and the breathing.

He sank down in the chair and put his head in his hands. "Now what do I do? I became a vampire for him. Now he isn't one anymore. I'm married to a nineteen year old boy."

Michael put a hand on Josh's shoulder. "We'll talk to him when he wakes up," the Druid said. "One thing I am certain of, Joshua, is that he loves you. Nothing can change that. No spell, no magic, no amount of adversity can change that. Have faith in him."

Josh nodded, then pulled himself together and stood up. He crossed back to the bed and stood looking down at Gideon. Then he bent and kissed the slightly-parted lips.

Those dark, pretty eyes fluttered open slowly, and the breathing became stronger. More colour stole into the cheeks.

"Joshua?" Gideon asked.

"I'm here," said Josh, squeezing his hand.

"What hit me?"

"Somebody sent you a spell in a bottle," Josh said. "We aren't entirely sure yet what its effect on you is." *Liar,* said an inner voice, which he ignored.

"Ah." Gideon rubbed his head. "A spell in a bottle."

"Yes."

"Thank God it wasn't a djinn." Gideon drifted back off to sleep.

When Gideon woke up, he was alone in the bed. He frowned a bit at that; but his memories of the previous night were hazy. There'd been a package...some sort of bottle? And then...he couldn't really remember. Somebody had said something about a spell? Obviously whatever it was had badly affected him, and Joshua had probably chosen to sleep on the cot in his office rather than disturb his lover after a trauma.

If only he could remember what the trauma was.

He got up, noting that he felt slightly dizzy. He had a distinct feeling of discomfort in the middle regions. Not exactly pain, almost more a pressure. As if...he shook his head. But that was impossible...

Nevertheless, the feeling was getting more insistent—to the point where his bladder was threatening to make its own arrangements. Who was he to argue? Maybe this was the residue of the spell, if it had been a spell, and he'd best eliminate the problem.

It had been a very long time since he'd last had to pee, but it wasn't something you forgot how to do. He was faintly disconcerted to see that it was red-tinged as it whooshed into the toilet. Well, guess that made sense, given his diet, but it made him feel dizzier and slightly nauseous. When it finally seemed to be over, he flushed the toilet, washed his hands, and then leaned his head against the bathroom mirror to recover his equilibrium.

A pale, tired-looking boy with disheveled hair stared back at him from the mirror.

Gideon raised his hand, noting that it trembled slightly, to touch the reflection. The reflection's hand rose to meet his. They'd never bothered to take the mirror out, after Joshua had been turned, because it was an antique, and it would have involved major renovation to remove it. Who was going to notice that the two occupants of the master bedroom didn't have reflections?

Well, apparently, one of them did now.

His breath was forming small clouds on the mirror.

A man made of less stern stuff might have fainted at this point, or at least thrown up. But Gideon Redoak had been toughened by more adversity than his fair share. He was shaking, but he held himself together. He stared at his reflection for a couple more minutes. There was no doubt whatsoever that he was breathing. He could feel his heart hammering away in his chest.

He was mortal. Human. A breather.

Prey.

Holy shit.

He took a brief shower and washed his hair, which made him feel marginally better. Then he left the bathroom without another glance at the mirror and pulled on some clothes. There was a mystery here, and he was going to solve it. Or at least find out how it had happened.

Someone knocked on the bedroom door. Feet still bare, Gideon sprang to answer it.

"Joshu..." his voice trailed off as he saw, not his beloved husband, but Michael Fairlawn.

The blond Archdruid shook his head. "Joshua is out cold, Gideon. It's ten in the morning."

"It's true, then," said Gideon, voice fairly steady. "I'm not a vampire anymore."

"It would seem not. Could I come in?"

Gideon nodded and they both went into the bedroom and sat down, looking at each other.

"How are you feeling?" Michael asked.

An elegant shrug. "I had to pee for the first time in three hundred and sixty-five years. How should I feel?"

"Do you mind if I have a look at you?"

Another shrug. "Go ahead."

Michael was gentle, but thorough. "You're still in a bit of shock," he said, when he finished. "Your heart rate's a bit accelerated. Understandably, of course. But otherwise you seem remarkably healthy."

Gideon stared at the floor. "I'm nineteen. I haven't aged mortally since I was turned. When I was a vampire, I could convince people that I was older. I'm not going to be able to do that anymore."

"No," Michael agreed. "But at least nineteen in 1641 was older than nineteen is now."

He got a look that was very reminiscent of the vampire Gideon had been. "Care to run that past me again?"

"You were not considered a boy, or even a teenager, in your own time. Therefore you conduct yourself as a much older adult. If you plead some illness that keeps you from public appearances, you should still be able to manage your business concerns by internet and telephone. Your voice still sounds the same."

"Does Joshua know?"

"Yes. Everyone does. Well, everyone in Oakwoods. I haven't

told anyone else yet."

"How...how did he take it?"

"He's very worried about you. And about what this will mean for your relationship."

"Why should it mean anything? I loved him when he was mortal."

"Gideon, it was one thing for Joshua to love you when you were an immortal vampire; then the age difference was meaningless. Now you are a human, young enough to be his son."

Gideon grimaced. "Ouch. But I still love him. It shouldn't make any difference how old we both are."

"I know." Michael touched his arm. "It's not just the age difference."

The Baron looked away. "I am not ready for that question, Michael. I only just woke up as a human."

"Yes, I know that, too. And Joshua will not press you until you think you're ready to discuss it. But Genevieve is here."

"Genevieve? When did she get here?"

"Very late last night, just before dawn, really. Josh asked her to come. He seemed to feel you might need to talk to her."

Gideon shook his head. "Let me have some time. I need to think. I would like to be human, just for a little while."

"Of course. Nobody will pressure you, Gideon. Now, do you feel up to coming downstairs, and maybe trying to eat something? That's why you feel dizzy. You're hungry."

"Eat...?" Gideon looked up. His stomach growled.

"We'll go slowly at first, to see how you adjust. Toast and tea would be my suggestion. Come on, I'll help you on the stairs."

They slowly made their way down to the kitchen. Evan and Mitch were sitting in the breakfast nook, the morning sun on their faces.

Gideon winced and blinked painfully. It wasn't that bright a day, but it hurt.

"I guess we'll have to get you some sunglasses," Evan remarked.

"I'll get you some toast," Mitch offered.

Neither of them mentioned how odd it seemed to have their employer join them for breakfast.

Gideon looked at the buttered toast on his plate for awhile.

"It'll get cold," Mitch advised him.

"Don't rush him," Michael said. "Take it slowly, Gideon."

After another minute, Gideon took his first bite, chewed, and swallowed. He had a sip of tea.

"Wow," he said, rolling his tongue around in his mouth. "So that's food." He ate a little more toast. "It's delicious." He closed his eyes. "I'd forgotten."

"Wait till you try chocolate," said Mitch, but Evan elbowed him into silence.

"Any bad effects?" Michael asked anxiously.

"My stomach's not quite certain what to make of it," Gideon admitted. "But it's not in danger of hurling it back out." He waited. "Seems to be settling. Is there anything besides toast?"

Grinning, Evan made some scrambled eggs and Gideon downed these with no apparent problems. He drank two cups of tea and enjoyed them thoroughly.

"That was different," he said.

"Here, boss," Mitch handed him a pair of sunglasses. "Thought you might want to go outside."

"Thank you, Mitch." Gideon put them on, since he was still squinting painfully in the sunlight that came in through the French doors.

He stood up, and everyone noticed that he'd stopped shaking. "I think I would like to go outside."

Evan opened the doors for him. All three of his friends watched from the kitchen as he walked out and looked at the Atlantic Ocean in daylight for the first time. Saw his house in daylight for the first time. Saw flowers blooming, a butterfly go by.

He shivered. It was late September, and the wind off the ocean was cold. He'd put on a t-shirt, that being the first thing to hand when he'd dressed, and he was chilly. Being human again had its drawbacks.

Someone was handing him a jacket. "Here," said Evan, kindly. "You might want this."

"Thank you. I see I have a lot to relearn."

"We're here to help you, no matter what, Gideon. Don't forget that. Shall I leave you alone for a bit?"

"Please."

Evan faded back into the house, and Gideon put the jacket on. That was better. He sat down on a boulder that commanded a good view of the ocean and watched the sunlight sparkle off the waves.

He wasn't all surprised to find he was weeping.

Eventually, there seemed to be no more tears. Gideon felt a little calmer, that cold hollow calm that comes when the tears stop. He sighed and got up off the rock, amazed to find himself stiff and cold. The stiffness wore off fairly quickly, though, as he walked around to the front of the house.

Oakwoods in the sunlight. It was beautiful. He had always loved his home, this lovely Georgian manor house, but he had never seen it in the daytime. The oak trees at the end of the drive were just turning colour, and the flowers in the garden had grown leggy and tired-looking, ready for their winter sleep. He heard a neigh shatter the quiet morning and, with a smile, went over to the stable. The smell of horse and horse by-product assaulted his nose, and made him sneeze. Despite this, he opened the stable door and went in.

Four pairs of dark eyes swivelled towards him. Four heads peered over stable doors.

"Calvin." Gideon walked over to the loose box containing his daemonic stallion. Calvin's glowing red eyes widened a little, and he shuffled back in his box, ears laid against his skull. "It's me, you silly great thing. Come here."

Calvin bared his teeth and shook his head. His ears did not come forward. A stamped hoof warned of what might happen if Gideon attempted to enter the stall.

"Calvin?" The Baron stared at his horse.

A whinny from the next stall over drew his attention. Buccaneer was thrusting his head over the stall door, inviting a nose rub. Gideon sighed and went over to greet Alex's young horse. Buccaneer was nearly ready to be broken to saddle; he'd achieved full growth and was raring to go. Deprived of Calvin, Gideon spent some time making friends with Buccaneer. He gave Victoria a cautious pat and scritched Damien behind the ears.

Then he realized he couldn't put off returning to the house any longer. He needed to use the bathroom again, for one thing; for another, he was hungry. The morning must have gone by already.

Lunch was a quiet affair. Michael had gone back home, telling them to call him if he was needed. Gideon wondered if Evan had warned Mitch not to ask too many questions; for both other men were silent unless spoken to. As for himself, Gideon wasn't sure what he wanted...did he want to be alone, or with other people? Did he want to be asked questions, or to be left unpestered? Good God, what was he going to say to Joshua? What would Joshua say to him? The inevitable question loomed over him, making him depressed. He hadn't even had a full day of being human again, and he knew that already everyone was wondering if he'd agree to be turned back into a vampire.

He didn't know.

But, at the moment nobody was asking him that question, so he was able to ignore it. There were several hours left of the day in which to explore and adjust to his new condition—or was it his old condition? He felt restless, confined to Oakwoods and the grounds. He wanted to see everything.

"So, anything you want to do this afternoon, Gideon?" Evan asked as he cleared the lunch dishes.

"Do you think…" Gideon hesitated. "I hate to ask. I don't want to inconvenience anyone."

"Just ask. It won't be an inconvenience."

"Could one of you drive me into town? I would like to see Fletcherville in the daylight."

"I can—" Mitch began, but Evan cut him off.

"I'll go," Evan said. "Mitch, you need to take care of the roses and walk the dog."

Pumpkin had jumped all over Gideon upon his coming downstairs, and now was lying under the kitchen table.

"Um, yeah, okay," Mitch said.

Gideon felt a little sorry for Mitch, but he understood why Evan wanted to be the one to drive him into town. It was a security risk, letting the master of Oakwoods be seen by day. People would wonder.

"Will it cause too much talk?" he asked, thinking this over.

Evan and Mitch exchanged looks. "Well, Fletchervillians tend not to ask too many questions about us," said the werewolf.

"I think it will be all right," Evan agreed.

Gideon bit his lip and sighed. So many complications, already! But he wanted to see the town. He didn't want to just sit around Oakwoods all afternoon and wait for something to happen.

The limo smelt and felt different, riding in it as a human. He discovered power windows, and was disconcerted to be told to fasten his seatbelt.

"You never bothered to tell me before," he complained, chafing in the confinement.

"You could never be killed by a car crash before," Evan replied, "barring extremely weird circumstances, of course."

"Oh."

"And please stop playing with the windows?"

"Sorry."

Fletcherville proved a little disappointing. It didn't look that much different in the afternoon than it did late at night. It was still a small Maine town, caught halfway between the fishing industry and the tourist trade. Familiar spots such as the China Clipper club, the community hall and the sheriff's office didn't garner much interest. Especially when Gideon felt he couldn't really get out of the car and wander around without having half the population wonder why he was doing it in the daytime.

"Well, what do you think of it by day?" Evan asked.

"It's a bit boring."

"But we like boring. Boring is good."

"It would be nice if I could get out of the car."

"I don't think that's a good idea, Gideon."

"No, I didn't think you would."

Evan glanced at him in the rear-view mirror, first for the novelty of being able to do so, and secondly to see his expression. Gideon looked resigned, but at least he wasn't actually sulking.

"I'm tired," Gideon said, realizing this was true. "Maybe this was too much for the first day. Take me back home, please."

"Yes, sir."

"You don't have to call me 'sir.'"

"You still sign my paycheck, don't you?" Evan turned the limo around and drove back towards the Cliff Road. "Just take it easy, Gideon. Don't try to do too much at once. Sure, it will be boring, but you've had a terrible shock. You need time."

"Yes, but will I get it?" Gideon cursed himself for speaking his biggest worry out loud.

Evan was silent for a couple of miles, until they reached the Cliff Road turnoff. "Nobody is going to push you to make a decision," he said finally. "But remember, even if they try, they want what's best for you. And for Josh. But if you feel anyone is pressuring you before you're ready, come and tell me and I'll smack them for you. Okay?"

Gideon watched the trees go by as the road steadily mounted the cliff. "Okay," he said, as they passed Ray's house. "He hasn't come by."

"I imagine he's busy trying to dissect the spell in that jar," Evan said. "He'll come by when he knows something, I don't doubt. And Michael hasn't told anyone else in the Brotherhood, and won't until you give him the go-ahead. Josh called Gen on his own last night."

The oak trees at the driveway showed the path to home. Gideon was feeling very drained now, too tired to think or guard his words.

"Yes. Just what I need. Someone else to make me feel guilty."

Evan stopped the car at the front of the house and got out,

then opened the door for his employer.

"Gideon," he said. "I can't begin to imagine what you're going through. I know it's been a dreadful shock. And I know you're tired, and scared, and unsure of what you want to do. I know you already feel pressured to say you'll become a vampire again, because it is what Joshua will want. And I know you're not sure if that's what you want. But there are two things you can be totally, completely sure of. Those are that Joshua loves you, and that Gen loves you. Neither will make you feel guilty. Got that?"

Gideon felt a little surprised to be addressed in the same tone Evan often used on his son Owen, but also acknowledged, deep down, that he'd deserved that lecture. He'd been ungracious and unfair.

"Got it," he said.

"Good." Evan switched back to his speaking-to-the-boss voice as they entered the kitchen. "Why not go upstairs and lie down for a bit? There are still a couple of hours before sunset; maybe you should try to have a nap."

"That sounds like a good idea. After all, I haven't had a nap in years."

Mitch laughed, and Evan grinned. Their employer, now much younger than either of them, made his way upstairs to the master bedroom.

Werewolf and Nameless One looked at each other.

"Think he's gonna be okay?" Mitch asked.

Evan sighed. "I don't know. He's scared. He's still in shock. And he's frantically worried that everyone is going to be on his ass to make him turn again."

Upstairs, Gideon peeled off his clothes but felt too unhappy and too tired to bother with pajamas. He fell on the bed just in his underwear, and lay staring up at the ceiling for some time before he finally managed to doze off.

Joshua was actually using one of the vampire-friendly guest rooms in Oakwoods rather than his office, since his office didn't have a shower. He woke up and stared at the tasteful decor for awhile before getting out of bed. He could hear a shower running down the hallway. Of course, Gen would be up. He wouldn't be able to lurk in this room, hiding from everyone, for very long. Why was he hiding anyway?

"Because I don't know what the fuck to do," he grumbled out loud. He sighed and went and took his shower.

He and Gideon were definitely going to have to talk; he

couldn't keep on wearing the same clothes. Of course, they were going to have to talk anyway.

He was just pulling on his socks when there was a knock on his door.

"Are you decent?" he heard Genevieve ask.

"Yes," Josh replied. "I'm also dressed."

She opened the door and looked at him. "That joke is older than I am," she said mildly.

Joshua smiled. What he saw in the doorway was a beautiful, slim, blonde Frenchwoman with bright blue eyes, who didn't look a day over 25. The fact that she was several centuries over 25 didn't show, unless you looked too closely at those eyes. She carried herself like a queen, even in casual slacks and light sweater.

No, like a Prince. Which was what she was, gender be damned.

"You'll never be old, Gen," Josh said, rising and giving her a kiss.

"My dear son." She returned the kiss. She had, after all, turned him; which made him her son. "They will be waiting for us downstairs."

"Yes. They will."

She delicately raised an eyebrow at him, but he just shook his head. He didn't know what to say to her. They'd talked when she had arrived, but not for long, just long enough to inform her of the situation. She hadn't had any advice to offer. In the five hundred years in which she'd been a vampire, she'd never known another who'd just stopped being one and become human again. She had, of course, known many vampires who had stopped being, period.

"Offer me your arm," she chided him gently.

"Oh, sorry." He did, and they glided down the stairs together.

They heard feet hit the stairs behind them. Quite likely only vampires would have heard that, since the feet belonged to yet another of the undead. They were feet encased in scuffed engineer boots.

"Hey ya gorgeous," called out the newest, though no longer the youngest, member of the Oakwoods Boys.

Gen turned, a smile stretching her lips. "Hey ya yourself, Francis."

"He's talking to me!" Josh objected.

"Oh, you wish. So, Gen, when are you going to go on that date with me?" Francis leered at her.

"Do be kind enough to run down to Hell and check the temperature, *cheri?* If it is getting chilly, then I will ride on the back of your Harley with you."

"Ha ha." Francis took his rejection in good humour, though. "So, what are we going to do about Gideon?"

"Do?" Genevieve and Joshua reached the main level of the house and both of them turned to watch Francis descend the last few steps. "Why should we do anything?" Gen asked.

Francis looked like he'd been smacked across the face with a dead mackerel. "Uh...you do know that he's suddenly not a vampire anymore, right? That's he's mortal. Human. A breath...."

"Yes, Francis, I know," Gen replied solemnly. "I do not need you to tell me what a mortal is. I have known a few in my time." She shot Joshua a look. "But I was unaware that the situation called for any action on my part. Or anyone else's part, for that matter."

"Uh..." If Francis could have patented that expression, he probably would have made a fortune. He looked at Joshua, and swallowed. "But...well..."

"We will protect him, of course," Gen stepped smoothly into the conversational chasm Francis had opened up. "If he wants to talk, I will listen. If he wants advice, I will give it to him. But I will neither force him to talk nor force him to listen to unwanted advice. It is up to Gideon to do something about the situation. Or to do nothing. It is up to us only to support him and remain his friends."

Poor Francis only looked more bewildered. "But..." he said again, and once more looked at Joshua.

"Francis," said Josh, kindly, "I am accepting Gen's lead in this. It is extremely difficult for me, trust me on this. But, you see, that's why she's Prince and I'm not."

"Actually, I very nearly named you my successor," Genevieve said.

"Gideon would have killed you."

"I know. That's why I didn't." She turned back to Francis. "All we can do, Francis, is be here for him, and for Joshua. Do you understand now?"

He scuffed his boots on the hall rug. "Yeah, I guess."

Josh put a hand on Francis's shoulder. "Thank you. For wanting to help me."

Francis nodded. "It's just...well, I don't care what that damn Bush thinks or what the fucking church thinks or anything else. You guys are one of the most...*married* couples I know. You make your relationship work. You have something real. I don't want to watch that fall apart."

"It won't," said Joshua, very firmly.

"Shall we join the others?" Gen asked.

Joshua offered her his arm again. Francis didn't have a lick of courtly manners, and had to take up the rear. But he enjoyed the view. *Lucky, lucky Jean de la Mare,* he thought.

The three of them entered the dining room, where the others waited.

"Genevieve." Gideon, looking rather odd in one of his business suits, since it had been styled for a middle-aged man, rose up to greet his mentor.

She gave him a very fierce hug and kissed his cheeks, then held him at arm's length.

"You look well," she said, almost accusingly.

"I had a good nap. I am still a little tired, but otherwise, I feel fine."

"Good," she said, and turned to greet Mitch and Evan.

That left Gideon and Joshua staring at each other. Everyone else was trying to pretend they either didn't notice or that they weren't actually in the room.

"Hey," said Josh.

"Hey."

Then, just like that, they were in each other's arms, and their lips met.

"I love you," Josh said when the embrace and kiss both ended.

"I love you, too," Gideon replied, eyes suspiciously shiny. "So...you don't mind?"

"Don't mind what?" Josh's arm encircled his husband's shoulders.

Gideon smiled. "That I'm a bit...indisposed."

"You're mortal. I'd hardly call that indisposed."

Mitch laughed, and, a second later, so did Gideon. That started everyone laughing, which got them nicely past the awkward stage. Soon they were all sitting down; the three who could eat enjoying the dinner, and the four who could not enjoying the company.

All of them enjoyed the look on Gideon's face when he tasted chocolate for the first time in his life.

He closed his eyes as he savoured the first bite, and his eyelashes fluttered. "It's incredible," he whispered.

"Don't forget to swallow," Mitch advised.

"Don't forget to chew," Evan corrected. "Then you can swallow. I don't think you're ready for the Heimlich."

"This is simply heaven," Gideon said, with a sigh. "Genevieve, you've never...?"

Gen looked at the dessert on offer, and shook her head. "No, I've never. I shall take your word for it that is wonderful."

"Oh, it is."

"So, how's Jean these days?" Evan asked Genevieve. Perhaps he was trying to take her mind off the lack of chocolate in her life.

"How is Jean, ever?" she replied. "He is Jean. He is still persisting in this pirate fantasy he's taken up. I swear I will buy him a parrot."

"Must be a bit of fun, though," Evan said. "In bed."

"Being told to prepare to be boarded tends to have the novelty wear off of it, *mon ami,*" Gen shot back, making Mitch and Francis look at each other and snicker.

"What did you do today?" Joshua asked Gideon, when the latter had finally surfeited on chocolate.

"I asked Evan to drive me into town, but I think that was a mistake. It tired me out, and we both thought it would raise too many questions if I was seen in town."

"Possibly, possibly not." Joshua reached over and took Gideon's hand. "The townies are pretty used to seeing us doing strange things."

"Yes," Gideon agreed. "But it was only the first day...it was too much."

"How much you must have enjoyed seeing sunlight again, though."

"I cannot describe it," Gideon replied simply. "Everything is different. The smells, the sounds, the textures. Sunlight reflecting off the waves. The way a flower opens. Everything." He touched Joshua's hand. "And you gave all that up for me."

"Yes," Joshua replied, feeling a bit wretched. He saw Gen's head come up as she caught his tone, felt Gideon's hand tighten on his. "But I'd had forty-five years of it, you know. You've had a day."

"I had nineteen years of it," Gideon corrected him.

"Centuries ago. You don't even remember it, not properly."

"No." Gideon stared off somewhere into a distance Joshua could not see. "There are things I do remember, but not the smells or the tastes."

"...and then he what?" gasped Francis, who was almost falling off his chair laughing.

"He rigged up some ropes above the bed," Gen said, "and he swings on them, with a dagger in his teeth...or sometimes a rose..."

"Sounds like a better story over there," Gideon remarked, mouth twitching.

Joshua smiled. "The story I want is right here."

When dinner was over, a slightly awkward silence fell over everyone in the room again.

"Come on, kids," Evan said to Mitch and Francis. "We have chores to do. Let's go do them."

"I was hoping he'd forget," Mitch complained to Francis.

"Fat chance of that," Francis sighed.

"Would you see to Calvin, Evan?" Gideon asked. "He won't let me near him."

"Really?" Evan looked surprised. "All right, I'll look after him." He herded the other two out of the room.

Genevieve stood up, and naturally so did both Gideon and Joshua. "I want to see the roses. Gideon, would you show me?"

Joshua looked at them and said, "Yes, go ahead, I need to work online for a bit."

"Of course," Gideon replied, repressing a sigh with an effort. But he and Josh kissed and Joshua murmured something in his ear that made him smile.

"He loves you," Gen remarked as she and Gideon walked from the dining room to the conservatory. "That has not changed."

"No. And I love him. And I know why you're here and what you're going to ask."

"Do you?" Genevieve stopped and looked at him. He had never felt frightened of her, even when he'd first been brought to her, but now...now she was a powerful master vampire, the Prince of France, and he was a mortal. "What am I going to ask, then?"

He did the smartest thing possible, and said, "To see the roses."

She permitted herself a smile. "Good answer."

She walked amongst the rows of blooms in silence for a few minutes. Gideon sat on one of the benches and watched her. He had forgotten how vampires looked to mortal eyes. You could spot the otherness, if you knew what to look for. The skin pallor could be explainable, but not the stillness. The economy of movement. The lack of breathing.

It was already second nature to him to breathe. Could he stop doing it again? Could he go back to that existence, living only by night, dead in the daytime, having to drink blood in order to survive?

The scent of roses was almost overwhelming in here, and it

was hot and humid in the glassed-in room. None of that had bothered him...before.

"You look troubled," Gen said.

"Just thinking. I haven't really had much time to think."

"No, I suppose not." She came and sat down beside him. "Gideon, I am here as a friend, *d'accord?* Joshua called me because he thought you might need friends who would support you no matter what. He is worried."

"I thought perhaps he had called you because...well...you turned him, after all, so..."

"Do you really think so little of him? And of me?" She didn't look offended, only a little sad. "That I would turn you against your will, without your permission?"

He hung his head. "Sorry, of course not."

"For one thing, it would be very awkward to have to behead myself for violating one of the most basic rules of the Council," she said, sounding slightly more good-humoured.

Despite himself, he heard himself say, "You could always throw yourself on a stake."

She cocked her head to one side, considering this. "Possible. But what if I missed?"

"It could get messy," Gideon said. "I am sorry, Genevieve...I didn't mean to imply you would force me to turn."

"Good. Because if I thought you had meant it, I'd put you over my knee."

He glanced at her and saw she was perfectly serious. "Um..."

"I am still your *maman, n'est ce pas?* And now you are young enough to spank."

"I hadn't thought of that."

She smiled and kissed his cheek. "My dearest son, I have loved you from the moment I saw you come into my library, with your hair chopped up by Evan, looking as if you thought I would eat you. You and I have weathered some horrible times together, and some truly wonderful ones as well. We will weather this adventure. No matter what, I will not stop loving you."

"Maman," Gideon said, and for a moment lay his head on her shoulder.

Joshua couldn't concentrate on the online auction he was following. He did manage to procur an item his client wanted, but he paid too much for it and cursed himself. He felt miserable. Twenty-four hours ago, everything had been fine, running smoothly, and their lives had been ticking away peacefully. Then that package had arrived.

The phone practically nudged him. He stared at it for a moment, debating with himself, then picked it up and dialled a number.

"Hello, Estella," he said to the person who answered. "How are you? And Eleanor?" A siren wail actually answered that question, and Joshua grinned through his worry. "Is Ray handy? Oh, he is? Okay, never mind, don't disturb him. I'm sure he'll get in touch when he has some news. No, everything's fine. Well, as fine as possible."

Sighing, Joshua hung up. Estella had said that Ray was down in his basement lab. That meant he was still working on the mysterious glass jar and its contents, trying to unlock the spell that had changed Gideon. Best not to disturb him.N

They really needed to tell the rest of the Brotherhood what was going on. It was unfair to keep their friends in the dark. But he'd have to get Gideon's okay to do so. Well, he'd have to talk to Gideon anyway...

There was a knock on the front door, and Pumpkin barked. Josh pried himself away from the computer. It wasn't like he was doing any good there anyway. He made his way downstairs. Evan had already opened the door to admit Michael and Mary and the twins. Pumpkin was leaping excitedly around the latter two, yapping her fool head off. Mitch, Francis, Gideon and Genevieve were all coming out of various rooms to see what the fuss was about.

"I think we need a Brotherhood meeting," Michael said, by way of explanation for bringing the family.

"Am I still a member of the Brotherhood?" Gideon asked.

"Of course you are."

Galen was staring at Gideon, despite his sister nudging him. "So it's true?" he asked. "You're, like, human?"

"It's true, Galen," Gideon replied.

"Whoa. Way cool."

"We need to tell the others," said Mary. She smiled at the woman behind Gideon. "Hello, Genevieve, it's good to see you."

"Bonsoir, Mary," Gen replied, smiling back. "And to you, too, Galen and Vivain."

They surged forward for hugs, or at least Vivain did while Galen pretended to be too cool to want one. He got one anyway.

"Yes, call a meeting," Gideon said to Michael. "Everyone should know."

"Ray's still working on the spell," Joshua said. "I just talked to Estella."

"He'll come for the meeting," Michael predicted. "Mitch,

where's the nearest phone?"

Mitch showed him the way, and Joshua got everyone else sitting down in the living room with drinks and nibbles in commendably short order.

Galen sidled up to Francis. "Dude..."

"Dude?"

"So, like, the Baron, he's a kid?"

"My age," Francis said a little stiffly, not liking being called a kid.

"Yeah, a kid," Galen nodded, grinning. At sixteen, he could afford to think of a mere three years difference as not being much. "Like us."

"Yeah, I guess," Francis nodded. "Odd to think of him that way."

Galen glanced over to where Gideon, in his nattily tailored suit, was talking to Mary. "We gotta do something for him."

"Such as?" Francis asked, a spark of mischief lighting in his eyes.

"Get him some cooler clothes."

"Hm, yeah, no shit."

But they didn't have long to plot before there was another knock on the door, and the remaining members of the Brotherhood of Darkness started coming in.

It was probably the oddest meeting they'd ever had. Everyone kept stealing glances at Gideon, as if to reassure themselves that the story was true. He got rather self-conscious after awhile, and tried his best to be invisible. This was embarrassing.

"And you just smelt it?" Alex was staring at Gideon, the story of the glass jar having just been repeated. "You opened up a jar that had come with no note, no idea of who sent it, and smelt it? Just like that?"

"I wasn't expecting it to be anything dangerous," said Gideon defensively.

"Are you insane?" Alex asked.

"Now, Alexander," Gen chided him. "We all make mistakes."

"Would you have done any differently?" Joshua challenged.

"Let's not argue," Michael stepped in. "Whether or not Gideon should have opened that jar is beside the point. It is done, and we have to deal with the consequences." He looked over at the scarred ex-black sorcerer, who'd been quiet until now. "Ray? Any progress?"

Ray Griffin looked up and around at everyone. "It's a powerful spell. Whoever sent that jar is a strong mage. It was designed specifically for Gideon. It may even have had a small compulsion spell on it, that vanished later, to make him open it and smell the contents." He gave Alex a look. "Probably he couldn't help it. I'm not having much luck so far tracing the jar or the spell. Somebody's got pretty heavy-duty wards."

Silence reigned as they digested this. Generally speaking, all mages knew each other or at least of each other. The idea of a magician powerful enough to elude detection was worrying. Especially a magician who could fool Ray Griffin.

"But you said it isn't black magic," Michael reminded him.

"It's...not," Ray answered hesitatingly. "Not precisely. I don't think there was an intent to harm."

"I'm mortal," said Gideon, drily.

"I'd noticed," Ray replied, equally arid. "But are you *harmed?*"

Gideon looked startled. "Well, I, uh..."

"See? I don't know what the intentions of mystery mage were. That makes it harder to dissect the spell."

Maggie got up and went over to Gideon. "So, how are you feeling?" she asked, taking Gideon's hands in hers.

"Confused," he replied. "A little scared."

"We're here," she said. "All of us."

"Thank you." Gideon looked around the room. "Thank you all."

Michael smiled. "We are the Brotherhood, after all."

"It's who we are," added Mitch.

Everyone laughed, and the meeting broke up.

"Can I talk to you? Alone?"

Genevieve looked into the anxious butterscotch-coloured eyes of the hovering Joshua and nodded.

"Yes, although there are only so many times I can look at the roses without raising comment."

"Please, Gen, I'm serious."

"Of course you are." She put her hand over his. "But not in the conservatory. Let's just go into the hallway."

"Okay."

They withdrew from the chattering group in the living room. Joshua paced the hallway, and since vampires don't often pace, it was a sign of his agitation.

Genevieve just stood stock-still and looked at him until he stopped.

"Sorry," he said.

"Joshua, of course you are worried. And probably frightened.

If you need to talk, then I am here. But I have already spoken to Gideon, and he does not wish to be turned back, or even to discuss it. You must have patience with him, and with the situation."

"I know!" Josh barked at her.

She raised an eyebrow, but made no other comment.

"Sorry," he said again. He sighed. "Damn it, Gen, I finally understand something, after all these years."

"And what is that?"

"When I got back the results...the night I went to Gideon and told him it was true, I was HIV positive...he wanted to turn me right then and there. We had a terrible fight."

"Yes, I remember. Gideon told me about it. You stormed out of the house, unable to cope with his reaction."

"Yes." His eyes were bleak. "Well, I finally understand how he felt."

"But Gideon is not dying, Joshua."

"How do we know? How do we know anything about him as a human? He's like a time traveller, Gen! He doesn't know his medical history, because there wasn't any such thing in 1641. Hell, he's probably carrying smallpox or something!"

"You do have a point," Genevieve conceded quietly, refusing to be ruffled by his agitation. "But it will gain you nothing to worry yourself so much and lose your temper. I will have a quiet word with Mary Fairlawn, if you like."

"Good idea," Josh grunted. Mary, as a nurse, would know what Gideon needed in order to protect him from the ills of modern society—and to protect modern society from whatever ills a mid-17th century transplant would have.

"I do have them every so often."

"Sarcasm, Prince?"

"It seemed fitting. Now listen to me, Joshua. This is a situation I have never before encountered. I have given you what advice I can. I cannot stay here very long, as you know, but if you need me, you know I will come at once if it's possible. But I am not the one you should really be talking to."

"I know." He looked at his shoes. "But Gideon thinks all I want to ask him is if he'll agree to be turned."

"Fortunately, I have persuaded him past that stage."

Joshua looked at her in admiration. "How'd you do that?"

"Prince secret," she said solemnly. "Actually, what you and Gideon really need to do is not talk."

He shook his head to clear it. "Huh?"

"Do I have to spell it out for you? Take him by the hand, lead him upstairs to bed, undress him, and make mad passionate love to him."

He stared at her for a moment, nonplussed. But then, Genevieve was not exactly a blushing virgin, and the French tended to be much more open about sex anyway. Her eyes were twinkling.

"But he's nineteen," Josh said.

"Yes. Think of the hormones."

A slow grin replaced Joshua's gobsmacked expression. "Are you sure it's Jean who says 'prepare to be boarded?'"

"Oh, go and get your husband and take him to bed," she snorted. "I will talk to Mary."

"Merci beaucoup, maman." He leaned down and kissed her cheek. "Will you be here tomorrow night, at least? Please?"

She nodded. "Yes, I will stay for tomorrow night, but then I must get back to France."

"Thank you. Okay, let's go back into the mob."

They returned to the living room.

Gideon had noticed his husband and his surrogate mother leave the room, and pretty much guessed what they were talking about. But he didn't have time to worry about it, because he was being beset with questions from the fascinated twins, Galen and Vivain.

"So, like, did it hurt?"

"What was it like to breathe again?"

"You gotta get some new clothes, you wanna come shopping in town with us?"

"Have you had any chocolate yet? Isn't it the best thing ever?"

"Are you gonna learn how to drive now?"

"Hey, you could, you know, go to college or something, that would be cool."

"Howcome Calvin doesn't like you anymore? That must be a bummer."

"Are you and Josh still married?"

"Leave him alone, you two," their father, laughing, collared them both. That was no mean feat, since they were both taller than he was. "Off with you."

Disappointed, the terrible twosome sauntered off to go plot with Francis and Mitch.

"So, how are you?" Michael asked Gideon.

"Ah, finally, a question I can answer," he replied with a brief laugh. "I'm fine, actually."

"Good. Just be sure to keep taking it easy for a few days, until your system adjusts. Be sure to get lots of rest, and eat properly, and stay warm and out of direct sunlight."

Gideon nodded. "Yes, all right. It does make sense not to rush things."

His head turned as Joshua and Genevieve came back into the room. He saw the look in Joshua's eyes. So did Michael.

"I'll round everyone up, shall I?" the Druid offered. He noticed his wife deep in conversation with Genevieve. Both women were casting occasional worried glances at Gideon.

There was a flurry of goodbyes. While Michael rounded up his offspring, Mary went over to talk momentarily to Gideon.

"I'll come by about midmorning to take you downtown," she told him.

He gave her a slightly wary look. "I don't think I'm ready to try that again."

She gave him a look, a look that said she had raised three teenagers and wasn't about to take any nonsense from someone young enough to be the fourth. "I'm taking you to the clinic. You probably have no immune system to speak of. You certainly don't have any of the vaccinations you should. God knows I shouldn't have brought the twins tonight, they're walking germ factories just in themselves. You'll probably end up with the flu, if you're lucky. You don't want to think about what else you could end up with. So you're coming with me and getting caught up on your shots."

"Shots?" he repeated faintly. He'd never had a needle in his life.

"I'll get Evan to hold you down, if necessary," said Mary sweetly. "Night-night." She gathered her two walking germ factories and her husband, and was gone.

"Evan, Mitch, Francis," Genevieve addressed the remainder of the Oakwoods Boys. "I have a burning desire to learn how to play Monopoly. Will you teach me?"

"Monopoly?" Francis stared at her. "Are you kidding?"

"Come on," Evan said, with a jerk of his head. "Game's down in the rec room, let's go show the nice lady how to play."

"Subtle," Gideon remarked as the foursome disappeared into the basement.

"What, you don't think Gen wants to learn Monopoly?"

"She'll have hotels on every property within half an hour. Who is she trying to fool?"

"I think," Josh said, offering his arm to help Gideon out of his chair, "that that was a ploy to let us be alone."

They kissed. Their arms went around each other, and Josh found himself lifting the shorter Gideon slightly off the ground.

Somehow they got upstairs to the master bedroom, though neither one of them could quite remember how. They were still wrapped in each other's arms. Joshua's mouth brushed Gideon's neck, and he felt his lover shiver.

"I don't frighten you, do I?" he asked.

"Maybe a little," Gideon replied. "Remember...remember I'm human now."

"I know." He ran his hand along Gideon's jawline. "I will not cross your comfort zone," he promised. "Whatever makes you uncomfortable, I will stop. I will try not to hurt you."

"I love you, Joshua."

Joshua undressed him slowly, trying to get used to the sight of him now with a pink tinge to his skin, the sign of blood coursing through his veins and arteries...no, maybe better not to think of that. He was warm to the touch, so different from vampire flesh...

So vulnerable. So fragile.

Things progressed slowly, each little step a small victory over Gideon's uncertainty and sudden fear. He was far more experienced now, of course, than he had been back when he'd been human the first time...did his body remember? Were all those centuries as a vampire locked away, unreachable perhaps, or could he summon them at will? It was not as if it was the first time he and Joshua had made love.

But it was as if it was the first time, because never before had the dynamics been like this, with Joshua the vampire and Gideon the human.

When that cold body covered his, he couldn't quite repress another shudder. And yet...he looked into those eyes and saw warmth. Love. Concern.

"I don't want to hurt you," Joshua said. He kissed and stroked and Gideon found himself relaxing. Trusting.

This was his husband, his truest friend, his lover. Joshua would not hurt him.

He felt a throbbing erection against his legs, and then they were as together as they could be, and he grasped Joshua to him and cried out in pleasure and pain. The night turned vivid colours as the waves of climax washed over them both. He fell asleep in Joshua's arms, heedless of the tears that wet his cheeks.

"Don't make such a fuss," Mary chided him. "I'll buy you lunch

if you stop flinching."

"I don't get a lollipop?"

"Okay, we're done for now."

"Thank goodness." Gideon reached to take his shirt back and gasped.

"It's going to hurt for awhile," Mary warned him, handing him his shirt. "You'll have to go back out to the waiting area and sit for twenty minutes before we can leave, too."

"Why?"

"To ensure against bad reactions. Which we can't be certain you won't have."

"You didn't tell me that before."

"It was need to know."

Gideon stared at her, and she smiled back at him. He shook his head.

"Tell me," he said, as he took a seat back in the waiting area, "do your children actually *like* you?"

Although Gideon's arm hurt considerably, he enjoyed the novelty of having lunch downtown with Mary Fairlawn. They ate the soup and sandwich special at the diner, and it was delicious for such a simple meal. Of course, Gideon found all food delicious now. He was a bit more prepared for the experience of seeing Fletcherville in the daylight. He was enjoying it this time—possibly being with Mary instead of Evan helped. Now that the vaccination ordeal was over, she was treating him as a friend, not as if he was one of her offspring.

"I suppose Gen will have to go back to France tonight," Mary remarked, once they had slices of blueberry pie in front of them.

"Yes," Gideon nodded. "It was good of her to come."

"She'd do anything for you, you know that. You or Joshua."

"I know," Gideon said humbly. "As I would do anything for her or Jean."

"My son wants to know what you're going to do about your wardrobe."

Gideon's brow wrinkled in puzzlement. "Why should I do anything about it?"

"Because he doesn't want to be seen hanging with anyone in Savile Row, apparently."

The brow wrinkled further. "Galen may be a tad high-spirited, and have crossed the line a few times in terms of his behaviour, but I doubt Sheriff Fletcher will hang him." As an afterthought he added, "Or me."

Mary laughed. "I see you're going to have to learn the

vocabulary."

"I have a perfectly good..."

"Oh, eat your pie."

"Shall we go for a bit of a walk?" Mary suggested as she left the tip. "How's your arm?"

"Sore," Gideon replied, "but not as bad as it was. Thank you for lunch."

"You're welcome. I always treat resurrected vampires to lunch. Come on, let's go stroll around downtown."

"That will take us five minutes," Gideon smiled.

"Pfft."

They wandered out of the diner and into the hustle and bustle of Fletcherville's main shopping district, all two blocks of it.

"I don't understand," said Gideon, looking at his hands. "How could it have just disappeared?"

Ray Griffin shrugged. "I don't know. I'd been examining the jar in my workshop and came upstairs to ask Estella something. There was a magical presence—we all felt it, even Andrei. I ran back downstairs and the silver box was empty. There wasn't a single sign of anything out of place, magical or otherwise—none. The jar was just gone."

The whole Brotherhood had gathered in Oakwoods once more, at Ray's request. He hadn't realized that confessing the jar had done a vanishing act meant everyone would be staring at him—everyone except the person most affected.

"Surely you have wards," Genevieve said.

He raised an eyebrow at her. He wasn't a vampire, so he didn't have to kowtow to a Prince—maybe just show a bit of respect.

"I do," he replied simply. "Whoever it was got around them. But I have some suspicions."

"And those are?" Joshua asked.

"Remember that the wrappings and packaging disappeared fairly quickly? The jar did something similar."

"But it took two days to disappear," Mitch objected.

"Two days in which I puzzled over it and shot every possible bit of magic at it," Ray said. "Without finding out anything much about it."

"It's crazy," Alex said. "Why would the mage or whoever sent it let it sit around for two days?"

"It's almost like they're playing a game," remarked Michael, frowning.

"Someone is playing a game," Ray said grimly. "We just don't know what the winning move is."

Everyone looked at each other with expressions of varying bewilderment, except for Gideon, who continue to study his clasped hands as though they might hold the answer to the whole puzzle.

"I am sorry to leave you with this dilemma unsolved, but I can spend no more time here, *mis amis,"* Genevieve said, her somber tone betraying her deep misgivings.

With that announcement, the jar was temporarily forgotten and everyone crowded around to say their farewells to the Prince. She took Gideon aside for a private chat, and what she said to him, he never revealed to anyone, even Joshua. But he did kiss her when they returned to the others, and for once not on the cheek.

"Je t'aime," he said, a bit huskily.

"Je t'aime aussi," she replied. "I can be here in a few hours if you need me. Be careful, Gideon. None of us want to lose you." She nodded around the room, said "au revoir," and left quietly.

"That is one classy woman," sighed Francis.

"Except when she's killing people, of course," Maggie said.

"So, um, Gideon," Galen spoke up, feeling a bit odd to be able to address the Baron this way, "if the bottle's vanished, does that mean you're permanently human?"

"I don't know, Galen. Certainly I don't seem to be turning back in any great hurry."

"But..." Galen looked like he wasn't sure he could say what was on his mind. "Dad? Is it okay if I talk?"

Michael regarded his only begotten son in faint amusement. "You and Vivain are full members of the Brotherhood now," he said, smiling at his youngest daughter to include her. She was whispering with Estella and Maggie, but looked up at the mention of her name. "Speak whatever's on your mind."

"Thing is," Galen exhaled with a whoosh, "thing is, you turned back into a human at the same age as you were, right?"

"Right," Gideon replied, wondering where this was going.

"So, well, you're nineteen."

"Yes?"

"You gotta stop dressing in three piece suits, dude."

Gideon surveyed Galen's attire. "So instead you suggest torn blue jeans and a t-shirt that claims the day is green?" Then he wondered why nearly everyone was having to smother a laugh.

"Galen," said Joshua, almost choking. "Maybe we can find a compromise, hm?"

"Clothing is not my biggest worry," said Gideon. "I have let business matters slide for two days, and people are starting to ask questions. How can I maintain the charade of being a business executive in his forties?"

"The internet is a wonderful thing," Estella said. "Not even a psychic could tell the changes in you from e-mail."

"Unless you start calling people 'dude,'" Michael added, grinning at his son.

"But I used to conduct most of my business at night," Gideon said. "Now I find myself far more active during the day, and wanting to sleep at night. Mostly sleep," he added, giving Joshua a slightly smouldering look.

"Nobody will notice," said Joshua. "That's the beauty of the internet. And there's fax, and phone, too. You'll manage. I doubt you've lost your business savvy and all that experience you have."

"No, that knowledge is all still there. But it has competition."

"Competition?"

"I was raised on a farm estate, and trained to be the Baron from an early age. I only saw London three or four times before I died, and under a set of fearsome prohibitions. I did not have much of a childhood, and nobody had an adolescence in the sixteen hundreds. I find myself wanting things I never had."

"Like what?" Vivain asked, leaning forward. This sounded promising.

"Fun," Gideon replied.

The twins looked at each other. Their father sighed, but said nothing.

"We've kind of lost track of the original conversation," said Ray. "Um...remember the jar?"

"But if it's disappeared," said Alex, "how can we learn anything more from it?"

"The result of the spell that was in it hasn't disappeared," Ray said, nodding towards Gideon. "We keep an eye on him, and try to come up with reasons why anyone, for good or evil, would have done this."

"Maybe somebody wants to throw the vampires in the Brotherhood into disarray," Francis suggested.

The mages and the other two vampires in the room looked surprised. That hadn't occurred to anyone, except, apparently, Francis.

"Possible," Ray admitted. "It's not like we don't have enemies."

"But in that case, why go after just Gideon?" Alex said.

"He's the oldest vampire among us," Francis said. "He's the second in command of the Brotherhood, and the head vampire.

Or was..."

"Yes, remember Uncle Rigo," Estella put in, coming over to join Ray. "The only one he had any respect for was Gideon, because of hierarchy."*

"Could your uncle be behind this?" Joshua had come over as well. The conversation had attracted the attention of the whole Brotherhood.

Estella shrugged. "Of course Uncle Rigo isn't a mage of any kind. That's not to say he doesn't know of one, or couldn't have arranged this. But he did promise not to interfere with the Brotherhood again."

"As long as Gideon was senior vampire," Ray added softly.

Estella went a little pale. "I will talk to Mother. She usually knows where Rigo is."

"But Gideon is still..." Alex's voice trailed off. "I guess he can't be, can he?"

"I fail to see how," said Michael. "I'm afraid you're senior vampire, Alex."

The Graf rose to his feet and went and grabbed Josh by the collar. "Turn him back!"

Joshua shook Alex off. "And that will solve the problem, how? Gideon wouldn't be senior vampire, he'd be the newest, rawest fledgling."

"Oh, shit." Alex went back and sat down. Maggie, feeling sorry for him, fetched him a brandy. "I'm not even two centuries old yet," Alex said. "I can't be senior vampire!"

"We could make you a Junior Woodchuck," Francis offered, and got kicked by Evan for his efforts.

"It seems we've stumbled upon a distinct possibility," said the Nameless One, ignoring Francis's yelp and glare. "This wasn't just directed against Gideon, but as a means of undermining the Brotherhood by rendering our top vampire out of action."

"Why not just stake me?" Gideon asked.

"That would be an open declaration of war," Evan said. "And our enemies have learned that we take war very seriously. We have defeated demons. But this...it's put us all off kilter, we're letting our guard down and we're all concentrating on trying to figure out why anyone would do this to you."

"Hmm," Gideon mused. "Yes, it's time to stop concentrating on just me and try and figure out who really hates the whole Brotherhood."

* Uncle Rigo is introduced in "Mistress Estella."

"Uncle Rigo," Estella sighed.

"Eric Bates," Ray said.

"Half the demons in Hell, probably," Michael contributed.

"The Prince of Belgium," Alex replied gloomily. "Possibly others."

"Is there anybody who actually *likes* us?" Maggie asked.

"Gen," said Vivain firmly.

The chattering went on, over and above Gideon's head. Nobody noticed that he sank down into one of the comfy wing chairs by the fireplace, head in his hands. Nobody, that is, except his husband.

Joshua came over and stood beside him and put a hand on his back. Not talking, just connecting, touching, comforting.

All around them, the Brotherhood speculated on the new possibility to explain the glass jar, listing their enemies and trying to pin down a likely suspect. Francis was ribbing Alex about senior vampiredom, and probably risking getting himself kicked again. The twins had their heads together, whispering, and their father was watching them in mild concern.

"You okay?" Josh finally asked.

"Alex was right," Gideon sighed.

"Alex was right?" Josh blinked. "What about?"

"I must have been insane to have opened that jar and smelled it. Look what's happened."

"You couldn't have known," Josh patted him. "Ray said there might even have been a compulsion on it. Cheer up, okay? Tomorrow's Saturday."

"So?"

"Nobody will expect you to be doing business, so you have a couple more days to settle in and think about what you want to do. Maybe you can have some of that fun you suggested."

Gideon's head came up. "I have no idea what I was thinking."

"Pfft. You were thinking that you never had any fun before you got turned, and now you want to try it out. Talk to Galen and Vivain. I think they have ideas."

"They will make me wear blue jeans. And possibly ride a skateboard."

"Get them to take pictures."

Gideon stared at his lover, then started to grin. So did Joshua. In a minute, they were both laughing, which stopped all other conversation in the room.

"I think that might be the signal to go home," said Michael, bearing down on his offspring. "Your mother should be home soon, anyway."

Everyone else got the hint. Francis, Mitch and Evan looked at each other and decided that this was a really good time to go muck out the stables or look after the roses or do something else that involved not being here.

"Come on," Josh said, holding out his hand once he and Gideon were alone. "Let's have some fun."

"Oh, I like the sound of that," Gideon replied, and took the offered hand.

Gideon had fallen asleep after he and Joshua had made love; sleep was yet another thing he hadn't readjusted to as of yet. He hadn't dreamt as a vampire, and now he was having dreams. For the first two nights, they'd been odd jumbles, memories of things that had happened to him as a vampire combined with processing the new sensations going through his body and, the previous night, culminating with a rather daft nightmare about being chased by a gigantic chocolate cake. Too many rich desserts on a stomach not used to them, he diagnosed, then forgot it.

Not tonight. At first he dreamed of riding Calvin; they were soaring through the air, surrounded by the Wild Hunt, horns blaring, oak leaves blowing past them on the damp wind. The Hunt landed deep in the Black Forest of Germany, a forest full of wild things, not all of them dumb animals. There were hunters in the Forest, other than the Wild Hunt.

Then with the logic of dreams, Gideon was alone in the forest, not even Calvin with him. He heard the myriad small noises of a forest at night. But it was no longer the Black Forest; now it was only a thin copse of trees huddled together for protection on the south slope of a hill. At the top of the hill was a ruined castle, of which the keep remained the only habitable part.

Not even the keep remained now, in the real waking world, but this was a dream, and Gideon moaned in his sleep. He knew every stone of that dreadful place. Even though he was shivering and frightened, he felt himself being pulled up the hill towards the great dark door that shut out the world. He was summoned and could not disobey.

His master's voice...

He stood in front of the great door. It looked like a castle door; bound with iron, hardened with age and fire, able to withstand sieges.

When it opened, the huge hinges creaked. There were torches burning inside, and their fitful, sputtering light cast strange shadows that shrank and stretched and danced across the flagstones.

Then one shadow detached itself from the rest, and became solid, and reached for him...

"Gideon."

"No!" he screamed. "No, no, no!"

A hand clasped his shoulder and he fought in blind panic. He felt his fist connect with solid flesh and heard someone go "oof."

"Gideon." The voice was different; slightly pained, for one thing. But warm, beloved, not dreaded.

"Joshua?" Gideon opened his eyes. "Ah, God..."

"Nightmare?" asked Josh, rubbing his stomach. Gideon had been raised to work, and could shoe a horse. He had a pretty hefty punch.

"I..." Gideon shook his head to clear it, and the bedroom slowly came into focus. There was no old door, no torches, and the shadows here were friendly. Of course, he was in bed with a vampire, but..."Yes."

"Want to tell me about it? You owe me for that poke in the ribs."

"Oh. Sorry." Gideon sat up. "I've got to go the bathroom."

"Go, then, but I still want to hear about the nightmare."

Josh watched his husband swing out of bed and stagger into the bathroom. There was the sound of retching, and he realized then what the nightmare must have been. He frowned.

"You okay?" he called out. He glanced at the time. Nearly dawn; they only had perhaps half an hour, if that.

"Fine," said Gideon, over the sound of the toilet flushing. He stared at himself in the mirror after washing his face and hands. He was pale; well, he hadn't gotten much sun, at Michael's insistence. But he looked like someone who'd had a fright. He tried to pull himself together.

He came back to the bedroom and got back into bed. In a low voice, reluctantly, he described his nightmare to Joshua.

"So you didn't actually see Corbeau?" Josh asked, when the recital had ended.

"No. But I knew it was him."

"He's dead," said Josh quietly. "Ashes and gone. You know that."

"My dream didn't know it." Gideon stared up at the ceiling. "What if I start revisiting that damn keep every night? What if I start dreaming about some of the things he did?"

"Forget it," Josh replied gruffly. "It was just a dream. Go back to sleep."

"I don't think I can, now."

"Well, then, stay up, and wait for dawn with me."

There were no windows in the master bedroom of Oakwoods. It was an inside room, protected from the rays of the sun by bricks and mortar and insulation and plaster in careful layers.

But it didn't take a window with an eastern view for a vampire to know when dawn arrived. There were those of the undead who were unaffected, or least not severely disabled, by the rising sun. Some could still function in daylight to some extent. It was all in the bloodline. Joshua's bloodline was de Monet, the blood of a Prince; and Gen was one of those vampires who had to sleep during the day. Plus, for a vampire, he was still quite young and not fully come into all the little tricks that come with age and experience.

When dawn arrived, he closed his eyes and died.

Gideon watched. He'd never, ever seen this happen before. The last two nights he'd been asleep before dawn; in fact, the first night, Josh hadn't even slept in the same room. The second night, Josh had already been dead when he'd woken up. That had been bad enough. This...this was terrible and frightening and made him feel like he wanted to go and throw up again.

One moment, there'd been the person he loved most in this world, and the next minute, there was a corpse.

He found he couldn't lie in bed next to...next to Joshua. Not like that, not having seen it happen. He got up shakily and was vaguely proud of himself for not being sick. He took a long shower, which helped a bit, and got dressed and left the bedroom without glancing at what lay in the bed.

Nobody else in the house was up yet, not even Pumpkin. Naturally, Francis would be asleep for the day, but neither Mitch nor Evan was stirring. Oakwoods was quiet, and for the moment, all his. He wasn't even familiar with his own kitchen, but managed to locate the necessities to make a cup of instant coffee—foul stuff, he'd have to find out how to use the coffee maker—and some toast.

He still marvelled over how wonderful food tasted. Not instant coffee, obviously, but the toast with jam was fabulous stuff.

He found a jacket and slipped outside, revelling in this rare freedom. The sun was just coming up over the Atlantic, striking the top of the cliff, lighting up the turning leaves on the trees so that the colours glowed. The air smelled of dead leaves and the sea. He heard the leaves crunch underfoot as he walked towards the stable, and each footfall wafted more scents up to him. It was all so beautiful.

There was movement in the stable. Horses are early risers. They looked hungry, so he pitched hay and poured oats into mangers, at least those mangers whose owners permitted this. Calvin still bared his teeth and laid his ears back when Gideon approached, so all he got was some hay heaved over the stall door. Gideon was strong, but not strong enough to control an enraged demon stallion.

He fingered some tack, wishing he could go for a ride. It was out of the question on Calvin, and Buccaneer hadn't been broken yet. He was still just a little too young, the bones in his knees not yet fully fused. Another couple of months, perhaps. There was Victoria, though she had a temper and a foal...but she likely needed the exercise.

"Would you let me ride you?" Gideon asked the mare.

She looked at him and thrust her head forward for the bit. He took off her stall headpiece and put on the riding bridle, memory serving him well since Calvin didn't tolerate a bit. She didn't even object when he cinched the saddle. Not quite believing his luck, he led her out of the stable, Damien following behind in a slightly bored way. Poor baby, he didn't yet know what was in the cards for him—it was nearly time to start weaning him.

Gideon swung himself up into the saddle with ease and chucked the reins. Victoria was a spirited mare, but she had no extra little secrets. Her hooves stayed quite firmly on the surface of the Cliff Road. Damien gave up following them and wandered back to the stable, content in the knowledge that his mother would return.

Oh, this was wonderful, riding a good horse through the fresh morning air, watching the sun come up and smelling the fall in the wind.

He almost forgot his nightmare.

Almost.

Victoria shied a little once, when they went past the signpost for the Cliff Road, but Gideon soothed her trembling. He dismounted and had a careful look around; Victoria might not have been magical but that didn't mean she couldn't sense danger. There was nothing except some dry leaves in a ditch by the sign. No trees where anyone could have been hiding. No sense of a life-form anywhere around, except maybe a rabbit or squirrel.

What Gideon didn't realize was that he was human now. Humans are not very good at sensing presences.

Something withdrew into deeper shadows, and watched.

It had been a full day. Gideon had found Mitch and Evan awake and preparing breakfast when he'd come back from his ride. He didn't bother telling them about the incident at the crossroads, since he hadn't seen anything. He knew exactly how that conversation would go. Mitch would tell him not to worry about it, and Evan would insist on going with him wherever he went. So he just kept quiet.

He'd gone for a walk along the cliff edge path, with Pumpkin frisking at his heels as if she was still a puppy, enjoying the crisp autumn day. He'd ended up at Fairlawn, and Michael and Mary had invited him in for lunch. Pumpkin had sorted things out with both Ruddigore and Orlando, the resident dog and cat, and was enjoying a bowl of borrowed dog food. The humans had hot beef sandwiches and veggies. The twins were astounded when Gideon tried Coca Cola for the first time—and disliked it. They would have lived on it if their mother had permitted it.

After lunch, Galen and Vivain persuaded Gideon to try a few things he'd never done. Michael just laughed and told him to be careful; Mary said she would patch up any damage. So feeling a bit odd, Gideon followed the twins outside.

Skateboarding did not go at all well.

Galen was surprisingly sympathetic. "Not everyone gets the hang of it," he said. "I guess it's just not for you."

"It's such a boy thing," sniffed Vivain disdainfully.

"So, what?" her brother challenged her. "You want to have a tea party with him and your dolls?"

"Don't be a dick. Let's get our bikes."

"Yeah," Galen nodded. "Come on, Gideon. If you can ride a horse, you can ride a bike."

Gideon learned a new phrase. "Road rash."

"Maybe we should get you training wheels," said Mary, as she tweezered the gravel out of Gideon's knee.

"Why can I not do these things?" Gideon asked. "I am not stupid, and I have perfectly good balance."

"You can't expect to master everything on the first try."

"Why not?"

"Because," said Mary patiently, spraying disinfectant on the abused areas, "you aren't a vampire anymore."

Despite the bruises and abrasions, Gideon enjoyed his afternoon with the young Fairlawns. They were patient, and sympathetic, and actually quite funny. He regretted having been so standoffish to them when they'd been smaller, although he'd never really enjoyed the company of small children.

By the time they decided to take a break for a snack, late afternoon, Gideon had mastered the bicycle. The skateboard, on the other hand, remained as unrideable as Calvin currently was. The three teenagers sat at the kitchen counter in Fairlawn, drinking milk and eating brownies, and talking. Gideon had never really just *talked* to Galen and Vivain before. He was learning all sorts of things about them.

Like how hard it was to blend in at a school full of mundane, ordinary teenagers when you weren't mundane and ordinary.

Like how much math sucked when you had zero talent for it, and how much you really wanted to be free of dreary homework and exams.

Like how your father was a hero, and your mother was too, really.

How much it meant to be a member of the Brotherhood at such a young age, and to be trusted to act like adults when at meetings or out on a mission.

Vivain talked about Hari, her...boyfriend...a lot. Galen didn't say much about Emily, who might or might not have been his girlfriend. Gideon got a bit confused about that. The whole world of "dating" was a total mystery to him. Sure, he and Joshua had gone out together before getting married, but he'd never thought of it as dating, and it certainly had not been what teenagers did. Galen made gagging noises when Gideon told him about his first real "date" with Joshua—at the ballet.

Their world was school, and soccer, and movies, and the arcade, and the ice cream shop. It was all a locked room to Gideon. With some coaxing, he told them a little about his own childhood. They were appalled.

"Didn't you even have any games?" Vivain asked.

"Bowls," Gideon said, a bit apologetically. "Although of course playing on Sundays was forbidden."

"Bowls?" Galen wrinkled his forehead. "You played with bowls?"

"He means bowling, moron," Vivain told him. "Right?"

"Right. You would call it lawn bowling now, or bocce, I think."

"But only old people do that," Galen snorted.

Gideon shrugged. "People were not generally encouraged to waste their time then."

"Well, then, let's find some more ways to waste yours now,"

said Galen, grinning.

"Yeah, to make up for it," added Vivain.

They ended up driving him into Fletcherville to try out the arcade. Ironically, Gideon had helped pay for this addition to the attractions of Fletcherville, along with the sports complex on the edge of town. He had wanted to give young people in the town something to do besides standing on streetcorners. But, apart from inspecting it when it had been built and fully furnished, he had never set foot in it. Certainly he had never played any of the games.

As he watched Galen throw basketballs towards a hoop that kept moving, or tried to challenge Vivain at the water guns, Gideon realized that he had not actually told anyone at Oakwoods where he was. He grinned. He was playing hookey! Of course, Michael and Mary knew where Gideon and the twins had gone, so it wasn't as if nobody knew. Still...he felt an odd thrill at being out without anyone knowing, doing something very silly and juvenile, and totally unlike the way he would have acted a few days ago.

He was having...fun.

"What do I do with these?" he asked a while later, showing his two companions his paper cup full of tickets that had churned out of the games.

"You hand them in over there," Vivain pointed, "and they weigh them, and tell you how many points you get. Then you trade the points for prizes. The prizes are pretty lame, though."

"Yeah, like you so totally don't have a shelf full of stuffed animals from here," said her brother.

"Oh, shut up."

Galen's pocket emitted an odd noise. It was almost like music, but very tinny and artificial sounding. Ah, a cell phone. Of course, Gideon had one, too, but it made a discreet ringing sound. It didn't blast badly-recorded Green Day.

"Yeah?" Galen had flipped his phone open. "Oh, hi Mom. Yeah, we're at the arcade. Oh, okay, I guess. See you soon." He closed his phone. "Mom says it's supper time and we'd better get our asses home. Let's go cash in our tickets."

"Is it really so late?" Gideon asked, and glanced at a nearby clock. "Oh, dear, Joshua will be up."

"So, what's he going to do, ground you?" Galen chuckled. "We'll get you home, no worries."

They took their tickets over to be weighed. Vivain was right, the prizes were lame, but Gideon had just enough points for a coffee mug, so he selected that. Clutching their prizes, they went out to the parking lot. Someone was leaning against the Fairlawns' car.

"Ah, the triumphant children," said Rigo Smith, though he only had eyes for Gideon. "Good evening...Baron."

"Rigo," Gideon nodded, stepping forward a bit so that he put himself between Rigo and the twins. "How are you?"

"As always," replied the gypsy vampire. "You, however, are not."

Gideon's eyes narrowed. "Is this your doing?"

Rigo laughed. "I am no bruja. But a Rom knows many tricks, yes? Perhaps I may know a few magic men, like your friend with all the scars."

"Or perhaps word is simply filtering through the community," said Gideon, "and you came to see for yourself."

A nod from the ugly vampire. "Perhaps," Rigo acknowledged. "But I am not going to tell you which it is. Because I no longer owe you any respect."

Gideon heard Galen shift his weight, as if preparing for a fight. He turned and looked at the teens. Vivain was pale, biting her lip; Galen was indeed clenching his fists.

"Don't be a fool," said Gideon in a low voice, though he knew Rigo could hear. "He's not interested in you two. Run. Get out of here."

"But..." Galen began.

"Go!"

The two siblings exchanged startled looks and took off like deer.

"No doubt they will run to your so-obliging sheriff," Rigo smiled, watching them. "But he, too, is human."

"If you lay one finger on me, Rigo, the Brotherhood will be down on you like a brick wall."

"But they are not here," said Rigo, his smile widening. "And you are no longer fast enough or strong enough to escape me." He was at Gideon's side before the Baron could even blink. "How careless of you, little boy," he whispered into Gideon's ear. "To come out at night to play when you are now only human." He put his lips on Gideon's throat, and Gideon could feel the prick of fangs. Not actual penetration, as yet, but the threat of it.

He was trembling, he realized, and pulled himself together. But the truth was that he was alone in a dark parking lot with a dangerous, unpredictable vampire.

This...this was what it meant to be human.

But Rigo was not quite as clever as he thought he was, and he had made a mistake in his victim. Gideon was no helpless target, unknowledgeable about vampires. He lived with vampires. He had been a vampire.

And he was strong. Not as strong as his captor, but stronger, perhaps, than Rigo realized. As the gypsy's fangs sank into his neck, Gideon pretended to sag so that his weight shifted. He was still holding his arcade prize—a fairly heavy, thick ceramic coffee mug in a square cardboard box, in a cheap plastic bag. Rigo had either not noticed this or dismissed it as an unlikely weapon.

It is amazing how much it hurts to be hit squarely in the balls with a ballistic coffee mug.

A strangled scream, part pain and part rage, escaped from Rigo and he momentarily let go of his victim. A moment was all Gideon needed. He swung his makeshift weapon again and hit Rigo between the eyes with it, then followed up with a kick to the groin that sent the unprepared vampire staggering back into the Fairlawn's car.

"I will kill you," Rigo snarled.

"Not in my town," said a voice from behind Gideon. There was the flash of a badge and the sound of a gun being cocked.

Two tousled redheads could be spotted lurking at the edge of the parking lot. Galen held up his cell phone to show Rigo.

A sneer escaped Rigo, even though he currently couldn't stand upright. "The posse arrives. Do you really think I am frightened of a badge, little sheriff?"

"No," replied Gainsborough Fletcher, sheriff and all-round good guy. "But I think you might be frightened of silver bullets."

"You do not have silver bullets in that gun."

"Want to bet?" Gains didn't take his eyes off Rigo, or let his gun waver. "You okay, Gideon?"

"He bit me," Gideon replied, hand going to his bleeding neck. "But he didn't get much."

"Good." Gains addressed Rigo again. "That's assault. I think I could even make a concealed weapons charge stick."

Rigo was keeping his eyes on the sheriff's trigger finger. It was steady as a rock. Something seemed to have happened to his mental powers over the minds of mere humans. Redoak had not been cowed, the twins had summoned help, and now the damn sheriff was not afraid of him.

"Might be hard to find a judge and jury," commented Alex's voice.

"So we'll have to do," added Ray.

The Brotherhood had arrived. Rigo couldn't keep his eyes on all of them. They looked pissed, even the babies.

"I am senior vampire now," said Alex, coming forward and standing over Rigo. Suddenly, he looked it. Tall, dark, handsome, no longer the slightly foolish gambler but a nearly two-centuries old vampire with the power of the Brotherhood behind him. "And you are trespassing, Rigo Smith."

Rigo's eyes flickered across the set faces until he found his "niece." "Estella?" he asked, reaching out a hand.

She passed little Eleanor to Josh tand walked up to her "uncle."

"Uncle Rigo, I don't want them to kill you. You protected me all those years I travelled with the fairs. But now you aren't protecting me, you're just trying to muscle in on the Brotherhood's turf, and take advantage of the situation. It would be a really stupid thing to die for." She turned and looked at Michael, who had been watching silently after ensuring his children were okay. "Michael?"

The Archdruid shrugged. "It's out of my hands, Estella. Alex is senior vampire; it is the vampires against whom Rigo has trespassed."

Everyone looked at Alex, including Gideon. He knew how he would have decided, were he still senior. But Alex...Alexander was broody and unpredictable. Sometimes he didn't think things through.

"One question," said Alex, addressing Rigo directly. "And I will know if you answer truthfully or not."

"Ask, then," Rigo spat.

"Did you do, cause, arrange for or otherwise, in any way at all, have a part in the spell that changed Gideon back to being human?"

Rigo looked a bit surprised at the question. "No."

"Then I spare your life. But I banish you from Fletcherville. Be gone."

"Goodbye, Uncle Rigo," said Estella, a bit sadly.

"Your mother will hear of this!" Rigo said, but it wasn't much of a threat.

"You heard Alex," said Gains, finger tightening ever so slightly, "and I ain't bound by any of the agreements of the Brotherhood. Get goin.' Nobody said you had to leave town in one piece."

Snarling and angry, Rigo Smith disappeared.

"Thanks everyone," said Gideon.

Josh carefully handed Eleanor back to her mother, then

rushed to Gideon's side. "Are you okay?"

"Fine," Gideon replied. "He did bite me, but I hit him and got free before he got much."

"You hit him?" Josh chuckled. "Poor Rigo. No wonder he looked so pained. I've felt your punch."

"I hit him with my coffee mug." Gideon spied the bag on the ground, and picked it up. There was a sad chinking noise from it that indicated the mug had paid the price for its role as protector against vampires.

"First time I've heard of that as an anti-vampire weapon," said Francis.

Gains had reholstered his gun. "Maybe I should start carrying mugs around. If you're okay, Gideon, I should get back on patrol."

"Yes, thank you, Sheriff," Gideon smiled at him. "You saved the da...night."

A quick smile from under the Stetson. "Glad to hear it. Just as well I didn't have to shoot, though."

"So, you don't have silver bullets in that gun?" Gideon asked.

"What in all the hells would I have silver bullets for?" Gains asked, and sauntered off into the night.

"Thanks, guys," Gideon said to the Brotherhood. "Especially you two," he added to Galen and Vivain. "You kept your heads and called everyone."

"Actually," Galen admitted, "we called home first, 'cause Mom would have killed us for being late for supper otherwise."

"There goes one suspect," Ray sighed later, as he and Estella put Eleanor to bed.

"I know," Estella agreed. "It so easily could have been Uncle Rigo. He knows a lot of very shady types, there could have been a dark mage amongst them."

"Hey," said the former dark mage who'd married her. "Watch it."

"You'll find out who sent that bottle, I know you will."

"Are you upset that Alex banished Rigo?"

"Better than beheading him. Wasn't Alex magnificent tonight?"

"I think he might finally be maturing. Adele must be a good influence."

"Poor Rigo, though," Estella said, almost laughing. "Hit in the balls with a coffee mug."

"Want to go for a walk?"

Gideon looked up gratefully at his husband and replied, "Sure."

He'd been human for a month now, and had experienced adventure, danger, the joy of eating, the unpleasantness of a bad head cold, a certain amount of fun with the Fairlawn twins, and quite a gamut of other emotions and incidents.

But what he enjoyed best was time with Joshua. Not just for sex, but just being together. That hadn't changed. The love between them had not changed. He could tell that Joshua was trying very hard not to become the dominant partner, or to treat him as a teenager. This made him love Josh all the more.

The two men went for a walk around the clifftop. It was mid-November now and the wind off the Atlantic was cold, promising snow. Gideon smiled despite his shivering; snow would mean skiing and snowshoeing for the teenagers at Fairlawn and no doubt they would drag him along with them—if he was still human by the time the snow flew.

The question had not arisen. Everyone in the Brotherhood was very careful not to ask it. Genevieve had not returned to Oakwoods since her initial visit, and whenever Gideon spoke to her by telephone, she merely asked how she was doing. She had been worried about the incident with Rigo, but Gideon had assured her he was fine. When he'd been felled by the head cold, she'd sent him a colouring book and crayons.

He'd drawn a moustache on a page depicting a woman who looked a bit like Gen and sent it back to her.

"What?" Joshua asked, looking at him as they stirred up the dead leaves.

"What?" Gideon responded, startled out of his reminiscences.

"You just laughed."

"Oh, just remembering that colouring book Genevieve sent me."

Josh grinned. "It's good she's gotten her sense of humour back."

"Yes." Gideon prodded at a tree root with his foot. "I almost tripped over that. I keep forgetting I don't have as good night vision now."

"I wouldn't have let you fall."

Gideon smiled at him and they clasped hands as they walked, now in contemplative silence, around the back of Valley Mansion. Lights were on and Joshua, with his supernatural hearing, could make out the strains of piano music and laughter. No doubt Alex was entertaining.

"Sounds like they're having a good time," Josh nodded towards the mansion. "I can hear music."

"Walls are too thick for me," Gideon said. "Let's not interrupt them.

Joshua took Gideon's hand again. "Your hands are cold. Want to go back?"

"No, not just yet. I'm fine."

"Here." Joshua stopped and unfastened the button at the throat of his cloak. "You need this more than I do," he said, positioning it around Gideon's broader shoulders.

It was a beautiful cloak. No red silk-lined black opera cape this, but a woven cloak of some strange material, light yet incredibly warm, covered with a pattern of fall leaves and acorns. It was Joshua's most treasured possession, and had been the gift of a god. The Oak King had taken quite a liking to Joshua, when he'd still been mortal.

"Thank you," said Gideon, whose gift from the same god had been compost for his roses. "Oh, it feels lovely."

Once more hand in hand, they strolled as far as the edges of Fairlawn, and stood watching the quiet house. There were fewer lights on here, and not even Joshua could make out any noise coming from within.

"All tucked up in bed," he said, glancing at his watch. "It is a school night, after all."

"From what Galen has told me," Gideon said, smiling, "I am grateful I never had to go to high school."

"Careful, or I'll send you to college."

"Oh yes? And how exactly would you get my academic record to show them?"

"I'd think of something. You could always take a high school equivalency exam. Think of how well you'd do in history."

"As long as nobody asked precisely how I know some of the things I'd answer..."

Laughing, they turned around and began walking back towards Oakwoods.

Just past Valley Mansion, Josh put his hand out and stopped Gideon. "Somebody's out there."

"And me without a coffee mug," Gideon whispered.

Joshua's mouth twitched. "Ssh." He strained to listen. "I don't hear breathing."

"If it's Rigo come back, and Alexander finds him, he's dead."

"Alex won't have the chance, I'll kill him myself."

Gideon glanced at Joshua. His husband's eyes were glowing faintly red, and his fangs had slid into place. Used to seeing vampire transformations, Gideon felt only a slight frisson. He found himself running his tongue across his own very human teeth.

They stood in the cold, dark wood, listening. Finally Joshua shook his head. "Jumping at shadows. Let's get inside before you get pneumonia and Mary has my head."

Gideon nodded, and they moved quickly along the path, almost breaking into a run when Oakwoods was in sight. Evan met them at the door, frowning at Gideon's flushed face and rapid breathing.

"I sensed something in the woods," said Joshua.

"I'm on it," said Evan. He disappeared into the basement for a minute, and came back up carrying a crossbow and bolts. Those were only the visible weapons.

"Be careful," Gideon told him.

The Nameless One nodded and slipped out into the night. "Lock the doors," he said, before taking off towards the woods.

"Where'd Ev go?" asked Mitch, ambling into the kitchen in search of coffee. "Have a nice walk?"

Gideon and Josh looked at each other. Now, in the safety of the warm kitchen, the incident in the woods seemed foolish. They didn't answer.

Evan returned an hour or so before dawn to a tense household. Both Mitch and Francis had finally been told about the sensed presence in the wood, and everyone was waiting to see what Evan's search turned up.

"Nothing," said the protector, accepting the coffee Mitch passed to him as he sat down. "I scoured those woods. Nothing but squirrels."

"It wasn't a squirrel I sensed," said Joshua.

A nod from the auburn-haired bodyguard. "I believe you. There was...something, I think. I could feel..." he shrugged. "As if there'd been something or somebody watching."

"But you didn't actually find anything?" Joshua asked.

"No. But I marked the spot I thought they'd been standing in. I'm no good at detecting magic. Get Ray or Michael over tomorrow to see if they can." Evan yawned.

"Go get some sleep," Gideon said. "And thank you."

"Right, boss. See you in the morning." Evan got to his feet and went off towards the stairs.

"I'd better get upstairs, too," said Joshua. "I can feel dawn approaching. Francis...you too."

The other vampire in the house nodded. "Yeah, time to close the coffin lid."

"Oh, please. Only losers sleep in coffins."

Chivvying each other, the two vampires headed upstairs. Gideon and Mitch were left at the table in the breakfast nook.

"Did you feel anything out there tonight?" Mitch asked his employer.

Gideon thought about it. "Maybe," he said slowly. "My senses aren't as acute as they were. I think Victoria sensed it the day I went out riding her and she shied at the crossroads. But tonight...I didn't feel threatened. I don't know if I really felt anything, frankly, or if I'm just imagining it after the fact."

"Maybe you should talk to Gen," Mitch suggested.

"About what? Some nebulous feeling of being watched? I will ask Ray to examine the woods tomorrow for signs of magic, and then perhaps we will know more."

"Yeah, good idea."

"We'd both better get up to bed, Mitch. Good night."

"Night, boss. Don't let the vampires bite."

"Very funny."

A curly brown head bent over a patch of earth, a thin, scarred hand carefully brushing the dead leaves away.

"Hm," said Ray Griffin, hand hovering an inch above the soil.

Gideon and Evan both watched, curious, but knowledgeable enough about magic not to interrupt.

"There was definitely someone here," said Ray after a minute, not looking up but still examining the soil.

Evan had already studied that patch of earth and found it devoid of footprints or other signs of occupation, and if Evan couldn't find a footprint, then there weren't any. But he said nothing of this. Magic left its own traces, and he was not that kind of tracker.

"I can sense..." Ray licked his lips. "Hard to say, really. Once again, it's that frustrating type of magic. Not black. Not white. Almost..." he shook his head.

"Like the jar," Gideon said.

A nod. "Yes, very like that." The mage stood up, brushing his hands off on the sides of his jeans. Estella was going to give him hell for that, no doubt. "I'm not used to mysteries like this, to be honest. I'm more used to magic that tells you what the hell it is."

"But you don't think it's malevolent," Evan said.

"No. I sense no such intent. However, I also don't think it's benevolent. Which is weird."

Gideon stared down glumly at the pile of leaves Ray had dislodged. "I'm getting a little tired of mysteries."

Evan gripped his employer's shoulder briefly. "We'll solve this one."

"That's an odd-looking leaf," Gideon said, still staring at the pile. He reached down and swept a couple of others off the one he'd been looking at.

"What the hell?" said Ray, also staring.

"What does it mean?" Evan asked, looking all around for an answer.

The leaf Gideon held in his hands was made of a soft, warm, woven material, as if it had fallen off of Joshua's cape, not a tree.

The Brotherhood sat around the large dining table in Valley Mansion, staring at the object in the middle of it.

A leaf, but not one wrought by nature. It was definitely the same cloth as Joshua's cloak. He'd checked the cloak frantically for holes or empty spots where a leaf might be missing, but the garment was perfect.

"So, he's watching us," Gideon said. "Watching me."

"But is he doing more than that?" Joshua asked.

The "he" in question was of course the Oak King, a Celtic deity of the lighter half of the year. Since it was now past Samhain, it should have been the time of the Holly King; but this admittedly did not seem to be the case.

Michael and Maggie, as the representative Celtic priests, were frowning at each other.

"The time of the Oak King is for growth, development, healing, and new projects," Maggie said. "He is the embodiment of the summer and the light."

"It's mid November," Ray pointed out. Any discussion of religion and deities made the ex-sorcerer uncomfortable. This could have been due to his previous affiliation with evil, or to the fact that he had actually met the Lord and Lady on a spirit journey and was slightly embarrassed about it.

"There is a belief that the twin gods do not actually die during their half-year hiatus," Michael said. "But that they remain to counterbalance their opposite. There is no reason why the Oak King could not be active in winter."

There were nods around the table, though Mitch and Francis both looked a little confused. Talk of gods of any description was not something they were used to.

"Do you think he's the one behind...that bottle?" Gideon asked, not quite wanting to sound dramatic by drawing attention back to his altered condition.

"It's possible," Ray shrugged. "We all know it took powerful magic. You don't get much more powerful than...well."

"A god?" Estella filled in for her husband.

"Uh, yeah."

"Why, though?" Gideon looked from Michael to Maggie, as if holding the Druids personally responsible.

"The Oak King does represent change," said Maggie, eyes twinkling slightly.

Gideon thought back to a party in England, now many years ago, when the Oak King had made an appearance. Joshua had still been human, and ailing. The god had wrapped him in that cloak and pronounced him a favoured mortal. Since he was no longer mortal, had he lost that protection? Was the King angry with Joshua for becoming a vampire, and had decided to turn Gideon mortal as some sort of punishment?

No, that made no sense, they'd had assurance that the Oak King had not objected to Joshua's turning.

"You said the Oak King's reign is supposed to be a time of growth." Alex turned to Maggie.

"Yes, that's right. Growth, development, and healing."

"Maybe he's giving Gideon a chance to grow."

Gideon frowned at his old friend. "What exactly do you mean, Alexander?"

"Well, you're only five foot six," Alex replied, grinning from the safety of the opposite side of the table. "Maybe you could have a late growth spurt now you're human, and stop being a shrimp."

A frantic visual search of the table yielded nothing within arm's reach that Gideon could throw.

Michael was rubbing his chin. "Actually," he said, giving Alex, then Gideon, both measuring looks, "apart from your being a total prat, Alex, that's not a bad guess."

Seeing everyone look at him, the Archdruid went on to explain that perhaps the jar had been sent, and the humanization spell cast, to teach some kind of lesson or drive some point home. Gideon felt slightly offended at the idea that he had needed a lesson of any kind. He and Joshua had been doing fine, hadn't they? They were still together. Their love had survived.

While others in the Brotherhood mulled this idea over, and discussed it in low tones, Gideon found himself looking at Joshua. His husband smiled at him, butterscotch eyes warm and loving. True, Joshua had had some trouble adjusting to being a vampire, but who hadn't? Gideon's first few years as one of the undead had not been exactly fun. Of course, Gideon had not had an exemplary turnsire. Joshua could not complain about his turndam. He had chosen her. Hadn't he, Gideon, been helping Joshua adjust? Hadn't he been patient with fledging woes and temper tantrums? He could not fathom any reason why anyone would think that he needed some kind of lesson.

"Gideon?"

He turned, startled; he'd been so lost in thought that he hadn't realized anyone had spoken to him.

"Sorry, Michael," he said to the Druid. "I was thinking."

"That's understandable." Michael smiled at him.

"Gods are a bit out of my jurisdiction," Evan was complaining, as Gideon tried to focus on what the rest of the Brotherhood was talking about. "How do I protect him if the Oak King tries something else?"

"There are ways of deflecting malevolent magic," Maggie replied. "I'll set him up with some basic spells, if you'd like..."

"I don't see anything dark around Gideon," Estella said. "I honestly don't think there is any malevolent intent at work. I would be able to sense that." She grinned slightly at Ray; their first meeting had been seriously tainted by her picking up on his bloody past.

"Can you see what is going to happen, Estella?" Gideon asked her.

A tense silence fell. Estella gave him a long, measuring look. "Do you really want me to try?"

"Please."

Ray gave his wife a worried glance, which she ignored. "Come into the kitchen with me, then, I can't read in front of all these people."

Gideon got up, putting his hand briefly on Joshua's as he passed, and followed Estella into the kitchen of Valley Mansion. Mrs. Jenkins, Alex's formidable housekeeper, was there, looking after baby Eleanor. She bundled the child off without a word when the seer and the ex-vampire came into the room.

"All right, let's sit down," said Estella.

Almost wishing he hadn't requested this, Gideon sat across from her at the small breakfast table.

"Don't be nervous," Estella told him, smiling. "I won't bite."

He rolled his eyes at her.

"Give me your left hand," she requested, and he did so.

"Are you happy with Ray?" he blurted out, having no idea why he asked.

She raised an eyebrow at him. "I thought we were here to answer questions about your future. But yes, I am. I love him very much. And Eleanor..." her eyes moved in the direction the housekeeper had taken. "I never expected Eleanor, but she's definitely an added bonus. Even if she does make her dirty diapers levitate and whack Andrei on the head."

Gideon laughed. "He loves you, you know. I can tell."

"Thank you for saying so." She smiled, then grew stern. "Enough about me. Let's see what your palm tells me." She turned his left hand over and gazed at the palm.

There was a leaf on it.

He was walking through a wood, and the oak leaves fell like rain around him. They brushed past his face, tickling him with their softness. They were not real leaves, but pieces of fabric, and they fell from a great cloak that obscured the sky.

Damien and Buccaneer frolicked in the leaves, kicking them up with their hooves. Calvin watched them disapprovingly from the top of an oak tree, which bowed under the weight of the great stallion, its acorns brushing the ground. Joshua ran laughing between the trees, occasionally stopping to scoop handfuls of the not-leaves, tossing them into the air. Galen and Vivain pelted him with acorns and fled on bicycles made of leaves.

At a castle made of acorns, he stopped and knocked on the door. It opened to reveal a carpet of oak leaves, and a man with a crown of leaves in his hair.

"Welcome, favoured mortal," boomed a voice.

"What do you want of me?" Gideon demanded.

The Oak King placed a hand on his shoulder and said, "Gideon, wake up."

For a King, the voice was oddly feminine. Gideon returned muzzily to consciousness, blinking up into a pair of blue eyes. No crown, of leaves or anything else, adorned that blonde hair, although it was tied up into a fairly severe knot of some kind.

"Genevieve?"

"The very same." She bent and kissed him. "You were thrashing and moaning; I thought it best to wake you."

He sat up, rubbing his head. He'd fallen asleep on one of the chairs in his library. He'd taken refuge in here after he and the others had returned to Oakwoods once the meeting at Valley Mansion had broken up.

"What time is it?" he asked.

"A little after midnight. Joshua asked me to come. He said you seemed upset after Estella read your palm, but that you would not talk to him."

"No." Gideon turned away from those compelling eyes. "I don't want to talk to you about it, either. And don't try any of that vampire mind whammy on me."

"I would not dream of it. Though if you continue talking to me in that tone, I might try some vampire hand whammy."

"Sure, go ahead, spank me," he muttered. "That will help."

Instead, he found a snifter of brandy pressed into his hand. "I find this a good cure for the sulks," she said, repressing a smile.

"I am not sulking."

"Ah, I see. Were you having a nightmare?"

"Yes." He thought about it. "No. Just...well, it was pretty surreal, to be honest. I think my mind was trying to make sense of what's going on, but couldn't quite manage it."

She sat down in the chair opposite from him and studied him, while sipping her own drink. "Joshua told me about the woods. Do you believe the Oak King is the one who sent that jar?"

"I don't know. I don't know why he would. But I don't know why anyone else would, either."

"Nor I."

They sat in silence, slightly awkward and slightly companionable, for several minutes.

"Gideon," said Gen softly. "How are you?"

"Scared shitless," he admitted. "Genevieve...*Maman*...I am so confused. I don't know what to think. I don't know why anyone, even a god, would do this to me. Even if I agree to be turned back into a vampire, I will start all over again at the beginning as a fledgling. I don't know if I can go through that again. Even though nobody says anything, I can feel them all looking at me. Pressuring me with their looks. Joshua has been wonderful, but I know what he's thinking...what they're all thinking. But I just don't know what I want!" Tears started to roll down his cheeks and he angrily brushed them away with his sleeve. "Look at me," he sniffled. "I cry at anything now."

"Gideon, *cheri*. Of course you are confused and emotional. I do not understand why anyone would choose to do this to you, but there must be a reason. Hopefully it is a good one. Just remember that you are surrounded by those who love you; and we are all worried about you. Talk to someone when you start feeling so lost."

"I thought that was what I was doing," he half-smiled.

"I am listening. Tell me about this dream."

He shook his head. "It was about…leaves. And the Oak King. But it was also sort of an echo of a nightmare I had the first night…walking through woods to a castle."

He saw her face alter, her mouth set. She knew what woods and what castle.

"Merde," she said, with feeling. Then she shook herself. "That is all in the past, Gideon."

"I know. But I can't dictate my dreams."

Gen got up and crossed over to him, and gave him a hug. *"Mon pauvre petit."*

"You're as bad as Alex," Gideon grumbled, to hide how touched he was by her sympathy. "Twitting me for being short."

"But you are short."

"At least I'm not blonde."

Her eyes widened. "Oh, you will pay for that…you had better run!"

Gideon was up and out of the chair and halfway out of the library, laughing. When she caught up to him, she gave him a kiss on the cheek and then raced him down the stairs.

She won, of course.

The rest of the Brotherhood had also gone to their assorted homes.

Ray walked Eleanor, trying to get her to fall asleep, while Estella talked to her mother on the phone. Rigo had vanished, which worried Chavi. It worried Estella, too. Eleanor babbled away to her Daddy, completely unconcerned by disappearing uncles, strange leafy portents, and unknown magic. Ray envied her. He knew he was in for a sleepless night, and probably so was Estella.

A palm covered by a leaf…

The twins went to bed without protest, making their mother stare up the stairs after them.

"Bad meeting?" she asked her husband.

"Odd," Michael replied.

A palm covered by a leaf…

"What do you think it meant?" Mitch asked.

Evan dealt out the cards. "No idea. Ante up, kids."

Francis and Mitch looked at each other and pushed forward piles of pennies. One cent stakes were all Gideon would allow them to gamble for under his roof.

"We should have asked Gen to sit in," Francis said, picking up his cards.

"She's busy," Evan grunted. "Let's play poker."

Alex Goldanias sat in his dining room, now empty but for himself, and poured a glass of wine.

"To the Senior Vampire," he said, a slight smile tugging at his handsome mouth.

Joshua, restless, vaguely unhappy, not wanting to play poker and not wanting to butt in on Gideon and Genevieve during their private conversation, went outside to stand staring out to sea.

Something walked out of the woods between Oakwoods and Valley Mansion.

The Druids and the twins were sequestered with Ray in his basement workshop. Galen was looking around with avid interest, since he had never been allowed down here before, and was very interested in the sword and the concentration exercises Ray did with it. Using a sword for anything but slicing someone else with was a novel idea. Vivain was studying the various herbs in jars and making mental notes.

Maggie and Michael had been invited because they knew more about fae magic than Ray did. It never hurt to give Galen and Vivain a chance to learn something new, and to learn more control over their burgeoning powers.

"What we really need," said Ray, "is a bit more evidence. Not that I would doubt the Oak King, but..."

The two Druids nodded. "He is a god," said Michael. "They're never direct and it's never wise to take them at face value."

"Right," said Maggie. "Plus we really shouldn't just go charging off into Eric Bates' place without proof he's behind this."*

"We probably shouldn't go charging off there anyway," Ray said. "If he is behind this, he'll be expecting an attack."

"So what do we do?" Michael asked.

"Draw him out. Give him bait he can't refuse, even though he'll probably suspect it's a trap. Not the twins," Ray added hastily before Galen could open his mouth. "I'll offer myself."

"It would never work. You've proven recalcitrant," Michael said. "Eric would never believe that you want to come back over to the dark side now. That's a point in your favor, by the way."

Ray smiled tightly. "Then we need someone he couldn't resist."

Maggie went white, even Vivain's face drained of colour, and

* The Brotherhood encounters Eric Bates in "Follow That Falcon!"

Galen looked at his father, then at Trevor.

"Not the baby!" An agonized whisper from Vivain.

"She will be in no danger," Ray said earnestly. "But if we make Eric and the Fae believe that we've all gone off chasing after them and left the baby with only minimal protection..."

"Which is what most of the Brotherhood was in favour of doing," added Michael, "so it wouldn't be unexpected."

"Minimal!" Maggie exclaimed.

"As Eric would see it," Ray said. "He's never been a great believer in equality among the sexes. Look how he treated Deirdre. In reality, we'll be waiting to spring the trap when Eric and or the Fae come to take the baby. It will be all right, Maggie. Eleanor will be perfectly safe."

"Which brings us back to assuming we're on the right track," said Michael. "Before we implement such a dangerous plan, we have to find out if it really is Eric and the Fae behind all this."

"How can you do that?" Vivain asked. "Didn't the jar disappear?"

"Yes, but we still have the results of the spell," Ray said. He took a little stoppered phial out of the pocket of his black jeans. It held a red liquid. "I had a little trouble getting this," he said, lips twitching. "Gideon has some pretty fierce protectors. But I managed to convince both Josh and Gen that I needed Gideon's blood to try and trace the magic."

"Didn't you have to convince Gideon, too?" Michael asked.

"No, not really; he was all for looking for the truth. Vampires just take blood a lot more seriously, I guess."

"Can we watch you do the magic?" Galen asked.

"Yes, if you stay quiet and out of the way." Ray took a plain white china plate off the shelf over his worktable and placed it carefully on the tabletop. He unstoppered the vial and poured out the blood slowly, chanting under his breath. He sat down in front of the gory plateful, staring into it and still chanting.

Michael felt his daughter's hand slip into his, and squeezed. He looked at Galen, who was watching the proceedings with considerable interest.

Ripples formed in the blood and threatened to slop over the edges of the plate. Ray spoke a stern word that sounded like a command, and the blood quieted.

"Yes," he said finally, after what seemed ages of staring at the red liquid on the white plate. "It is Eric...augmented by something extra. Probably the Fae, but their powers are not known to me. It wasn't a study Matthew encouraged. Wonder how Eric came to hook up with them...odd." He looked around at the Druids. "Can either of you scry in blood?"

"I'll try," said Michael, letting go Vivain's hand and walking over to the table. He took Ray's place in the chair and looked into the pool on the plate.

"Hm," he said after a while. "There is definitely something here. Not human magic. It feels like the Fae...like Unseelie..."

As soon as Michael spoke the word "Unseelie," the blood on the plate split in half like the Red Sea, shot up into the air, and fell back down again, splashing everyone in the room.

There was a long silence while people tried to wipe off the blood.

"I'd say that was a yes," Maggie laughed shakily.

Estella joggled a fretful Eleanor in her arms and bit her lip. "This will be okay, won't it?"

"You'd be the one to know," said Mitch.

"Oh, bite me," Estella snorted.

"Incidentally, Estella," said Francis as they started walking towards Oakwoods, the agreed-upon waiting spot, "how do you think your uncle found out about Gideon?"

She looked at Francis in some surprise. "Francis, Gideon went into town in broad daylight more than once. He was seen eating lunch in a restaurant. You know how people in a small town gossip. I have no doubt at all that the news found its way to quite a few unfriendly ears. I'm surprised we haven't had trouble with more than Uncle Rigo, frankly."

Francis shrugged. "Maybe the way Alex handled him scared other people off."

"Could be."

"I bet our efforts to beef up protection, and find out the cause of that spell, and yes, Alex's actions with Rigo, warned off hostile intentions," Maggie agreed. "Maybe even kept Eric and the Fae from trying anything new."

"Or they're waiting for us to let down our guard," said Mitch gloomily.

"Also possible," Maggie nodded. "Like, say, tonight."

"Yeah." The werewolf looked uneasily up and down the road. "I hope that lot know what they're doing."

"Of course they do," Vivain spoke with supreme confidence. "Dad's with them."

Maggie gave her a hug and they all went back inside Oakwoods.

"This place doesn't feel right with Gideon not here," Estella observed, setting Eleanor down in the portable playpen set up in the living room.

"How long do you think we'll have to wait?" Francis asked Maggie.

"No idea."

The adults and teenager settled down as much as possible, and waited.

The van that had loudly and slowly driven down the Cliff Road winked out of mortal sight just outside Fletcherville.

"That should convince anyone watching that we really have left," said Michael. "They'll think we've used some kind of magic shielding or teleporting spell—unless they suspect something and try and trace us."

"Doesn't hurt to be paranoid," said Ray. "I left a false trail to indicate that we just shielded and kept going. Hopefully that will put anyone off the scent. The Druids and I have us pretty heavily warded."

"Wards can be broken," Genevieve murmured. She was watching Gideon, who had gone a bit pale and quiet.

"I know," Ray answered. "We'll have to hope they aren't."

"What I don't understand," said Gideon, "is why me."

"Eric knows he can't take me out," Ray said. "Michael's too obvious a target, as our leader. I think that's why he went for you. Taking out our senior vampire, one who's proven himself strong, a fighter, a good leader, would weaken the Brotherhood. He probably had more planned but didn't reckon with our reaction to what happened to you. Or possibly he found out that dealing with the Unseelie Court can be dangerous. It's hard to say. But I think he'll find it impossible not to rise to the bait we're offering. Especially if he's still in league with the Fae."

There were nods all around the van.

"I guess that makes sense," Gideon sighed. "Not that I'm happy with having been a target."

"But you haven't shown yourself weakened by it," Michael said. "You've risen to the challenge and proven yourself still the man you always have been. I suspect the idea was for you to just crawl off somewhere, not fight back."

Gideon sat up just a little straighter. Galen gave him a thumbs-up.

"I guess now we wait," Alex said.

"Indeed, senior vampire," Gideon said to him.

"Oh, stop that."

"Boys," Genevieve said. "Don't make me come back there."

The hours had crept past. Nobody was doing much talking. Nobody was hungry, or thirsty. They just sat and looked at each other, and waited.

There was a neigh from the region of the stable. It sounded like a warning.

"Calvin," said Mitch.

There were voices just on the cusp of hearing, just outside the walls of the house. A wind blew up, scattering snow, twigs and other debris past the windows.

"And it's not even midnight yet," said Francis with a humourless laugh.

"No sense of timing," Maggie quipped nervously.

"Is that the Fae doing that?" Vivain was so pale that her freckles stood out.

"Yeah, seems to be their style," said Mitch, the only person in the room who had fought the Fae on their last invasion of Oakwoods.

"Right...we ready, then?" Maggie picked up a sword.

Steel...or iron. Those were the weapons to use against the Fae. The outside of Oakwoods had already been protected with rowan and St John's wort, plus spells woven by the Druids and incorporated into the existing wards.

"Where do you think Bates is?" Estella asked.

"No doubt ready to break in here the moment he sees the wards breached," Francis replied. "Remember, Ray told us he doesn't have much magic of his own."

"Right. So let's lay the trap." Maggie stood up, holding the sword. "Eric and the Fae both learn a lesson tonight. Never mess with the mommy."

"Damn straight," said Estella.

She and Vivain took up their positions protecting the playpen, where Eleanor sat in splendour amongst blocks, rattles, stuffed toys and a large plastic ball. Mitch, Maggie and Francis went charging outside, ready to tackle the Fae...leaving the French doors wide open.

It only took three minutes before a smiling—though much greyer and thinner—Eric Bates strode through the opening thus provided.

"Hello, Estella," he said. His eyes flickered to Vivain. "And what do we have here? A junior Girl Guide?"

"You're not welcome here, Bates," Estella said.

"Aw, you hurt my feelings. Didn't I show you every hospitality when you came to visit me two years ago?"

"We are not without protection," Estella warned him.

He laughed. "Ah yes. A werewolf, a vampire and a Druid. All the rest of your gallant Brotherhood, including your dear husband and the father of this delightful little girl," he glanced down at Eleanor, "are off looking for...well, me. I've learned how the Brotherhood works, my dear ladies. They all go haring off to the rescue or to the battle without a thought that such a reaction might be just what the enemy wants."

"Yes, I'm afraid we are rather set in our ways."

"How heroic...but I am afraid that the Harry Potter solution does not work in real life, ladies. While the Fae are distracting the three valiant fighters outside, I will take what I came for." He once more glanced down into the playpen.

But Eleanor was not an ordinary baby. She had developing magical talents, which were being channelled by her parents but still tended to manifest in unusual ways. A full diaper magicked itself off her and hit Eric in the face.

Enraged and dripping, Eric frantically rid himself of the diaper. "No six month old could do that!" he howled.

Vivain looked puzzled.

"You forget who's six month old that is," said a voice from the open doorway. "She's my and Estella's daughter."

The cavalry had arrived.

Francis, Mitch and Maggie had been fighting, greatly outnumbered, although they had the advantage that all they needed to do was touch their opponent, barely break the skin, and the Fae would die in agony from cold steel. However, a couple of the faery warriors had arrived armed with silver daggers. While these were not a problem for Maggie, they hurt Francis badly and could kill Mitch.

"Silver, shit," said the werewolf, managing to knock the deadly weapon out of a faery's hand by removing the hand.

"Be careful," Maggie warned him. "Francis, you okay?"

The vampire nodded, but his forehead was drawn with pain. He'd taken a stab wound to the ribs from a silver dagger. It hadn't incapacitated him, but it was making it harder for him to fight due to the pain.

"Since when do you guys make deals with witches?" Mitch demanded of the Fae he was currently fighting.

"He can get us what we want," his opponent said.

"You still after Calvin? Give it up already."

"The horse is nothing. We will take the baby for our payment."

"Need a little help, Mags?" There was Alex, grinning, stepping over some dead faeries.

"What kept you guys?" Maggie asked.

"Gideon and Alexander were arguing in the back seat," said Genevieve, stepping forward while at the same time casually taking down one of the Fae who was trying to behead her. "You know how they are."

Alex was busy fighting his way to Francis's side, in order to help the weakening young vampire, and pretended not to hear this.

Gideon looked around at a very familiar sight—faeries in his garden. Really, this was getting old. He grabbed the nearest one. "Take me to your leader."

The Fae gave him a startled look, but Gideon was as serious as he was clichéd. He was taken to a wild-looking female guiding the fighting from the edge of the forest.

"You trespass here," said Gideon to her, without preamble. "This household and all within it are under the protection of the Oak King."

"And what is he to me?" asked the Faery. "He is neither Seelie nor Unseelie, and so not my concern."

"He is still a god of the old peoples, and as such, should be respected by you."

She yawned. "Next you will tell me you are a personal friend of King Herla's and have ridden with the Wild Hunt. Yes, I know this. It still causes me no concern. Herla and the Hunt are far from here tonight...and you are mortal."

"Yes. Why?"

"You denied us our rightful property. You slew our people when they came to claim that property."

"Calvin is his own master," Gideon replied angrily. "He chooses to remain here of his own will."

"But he has not let you ride him since you opened that jar, has he?"

The Baron's eyes narrowed. "You made that a part of the spell, so that I would be willing to give him back to you because I can't ride him. It won't work. He's been letting me into his stall and I can touch him. Being allowed to ride is only a matter of time. Your spell was not perfect, my lady."

An unmistakable look of anger flashed in her eyes. "The horse no longer matters," she said. "We want changelings. Our people dwindle."

"If you would stop sending them on senseless missions where they are bound to be killed, they might not dwindle quite so quickly."

"You and the others were not supposed to be here. We were promised the baby would be left poorly defended."

Gideon leaned on his sword and gave her a pitying look. "And you believed Eric Bates." He shook his head. "Why did you ever deal with him? I thought the Fae don't normally make deals with human witches."

"We did not have the power to make and send you the jar, or to make it disappear. We needed a witch. He agreed to give us a baby in return for our spell to make you human again."

"And is that spell reversible?"

Everyone had stopped fighting to listen; the fae because it was their Lady who spoke, the Brotherhood because of the importance of this conversation to Gideon. Alex had taken Francis inside for Michael to tend to, but had not returned; at the moment, nobody on the outside could spare a thought for what was happening indoors.

"Perhaps," said the Lady.

"Perhaps?" Gideon glared at her. "It is either yes or no, Lady."

"Give us something we want, Redoak."

"I will not give you a child, even if you kill me," said Gideon. "And you can try to kill us all to reach the baby, but you will never make it. You can't have Eleanor."

"So I had concluded. But there is still room for negotiation."

Gideon sighed. "You still want Calvin. Tell you what; if you can get him to go with you, he's all yours."

The Lady shook her head, her crown of leaves and berries threatening to tumble off. "No, we realize he would be of no use. He is bonded to you. The bond was warped for awhile but not broken. We will take his foal."

A vision of Jean's expression when he learned that Damien had been bartered away flashed across Gideon's mind. It would be a pretty poor bargain for an end to the spell.

"No," Gideon said. "This foal is already bonded. He is not my property to give you, as he has already been given to another. You can't have Damien. But I am prepared to offer you Calvin's next foal."

The Faerie looked at him for a long time, trying to see if he was telling the truth. "And will there be more foals?"

"Genevieve de Monet and I have been discussing a breeding

program," Gideon replied. "She wants Calvin's bloodline, and will put him to as many of her mares as possible when they come in season. There will be more foals."

"Then we will take the next five, in return for giving you the counterspell."

"I can't do that. I have promised Genevieve foals. Five is too many, from her mares."

"The next three, then."

"Two."

"Done," said the Lady. "But you need the witch to complete the spell. Only he can make the bottle."

"Then I'll just have to hope nobody's gone and killed him," Gideon sighed. "Take your dead away, Lady, and send the others home. I will talk only to you, not to an army."

"Very well." She clapped her hands, and the host vanished, as did the corpses.

"Your word that you or any of the Unseelie Court will not invade my gardens or house or grounds or stables again, that you will make no further attempts on my self, my horses, my friends, or anyone in the Brotherhood or their families."

"You drive a hard bargain, Baron Redoak."

"Yes, but I am in the driver's seat."

"Oh, very well! I do so swear. My word on it. The word of a Faery Lady."

Gideon nodded. "Good. Now, let us go see if they have suffered the witch to live."

Eric had started backing up when Ray and Michael came into Oakwoods. He was trying to sidle closer to Vivain and the playpen—two potential hostages—but found Estella blocking his way.

"I curse you, Eric Bates," she said quietly. "The curse of a Rom. If you ever touch a child again, your hand will shrivel and die. If you ever move against any of the Brotherhood again, your heart will shrivel and die."

"That's my wife," said Ray cheerfully.

"If you kill me, Griffin," said Eric, facing his old enemy and ignoring Estella, "then the Baron remains human. He can't be turned back the regular way, you see. It won't take again. Only a reversal of the spell will do it. And for that you need the cooperation of the Fae...not much chance when your Brotherhood is slaughtering them out in the garden, hm?"

"What can you possibly have hoped to gain from all this,

Eric?" Ray asked. "You know that you'd have had to kill us all to get at a child, and you just don't have the firepower. Is that why you bargained with the Fae?"

"I just wanted your daughter," Eric replied. "The Fae could have taken the twins. I wanted your daughter to replace Deirdre."

"That's sick," said Estella, looking a bit ill. She had seen what Eric had done to Deirdre.

"Wouldn't have happened," said Ray calmly. "Just forget it, Eric. For once in your life, admit defeat graciously."

"No. I am not defeated. Your precious Baron is still a human, and the senior vampire of the Brotherhood is a..." Eric stared as the doors from the back opened and Alex came in, carrying Francis.

"Michael," Alex said, ignoring the odd tableau before him and carrying Francis over to the Druid. "He's bad; do you have any of that salve for silver wounds?"

"Yes," Michael said. "I always have some on hand in my bag, considering what you lot get up to. Lay him down over there, Alex, gently, and I'll tend him."

Alex did as directed, giving the now-unconscious Francis a pat on the shoulder. "You'll be fine," he said. "And that's an order from the senior vampire." Then he finally turned and looked at Eric. "By the way, we have excellent hearing. What exactly am I, Mr. Bates?"

Eric licked his lips. Alex was very tall, and right now, extremely menacing. His fangs were out.

"There's no noise from the garden," Maggie said. "The fighting has stopped."

"Impossible," Eric said. "The Fae outnumber the Brotherhood."

"But we have steel," said Alex, almost purring. "They must be growing tired of dying."

"So, we get to kill you now," Ray smiled. "Definitely."

"Kill me, and the Baron stays mortal."

"So you've said. Maybe that prospect doesn't bother him, hm?"

"Might be better to ask." Gideon was leaning against the doorjamb, with a tall Faery who looked a bit windblown beside him. The remainder of the Brotherhood and Genevieve lurked just behind the twosome, looking anxious.

Everyone fell back without meaning to as Gideon came in. He was still carrying his sword, dripping fae blood, and he looked grim and deadly. Nobody would doubt now that he had been a vampire for nearly four hundred years. There was no trace at all of youth in his face.

He walked right up to Eric Bates and raised his sword. Eric flinched, but Gideon rested the point of the blade against Eric's heart.

"The Lady has sworn her vows," said Gideon in tones that would not have been out of place in a Council of Princes meeting. "I will give you one chance to swear yours."

Eric's eyes darted around the room, and met no sympathy, not from the twins, not from Michael, not from Estella, nowhere.

"What vow is this?" he asked.

"Give me the jar that will hold the spell to reverse the one put on me," Gideon demanded. "The Fae will do the rest."

"You broke our bargain!" Eric screamed at the Faerie Lady.

She shrugged. "I have had a better offer. You had best do as they ask, witch."

"Easy on the witch," Ray said, sparing her a glance. "I'm one."

"You? You are more than mere witch. You are a mage. This one..." she shrugged again. "No real power."

"Of course not. He steals it from other people. But he has enough to do our bidding, I think. Eric, give Gideon the jar."

"Why should I, if you are going to kill me anyway?"

"Because there are good ways to die, and bad ways to die, and I for one don't really want to see Francis and Alex drain you dry and Mitch chew up what's left."

Mitch, hovering behind Gideon, looked offended. Evan clapped a hand over his mouth to keep him quiet.

Eric looked trapped. "I..."

"And I will know if the jar is something malevolent, or intended to have a different effect than what we want. So don't try anything devious." Ray stared at his old enemy. "Go on, do the magic."

The air shimmered, and a dark blue jar appeared. It seemed nearly the same as the green one that had caused the devampification in the first place. Ray's hands mysteriously acquired black leather gloves, and he picked up the jar off the floor where it settled. He examined it carefully.

"Seems all right," he said. He took it over to the Faerie Lady. "Everything copasetic with this?"

She looked at it without touching it. "Yes." At Gideon's measuring glance, she added, "My word on it. There is nothing harmful, nothing that should not be here."

"Thank you." Ray turned and looked at Eric. "There. You did one good deed in your life. I doubt that's enough to get you into heaven, though. Just as well, really. Alex, kill him."

I didn't know who else I could talk to.

I mean really talk, without them interrupting, or thinking of something else, or wishing they could have another drink, or smiling at me in that faintly patronizing way, or looking uncomfortable. I know you won't interrupt, or have to go to the bathroom, or judge me one way or the other. I know you will listen.

It's March already. More than two months into the new year. There are strange things happening. Frightening things. Vampires being killed. Eric being taken, and Ray being shot. Good things, too, of course. Genevieve and Jean are finally engaged to be married. I thought that would make you smile. You always said you thought they should.

Well, you know what happened to me. Here I am. Human. Mortal. Not just an ordinary person, no. Ordinary people don't suddenly become mortal after almost four hundred years as a vampire. And I can't be turned back. Not by another vampire. Because this was done to me by magic, it has to be undone by magic.

So, there's a jar. Almost identical to the one the first spell came in. It's sitting in the china cabinet in the formal dining room, right beside Spode and Wedgewood, as if it was another antique Joshua picked up somewhere. All I have to do is open it up, and hey, presto, I'm a vampire again. The same vampire I was before. The same bloodline, the same history. The same master.

But I don't know if I want to do that, to open the jar. Of course, I should never have opened the first one. It's too late for that.

I had less than twenty years as a human, and four hundred as a vampire. I can remember things, some with such clarity that it hurts, and other things I've had to discover all over again. How sunlight feels. The taste of food. True colours. But sometimes being human is like being blind and deaf. I can't see much at night. I can't hear the fall of a leaf or the sound of lungs breathing.

Nobody says anything. They're all so careful not to say anything. Not to pressure me. I can't hear thoughts anymore, stupid deaf human that I am now, but I know what they are all thinking. What an ingrate I am. How careless, how reckless; wanting to stay human when humans are so vulnerable. They want to remind me that Joshua agreed to be turned out of love for me, so that he would not die and leave me alone. Now the situation is reversed. But I'm not dying. I'm quite disgustingly healthy, which annoys Mary Fairlawn because she thinks I should have caught about fifty diseases by now. All I've had is a cold. Perhaps there is some lingering protection from my years as a vampire, perhaps it is the faerie magic. I don't know. But I'm twenty years old, and healthy, not forty-five and...not healthy.

I didn't have much of a life, as a human, the first time around. You know that. We talked about it. And this world...it is so much different from the one I knew. So many more possibilities. All the experiences, waiting. Yes, I can die. There are dangers. But there are dangers to vampires, too. Especially now. We don't know where or when these killers will strike again. There are no guarantees, no promises.

You knew that. You made your choice. At the time, it seemed cruel, but I loved you, and so I accepted your choice. It took me a long time to understand. Now I do, and I ask your forgiveness. I know you cannot help me make my choice. It is mine, and mine alone. It's only been a few months. I just wish everyone would... back off, as the youngsters say, and let me just get on with things, living my life. Give me more time.

Time. Ironic, isn't it? I had scads of it half a year ago. Now I see clocks ticking in everyone's eyes. No, more like hourglasses with the sand running.

You, of course, are beyond the reach of time. That was your choice.

Thank you for listening.

Sleep well. I will always love you, Jonathan.

The Adventures of the Brotherhood of Darkness

Daven's Stream.
(1998)

There was blood. More blood than he'd thought, black in the moonlight, steaming and stinking as it leaked from both his own body and the carcass of the man he'd just killed. Groaning, his muscles protesting, he dragged himself to his feet. The night went spinning, the moon mocking his weakness, and a thin bitter stream of vomit trickled from out of his mouth to join the blood on the ground. His lungs ached as he tried to take in more air. But half his life had been spent in learning to control his body, to marshall his resources; and the moment of weakness passed.

Limping, hand clutched over the worst of the seeping wounds, he approached the fallen, broken body of his foe. Warm liquid coated his fingers and he cursed. Cursed the man who lay at his feet, the large body now rendered harmless, the once white hair clotted with blood and brain matter. Matthew had died hard, a hard death for a hard man. His killer...no, his executioner...knew that life had ceased in that still form. No one, no matter how powerful, could sustain such injuries and still live. But he kicked the sole of the nearest boot, the motion sending shock waves of pain through his own body. If he did not find medical help soon, his victory would be meaningless.

The fight had been on more than the physical plane, and he was exhausted, his strength gone, his reserves strained to their limit. Lights flashed on the periphery of his vision, the dancing phosphorescence of impending unconsciousness. He couldn't afford to pass out. The monumental struggle that had taken place had attracted attention, there were *things* waiting on the perimeters of the circle. There would be those who would seek to avenge

Matthew's death, and news of death travels quickly. To pass out here would be to die.

But his training was so well imbedded that he broke the circle with the proper ritual, and warded himself as well as his fading power and strength allowed. This left him barely able to walk, but his physical wellbeing was not as important as the magical. The burnt ozone smell of magic tingled in his nostrils, blocking out the less pleasant effluvia of death, of tortured flesh, even of the scuffed earth where the battle lines had been drawn. The *things* on the edges made way for him to pass, sharp eyes watching him, small snuffling noises and scrabbling claws marking their movements. One sign of weakness and they would be on him. Flared nostrils showed they scented blood; luckily the smell of death was more enticing to them than that of still living flesh.

"Bon appetit," he muttered wearily, pushing his way past them, putting the circle and the dead Matthew behind him. He closed his ears to the sounds of feeding.

Rebellion had been a long time coming to Raymond Arthur Griffin, but when it had flared, it had been deadly to his master.

He had a plan. Had to have, or else this would have been his death, too. Just get through this part, past these tall shadows of trees, the scent of pine, of death, of blood, of magic, through the dead needles and leaves that squelched and crunched underfoot, trail of blood, of spent magic behind him, things moving in the shadows, through this part, through this damned bloody night.

Cold metal, moonlight glancing off chrome and glass, smell of gasoline, of rubber. It took him a minute to form a word for what blocked his escape route. "Car." Could he drive? Was it advisable when he couldn't even remember what this machine was called? Something scrunched in the undergrowth behind him, snuffling, a deep growl hungry for blood. It was the car or death.

Small strips of shaped metal dangling from a knob beside the wheel, he could see these through the glass. Keys. Window. Steering wheel. He forced himself to remember the words, to fumble at the handle (yes, handle, that was the word) and pull the door open. The movement made him teeter, more blood dripping. Something in the woods licked its lips. He slid into the seat behind the wheel with a surge of new strength called self preservation. He hadn't gone to all the trouble of killing Matthew only to succumb to the feeders. Pull the door closed, never mind how it opens the wound in the shoulder, how it hurts muscles that surrendered hours ago.

Turn the key. Foot goes on this pedal, here. Smell of gasoline, rumble of engine coming to life, vibrations sent through aching, aching body. Turn the wheel. Concentrate. Lights. Concentrate.

It was a nightmare, but so was dying.

Matthew had not known why this battleground had been chosen, other than its distance from human habitation, its being on a ley line for drawing power. It was also near a road where the car had been hidden, and the road led to sanctuary, of a sort. A place Ray had heard whispers of, from discontented coven members, whispers reeking of fear and bad whiskey. A safe place.

Daven's Stream. He'd thought they'd said Daven's Dream at first. Not a true sanctuary, but a safe house, somewhere he could at least recuperate—until they came looking for him. And they would.

A farmhouse, fields of black wheat rippling in the moonlight, smell of cow, of fresh earth, no blood scent. The car seemed to turn of its own accord into the rutted driveway, more jolts to a badly wounded body. He had not the strength to open the door, to speak to the people who came out of the farm house. Hands reached for him, voices, too loud, exclaiming, but no questions, simply help offered. Somewhere along the trip into the farmhouse, the blackness claimed him.

He came to in a bed, bandaged to the eyebrows, feeling warm and safe for the first time in far too many years. The blood smell was gone, replaced by antiseptic, sun-dried sheets and apples.

Daven had explained the farm to him. It was no sanctuary, no refuge for such as he. It was a place to rest, yes, welcome to all Wiccans or magic-weary, but for a killer, for one fleeing from darkness into darkness, there was no safety. They could not protect him, and for the safety of those who did need the farm, he must move on. He understood, only too well. But they tended him well, treated him fairly, mended his wounds and let him gain his strength back. He and Daven had many talks, he was given advice which he would later take. He milked a cow, rode a horse, played with the tumble puppies and children; all part of the healing. When it was time to move on, he did so without regrets and with a wholer heart.

He stayed in touch with the kind, wise people on the farm, would occasionally send them someone in less dire straits than he had been. But he never forgot that night of blood, either, the stain that would not let him be a part of the farm community.

He was still a marked man.

Seven years.

There was no significance in the number, merely coincidence.

The insistence of non-magically endowed people in imbuing the number seven with deep occult meaning never failed to amuse and mystify the truly gifted. There were numbers that had such meanings—three and five, for example. But seven meant nothing, particularly.

Seven years.

It had a historical, personal meaning to the man behind the wheel of the car. Seven years had passed since he had last taken this trip. He'd been coming from another direction, then. It had been night, and he had been badly wounded. But journeys aren't always about the details, like time of day or the highway number.

Seven years.

A nightmare lifetime before that, twenty-eight years of terror. Perhaps the number had power after all, four times seven...exactly half of which had been spent under a thick cloak woven of blood and the shadows of night, woven of black magic and sharp, cruel words, woven of hate.

For the first fourteen years of his life, Raymond Griffin had lived with the knowledge that his father hated him for being a witch. The powers he manifested, untrained, afraid, the raw magic stinking in his nostrils; these brought on the temper tantrums, the bullying, and the beatings. He had been shielded from the worst of it for a few, sunshine-brilliant years by his mother. His father was stronger, and killed her, though it was made to look like an accident, just like all the black eyes, bruised ribs, broken bones, and broken heart of the boy. His mind, diamond hard, already building defenses before it knew the word "wards;" this alone could not be broken or bent.

He knew, with every aching, weary muscle, how leather felt when brought down with anger on bare skin, how a fist felt smashing into cheekbones, into soft abdominal tissue, how it felt to have your own father turn a blowtorch on your back and laugh as the skin melted and you screamed and screamed and screamed.

How it felt to have him spit on you as you writhed on the ground, and snarl, "You burn witches."

Fourteen years in that hell, and he had only traded it for another kind.

Feel of rope in hands, strands like snaky splinters; muscles aching to hold, newly healed back screaming in pain as a too-thin body wiggled out the bedroom window. If he closed his eyes now, twenty-eight years later (multiple of seven again), he could still feel the jolt as he had landed on the ground beneath his window.

Another teen runaway, another statistic. He never found out what his father told the authorities. “Bad to the bone, tried to raise him right, ungrateful little brat, took everything from my wallet, you catch him, throw him in jail, he’s not my son anymore.” Another lost face in the crowds of hungry lost faces on the street.

The streets are not mean. Streets have no personality, they are simply thoroughfares. It is the people who throng them who make them mean, the cold faceless ones who pass the shivering young stranger who are mean. It is the system, with too many cracks in it, potholes, where the lost can slip into the shadows, never to be found; the system is mean. The streets are only streets.

Ray became another thin boy on the street corner, dressed in stolen leathers painted with gang colours, bumming cigarettes, learning to hotwire cars and use a knife. The city effluvia of car exhaust, rotting fruit, dog shit, human urine, old wet newspapers for a bed...these became his identity; the steady hum of traffic, horns honking, swearing, gunfire, his lullaby. The gang was impressed by his scars, no one they knew had ever been burned by a blowtorch. “Bad trip, man. Bad trip.”

Yet there was no sense of family here. Even though he had learned to suppress his magic, Ray was different, and the gang sensed it. Almost feral, they could smell that he was different, dangerously so; no name to put on it, but he made them uneasy. He had little time in the colours—they came, the street sweepers, the do-gooders, rounded up the gangs, broke up friendships, connections, the only sense of community these ragged children had.

No father came to claim Raymond Griffin. Unwanted, he drew back into the comforting shadows, biding his time. His power was hungry, demanding to be fed, trained; and it called out. It was heard.

Seven years.

This time it was daylight, the gentle gray of a fall day when rain threatened, but not seriously. The leaves had not yet turned, and hung tiredly from the trees, dusty green globs in the haze. The rain was needed, Ray noticed, the ground was dry, the crops withering. It had been a long, hot summer.

Seven years.

He was not fresh from battle, knife wounds suppurating, psychic and physical energy drained, the taint of a man’s death in his clothes, his mind. He was older and perhaps wiser, certainly far more experienced, certainly sadder. A falcon perched on the back of the passenger seat this time, watching the road with avid, beady eyes. Andrei knew better than to act up in the car.

Seven years.

Ray turned down the driveway, smiling when he noted that it was still rutted, still jolted the car. This time, he had no injuries to be aggravated, though it still did not do his perpetually bad back any favours. He remained fully conscious when people poured out of the farmhouse to greet him. He found himself wrapped into a hug that included Daven, Daven's wife Nora, and at least two of the kids. Laughing, he broke free.

"Daven, Nora," he said, smiling. "It's good to see you."

"Ray," they chorused. "Come inside, come inside. It's been too long."

He found himself in the kitchen, clean white butcher block table, green linoleum, pine cupboards. The wonderful aroma of coffee and apple pie assaulted his nose, he found himself hungry. Food and coffee were produced, and the family sat down at the table to gaze at their visitor.

"I feel like the prodigal son," Ray complained, but his eyes twinkled. He had not looked for such a welcome here.

"We're happy to see you," Daven replied. "We enjoy your letters and notes, but it's good to see the flesh, too."

"What little there is of it," Nora said predictably.

"Not you, too!" Ray protested. "I eat quite well, I just burn it all off."

"Still smoking?" she asked, frowning.

"Quit." He laid his hands out on the table, palms up. "Now stop being a Mom, and tell me how things are here."

They caught each other up on what they'd been doing for seven years. Ray exclaimed over the Lawford children. Those who had been toddlers seven years ago were now preteens, and the preteens were young adults. The Lawfords had six kids in all. "Farm's good for growing all kinds of things." Ray talked about the Brotherhood, knowing that he could trust this family.

Daven looked at him sharply. "And there's been no sign of anyone coming to make you pay for what you did?"

"Not so far," Ray shrugged. "It could be that they find the Brotherhood and the wards on the Road a bit intimidating, but even when I'm alone, with only Andrei here, there's been no attempt at revenge." He drank some coffee. "Yet."

"Seven years..." Nora said thoughtfully. "Surely they would have done something by now."

“With them, one can never be sure,” Ray said. “But I won’t stay long, I will not bring danger to this place. I just wanted to see you again,”

“We’re fine,” Daven replied. “Now then stay a spell, okay?”

“What kind of spell?” Ray asked, and they laughed.

But he knew he wouldn’t stay long, because of the “spell.” Because of the damned magic.

A Novel Experience
(2000)

Gideon stood in the doorway of the den in Valley Mansion, waving his hand in front of his face. A thick blue fog of cigarette and fireplace smoke obscured the room to the point where Gideon wasn't sure if he should hail his friend Alex or a London cab.

In the centre of this thick cloud, a tall, muscular, handsome man could just barely be seen. He was hunched over a table much too small for him, his fingers hammering at something that the smoke hid. The tapping of typewriter keys betrayed his activity to his observer.

Gideon paused. He hadn't been aware that Alex *could* type. Whatever could he be working on so industriously? Alex had always been allergic to work.

The Baron politely cleared his throat. "Good evening, Alexander. I think you should check your flue, not to mention your smoke alarm."

Alex's head jerked around. He struggled to his feet, disentangling himself from the typewriter table and nearly overturning the full ashtray that balanced precariously on one side of the table. A half-smoked black cigarette dangled from the tall vampire's lips. He snatched this and scrunched it out in the ashtray.

"Gideon," he said, forcing his voice to be nonchalant. "I didn't hear you come in. Mrs. Jenkins didn't..."

"I let myself in. When you've been friends with someone for over a century and a half, you are permitted certain liberties."

"Oh. Of course, you're always welcome..."

"I haven't seen you for quite some time, Alexander. I wanted to be sure you were well."

Alexander's physical well-being had not changed since 1815, of course. He was a vampire. He was safe from the illnesses that felled mere mortals. However, since his cousin Janine had returned to Toronto, Alex had been very quiet. His friends were worried about him. He was prone to fits of suicidal despair and self-hatred. He'd fallen into one of these black moods after Janine's departure, but he had shown signs of coming out of it. Just when his friends had started to hope for his recovery, Alex had once more retreated behind the gloomy gray walls of Valley Mansion.

"I'm fine," Alex replied to Gideon's concern. "I've been... working."

The Baron raised an eyebrow. "You?" he asked in that incredulous tone that only very good friends can get away with.

"Yes, me," Alex snorted. "I've been taking...correspondence courses."

A lesser being than Gideon Redoak would have let his jaw drop. As it was, the other eyebrow joined the first one in elevation. "Correspondence courses?" he asked, floored. It was as if Pumpkin had told him she was going to university. One of the inescapable facts about Alex was that he wasn't one of the brightest vampires to get out of the coffin.

Alex was nodding. "Yes. Correspondence courses. It's interesting," he said defensively.

"In what?"

Alex's hands searched for his gold cigarette case. "Philosophy. Political science. History. I've been taking several courses, to see if there's one thing that suits me." He extracted and lit one of his custom-made cigarettes.

"And is there?" Typical of Alex, to be unable to stick to one thing. That he was attempting this at all was astounding.

An eloquent shrug, accompanied by tobacco smoke. "You'll see," Alex said enigmatically.

Gideon knew that was all he was going to get out of his friend. He longed to have a look at the typewritten pages Alex had been churning out, but that would be a violation of privacy.

"So, you have found a way to spend your time," he said instead. "I'm glad. I hope it proves worthwhile."

"You mean you hope it keeps me from being suicidal," Alex commented wryly. "Gideon...I miss Janine. I missed her terribly when she was first gone. It's not as bad now; I can talk to her on the phone without breaking down afterwards. However wrong our relationship was, it was still a relationship. I need...something to fill the void. I know I'm not very smart, but I thought I could handle a couple of correspondence courses."

"I think it's an excellent idea, Alexander," Gideon's voice was sincere. "If you need any help at all with them, please ask. Maybe you'll be the first member of the Brotherhood with a degree."

Alex laughed. "I doubt that," he chuckled. "But thanks for the encouragement." He flung the remainders of his cigarette into the fireplace. "Manners!" he slapped himself on the forehead. "Come and have a drink, Gideon. I'll tell you Janine's latest news."

Gideon agreed, and they adjourned to the leather couch. Alex poured brandy and steered the conversation towards Janine and her doings in Toronto. When Gideon took his leave an hour or so later, he was satisfied that Alex was not only surviving, but finding an interest outside both his departed cousin and himself.

Good for him! But Gideon still wanted to know what Alex had been typing.

Mitch enjoyed reading the Vampyres email list. Often he engaged in exchanges on it, especially when he had a chance to tease or send up his boss. He particularly liked reading the book reviews posted by the MadBibliographer. He'd acquired a taste for vampire fiction and purchased books based on the MadBib's reviews.

He sat down in his office, played briefly with the toy cars he kept on the computer desk, then logged on to his ISP. There were several messages in his mailbox: a few personal notes, some spam, and a smattering of posts from Vampyres. The list was certainly much quieter than it had been. There were two book reviews from the MadBib: one for a Buffy spin-off that didn't sound very good, and one for a first novel from a new author.

Mitch reached the concluding sentence and let his breath out with a whoosh; only then aware that he'd been holding it. He rubbed his eyes and reread the review, to make sure he hadn't misinterpreted it.

"Holy shit," he said. He had to read this book, to see if it really was that...he couldn't finish the thought.

He sauntered out to the parlour, where he found Evan doing the dusting.

"I'm going to make an office supply and bookstore run into Bangor," Mitch said casually, as if he'd just discovered a burning need for paperclips. "Need anything?"

"Mmmm." Evan's expression indicated suspicion. "Pick up some stamps."

"Stamps. Gotchya."

"This came up very suddenly, didn't it?"

Mitch shrugged. "Okay, I'm bored. I want to drive to Bangor. Sue me."

He left Evan to the dusting and made his way upstairs, Pumpkin and Smoke trailing hopefully behind him. He found Joshua in the latter's office, carefully examining an elaborately carved chair.

"Is it real?" Mitch asked, watching his friend peering at the carvings through a magnifying glass.

Joshua looked up and smiled. "It is assuredly a real chair." At Mitch's snort, he grinned slowly, then relented. "I have doubts about the carvings."

"Oh." Mitch's chief interest in furniture was how much abuse in the form of being sprawled in, kicked back, or in extreme cases chewed on it could take. "I'm driving into Bangor. Need anything?"

Josh shook his head. "No thanks. Got cabin fever?"

"Something like that. There's a book I want to get, and I doubt I'll find it in Fletcherville."

"The MadBib write one of her usual scintillating reviews?"

"She certainly made it sound like this is a must-read. Besides, I need a bunch of stuff like computer paper and stamps, and it's cheaper in Bangor."

Josh didn't bother to mention that the amount of time and gas spent driving to midcoast Maine's largest city more than cancelled out a dollar's difference on the price of computer paper. Mitch wanted to go. There was no harm in him doing so.

"Have fun," Josh said, getting back to examining the suspect carvings.

Mitch ended up having to take the two younger animals with him. Warg spent most of his time sleeping these days, but Pumpkin and Smoke were always ready for an outing in the ATV.

Once Mitch got out of Fletcherville and hit the highway, it was a little more than an hour to Bangor. He found a park and took the animals for a run, then left them in the ATV with a window cracked open and some food and water. He did his office supply shopping first, then hit Barnes & Noble.

Jackpot! They had *Stormwings* in stock. He bought a copy, picked up a couple of other books that looked interesting, and lugged his purchases back to the ATV.

He couldn't wait to read the book.

It was even worse than Mitch had anticipated. Not in the sense of badly written; indeed, the writing was more than competent and verged on the excellent on occasion. No, it was not the writing. It was the story itself.

The plot was fairly standard: boy meets girl, boy romances girl, boy turns out to be a vampire and girl freaks. But the situation and the characters were what made Mitch gasp at every page turn.

Whoever the hell Sandy Daniels was, he or she knew some pretty key stuff about the Brotherhood in general, and about Alex in particular. This novel, barring a few trivial details and some transparent personal name changes, was about Alex's stormy love affair and stormier break-up with Brier Snow.

They were all there. The brooding Byronic vampire, the shy art teacher who falls for him, the vampire's gay best friend and that friend's lover, the mysterious Druids, the black-clad sorcerer, the muscular bodyguard, the puppyish young werewolf...

Mitch knew he had to tell Gideon about this book...by long-distance phone call from Japan, preferably. He looked up from the final pages, with their maelstromic parting scene that yet contained a kernel of hope for reconciliation, and saw that it was nightfall.

He, Gaylord Algernon Pritchard, had a solemn duty as a member of the Brotherhood of Darkness to protect and preserve said Brotherhood, and to make any threat to their security known to them.

This book was a threat—not so much in itself as that it demonstrated the fact that an outsider knew the secrets of the Brotherhood. Somewhere, somebody who knew about Alex and Brier had turned their tragedy into a novel. This Daniels person had dangerous information. It might not stop at just a novel.

Who could have betrayed them like this? The few ordinary humans who knew of their existence were all trustworthy.

Mitch decided he had no choice but to tell Gideon about *Stormwings*, and to get the Baron to pass the information on. Buoyed by this decision, he went down to dinner.

Gideon agreed amiably to Mitch's request to speak to him alone after dinner. They withdrew to the downstairs office, and Gideon shut the door.

"You have my full attention," he assured the werewolf.

Mitch toyed with one of his Matchbox cars, making the tiny rubber wheels spin with his index finger. "You won't like this."

Gideon looked patient. "I don't know that until I've heard what it is."

Mitch sighed and put the car down. He handed Gideon the novel. The Baron studied the cover illustration of a pretty girl being menaced by a darkly handsome man whose cloak spread behind him in a not-very-subtle suggestion of wings.

"A novel?" Gideon asked, sounding as if he'd never seen one before. He turned it over to study the publisher's blurb. "A vampire novel?" He raised his eyes up to look at Mitch, noted the young man's unusually sober expression, and went back to the blurb.

"'Welcome to Shadowfall Manse, where dark secrets lurk in the cellars and in the heart of Comte Philippe Danescu. When pretty young Bianca Thorn is drawn into the Comte's tormented world of vampires and magic, her life is changed forever.'"

"It gets worse," Mitch said gloomily. "And I don't mean the writing."

Gideon sat down in one of the swivel chairs and opened the book to read aloud at random.

"There were far more women in the casino than would have been common or allowed in the previous century. The older ones wearing deceptively expensive gowns tended to be serious gamblers. Those who boasted younger faces and more daring necklines often had other objectives. One of the latter spotted Philippe and Damien and obviously liked what she saw—at least the taller half of it.

"As Philippe walked past her chair, the young woman, overcome with self-consciousness at his unexpected approach, knocked her beaded evening bag off her table. Philippe paused and gracefully swept the bag up from the carpet.

"'I believe you dropped this,' he said.

"'How clumsy of me.' She smiled invitingly at him. She took lipstick and a compact from the bag, and fixed an already perfect face. Philippe observed these ministrations with an appreciative smile. When she glanced shyly up at him, he gave her a neat bow.

"'Hello. I am Philippe Danescu, at your service.'

"'She held out her hand. 'And I'm Bianca Thorn.'"

There was a moment of appalled silence. Gideon's troubled dark eyes met Mitch's blue ones. "Is it," he asked softly, "all like this?"

"Yeah, boss. It's all like that. Only the names have been changed to protect the guilty."

Gideon leafed through a few more pages, discovering passages about a young werewolf named Rich and a meeting of the Fraternity of The Night. He closed the book and looked at Mitch. "Thank you for bringing this to my attention. I think I should read the whole thing at once."

"I think you should, too," Mitch agreed. "I guess I should have bought more copies."

"Why?"

"Because everyone in the Brotherhood is going to want to read this. We're all in it."

Gideon shuddered. "Who is Sandy Daniels? Any guesses, young Rich?"

Mitch shrugged. "Sorry, Baronet Kirkwood, but I have no idea."

"Ah, well. Perhaps my lover Jericho might know something."

Holding the book as if it might bite, Gideon departed from the office. Mitch sagged in relief. There hadn't been the scene he'd been half-expecting, even though he knew Gideon would never make a scene.

Gideon and Josh traded *Stormwings* back and forth until the wee hours, reading each other voice passages out loud and hunting for clues to the identity of the author. The standard "about the author" insert told them nothing. The only information to be gleaned from the single sentence was that *Stormwings* was Sandy Daniels' first novel. There was no hint as to the gender, location, age or appearance of the author.

"I think it's a man," Joshua ventured.

"Why?" Gideon asked.

"Just some of the phrases used, and the sex scenes..."

"I think it's a woman. Some of the passages are reminiscent of torrid romances."

Josh mulled this over. "Men write romances, too," he pointed out. "But maybe you're right. Our relationship—I mean, the relationship between Damien and Jericho—is treated more sensitively than you'd expect a straight guy to write it."

"And 'Sandy' sounds more like a woman," Gideon said.

"Mmm. I have to admit that I rather like the sound of 'Jericho Pengallon.' Pretty clever, changing 'Joshua' to 'Jericho.'"

"I can't say I'm overly fond of 'Damien Kirkwood,' however."

"You're just mad that you got demoted to a mere baronet."

"'All baronets are bad,'" Gideon quoted, eliciting a laugh from his partner.

"Seriously, Gideon, you'd better tell Michael about this."

"I think it might be more appropriate to inform Alexander that someone is turning his personal life into a tawdry novel."

"He'll probably hang himself."

"We must find out who this Sandy Daniels is," Gideon said firmly.

"How? The publisher won't tell you anything if the author doesn't want the information to get out."

"If you want to find something out, my dear Josh, you ask an investigative reporter."

"Ah. And I know that you meant that quite literally."

"I shan't be able to ask anyone anything until sunset," Gideon pointed out with maddening logic.

"Oh, all right. I'll go talk to Fox. *And* Michael."

"In the meantime, though, Damien Kirkwood would like to speak to Jericho Pengallon."

"Yes? What about?"

"Care to make the walls come tumbling down?"

Joshua shoved aside a filthy coffee mug, an ashtray crammed with cigarette butts and gum wads, a pile of papers of assorted sizes, colours and ancestry, and miscellaneous other debris. The occupant of the desk he was performing urban renewal on watched him with deep suspicion.

"Hey," Fox Fletcher objected. "You're disturbing the ecosystem. It took me years to develop some of that strata."

The battered investigative reporter for the Fletcherville Gazette had become a friend of the Brotherhood more or less by accident...the accident involving his fascination with Janine and his misguided attempt to rescue her from the clutches of her vampiric cousin. He had nearly been the one who needed rescuing, but the misunderstanding had been cleared up and Fox was now firmly in their camp.

As long as nobody mentioned Janine to him.

"Do you know anything about this?" Josh asked Fox, plunking the now well-thumbed copy of *Stormwings* down on the cleared space on Fox's desk.

Fox's right hand, which was lacking two fingers, reached for the book. "It's a book. It's made of paper, which is derived from the murder of innocent trees, and ink, which is derived from the murder of innocent soybeans or whatever the hell is trendy right now. Do you want to know how books are printed and bound?"

"I'm not unaware of the process. I want to know if you know anything about this particular book."

Fox examined it. "Bought at Barnes & Noble in Bangor...nice alliteration, that."

"Fox..."

"Okay, okay, it was just a joke. No, I don't know anything about this book. I've never seen it before, and I don't tend to read the book review columns. Something wrong with it?"

Joshua explained, tersely. Fox whistled.

"No wonder you're so tense. You want me to find out who Sandy Daniels is, right?"

"Yes. Someone has betrayed us, Fox."

The reporter frowned. "Now, this is before my time. I didn't stumble across your secret until Brier had headed for the hills of North Dakota...but could it be her?"

"I thought of that myself," Josh said. "She certainly seems the obvious suspect on the face of things, but somehow, I don't think so. You'd have to ask Alex, though; none of the rest of us really got to know her very well."

"I'll nose around, see what I can find. Can I keep the book?"

"We only have one copy, and I still have to show it to Michael."

"Maybe I can pick one up, then," Fox handed the novel back to Josh. "Are you guys going to get really upset about this, like Donovan-level upset?"

Josh repressed a shudder at the reminder of the evil mage whom they—Gideon, actually—had wiped out. "I doubt it. Depends on who this author turns out to be."

"Good luck," Fox said.

"You, too." Josh departed, clutching the book, and drove back to the Cliff Road to go talk to Michael.

Michael's desk in the library was only slightly less cluttered than Fox's had been. His coffee mug was cleaner, and there was no ashtray since the Archdruid had given up smoking. But the carefully developed strata and entire miniature ecosystems were in full evidence. Josh was fairly sure he saw one of the piles of paper shift independently of any air current or gesture on Michael's part. There was a rubber ball on the desk, even though the children were banned from this room.

When Josh explained his mission, Michael looked up and ran a hand through his blond hair, disarraying it. "We'd better order multiple copies," the Druid observed wryly.

"Mitch already thought of that," Josh said. "He figures everyone will want one."

"Has anyone spoken of this to Alex?"

"Not yet. There hasn't been time. The review only came out yesterday."

"The MadBib isn't aware of Alex's relationship with Brier, but how did the 'Fraternity of The Night' escape her notice?" Michael wondered.

"Maybe she just thought it was coincidence, or something."

"Likely. Will you leave it here, with me, so that I may read it?"

"Sure. I've talked to Fox Fletcher, he's going to see if he can track down the author. He thinks it might be Brier."

Michael's expression was dubious. "I should think that highly unlikely, actually. Someone really has to break this to Alex..."

"Gideon will do it. He's Alex's best friend, and he won't get all emotional about it. Alex is probably going to go ballistic, though. This is his private life."

"It even looks like him, a bit, on the cover," Michael mused. "Whoever this author is, he or she has a lot to answer for."

"Fox is worried that we're going to do a Donovan on Sandy Daniels if we find her."

"That depends on Alex, I imagine. Gideon may have to hold him down."

"The Brotherhood may take turns. After all, we're all in this book."

Michael nodded. "Even the twins, which is carrying coincidence much too far. Thank you, Josh. I'd better start reading this soonest."

"Sure. Enjoy." Josh let himself out of Fairlawn, stopping briefly to pet Ruddigore the Irish setter, who was sprawling in the hallway outside the library. The house was otherwise empty, the kids being in school and Mary at work.

Satisfied that he had done his best for the cause, Josh went home and waited for sundown.

For the second time in less than a week, Gideon found himself calling on Valley Mansion. This time, he knocked and allowed Mrs. Jenkins, Alex's long-suffering housekeeper, to announce him. When he reached the study, it was a tad less smoke-filled than it had been on his last visit, but little else had changed. The typewriter table with its cascading sheets of paper was still set up against one wall. Alex was studying a book rather than typing, but he had obviously just left off working on something—the keyboard was still steaming.

"You caught me taking a break," Alex grinned at his old friend as Gideon entered the room. "I'm getting typist's cramp." He flexed his long fingers carefully. "Look, I'm getting calluses."

"I don't think we can get calluses, Alexander," said Gideon mildly. "How are your courses going?"

"Quite well, actually. I'm enjoying them."

"Good. But that isn't why I came over."

"Oh? Is something up?"

"Do you know the expression 'my life is an open book?'"

Alex looked puzzled. "Is this some sort of trivia game or

something, Gideon? I'm familiar with the expression, why?"

Gideon tossed him a copy of *Stormwings*. "Open this, and that old saw will be literally true."

Alex stared down at the paperback in his lap. Gideon couldn't read the younger vampire's expression, which worried him. "Explain."

"Whoever wrote this novel had intimate experience of your relationship with Brier, the breakup of that relationship, and of the membership and function of the Brotherhood."

"You mean...the plot of this novel...?"

"Precisely."

"But that's absurd."

"You are holding the proof in your hand, Alexander. I would suggest you read it."

Alex sighed and thumbed the pages of the paperback with all the enthusiasm of a true bibliophobe. "When," he asked slowly, "is the meeting of the Brotherhood to discuss this?"

"Tomorrow night. We had to give everyone time to read it, first. Mitch had to drive to Bangor and buy several copies."

"I hope everyone reimburses him."

"You owe him seven ninety-five."

Alex snorted. "I'll pay him tomorrow night, then. I don't think I'm going to like this, but I'll read it. Who the hell is Sandy Daniels?"

"We're trying to find that out. Joshua asked Fox Fletcher to look into it."

Alex nodded. "When he finds her, she is going to be one sorry author."

"We don't know that it is a she."

"Pronoun of convenience. Well, if you don't mind, Gideon, I have some schoolwork to do before I can read for displeasure."

"Of course. I will see you tomorrow night, then. Good evening, and happy reading."

A bitter laugh followed him out.

The conversation level in the meeting room at Fairlawn the next night bordered on violating the town noise bylaw. Everyone wanted to talk to everyone else, to see what they had thought of *Stormwings*. Mary crossed over to where Alex stood, looking calm despite the disruption in the hive, and politely collared him.

"How do you feel about this?" she asked, displaying her copy of the hotly controversial novel.

"It certainly seems to be far too much for mere coincidence."

"You know what I meant," said the nurse, giving him a look.

"Are you upset, angry, hurt...?"

"Mostly numb," Alex replied. "I don't really know why this has happened. I don't know what to think."

Mary gave him a quick hug, then returned her chair as Michael came into the room. The Archdruid took his place behind his desk, and the angry hum of conversation slowly dwindled. The Brotherhood took their seats.

They were all looking at him, Alex realized. Some sympathetically, like Josh and Mary, some quizzically, like Ray and Maggie, some as if they thought this whole thing was funny, like Mitch and Francis. Mostly they were looking at him to wait for his reaction.

Fox Fletcher was the last person of all to come in. He sat down near the door, quietly nodding to one or two people. Michael cleared his throat and expertly herded together everyone's wandering attention.

"You all know why I called this meeting," Michael said. He held up a copy of *Stormwings*. Gideon privately thought that he was getting sick to undeath of that cover illustration. "We are here," the Archdruid continued, "because of this. The MadBibliographer reviewed it for her column, Mitch read that review and recognized the similarity to events that occurred within the Brotherhood, and went out to buy the book. It is not just similar. It is identical, save for name changes and perhaps the odd minor detail. That indicates dangerous knowledge on the part of Sandy Daniels. Whoever that may be. Fox?"

The scarred reporter shook his head. "Josh set me on the trail, but the publishers aren't talking, even when I threatened a lawsuit. Seems an author is entitled to have a pseudonym, and to not have their real identity revealed if they don't want it to be. Craig Books isn't talking. I couldn't even find out if our Sandy is a guy or a girl."

"Sandra, probably," Maggie said. "A woman wrote this."

"A guy," Evan argued. "There's a fight scene in here that had to be a guy."

Michael interfered before squabbles broke out. "Whether the author is man or woman or transgendered gerbil," he said, getting a brief laugh, "we still have the problem of this book to contend with."

"But Michael," Mary said, "it's a novel."

"Yes," the Archdruid agreed.

"Everyone who is reading it will know it's fiction," Mary went on to point out.

"Good point," Ray said. "Nobody in their right minds would think that any of this is 'based on a true story!'"

"Especially the part about the cynical former high priest of black magic," Francis teased.

"I'll admit your point," Michael nodded at Mary, ignoring the other two. "But we still must face the fact that the author of this book knew about Alex and Brier, knew about the Brotherhood, and wrote about them in very thin disguise. My counterpart in the novel is named Rafael Greensward. Another archangel, and a synonym for 'Fairlawn?' The other names are as transparent. This Sandy Daniels is laughing at us."

Nobody in the room was laughing as that aspect sank in. Eyes once more turned to Alex, who seemed on the whole unconcerned. He shrugged.

"Alex," Michael's voice was gentle, but uncompromising. "could it have been Brier who wrote this?"

"Not a chance," Alex replied promptly. "Look at the way it ends. With hope for a reconciliation. There's no hope at all for one with Brier, and she certainly wouldn't have written the story that way. Assuming she'd write a vampire novel in the first place, which I doubt. She did not leave me solely because I have black moods, you know. She left because she hates vampires. Why would she write a vampire novel?"

The members considered these words. It was a valid argument.

Gideon's eyes narrowed slightly as he studied Alex. Why wasn't the broody Count more upset over this? It was his life, his love affair, that had been turned into a trashy paperback. Nobody else seemed to find anything wrong with Alex's reply, though.

Maggie said, "But who else, other than Brier, knows the details of the affair?"

"Well, I do, of course," Alex said, "And Gideon and Joshua, and the rest of you know enough about it to have written the book." He smiled to show he was kidding. "Otherwise...it's quite a mystery, isn't it? But as you," he bowed to Mary, "pointed out, it's a novel. Fiction. It can't hurt us."

"I would still like to know who this Daniels person is," Michael said. "If anyone has any ideas how we can find out...?"

Fox shook his head. "The publishers ain't talkin'," he reemphasized.

"We could use mind control," Francis suggested.

"No," said Alex. "That's dishonourable."

"So?"

"We will see if we can pursue this through more mundane

methods first," said Michael. "I'll see what I can find out. I have contacts in the publishing business. So, unless anyone else has something to say...?"

Nobody did, and the meeting broke up.

Gideon was getting tired of standing in the entrance of the den at Valley Mansion, a haze of cigarette smoke clinging to his clothes, watching Alex pound away at the typewriter keys. Déjà vu wasn't even in it.

Two nights had passed since the meeting, and nobody was any further along on identifying the author of *Stormwings*. But Gideon knew, or had a very shrewd guess.

"So," he said, watching Alex's head whip round, "how are the correspondence courses going?"

"Fine, fine," Alex replied, standing up and threatening to topple the pile of typed papers.

"Tell me...would any of that correspondence be with Craig Publishers?"

Alex blinked. "What?"

Gideon extended his copy of *Stormwings*. "I think I would like the author to autograph this."

Alex sagged. There was a lot of Alex, six feet four inches of him, and it took him some time to sag. "Damn you. How?"

"Simple deduction, actually. Who else knew all the details of that relationship, other than Brier? And the transparent name changes...nobody thought to look closely at the author's name. Maggie thought that Sandy was short for Sandra. But it's also short for Alexander. And it is not hard to get Daniels out of Goldanias." He clenched the book tightly as he confronted his friend with a hard look. "Why, Alexander?"

"I couldn't think of a better pseudonym?" Alex saw the flash of anger in Gideon's eyes. "All right!" he shouted, then calmed. "It's true that I've been taking correspondence courses—in creative writing. One of the exercises was to take a bad experience in your life and turn it into a story, distancing yourself from it. So I did that with Brier. The instructor actually called me on the phone, he was so impressed, and urged me to turn it into a full-length vampire novel. He was really blown away by the fact that I'd made my fictional counterpart a vampire. He seemed to find that deeply symbolic." His expression was wry enough to make whiskey out of. "So I wrote *Stormwings* in about a month, and sent it to him, and the next thing I know, I'm signing a publishing contract."

"You have risked exposing us all."

"No, I haven't. It is, as Mary pointed out, a novel. Fiction. The fictions of a demented Romanian. Nobody will think it's real."

"Supposing Brier reads it?"

Alex, who had started pacing as he grew more agitated, froze mid-stride. "She won't," he said, almost under his breath.

"You should tell Michael that you wrote it," said Gideon after a minute.

Alex threw himself dramatically on the sofa. "I suppose. I've done nothing wrong! I never lied. I just didn't tell the truth."

Gideon's expression showed what he thought of such dubious honesty. "If someone had asked you outright if you knew who had written this, would you have answered?"

A shrug. "Nobody did." A long-fingered hand reached out for Gideon. "Give me your copy. I'll sign it for you."

The Baron found himself handing over his copy of *Stormwings*. Alex rummaged for a pen, scrawled something, and handed it back. Gideon read the inscription.

"To my best friend, Baronet Damien Kirkwood, with my highest regards. Sandy Daniels."

Despite himself, Gideon was smiling. "Joshua says he likes the sound of Jericho Pengallon."

"Tell him to come over and I'll sign his copy to Jericho," Alex grinned.

It was impossible to be angry with Alex. He was right, the world would regard *Stormwings* as no more than fiction. Well, most of the world...Gideon wondered how many of their supernatural associates read vampire novels. No doubt they'd find out.

"You end it on a hopeful note," Gideon said gently, closing the cover of the book on Alex's signature. "Do you really think there is hope of a reconciliation with Brier?"

Alex stood up. He put a hand on Gideon's shoulder, briefly. "Not a one."

"Then, why...?"

"It is," Alex sighed, "fiction, after all."

Fairy Gothmother
(2001)

A wreath of aromatic blue smoke hung in the still air of the paper-strewn room. Fingers tapped at a typewriter (think of it as a combination of a keyboard and printer without the monitor or CPU in between if that will help, kids). An ashtray full of the detritus of a smoker wobbled precariously on the edge of the desk. The butts were black, and slightly thicker than those of an ordinary cigarette, for the industrious typist smoked a specially-made panatela that was soaked in rum and then rolled on the creamy white thighs of...absolutely no human woman. They cost enough, though, that they ought to have been.

Long, tapering fingers on a long, tapering hand reached for the latest finished sheet to roll it off the platen (look, kids, if you keep interrupting to ask me what the parts of a typewriter are, I'll never finish the story). It was the sort of hand, in itself not very far from creamy white, that likely once would have been called "aristocratic." In this enlightened politically correct age, however, we would merely say...well, actually, there isn't a politically correct way to describe that hand. It was undeniably aristocratic. It had breeding, that hand, the sort of breeding that leads to military officers, high church officials, stuffy-looking balding men cutting ribbons or laying cornerstones, and hemophilia.

That long pale hand reaching for the paper had possibly cut ribbons, but only of the sort holding together expensive little boxes containing gifts of minute size and staggering price tags, or else expensive little dresses containing young women of a very similar description. It was not a hand that had ever laid a cornerstone, although as for the young women, one may take it for granted that...never mind.

Hemophilia was not a problem suffered by the owner of that hand. Nor was male-patterned baldness. The thick raven-black straight-as-a-plank hair on the head of the hand's owner showed no trace of crop circles or a retreat from high tide of the scalp.

Still, despite its disappointing lack of the sort of qualities we have come to expect of the modern aristocracy, there was no denying the birthright of that hand. The rest of him must also be considered for a complete inventory. That black hair, mildly distressing for its lack of a Byronic wave or boyish curl, sat atop a very arresting head. A long, high forehead, the effect somewhat blunted by the midnight locks of hair. Good, high, sharply defined cheekbones (breeding again; you want good cheekbones, you have to breed them). A high-bridged, straight nose, made specifically for sneering down at the lower classes. Full, sensuous, heavy red lips and straight, even white teeth (ignore the hint of fangs for the moment, we'll get back to those). The mouth seemed designed for crushing the lips of willing women. A powerful jaw, set in a line that shrieked of stubbornness and pride. A strong, handsome face.

And the eyes. Perfectly shaped, perfectly spaced, and storm-gray. Picture the sky as a rip-snorter gathers and the reflection of that in the waiting sea. Yes, just that shade of angry pewter. With those eyes in the equation, the description of the man at the typewriter can be upgraded to "beautiful."

He was dressed in a crisp short-sleeved button-down shirt, the sort that for some odd reason is advertised by a man with an eye patch. Equally crisp twill pants and leather loafers completed his deceptively simple garb. This is not a man you can easily picture in jeans and a T-shirt.

A gold watch flashed on his wrist as he reached for the piece of paper. The cluttered smoke-polluted room in which he worked was the study of a large gothic-style stone mansion, complete with tower.

He never went into the tower anymore. All the doors to it had been locked. No, there was no mad first wife hidden in those now dusty rooms.

Alexander Goldanias' first (and only) wife had died many years ago. More years had passed than that handsome, wrinkle-free face revealed. He did not know when Katrina had died, nor when their sons had, for he by then was far away and not the same husband and father they'd known.

Becoming a vampire tended to involve nasty inconveniences like being forced to abandon your family.

He hesitated over the pile of pristine white paper awaiting the attention of the typewriter. He'd already pounded out two chapters of his new novel tonight, it was time for a break. Let the publisher and deadlines go hang. The world had waited this long for the sequel to *Stormwing,* it could wait a little longer.

"I'm going out, Mrs. Jenkins," he said as he left the morass that was his study and strode purposefully through the ill-lit halls of his home.

"Yes, sir," called a calm disembodied voice from whatever room the housekeeper currently occupied.

Alex had always suspected that her reply would be "Yes, sir," had he announced his intention to jump off the cliff or fly to the moon. Nothing perturbed Mrs. Jenkins. He hastily amended that to "almost nothing." She'd been very perturbed indeed when she'd discovered what her employer had done to his cousin.

No. No thoughts. Those were all to be channelled into the new book, working title of *Killing Cousins.* No thoughts of why the tower rooms were locked, no thoughts of why Valley Mansion's halls echoed with his footsteps. No thoughts at all allowed, not even to acknowledge that he was spinning his wheels in neutral.

Speaking of wheels, the modest returns from the sales of *Stormwing* had bought him new ones. Persuaded to trade in the overly ostentatious and impractical Rolls Royce, Alex had actually scaled down. A new Audi sat in the driveway, gleaming black in the pooled light from overhead.

Alex got in and drove. He was almost tempted to stop at one of the other houses on the Cliff Road to visit. But he did not, reluctant to disturb the residents at...good lord, three in the morning.

So, not much of the night left. Fletcherville was not exactly a jumping all-night hot spot. To Alex's knowledge, only the gas station and one convenience store were open at this hour. Fletcherville tolerated the Cliff Road Crowd, who kept peculiar hours, but didn't believe in catering to them.

It wasn't until Alex was on the coast highway (the scenic route through Maine!) that he realized he'd left his cigarette case on his desk in Valley Mansion. For a moment, the air inside the car turned blue. Then he relaxed. He'd survive a couple of hours, all the time he had before dawn, without a smoke. His addiction was purely psychological, after all. He was beyond all physical cravings except for the stuff that maintained his existence.

The blood is the...oh, you know the rest.

He turned the car stereo on, but failed to find an appropriate song. Not one station was playing "Sympathy for the Devil," "Bat

Out Of Hell," "Bloodletting," or even "The Moon Over Bourbon Street," proving once again that life fails to provide a soundtrack. Refusing to settle for "Who Let the Dogs Out" (he was not a werewolf, thank you very much), Alex turned the radio off again.

It was pleasantly pointless to be out driving nowhere with no aim in mind; Alex made a mental note to try this again sometime. Not to plan it, of course, for that would make it a chore. Just sometime when he was feeling pent up and frustrated. Loneliness was the ache of a ticking clock.

No. Save it for the novel. The plot of *Killing Cousins* (stupid title, must find a better one) was Alex's steamy affair with his cousin (a distant cousin, separated by several generations, incest had not been the issue) and the tragic results. He missed her. It had been a mistake of epic proportions, but he missed her. What really hurt was the suspicion that she didn't miss him. He'd left that out of the book. Naturally, all the names had been changed to protect the guilty.

He'd tried to find some sort of balance in his life since. Writing and publishing *Stormwing* had been a huge boost for him; the fact that sales had been modest and nobody was begging for the movie rights was unimportant. He'd achieved something unexpected and he was determined to find a way to keep himself from backsliding.

What he really needed was a more radical change. He'd tried spending some time at his villa on a private island off of Venice, but he'd been too lonely there.

"Damn!" Alex said out loud as the car's headlight beams flashed off a highway sign indicating yet another deserted tourist attraction. "I don't see why the hell vampires can't have wishes granted. Why don't I have a fairy godmother?"

"Because you never asked for one before, idiot," said a voice from the passenger seat.

Alex was wearing his seatbelt. An Audi has good brakes. These two factors prevented him from meeting the hood of his car from the wrong side of the windshield.

"You really shouldn't slam the brakes like that, moron," growled the voice from the passenger seat. "You could've caused an accident."

Alex gripped the steering wheel, which creaked ominously, and stared at the trees and quiet houses in the headlight beams. He was grateful for his vampiric state of being for the first time ever since he'd been turned. Had he still possessed a beating heart, it'd probably have gone into cardiac arrest.

Slowly, delicately, he turned to look at the seat beside him.

A young goth girl with the standard Cleopatra haircut, a black ruffled poet's shirt, a PVC micro-short skirt, large-meshed, artistically ripped fishnet stockings, and army boots gazed calmly back at him from under several pounds of make-up. She had a nose ring with a chain that attached it to an earring, and a spider web tattoo on her left hand. She smelled faintly of incense and leather, but not of blood or sweat. Whatever she was, she wasn't human.

"Who the hell are you?" Alex snapped. She'd given him a bad shock.

"I'm your fairy godmother," the apparition snapped back.

"My what?"

"Fairy godmother. Something wrong with your hearing?"

"No, of course not. But you don't look like a fairy godmother."

"Yeah? You're an expert? How're we supposed to look?"

Of course Alex knew the answer to that. Fairy godmothers were supposed to be cute little old ladies with curly gray hair and flouncy dresses who waved magic wands and said things like "bibbety bobbety boo." Weren't they?

That was about the time his brain started screaming that there were no such things as fairy godmothers. Right. Just like there were no such things as vampires?

"Well?" demanded the black-clad total stranger sitting in the Audi. "How is a fairy godmother supposed to look, Mr. Expert?"

"More...twinkly?"

"Sorry. You ain't Cinderella, so no twinkles. I'm it, and I'm overbooked. Lot of vampires out there. Now, let's get to it." Out of a backpack that Alex was prepared to swear hadn't been there a second earlier, she pulled a thick file folder brimming with papers.

"What's that?" Alex asked.

"Your dossier, Einstein. You think they send us in with no info at all on the clients? Now shut up and let me read."

Alex winced at the size of his file and tried not to think about the contents. This proved difficult, since his fairy godmother read the juicier bits out loud as she came across them.

"Born 1780. Difficult child, stubborn, disobedient, often punished. Hah! Given choice between military career and marriage. Chose marriage." The raccoon-ringed eyes bored into his. "So, thought you'd make some woman miserable instead of trying to be a soldier? Typical."

"I..."

"Shut up. Two sons, mm hmm. Couldn't wait to knock her up, I see. Cheated on the wife. That doesn't surprise me. Drinking, gambling, spent more time in taverns than at home. No surprise there, either. Fell ill due to the activities and the fact that the mistress was a vampire. Stupid male! Wifey nursed you back to health. Well, sign her up for the sainthood."

"Don't you speak a word against Katrina!" Alex slammed his fist on the dashboard.

"Keep your shirt on, Galahad, I'm not her fairy godmother. Where was I? Oh, yeah. You decided to be a good little hubby and daddy from then on, so you went to break it up with the mistress. Gold star for you. But, boo, hiss, she was a vampire. You got turned in 1815 at the age of twenty-five."

"Don't remind me," Alex shuddered.

"She abandoned you. Nice sense of irony. You fled to Paris, got taken under the wing of a couple of older vampires like Jean de la Mare and Gideon Redoak." A plucked eyebrow went up. "Oh, so you already had a fairy godmother."

"That's not funny."

"Weird reaction. It says here that you're homophobic. Not to mention a selfish pig, suicidal, bipolar..."

"I am *not!*"

"...antisocial, a smoker..." she flipped some pages. "You screwed and turned your own cousin? Sicko. You need a psychiatrist, not a fairy godmother."

"But she..."

"Shut up. You wrote a novel. *You* wrote a *novel?*"

"Yes, I did."

"Hm. Maybe there's something I can work with, after all." She continued to read in silence, occasionally pursing her lips.

"I don't run with scissors," Alex offered weakly.

She didn't even spare him a glance. "You sure as hell don't play well with others."

Alex wanted desperately to change the subject from his defects. "What exactly does a fairy godmother do?"

The female in question slammed the dossier shut. "Well, getting you to the ball so that Prince Charming can fall in love with you doesn't seem to be an option." She drummed her fingers on the file folder. "You're the one who asked for a fairy godmother. What do you want?"

"Change. A new focus for my life."

"Hm. Well, I like a challenge, and you certainly are one. From what I'm reading here, I think what you need is...no, that won't do."

"What won't do?"

"Never mind. I'm going to try something radical. What's a really wild, romantic lifestyle you've always wanted to try? Name anything."

Alex wasn't certain what was more wild than being an international playboy vampire, but he gave it a try. "Pirate?" he hazarded.

"Typical male fantasy, but if that's what you want..."

Feeling a bit stupid, Alex said, "What are you talking about?"

"You'll see. Now, you'd better get your ass back home, because it'll be dawn soon and that will make all this pointless."

"Damn." Alex started the engine and pulled a U-turn. "Would you like..." but he was addressing an empty seat.

"Oh, hey, I almost forgot." She was back. "You get into trouble, just yell 'Noni.'"

"Noni?"

"It's my name, okay?"

"Listen, Noni, I..." but she was gone again.

Shaken, Alex drove as quickly as he dared back to Valley Mansion. He said nothing to Mrs. Jenkins about his peculiar encounter with a fairy godmother, just bid her good morning and took himself down to his bedroom. Maybe tomorrow night, he'd talk to Michael about all this.

He woke up thinking that the Atlantic sounded much louder than it normally did, as if the waves were lapping at the walls of Valley Mansion. But that was impossible. It was a hundred feet above high tide. What was that sound he'd just heard? Someone shouting? He sat up and cracked his head on a ceiling beam.

What the hell was going on? Rubbing his head, trying to blink his eyes back into focus, Alex swung his legs out of bed. Or, he tried to. They seemed to be trapped in some kind of net. The more he struggled, the more enmeshed he became, at one point turning completely upside-down. Finally he broke free of his bonds and landed with an unceremonious thump on the plank floor.

Plank...floor. Head still throbbing, Alex took in his surroundings. The "net" was a hammock. His bed, his bedroom, his very house had vanished. He was in a tiny little room (his brain wanted to use the word "cabin" for some reason) containing the hammock, a large, rough-hewn table with a couple of stools and some clothes piled in a corner. The table held a brace of flintlock pistols, a sword, two knives, an empty wooden bowl, a couple of lanterns and some large sheets of what looked like parchment with charts drawn on it. That was pretty much it for furniture and decor. And he'd always thought his bedroom had been Spartan.

There was a strong smell he couldn't quite identify, like the way air smells after fireworks. Other odors were easier; the sea, lantern oil, old wood, wool, leather, a dozen more assaulted his nostrils.

He'd gone to bed naked. Now he seemed to be wearing black wool knee breeches and a loose, badly stained red shirt; both of which had laces rather than buttons or zippers. A quick glance at the corner strewn with clothes showed him a pair of boots and a long coat that seemed a bit rusty.

His hand, trembling a little, touched his upper lip. Yes, there was a pencil-thin moustache there that probably looked rakish as all hell.

"Yo ho ho," Alex muttered. He had more than a sneaking suspicion that no real pirate had ever had an Errol Flynn moustache, but whatever. Real pirates probably never said "Yo ho ho", either.

He pulled on the boots and looked over the other items available.

He was just buckling on the sword belt when someone pounded on the door.

"Cap'n! Sail off the starboard stern!"

Uh...starboard was right and the stern was the back end of a ship. Right?

"Order all hands on deck!" Alex called out. "I'll be right there." He had no idea if "I'll be right there" sounded sufficiently piratical, but he couldn't think of anything else.

It apparently satisfied the knocker, for he heard boots tramping off. He thrust the knives into his boot-tops, the pistols into the sword belt, and his tongue firmly into his cheek. He opened the cabin door and manfully strode toward the main deck.

He arrived just as an enormous swell took hold of the ship and swung it up and down precisely like one of those amusement park rides.

You haven't forgotten that Alex is a vampire, have you?

It's not entirely true that vampires can't cross running water. Like every other "fact" that's "known" about vampires, it depends on a number of factors. Bloodlines, the limitations of the individual vampire, the definition of "running water;" these all must be considered. Alexander came from an ancient and noble vampire bloodline. Unfortunately, it was an ancient and noble bloodline that had a little H_2O problem. Add to this the fact that Alex hadn't been on a boat larger than a motor launch in nearly a century.

He had no time to take in little details like the size and type of ship he was on, the components of her crew, or even the fact that it was just barely dusk and a stiff nor'wester was making the sails billow and crack. Nor was there time to grab onto a handy non-moving object.

Six feet, four inches of Romanian vampire hit the deck. For the second time in less than half an hour, Alex's head connected painfully with a large amount of well-seasoned wood. The rest of his body suffered from the sudden impact, too, but he was too busy choking back vomit to notice.

"Cap'n?" There was a hand on his elbow, trying to help him up.

The ship groaned and creaked as another wave rocked her. Possibly it was Alex who groaned and creaked. With the assistance of the hand at his elbow (focusing his eyes was out of the question), he was able to get up as far as his knees. Hands clutching the damp, rough wool of his breeches, head down, black hair hanging limply over his eyes, he was scarcely the picture of a dashing, romantic figure. The wool prickled his palms. That peculiar odor was swirling around in his nose and the back of his throat, making his nausea worse.

"Cap'n?" The hand was trying to tug him to his feet. "The crew's awaitin' orders, Cap'n."

Ah, yes. The crew. They were probably on the verge of mutiny by now. Swallowing the acid reflux in his throat, Alex managed to stand up without throwing up.

Approximately twenty men, young, middle-aged and gray-haired, were standing on the deck, staring at him. Their ragged clothes were stained with salt rime, grease, blood and general grime. Many had matted, filthy hair. All except two young sprats had unkempt beards. The accumulated stench of them threatened Alex's hard-won equilibrium.

They didn't look as if they'd break out into a chorus of "Come friends, who plough the sea" anytime soon.

Alex turned to look at the rest of the person whose hand had helped him up. He beheld a short, stocky, dark complexioned man with wild gray hair and beard. This creature was dressed in a too-small jacket that might have once been navy blue and what looked like the remnants of a plain white kilt. A jagged white scar divided his face into uneven fractions; parts of his features seemed to be sliding off. He was lacking an eye, but hadn't bothered to disguise this deficiency. In fact, nearly all of the crewmembers seemed to have been mutilated in one way or another.

Alex nervously did a mental check of his own limbs and features; all were intact.

"Okay, Noni, what the hell do I do now?' he muttered inwardly.

And he knew. Just like that.

"Mr. Jackson!" he barked.

The one-eyed mulatto saluted. "Aye, Cap'n?" Was that relief in his voice?

"Details on the ship approaching, Mr. Jackson!"

"She's a Spanish galleon, Cap'n, flying the royal ensign."

"Unescorted?"

"Aye, Cap'n."

Now Alex knew perfectly well that a ship flying the Spanish royal ensign would not be unescorted. He didn't know how he knew that, but there seemed to be an unprecedented pool of information in his mind, no doubt the interference of his fairy godmother. He took an unnecessary deep breath to steady his nerves and his stomach. That post-fireworks smell was stronger than ever.

"Mr. Jackson!"

"Aye, Cap'n?"

"Why do I smell gunpowder?" As soon as he said the word, he knew that was what he smelled. Not unusual on a fighting ship, of course, but not in that quantity.

There were sidelong looks being exchanged among the scurvy crew. The ship pitched on the rolling waves, but Alex managed not to pitch in the opposite direction. He was getting the hang of this. If only the ship didn't make quite so much noise! Sails cracking in the wind, timbers creaking, the slap of waves on the hull...wasn't sailing supposed to be quiet?

"Waters, Cap'n," said Mr. Jackson.

"Huh?" Alex blinked, drawn back to the situation at hand.

"Waters." Mr. Jackson's gnarled hand pointed out one of the two beardless boys. He looked about fourteen under the grime. "He broached a powder keg, Cap'n. It mostly went overboard, but some got into the deck."

Staring down, Alex could make out black grains embedded into the sun-and-salt bleached planks.

Oh, wonderful. They were in distinct danger of being fired on by the Spanish, and the entire deck was drenched in gunpowder. Well, he'd wanted a radical change, hadn't he?

Time to show this crew who was captain around here. "Come here, Waters," he snapped.

The boy blanched beneath his coating of dirt, but obeyed. He was tall and gangly, with what might have been blond or light brown hair and hazel eyes set in a thin, frightened face. “Cap’n?” he stammered, not daring to meet Alex’s eyes.

“Is there any particular reason why you spilled gunpowder all over the deck, Waters?” Alex asked. Lightning flashed in his storm cloud eyes.

“No, Cap’n,” Waters swallowed. “I was careless, Cap’n.”

All eyes were on Alex, waiting to see what he would do.

It hadn’t started out as a tsunami. Technically, it still wasn’t one. But it was one hell of a big wave. The kind of wave that gives surfers either wet dreams or nightmares. It roared through the ocean, zeroing in on a pathetic little construction of planks and nails that called itself the pirate ship Ravaged Maiden.

Unable to maintain his newly discovered sea legs, Alex pitched right along with the ludicrously named ship. He slammed into the unfortunate young Waters, half-crushing the boy.

“Let that be a lesson to you,” he admonished the lad, as he struggled to stand up.

Waters groaned. Undoubtedly, he’d expected to be flogged or keelhauled, not fallen on by his captain. The remainder of the crew was looking puzzled by this unusual punishment. Alex managed to stand upright and draw his sword, wondering what on earth to do next. The helpful voice in his head was silent.

Something round and hot sailed overhead. The other ship (still off the starboard stern) had started firing on them. Cannonballs plunked down into the roiling ocean all around the Ravaged Maiden. The pirates cursed.

“Return fire!” Alex shouted. “Man the guns! Bring her about and we’ll show those dogs!”

The first mate looked at Alex. The vampire grinned maniacally. This was suddenly fun, like being a pirate should be—if you were eight years old and playing pirate on a plank in your swimming pool. Another cannonball smashed into the ocean beside the Ravaged Maiden.

The Ravaged Maiden did some more creaking and groaning. One of the crew was nearly twisted in two at the wheel. (Tiller? Who gave a damn at this point?). Even Alex could tell that the pirate ship was turning to face the other vessel. Cannonballs continued to fly, and now the pirates were returning fire. Clouds of smoke obscured the deck. Either the other ship didn’t have its range yet, or they were the world’s lousiest aims, however. Not one ball had yet hit...whoops.

Splintered wood flew towards Alex’s face and he instinctively covered his eyes. Jackson screamed some indecipherable orders. The sound of cannons firing was so loud that the first mate might as well have been praying or reciting poetry, but the crew seemed to know what to do. Alex stayed where he was, up against a solid barrier.

With a sort of awful inevitability, the pirate ship drew steadily closer to its opponent. The aggressive ship was striking its Spanish royal ensign and raising...Alex nearly giggled. They were running up the Jolly Roger. It was another pirate. No honour among thieves, indeed.

The ships were now too close for cannon. Pistols and muskets were being fired, and flaming braziers appeared on the deck of the other pirate. Uh-oh. There was all that gunpowder ground into the deck of the Ravaged Maiden. Sure enough, arrows were being lit in the braziers.

"Grappling hooks!" Alex screamed to Mr. Jackson, who relayed the orders to the crew. The two ships drew together with ominous crunching noises. "Board her, men!" the vampire captain commanded even as flaming arrows thunked into the Maiden's decks.

He put his long knife between his teeth, managing to somehow avoid cutting his lips or severing his fangs, and grabbed a stray rope. "Always wanted to do this," he said incoherently past the dagger. He leapt off the railing of the Maiden and swung on the rope over to the rival pirate ship, brandishing his sword.

The trouble was, he discovered, waving his arms and coughing as smoke overwhelmed him, that he could not tell the difference between his own crew and that of the other ship. He fought against all comers, sword dancing like Michael Flatley on speed, a sneer curled on his aristocratic lip and a twinkle in his eye.

"Have at ye!" he cried out. "Arrr!"

He was having so much fun that it took awhile for the smell of smoke to filter into his consciousness after it had filtered past his nostrils. But eventually his vampiric self-preservation kicked in and he stopped dueling against his current opponent and paused to have a good look. Not only was the Ravaged Maiden on fire and burning to the water line, but so was the attacker. The deck was burning, not ten feet from where Alex stood.

Time to make an exit.

"Noni! Get me out of here!" he called out, as his opponent noticed his distraction and ran him through.

"You sure give up easy."

He was sitting on his typing chair in his study in Valley

Mansion, still dressed in the ragged pirate costume. Blood dripped from the sword thrust in his chest. The smell of smoke in his nostrils made him jumpy, looking for the source. His eyes fell on his fairy godmother, who was perched on the leather couch. She was dressed exactly the way he'd seen her last. She looked as out of place in Valley Mansion as Alex did.

"Nice place," she said, then screwed up her nose at the sight of the full ashtray. "How can you smoke those things?" she asked, producing an unfiltered clove cigarette from midair and puffing on it. "So, why'd you yell?"

"The ship was on fire," Alex said. "And I got stabbed."

She raised an eyebrow. Clearly, she didn't regard this as an adequate explanation for wimping out. "Didn't you have a good time?"

"The ship was on fire," Alex repeated. "I have a sword wound in my chest."

"Is that all?"

"No, it's not all!" He leapt to his feet and started walking towards her. "I am a vampire! I don't get along with running water! I don't know one damned end of a boat from another!"

"Ship."

"What?" He stopped in his tracks, a foot away from her.

"Ship. A boat is something you pick up out of the water and put on a ship."

Alex wanted very badly to say that he didn't give a damn what the technical terms were, but something in Noni's expression made him choke the words back. She, whatever her faults, was a powerful occult being. The next time she plunked him down somewhere without warning, she might not wait until after dusk to do it.

That reminded him. "What if I'd stayed on that ship until morning?" he asked.

She met his eyes. Hers were very dark, expressionless behind the mask of make-up. He suppressed a shiver. "I'm your fairy godmother," she reminded him acidly. "I'm not in the business of trying to get you fried. Have a little faith."

"What are you in the business of trying to do?" The question came out before he could stop it.

"That's up to you, remember? You're the one making the wishes."

"How about a little advice on what to wish for?" Alex sank down into his chair. "I couldn't seem to make piracy pay."

Noni blew a smoke ring at him. "I don't give advice," she said.

"That's cheating. What do you want, Alex? Adventure? Romance?"

"Anything that doesn't involve boats," he said, carelessly. "Oh, sh—"

"—it." A few scraggly palm trees swayed above him. Waves lapped at a dismal little beach. He was on an island. A small island, apparently, to judge from what he could see.

"Very funny, Noni," he growled. "Now get me the hell out of here."

He failed to reappear in his comfortable study. Oh, right, she'd only help if he were in trouble. Apparently, being cast away didn't count as being in trouble. Could he build a sun-proof shelter? He rolled his eyes and looked up at the star-strewn heavens for help. Alex had never built so much as a Lego house in his existence, let alone something as complicated as an entirely light proof shelter. He was still in his pirate clothes, without a tool save for the sword and long knife. The chest wound had healed, but there were blood stains on his shirt. He had no watch, no maps, no compass, no handy signal flares, no cell phone and... damn, no lighter and no cigarettes!

As soon as that thought struck him, he desperately craved a smoke. "Noni? Can I at least have my cigarette case?"

That slim gold lifesaver failed to manifest for him. Damn. Sighing deeply, Alex set out to explore. Palm trees, rocks, bushes, and a smallish hill, hardly anything interesting. There was a bit of a lagoon on one side of the island, but Alex didn't swim. There were some dark smudges on the horizon that were likely other islands, but even if he did swim, they were too far away. He knew enough about oceans to know that distance was deceptive and that even warm ocean water could be deadly. For one thing, there were probably sharks and jellyfish and eels, none of which cared if you were a vampire. He'd never liked seafood when he'd been human, he desired to be seafood even less.

He wondered what the other members of the Brotherhood would have done in this situation. The magic users wouldn't have any problems. He comforted himself with the thought that at least the other vampires would have been equally helpless. But none of them had a nicotine addiction.

Stop thinking about cigarettes! His hand went habitually to his pocket, except that he didn't have a pocket in that location at the moment and there was no case or lighter there, anyway. Maybe he could roll some dried palm leaves and—what a ridiculous idea. How would he light it?

In one way, he was slightly better off than the average

castaway human. He didn't need fire or food. He did need shelter and blood. Where was he going to get blood? Noni seemed to have neglected a few little details. As of yet, he wasn't hungry, but long enough on this stupid island, and he would starve. A starving vampire is not a pretty sight.

Still, the problem of what he was going to do in sunlight was more pressing. His walk around the island had not shown him any handy old castles or abandoned huts or even a cave. There were rocks and trees and vines; he had the vague notion that somebody could probably do something very clever with such raw materials. Pity that Alexander Philippe Goldanias wasn't that somebody. He'd have cheerfully traded his new car for Bob Villa. Or even for Francis, who had built his own shack several years ago and it at least was still standing.

He went for another walk around the island, exploring the laughable hill and the pathetic jungle. Wildlife on the island seemed confined to a few birds that laughed at him, several insects, and a large spider that he decided to leave well enough alone. No mammals. No blood. Damn.

There was also a depressing lack of a handy Time-Life "build your own light proof shelter using only a pirate sword, long knife, palm fronds and rocks" do-it-yourself book. There were coconuts and some berries on the bushes and fish in the lagoon. This was the downside of not being human. He could eat the berries and the coconuts, but they wouldn't provide him necessary nutrition he only got from mammalian hemoglobin.

Why, oh, why had he spent his formative years in sloth and indolence, drinking, gambling and whoring, instead of volunteering for Habitat for Humanity or at least studying architecture?

His fifth walk around the island, he started singing to himself and talking to the spider as he passed it. The eighth walk, the spider went and hid rather than listen to him again. The birds were nearly killing themselves laughing in the palm trees.

By his twelfth time around the island, Alex realized that Noni had worked some fairy enchantment on his predicament. It definitely should have been morning by now, no matter what time of night he'd been marooned; yet the stars still twinkled above in a black velvet sky. So the need for shelter was eliminated.

But he was bored out of his mind, having nicotine withdrawal fits, and worried about the fact that the birds were all gathering in one tree, staring down at him and whispering to each other under their wings. One of them squawked at him. He threw a stone at it and missed by a country mile.

It splashed into the lagoon, starting a ring of ripples that undulated across the dark water, lapping against the hull of the pirate ship that was gaining rapidly on the island.

"Noni!"

"What?"

Alex clutched at the side of his typing table, toppling the overloaded ashtray and causing a minor avalanche to the floor. He didn't care.

"That wasn't funny," he snarled, grabbing for his cigarette case. He extracted and lit one of his specially made panatelas and took a deep drag on it, feeling his whole body tremble.

"You should be a bit more specific next time," she sniffed, leaning back on the couch.

"Next time? Why would I be stupid enough to make another wish?"

"Because three is traditional?"

"You're a fairy godmother, not a genie."

"Because how often do you get wishes granted?"

"But everything I wish for turns out wrong. I'm obviously as bad at wishing as I am at everything else."

"You're not bad at everything, moron."

"Oh, yeah? I'd like to know something I'm good at."

"Granted!"

Alex groaned as the scenery changed. His comfortable study faded out and he was in what looked like a hotel convention room. At least he was no longer in a ragged, bloodied pirate costume. He wore a neatly tailored suit, shirt and tie and good shoes. People were gathered around, shoving things towards him. With a sinking feeling, he recognized copies of *Stormwing.*

"Mr. Daniels." It was like a tribal chant. "Mr. Daniels, would you sign this, please? It's for my son, my daughter, my aunt, my poodle. Mr. Daniels, where do you get your ideas? Are the characters based on anyone you know? Mr. Daniels, are there plans for a sequel? Why did you make your hero's best friend gay? Are you gay? Do you believe in vampires?"

Alex stopped backing away from the admirers and stared at the person who had asked this last question. She was a short, plump middle-aged woman with short fair hair, wearing a Forever Knight t-shirt.

"Actually," he said, just to her, "yes, I do. Excuse me, I need to call my agent."

He turned and ran. When he'd covered enough distance, he called out for Noni to rescue him.

"Can't handle fame, huh?" the fairy godmother blew clove cigarette smoke at him. "Nothing makes you happy."

Alex sank into the nearest chair. "I was just asked if I believe in vampires. Be glad they didn't ask if I believe in fairies."

"I'm doing my best. You're the toughest case I've ever had."

"Do you not enjoy the challenge?" Alex asked, grinning at her as he lit another slim black panatela.

"No."

Their eyes met, glaring, then they both looked away at the same time.

"So now what?" Noni asked. "Cowboy? Cavalier? Cossack?"

"Are you stuck on the letter C?"

"What do you believe you are good at, Alex?"

He shrugged. "Good at being a defunct type. The international playboy gambler seems to be a specter of the past."

"Playboy?" she snorted. "Oh, yes, I've seen your way of handling women. As smooth as gravel, you are."

"Not all women are as irritating as you."

"Let's see you in action, hotshot."

He was wearing a burnoose and a turban. He was entering a tent in which a scantily clad, slightly plump woman with too much eye make-up was lying in an abandoned posture on a long fainting couch. Desert winds howled outside the tent, except that they weren't howling because although the tent shook in the wind, there was no sound. There was also no colour. Everything—the tent, the couch, the scanty outfit, the woman, the burnoose—was glorious black and white. The woman was probably beautiful in colour, she had long fair hair and nice curves.

"What the hell?" Alex asked. His lips moved, and that was what he meant to say, but no sound came out.

Words appeared on a card projected onto the tent wall. "Have no fear, my desert blossom, I am here to rescue you!"

The woman read the words, and looked at Alex. "Who the hell are you?" her lips formed.

The tent wall accordingly projected, "Ah, my hero! But beware the evil sheik Jafar al-Wampyr, for he will kill you if he finds you here."

Alex stared at the shaky projection of words, then looked down at the woman. She shrugged. "Jafar al-Wampyr?" he repeated incredulously. "Are you kidding?" He moved his lips carefully, so that she might be able to read the actual words he was forming.

The tent, on the other hand, cheerfully interpreted his

response as "Hah hah! I laugh at that pathetic villain! He shall not defeat me and my stalwart brothers of the desert!"

"What brothers of the desert?" said the woman's lips.

"Oh, you are so brave, my hero! Kiss me!" The tent wall interpreted.

"Okay," Alex grinned and kissed her. Even in black and white, she was pretty and he was on trial to see how well he did romancing women.

"What are you doing?" she mouthed at him when her lips were free. "Who are you?"

"Oh, there is no time, my brave, passionate fool!" This was from the tent, which Alex was beginning to dislike quite intensely. "Jafar al-Wampyr will be here any moment!"

"I'm Alex Goldanias," he told the woman. "Who are you?"

"I fear nothing! Bring him on!" This, predictably, from the tent.

"Deb Haydon. Nice to meet you, I think. What are you doing here?"

They were getting quite adept at lip-reading and were actively ignoring the tent, which interpreted Deb's response as "I hear his evil steps outside the tent. Quickly, my love, draw your scimitar!"

"You wouldn't believe me."

"Never fear, my desert rose! I will protect you!"

"I'm not even sure what I'm doing here."

"Oh, he is coming in! Help, help!"

Indeed, the tent flaps parted and a tall, menacing figure in a hooded black burnoose entered.

"Hah hah, my pretty!" chortled the tent wall. "You think your true love can protect you from the evil sheik Jafar al-Wampyr? I shall challenge him to a duel to the death on the sands!"

All three of them stared at the wall. The black-clad intruder had not, as far as could be determined, actually said anything. He cast his hood back and drew closer to the projected card.

"What the hell is that?" he asked, turning around.

Alex's jaw dropped. Jafar al-Wampyr had shoulder-length platinum blond hair and eyes that looked like they might be blue if there was colour in this peculiar setting. He had the sort of beautiful features usually seen on figures on Christmas cards with captions like "Hark" or "Fear not," but he also had fangs and undoubtedly there was a heavy-metal rock band's logo somewhere on that burnoose.

"Francis?" Alex asked.

The tent wall projection wavered a bit, but gamely shot up the words "Your evil ploys are at an end, Jafar al-Wampyr! I, the Son of the Desert, challenge you for this fair maiden."

"Alex?" The younger vampire shook his head. "What is going on here? One minute, I'm walking out to my Harley, next minute, I'm wearing a damn dress and everything's black and white." He noticed Deb Haydon. "Hey," he nodded. "Francis Calvert."

"Deb Haydon," she said faintly.

They all turned to the tent wall. It flickered and began to project, "Your puny efforts strike no fear into me, Son of the Desert! I am Jafar al-Wampyr, possessor of the secret of—" and then it gave up and smoke rose from the tent wall.

"Did you, by any chance, happen to wish for a fairy godmother?" Alex asked the confused Deb Haydon.

"How'd you know?"

"Fairy godmother?" Francis stared at them both.

"Long story," said Deb.

"Be grateful you didn't ask to be a pirate," Alex told her. "You really don't want to go there."

"I just wanted a little romance in my life," Deb sighed. "Something out of the ordinary."

"I wanted a change from routine, too," Alex nodded. "It does prove what they say about wishing is true."

"Why is everything monochrome?" Francis asked. "Where are we, anyway?"

"Somewhere that our respective fairy godmothers cooked up," Alex grunted. "Say," he said to Deb, "your fairy godmother wouldn't happen to be a smart-mouthed punk girl named Noni, would she?"

Deb sat up on the couch. "Yes. Looks like she's got a hell of a sense of humour."

"Where do you live?" Alex asked, sitting beside her.

"Boston. How about you?"

"A little place in Maine. Do you like vampire novels?"

Francis snorted. "This is all very cute and romantic, but I've got a hot date waiting for me at the China Clipper. So can we get the fuck out of here?"

"I've never read any," Deb admitted. "But I've seen a couple of vampire movies. Why?"

Francis threw up his hands and stormed out of the tent. He was back in under a minute. "There's nothing out there. Literally nothing. Seriously creepy. Can we go home?"

Having discovered a serious lack of writing materials to get Deb's phone number, Alex sighed and agreed. "Noni!" he called out.

And he was back in Valley Mansion, dressed in his usual clothing, without either Deb or Francis.

"What was that all about?" he demanded.

"Testing your playboy instincts," Noni said.

"As Rudolph Valentino? Wasn't he gay?"

"It was supposed to be a romantic setting! Most guys would kill to play the Sheik."

"I liked Deb Haydon. Can you get me her phone number?"

"You haven't learned a damn thing from all of this, have you?" she demanded, getting up and glaring at him.

"Yes. I've learned that having a fairy godmother can be hazardous to your health."

"Fine! I'll just go away and let you go back to your miserable existence, then."

"Fine!" Alex yelled back at her.

And she was gone, leaving only a hint of clove and PVC in her wake.

Alex searched the entire house, even the locked tower rooms. He apologized for disturbing Mrs. Jenkins. There was no sign of Noni. He picked up the phone and called the China Clipper, asking the receptionist if she'd seen Francis Calvert come in that night. She had, and asked if there was a message, but Alex decided against it.

Had it happened at all? He went back to his study, a bit perplexed. Maybe it had been a dream, although vampires weren't noted for having them. And there were those unfiltered clove cigarette butts in his ashtray. He looked at the pile of papers beside his typewriter. At least he had a few new ideas for *Killing Cousins.*

The telephone rang, and he strode towards it. "Got it, Mrs. Jenkins," he called out and picked it up.

"Is this...Alex Goldanias?" asked a hesitant female voice.

"Speaking. Who's calling, please?"

"This is Deb Haydon. We, uh... met in a tent?"

A slow smile began to form at the edges of Alex's handsome mouth.

"Thanks, Noni," he whispered.

There was a definite twinkle in the air.

Mistress Estella
(2003)

The dishes clinked in the drainer as Ray Griffin finished tidying up from dinner. A mundane, domestic sound from a mundane, domestic chore. Bachelor he might be, but that was no excuse for not doing housework, at least the more obvious kind. There were probably dust bunnies evolving their own species behind the couch.

The key word there, he reflected as he left the dishes to drain dry (there were limits, after all), was "bachelor." These days, that word seemed to conjure up a bevy of Hollywood-eager women vying to be contestants with a man as the prize. Or was it the other way around? He found reality TV too damn depressing to pay much attention; it all came down to human beings being treated like objects. At any rate, he certainly wasn't the type of bachelor that they made TV series about. At least not reality type TV series with women trying to be the one he picked. More like, he thought without bitterness, the type of TV series with the word "Dark" in the title, involving women trying not to be the one he picked.

There weren't very many bachelors around who were former black sorcerers, complete with a collection of stomach-churning scars, a nifty tattoo of a pentacle, a gold earring, a falcon familiar who'd been conjured out of his own blood and pain, and an underground workshop hollowed out of a cliff. There probably was enough material there for a TV series, Ray thought as he tossed some meat scraps to said falcon, but nobody would call it reality.

Andrei shrieked, and flapped over to land on his master's shoulder.

"How about some TV?" Ray asked.

The falcon shrieked again, which Ray generously translated

as "Sure, as long as it's *Animal Planet.*"

Andrei launched himself off Ray's shoulder and into the living room, where he settled on a specially built perch. His master followed.

As he sank into his favourite chair in front of the idiot box, Ray found himself violently longing for a cigarette. It had been six, no almost seven years since he'd quit, and still the cravings caught him off-guard. It would have given his hands something to do as he watched TV and contemplated the long, lonely evening, one in a series of long, lonely evenings stretching into the echoing abyss of...

"Ring. Ring. Ring."

Damn. "Hello?"

"Hello, Ray." Mary Fairlawn's terminally cheerful voice greeted him.

"Hi, Mary. How's everyone at Fairlawn?"

"We're all fine. I'm just calling to make sure you remembered that you're coming over for dinner tomorrow night. I'm making fried chicken."

For Mary Fairlawn's fried chicken, grown men had been known to crawl on their knees up mountains. She didn't make it very often, on account of a cholesterol count in the outer stratosphere, but when she did, she invariably invited Ray to come and share it. She seemed to think he needed fattening up.

"Of course I'll be there, Mary. Can I bring anything?" It was a ritual question.

"Just yourself and Andrei," was the ritual answer.

"Okay, I'll be there at six."

He hung up, and turned on the TV. The long, lonely evening, one of a series of long, lonely evenings, stretched out before him into the echoing abyss of...

"Knock, knock."

Damn.

He got up, noting that Andrei hadn't stirred or given him warning. That's how he knew who to expect even before he opened the door.

"Hey, Ray."

"Hey, Francis," he nodded, standing aside so that the blond young vampire could come in. "What's up?"

"Nothing much," Francis shrugged, zipping off his leather jacket and struggling out of his engineer boots. "Just thought I'd drop over and see what you were doing."

"As a matter of fact, I was contemplating the long, lonely

evening, one in a series of long, lonely evenings stretching into the echoing abyss of dismal eternity."

"Man, you have got to stop reading Kafka. What's on the tube?"

Francis didn't have satellite TV. (Nobody out on the Cliff Road had cable, it was too far from town, but nearly everybody had a dish). He lived in a ramshackle, self-built shack next door that barely had electricity. As a result, he spent a lot of time with Ray. The mage didn't mind; it was company, of a sort, even if the shows they watched tended to be heavy on the jiggles and short on plot or character development.

"I promised Andrei I'd let him watch *Animal Planet,"* Ray said.

"You're spoiled," Francis informed the falcon, who shook his wings at the vampire. "Hey, I brought the beer this time." He held up a six pack.

"Make yourself at home," Ray said.

Francis did so, flopping sideways onto the couch, cracking open a can, and taking possession of the remote. He had a hole in one of his socks, Ray noted—another bachelor.

Of all the Brotherhood, Francis was Ray's closest friend, and a total mystery. He knew the stories of all the other vampires; he knew how Mitch Pritchard had become a werewolf; he knew the Druids and their long, tangled history. All he knew about Francis was that the boy had become a vampire at age 19 (mental age about 12 and a half), and that it had been a woman who had turned him. Francis refused to talk about anything else—who he had been, who his family was, even where he'd been born. His accent was New England, but that covered a lot of territory. His name—Francis Xavier Calvert—seemed to suggest that he'd come from money, and he was rather pretty for a male, but he didn't behave like someone who'd grown up rich.

Ray shrugged. One of these days, he was sure, Francis would open up.

However, what he said tonight was "Let's go to the fair."

"The fair?" Ray's eyebrows quirked, stretching one or two of his myriad scars in interesting ways. "That's for the kids and the tourists."

"So? I'm a kid. You can be a tourist if you like."

Ray sighed. Francis was his best friend, but he was also as annoying as hell, and half his schemes ended up causing trouble—usually for Ray. "The accidental tourist, maybe," he said wryly.

Francis just grinned. It was absolutely useless to try and

make him feel guilty, even about the time a few years ago when he'd caused a motorcycle accident that had left Ray with a badly broken leg.

"Come on, Griff," Francis coaxed him. He knew that Ray hated being called "Griff." "It'll be fun. We can play Whack-A-Mole."

Ray thought about it. Usually the only Cliff Roaders who went to the annual Fletcherville Summer Fair were the Fairlawns. Likely even they weren't going this year. Galen and Vivain were a bit too old now for kiddie rides and cotton candy.

"We'll surprise the hell out of the townies." It was a feeble protest, and Ray knew he'd lost.

"I hear they have a wicked good fortune teller," Francis said.

"You've been here too long. You're talking like a Mainer. 'Wicked good?'" Ray shook his head. "If you say 'Ayeh,' I swear I'll turn you into a toad."

The perennially young vampire laughed. "Come on. We'll take the bikes, they'll be easier to park."

Shortly thereafter, two motorcycles roared down the Cliff Road towards the town. The fair was set up behind the civic centre in the large park, both of which had been established with generous donations. The donor wished to remain anonymous. Ray and Francis and the townspeople, should they wish to admit it, knew perfectly well that the donor was Gideon Redoak.

The fair was easy to spot—just head for the spider web of lights that delineated the Ferris wheel. Orange-vested volunteers with flashlights directed traffic to available parking. Ray and Francis left the bikes where they were told. Francis' Harley quietly dripped oil and rust onto the gravel while Ray's beautifully restored Norton Commando did nothing so socially unacceptable.

"That bike of yours is an absolute sin," Ray commented as they queued up to pay their admission fees.

A shrug was his only answer. It cost them five dollars each to get into the fair. A sign assured them that all proceeds went to charity. Inside the snow-fence gates, booths and rides lined what were normally soccer fields and baseball diamonds. Most of the rides were for the under-ten set, but there were a few for adult thrill-seekers. The Ferris wheel was popular with young couples hoping to get stuck up at the top.

"Hey, water guns!" Francis was examining the various games where idlers could spend twenty dollars trying to win a stuffed animal worth five. "And they've got that balloons and darts thing."

"I thought you wanted to play Whack-A-Mole."

"Yes, but one must savour the anticipation. You can't rush

right into Whack-A-Mole. You have to save it for later, so as not to ruin the purity of the moment."

Ray crossed his arms. "Francis, have you ever considered therapy?"

"Let's try the good old tossing rings onto bottles game," said Francis, as if he had not heard.

"You can't win at that game. It's rigged." But Ray followed Francis anyway.

"All proceeds to charity, remember?"

Even so, Ray found himself studying the array of bottles and multi-coloured plastic rings. Gaudy stuffed animals hung from the supports of the booth, lures to the unwary. You had to get a ring on one of the specially marked bottles to win a prize. It wasn't utterly impossible, just highly improbable.

Francis paid for a handful of plastic rings and handed half of them to Ray. "Bet I win something before you do."

"What's the bet?"

"A six-pack. And no cheating."

It was Ray's turn to look innocent, or at least as innocent as his hard-bitten appearance allowed. "What do you mean, no cheating?"

"No using magic to help you win."

"I'd never dream of it."

"Yeah, right," the vampire grunted.

"Okay, then," the mage nodded. "No using your vampire mind whammy powers to make them think you've won."

"Deal."

They'd attracted a small crowd by now, though fortunately none of them had overheard this exchange. The sheer novelty of seeing two of the usually reclusive Cliff Road Crowd had drawn the spectators. While the Fairlawns were frequently spotted in town, Ray and Francis were far rarer sights. Fletchervillians couldn't resist getting a good look. A few tourists had drifted over as well, to see what the townies were looking at.

Francis grinned and waved at the spectators, loving the attention. A handful of teenage girls perked up and waved back at the pretty boy. Ray wished he had a hat to pull down over his eyes. He threw his rings, missing the targets.

The vampire stopped hamming it up and tossed his rings. The first four missed. One did snag a bottle, but not one of the marked ones. The sixth, however, settled perfectly over the neck of a prize winner.

"We have a winnah!" the booth operator shouted. "The young

man wins his choice!"

Francis looked startled, but rallied admirably. "I want the blue dinosaur."

A gigantic blue dinosaur was unhooked from the ceiling and handed over. It was more than half the size of Francis.

Ray fought a laugh and lost. "How the hell are you going to get that home?"

Francis looked at his prize in some dismay. The Harley did not have a sidecar. Then he remembered the teenage girls. One of them was still hanging around, trying not to look hopeful. He picked up his prize and carried it over to her.

"Would you like to have this?" he asked her.

"Yeah!" Her expression made it clear that she thought the dinosaur was second best.

"I'll trade you for your name and phone number."

Back at the booth, Ray exchanged amused looks with the operator.

"How'd he do that, anyway?" asked the carny. "It's almost impossible to win this game."

Ray shrugged, enjoying himself hugely. "Maybe it was magic."

"Sure."

"I hear the fortune teller here is pretty good," Ray said casually.

"Mistress Estella," the carny nodded. "She's kind of spooky."

Ray put this down as advertising hyperbole. He didn't really want to go to a fortune teller. But he knew, without even consulting Mistress Estella, that his very near future included a visit to her. Francis really wasn't that subtle. They'd come here to see this "wicked good" psychic, not to win stuffed animals or throw up on the Tilt A Whirl.

Which was why Ray was determined to torment Francis. It had already cost him five bucks and a six-pack to be named later, but it was worth every last cent.

Francis didn't win every game he played, or even every second game. That would have made him suspicious. But by the time he'd traded up to an enormous St. Bernard at Whack-A-Mole, he'd run out of potential girlfriends and was reduced to donating his prize to a six year-old boy.

"Happy now?" Ray asked. The most he'd won was a small stuffed donkey in a silly hat, which he kept.

They were walking past a booth selling the usual fairground snacks. The smell of sugar and popcorn wafted tantalizingly on the night breeze. Francis stopped and sniffed, and an odd, almost wistful expression appeared on his face.

"Happy?" he repeated. "No."

Ray instantly regretted the bit of fun he'd been having with his friend. Francis seldom expressed his feelings about being a vampire. To be here, among this happy, sweating, breathing, eating, living crowd of humans and never, ever, really be a part of it...

"No," Francis repeated, the look vanishing. "I really wanted that St. Bernard."

"Oh, for...come on! Let's go see this 'wicked good' fortune teller of yours. Maybe she'll tell you that you're going to win ten more prizes at the water guns."

The fortune teller's tent had a line. Apparently Francis was not the only one to have heard of Mistress Estella's reputation. Ray left Francis in line and went to get something to eat. Tactfully, he finished his hot dog before rejoining the vampire.

The line moved slowly, giving Ray lots of time to reflect on why he was so reluctant to do this. Odds were that Mistress Estella was an outright fraud. It was possible that she might have a touch of the Sight. Many psychics had it, in small measures. A touch of the Sight, a dose of intuition, some good guesswork and a fair knowledge of human psychology, and you had a "wicked good" fortune teller. No possible threat to Ray or the Brotherhood.

So then why were his senses, honed by nearly thirty years' accumulated training and practice in the occult, screaming at him to get the hell away from here?

Francis didn't seem to feel it. But then, he was a vampire. His senses were different, attuned to other stimuli. With all of these people around, the smell of their blood would be nearly overwhelming. Given Francis' oaths not to attack humans within town, it must have been like being stranded in a pasta bar while on the Atkins diet.

Suddenly, it was their turn to go in to see Mistress Estella.

The tent was dark, lit by a few candles. A table with two chairs, one on either side, stood in the middle. Two more chairs sat against one wall of the tent, along with another long, narrow table. There was no crystal ball anywhere in sight. Nor was anything within the tent particularly occult-looking. Not one star or moon. No pentacles, incense, Eye of Horus, pyramids, wizard figurines or dream catchers. Ray felt his hackles rise. Only one kind of person was as supremely confident as all that. The only type of person who could do away with all the paraphernalia was the type of person who didn't need it.

"Mistress Estella travels light," Francis remarked.

"Visit as many summers fairs as I do," remarked a voice, "and you'd travel light, too."

They both turned. A woman had entered through a side flap of the tent. *Without either of us noticing,* Ray thought. It wasn't a happy thought. It's hard to sneak up on a vampire.

She was rather ordinary-looking, really. No beauty of the ship-launching variety. Neither tall nor short, dark nor fair, fat nor slim, voluptuous nor flat-chested. Her hair was black, her eyes brown, her features Middle-European, her accent pure Middle-American. She wore a white frilled blouse, a flowered skirt, and sandals. Her long hair hung in a pony tail. She had two small gold hoop earrings, but no bangles and no scarves. It was possible that she was a gypsy. It was equally possible that she was a check-out girl at the local supermarket.

"Well, now," an amused smile tugged at her lips as she looked them over. "Who wants to go first?"

"Oh, Ray's the only one here for a reading," Francis replied. "I'm just here to make sure he gets it."

"Then sit over there," the fortune teller indicated the chairs over to the side, "And keep quiet."

She watched Francis comply with this request, her eyes narrowed. It wasn't the usual look that young women gave the beautiful vampire.

Mistress Estella (and Ray couldn't help the stray thought that the name sounded more like a dominatrix than a palm-reader) turned to her customer.

"Cards or palm?" she asked.

"Don't I have to cross your palms with silver?"

"I prefer paper money," Mistress Estella answered. "It's easier to carry. Five dollars for palm, ten for the cards."

Ray looked in his wallet. It echoed. "Palm."

They sat down at the table and he showed her his left hand. It was as if he had handed her something with a live current running through it. Her eyes widened and she gasped, dropping his hand.

"Who are you?"

"Raymond Griffin."

"That is only a name you wear."

"It's the only one I've got." Ray was really wishing that he'd listened to his instincts.

"Let me see your palm again."

Francis stirred on his chair. "You don't have to, Ray. This was a mistake. Give him his five bucks back, and we're out of here."

"I told you to keep quiet!" Estella snapped at him. She took Ray's hand again, turning it palm side up, flinching so slightly that he almost didn't catch it.

She didn't talk about the length of his life line, or trace the heart line, or study the patterns of swirls and whirls. She didn't comment on the old scar that marred part of his palm.

"There is blood here. Power bought with blood. The power always has a high price. There are echoes in this hand, echoes of screams. This hand has done evil. But its wielder is not evil. Your past is written clearly here." Her eyes briefly met his, and he saw...pity? Understanding? Horror? "But it is your past. You have spent too long doing nothing, remembering the past, and going nowhere. There are many choices, paths ahead of you."

"How do I know which is the right one?" Ray asked.

"Simply choose. This stasis is not a choice."

"So you can't actually see my future?"

"If you do nothing, then you have none. The future is unclear because you dwell on your past. You must act to make a future." She released his hand, unable to suppress a look of relief. "This reading has ended."

Ray stood up, a bit shakily. "Thank you. I think."

"Sheesh, you call that fortune-telling?" Francis scoffed. "Read my palm, Estella!"

Her eyes blazed with anger and contempt. "There is nothing there to read. You have no future. You are dead."

"Not too many dead guys drive a Harley," Francis retorted, unruffled.

"Vampire," she spat. She looked at Ray. "Consorting with the dead is one reason why you are caught in this stasis. They do not learn, do not change. It can be contagious."

"Francis is my friend," said Ray quietly. He looked at the vampire. "We're leaving." He turned to Estella. "That's one choice."

They walked out of the tent. Ray was almost surprised to find that the fair was still in full swing. Rides whirled, bells rang, children ran laughing.

"What the fuck was that all about?" Francis asked.

"She has the true Sight," Ray said. "Among other things."

"She knows I'm a vampire. Should we do something about that?"

"I doubt very much that she'll tell anybody."

Choices. Paths. No future if he stayed in place and did nothing, but no hint of what it was he should do instead. He looked at his hands.

There is blood here. Power bought with blood.

"You okay?" Francis asked. "That was a pretty weird reading. I thought it would be the usual 'you will meet a pretty girl, fall madly in love, and have eighteen children' crap."

"Why on earth would I want eighteen children?" Ray asked, distracted and aghast at the thought.

"Well, it would certainly be a choice," Francis grinned.

"Fuck off."

"That would be another choice, yes."

"At the moment, I'm choosing to go home," Ray said, striding towards the parking area.

Francis opened his mouth to protest, decided that it would probably be the single most stupid thing he'd ever do, and firmly closed his mouth again. "Home's good with me," he said with uncharacteristic meekness.

There are echoes in this hand. Echoes of screams.

Ray arrived home safely, shooed Francis on his way, fed Andrei, stripped out of his clothes and went to stand under the shower. The water swirling down the drain refused to surrender to narrative drama and turn red. But it was a sleepless night.

You have spent too long doing nothing, going nowhere.

The next day he drove back to the fairgrounds, but he didn't have ten dollars to go and see Mistress Estella again. He wasn't even sure he wanted to, but he needed to talk to someone.

Not Francis. Francis was a drinking buddy, a pal, the kind of guy you hung around with in high school. Ray had never actually gone to high school, but the analogy held. He couldn't talk to Francis. No, there was only one person he could trust with this. The person to whom, sooner or later, everyone in the Brotherhood turned.

"Walk with me," Michael said.

This was his usual routine when someone came to him with a problem. Walk through the gardens at Fairlawn, let the ritual of the walk order your mind and put things in perspective. Let the beauty of the gardens, now a kaleidoscope of summer colour, ease the urgency until you could speak clearly. Let the garden heal.

"You've been to see the fortune teller at the summer fair," Michael said as they reached the outer edge of the gardens.

"Francis told you," said Ray.

The Archdruid chuckled. "So, you are prepared to grant Estella the Sight, but not me?"

"I...sorry."

"Actually, Francis did tell me. I don't read thoughts unless I've been invited to. Does this Estella truly have the Sight?"

"She knew that Francis is a vampire."

Michael dismissed this evidence with a wave. "That could simply be acute observation skills. All that's needed is to notice that he doesn't breathe."

They do not learn, do not change.

Ray shoved his hands into the pockets of his jeans. "She has the Sight."

"Ah."

The really comforting thing about Michael was that he knew when not to ask questions.

"Am I achieving anything by staying here?" Ray asked.

"It is not always necessary to achieve. Sometimes it is merely necessary to be."

"Thank you, Yoda."

Michael sighed. "Sorry, didn't mean to sound so utterly Zen. What exactly did she tell you?"

"That I have no future as long as I remain unchanging."

"But you have changed," Michael pointed out. "I remember a young man who was so afraid that he hid behind arrogance and bluster. Where is he now?"

A wry smile answered him. "Still here. Just older and wiser."

"Wiser implies learning, which implies change."

"Ah, but lately?"

"Do you feel the need to change?"

"I didn't until last night."

Michael contemplated a riotous display of begonias in silence. Ray fidgeted, but managed to hold his tongue.

"What else did she say to you, Ray?" the Archdruid asked the begonias. "Why do you have your hands in your pockets?"

This hand has done evil.

"You noticed." Ray took them out, trying to look casual.

"You're not going to go all Lady MacBeth on us, are you?" The words were light, but his tone wasn't.

"I hope I'm a bit more stable than that."

"She told you that you have blood on your hands, didn't she?" This was not asked of the begonias.

"It's true."

"Yes," Michael nodded. "But so what?"

"What?"

"She also told you that you are not evil, am I right?"

Ray's head lifted. "How did you know that?"

"Because you aren't evil. As for the not having a future if you don't change or make a choice..." Michael shrugged. "It's not something I really like to do, trying to see the future. The temptation to change it or force it to come true is sometimes overwhelming. Still, there are things I cannot help knowing." His expression was unreadable.

Ray wasn't insensitive enough to ask what those things might be. "She told me that simply making a choice was the right answer."

"Don't choose simply for the sake of what some fortune teller said," Michael answered, again speaking to the begonias. "Know what the choices are first, and consider the consequences. Make it an informed choice, not an impulsive one." Michael turned to look at his friend. "No more snow banks, Ray."

"I promise."

"What did she tell Francis about his future?"

"She said he didn't have one, because he was dead. She told me that consorting with the dead was one reason why I didn't change, because they never do."

"Ah-hah. There, you see, she doesn't know everything. Vampires can change."

"I wish Francis would change his socks more often."

"She disturbed you very much, didn't she?"

"Yes."

"Then likely she spoke to something deep inside of you, a need for change, for choices, that you have not admitted to yourself. Give yourself some time to think this over. I wonder if I should go and see Mistress Estella."

"She would most likely refuse to talk to you. She flinched when she held my hand, and she wouldn't touch Francis."

"If she backed away from a harmless boy vampire, perhaps I should send Alex or Gideon to see her."

Ray found himself smiling. "I had no idea you were so vindictive."

"When one of my friends is disturbed, and another one insulted, I can be. Go on home, Ray, and try not to let this disconcert you. If you feel yourself becoming obsessed with what she told you, come and see me. I shall speak to Francis, as well."

"I don't think it bothered him very much."

"Nobody likes to be told they have no future, Ray," Michael's rebuke was mild. "Not even the undead."

"No, I guess not. Thanks, Michael. You've helped."

"That's what I'm here for." Michael had to resist the urge to give Ray a hug. The mage didn't like to be touched unless he initiated the contact. It had been brave of him to let a total stranger touch his hand, and look what had happened! If Michael had had Mistress Estella nearby at that moment...he shook his head. Michael didn't know what he'd actually do to the fortune teller. He was not a man of violence. Not for centuries, at any rate.

Ray went home to feed Andrei, then decided to take the falcon out for some exercise. Andrei liked the beach, and the one below the cliffs was currently inaccessible due to a little thing called high tide. The public beach in Fletcherville would still have some sand, and the locals were more or less used to the sight of the falcon chasing the lure along the shoreline. He put Andrei in his cage and the cage into the car—trying to drive a motorcycle while hanging on to an excited falcon wasn't highly recommended.

There were some people on the beach, this being midsummer, but few of them paid much attention to Ray. He knew he looked odd in long sleeves and jeans on a beach in late June, especially all in black. Something else for the tourists to gawk at. He shrugged. He set up the perch in the sand, really pounding it in so it wouldn't collapse under Andrei's weight, and let the falcon out. Shrieking with excitement, making some heads turn, Andrei flew up to the perch and stayed there, watching Ray intently.

Ray walked down the beach to a spot perhaps thirty yards from the perch. A few spectators gathered to watch, falconry not being a common sight on a beach, but neither Ray nor Andrei paid them any heed. The human put on his falconry glove and started to swing the lure. Andrei's eyes followed it until Ray whistled the signal. The falcon launched into the air, soaring over the heads of the spectators, making some of them duck. He flew past the swinging lure, faking a snatch at it, and issuing a shriek of falcon laughter. He spiralled high into the sky, then came diving down and snatched the lure neatly in mid-swing, carrying it back to his perch. Another whistle, and he flew neatly to Ray's glove, bloodied corpse in beak, gulping it down.

People applauded, and Ray grinned. "Shows are at two, four and six daily. Pay what you can."

A few people laughed, even fewer made gestures as if to hunt for coins. Though he was sorely tempted to accept the offers, Ray shook his head to show he'd been kidding. If any of Fletcherville's finest had happened to be on the beach, he could get in trouble for soliciting. They'd just love to pin something on one of the Cliff

Road Crowd.

"Don't I have to cross your palms with silver?" asked a familiar voice from the small crowd.

Ray looked over, and sure enough, there was Mistress Estella, still plainly dressed, taking a scarf off her head.

"I prefer bills. They're easier to carry."

"I believe what I said is that I prefer paper money." But she smiled.

Andrei ruffled his feathers at her. She wore shiny hoop earrings again, and the falcon loved shiny earrings. Ray had the scars on his ear, next to his own earring, to prove it.

"You might want to cover up with that scarf again," Ray said as the rest of the crowd, sensing that the falconry demonstration was over, started drifting away to their own pursuits. "Andrei wants your earrings."

"Andrei? That's an odd name for a falcon, considering it means 'manly.'" Estella put the scarf back on, covering the earrings.

"It can also mean brave," Ray said calmly. "Besides, why can't a falcon be manly? Men can be hawkish."

"I suppose, but that's not a real falcon, is it?"

Andrei slurped down the last of the dead critter that had been the lure, looking remarkably like a real falcon. Ray raised his glove and the falcon took off, looping around Estella, and flew back to his perch. He still looked like a real falcon.

"I won't ask how you know," Ray sighed, scuffing sand over the slight mess Andrei had made on the beach. "Should I bother to ask why you're here?"

"Aren't gypsy fortune tellers allowed a day at the beach?"

"Are you really a gypsy?"

"Does it matter?"

Ray didn't glare at her, though he was considering it. Magic itched along his fingers, begging to be used. She'd be a particularly fetching toad, for example...no. For one thing, he couldn't really turn someone into an animal. For another thing, he couldn't use magic in public.

"Don't you have a tent you should be in?"

"I only work after sunset. Something like your friend, the dead thing."

"Francis isn't a dead thing. And that's not really something you should say on a public beach, anyway."

She drew back the scarf again, risking imminent falcon attack on her ears. "You don't like me." This revelation did not appear to bother her.

"You've given me very little cause to, so far. Now, excuse me, I should get Andrei back home before it gets dark." He started walking towards the perch, from which Andrei was watching them both suspiciously.

"It's the middle of the afternoon," Estella pointed out.

Ray stopped and looked back at her. "What do you *want?*"

"From you? Nothing."

"And you shall receive it. In abundance." He stalked falcon-wards.

"Rocky Horror Picture Show!" she called after him.

He grit his teeth and ignored her. Andrei ruffled his feathers and shrieked. It sounded like laughter.

"Great, you, too?" Ray asked his falcon familiar, with a sigh. "Come on, let's get out of here." He held up his gloved hand, to get Andrei to jump on it for easier ingress to the cage.

But Andrei didn't want to go. He ruffled his feathers, screamed, and hopped into the air. Ray swore at him, which didn't help. He could see Estella, standing where he'd left her thirty yards down the beach, and she was laughing. *Great, just fucking great.*

Andrei flew towards her, aiming for those enticing earrings. A large brown falcon suddenly swooping at her ears disconcerted her, and she ducked and gave a yell.

"Don't move!" Ray called at her, but the wind snatched his words away. "Oh, damn." He whistled and took another bloody lure out of his bag. "Andrei!" He mimed pulling a scarf over his head with his free hand as he waved the tiny corpse of a field mouse at the falcon to get Andrei's attention.

With another of his laughter-imitating shrieks, the falcon obeyed. Ray shoved him hastily into the cage, snack and all, absently-mindedly wiping the blood off on his jeans. With Andrei safely locked up, he walked over to Estella.

"I told you he wanted your earrings."

"It's rude to say I told you so," sniffed the fortune teller.

"It was a choice to say it," Ray's smile was wicked.

"That isn't what I meant, and you know it!" she snapped, sounding now far more like a supermarket check-out girl than a fairground clairvoyant. She straightened her scarf, tucking the earrings back out of sight. "I can't help what I see," she said, more calmly.

"Perhaps not. But perhaps you could be a bit more diplomatic in how you phrase some things."

She glared at him. "The dead belong buried. I don't like vampires."

"Have you ever actually gotten to know one?"

"Yes." Somehow, that one word, one syllable, told an entire story. Ray wished he knew what it was. Obviously, for a start, she'd met the wrong vampire.

"What—"

"Don't."

He shrugged. "It's your choice."

He walked back to the perch, which he pulled out of the sand. With it tucked under one arm, and the other hand holding Andrei's cage, he started to walk to the car. A vocal accompaniment from the cage informed him that the falcon was not happy with this situation.

"He sounds upset," said Estella.

She'd caught up to them while Ray was struggling with the perch, and was trailing behind the mage slightly as he walked to the car.

"I don't like being followed. He's picking up my mood."

"I'm not following you. My car is here, too."

"Fine, whatever."

He turned his back, determined not to speak to her again. This lasted approximately five minutes.

"You never did answer my question," she said, sandalled feet slipping in the heavy white sand on a slight slope that lead up to the beach parking lot.

He sighed, set down Andrei's cage and the perch, and turned to give her a hand up. She didn't flinch from the contact this time, but maybe she didn't have her Sight turned on, or something. Ray didn't have a lick of that kind of power; he had no idea how it worked.

"What question?" he asked.

"Thanks." She gained the top of the hill, and smiled at him. Then she realized her hand was still clasped in his and gave him a look. He released her with an evil grin.

"What question?" he repeated.

"Who are you?"

"Just a guy in stasis who hangs out with dead things and has a falcon that isn't a falcon. There's my car. Been lovely chatting with you, but I really must get Andrei home. *Buffy the Vampire Slayer's* on tonight, and I have to cheer for the vampires."

He left her standing on the edge of the parking lot, staring after him.

Dinner at Fairlawn had been wonderful; the best part was no dishes to do afterwards. Well, no, the best part was the fried chicken—and not having to eat dinner alone. It had been a fun evening, after an odd afternoon.

Ray thought about that encounter with Mistress Estella. Was she following him? Though his early experiences in life had left the mage with a healthy dose of paranoia, he doubted it. She couldn't possibly have known that he would come to the beach that afternoon, could she? Well, she was a psychic, but he'd have to be extremely paranoid to believe that she was using her clairvoyance to spy on him. It had just been coincidence.

Too bad he didn't believe in coincidence.

The phone rang in the middle of this train of thought. It was Michael, sounding a bit worried. "Is Francis over there?"

"Not unless he's hiding," Ray said. "I haven't heard from him tonight."

"He's not at home. I dropped by to talk to him about that fortune teller."

"He met about ten girls at the fair, Michael," Ray fought a grin. "He's almost certainly out with one of them."

"Ah." The Archdruid sounded relieved. "If he stops in to see you on his way home from tomcatting, tell him I want to talk to him, okay?"

"Sure."

"How are you doing?"

"Oh, fine. Thanks again for dinner. I was just going to go downstairs and do some work."

"I won't keep you, then." Michael didn't entirely approve of Ray's workshop, but knew better than to criticize another magic-user's techniques. "Good night."

"'Night. Love to Mary and the offspring."

Ray hung up, vaguely worried himself. Michael wasn't the sort to panic over nothing. The Druid was extremely sensitive; he might have picked up something out of place at Francis' shack, making him concerned over the vampire's absence. It was still early in the evening, though, and this was boring little Fletcherville… how could Francis possibly have gotten into trouble?

Aside from being Francis, of course.

Shrugging, Ray decided to take his own advice and not worry about it. Francis was a big boy and had been a vampire since 1968; he could take care of himself. Admittedly, he was practically a fledgling compared to, say, Gideon; but he was still a vampire. There wasn't much that could hurt the undead.

As he walked down the stairs that led to his underground workshop, Ray tried very hard not to think of the things that could harm vampires. He didn't need the distraction of worrying about his best friend right now. He had meditation exercises to do, and for that, he had to have a clear mind. Lack of concentration could kill the unprepared magic-user.

The workshop had been built into a natural cave in the cliff when Ray's house had been constructed. It was sparsely furnished. A worktable, the surface scarred almost as badly as its owner, with a bookshelf above it and a hard wooden chair, were the only furniture. The bookshelf held material that, a few scant centuries ago, would have gotten Ray burnt at the stake. On the table were a candlestick with a stub in it, surrounded by wax, a plastic skull that yelled out "Happy Halloween!" if its button was pressed, and a small metal box that appeared to be covered with frost. A few assorted dried herbs in mason jars were shoved in randomly among the books. A sword, edges sharpened and gleaming, leaned against the far end of the table. Otherwise, the workshop shared something with Estella's tent at the fair. There were no pentacles, no occult signs and symbols, no other magical paraphernalia at all; not so much as an athame.

Ray had a knife in his pocket. It had three blades, a corkscrew, a bottle opener, and a device for taking the stones out of horses' hooves; all tucked into a staghorn handle. It was the only thing he owned that had been his mother's, handed down to her by her father and carefully kept all these years. It was consecrated to absolutely no gods, but the three blades were seriously sharp. It had served him well, and was the only knife he needed.

He sat down in the chair and lit the candle. No matches or lighter required. He tried to clear his mind of all its baggage from the past few days: the fair, Mistress Estella's reading, his talk with Michael, the meeting on the beach, vague worries about Francis. Damn and double damn, it wasn't working. He found himself reaching towards the cold metal box. It contained drawn cards called Trumps, through which Ray could contact the person represented on them.

No. If Francis was out with a girl, he would not appreciate being interrupted by a Trump call. There was nothing wrong. Let it go, and concentrate on the task at hand.

The candle flame danced, though there was little air current down here. Ray concentrated on his breathing. In, out, in, out, in, out. Let the worries go. The past was the past and could not be altered. The future is unknown, fortune tellers be damned. The present is this room, this candle, this exercise. Nothing else mattered.

His mind calmed, peace achieved, Ray rose from his chair. He picked up the sword from its resting place and slowly went through a series of exercises with it, as if fencing with an invisible partner. Finally he finished by holding the sword in *en-garde* position...and releasing the hilt. It hung, unsupported, in mid-air, only the power of his mind holding it in place.

Nobody at all had taught Ray this exercise. He'd made it up himself; found it was the best way to concentrate his mind. When he really needed to fine-tune his control, he would lie naked beneath the suspended blade, one careless moment away from self-disembowelment or castration. One or two of his scars were from lack of concentration with the sword exercise, but fortunately all the important bits of him still functioned.

While he stood there, holding the sword with his mind, open to the power that coursed through his blood, Raymond Griffin knew that his friend Francis was in serious trouble.

Francis had woken at the crack of dusk, as usual for a vampire. He hadn't lost any sleep over the encounter with Estella, but that was because he didn't sleep as mortals defined the word. But he was perturbed at what Estella had said. Not so much on his own account; the idea of lacking a future just because he was dead was laughable. If that was true, then he hadn't had a future since 1968. No, that wasn't it. She'd really upset Ray and Francis didn't like it when his friends were upset. He decided to pay the fortune teller another visit.

Since this was a professional visit, he put on the jeans with the fewest holes in them and a clean Metallica t-shirt. It was, theoretically, possible to dress Francis up, but even in a tux he still acted as if wearing jeans. He tugged on his boots and threw on his leather jacket, then went out to swear at the Harley until it started. He never bothered with a helmet. What was the point?

The fair was going full Tilt-A-Whirl when he arrived. This time, Francis ignored the lure of the games and the smell of food. There weren't too many people lined up at Estella's tent. Grinning to himself in anticipation of the encounter to come, Francis joined the line.

Nothing much happened until it was his turn to go into the tent. As he entered, Estella drew in a breath. But whatever she had to say remained unspoken, as a shadow in the tent moved and stepped in behind Francis. The young vampire tried to turn to look at this unexpected company.

Then the person behind Francis reached out, seized the

young vampire's right arm and twisted it behind its owner's back in an unbreakable "come-along" grip. Francis yelped, but a hand went over his mouth.

"Don't make a fuss, boy," hissed a voice in his ear. "I just want to talk to you. Not a word, Estella!" he warned the fortune teller. "Go and sit down over there."

She did as she was told, her eyes broadcasting an apology and appeal to Francis.

Francis couldn't break free. He should have been able to slip out of that grip like an eel; instead he found himself being held so tightly that he'd have had a problem breathing had he still needed to. The hand over his mouth had no blood smell; neither did the hand's owner.

There was a new vampire in town, and he was a lot stronger than Francis.

Francis fought. He bit, he kicked, he squirmed. His captor only laughed and increased the pressure of his hold. Finally, though, the stranger had had enough.

"Stop fighting me, boy," he snarled, "or a mortal dies for every kick."

Francis had to believe him, for the sake of the fair-goers. This was one powerful vampire, and not only in size. The last time there'd been a vampire of this magnitude in Fletcherville, it had taken the whole Brotherhood to kill him. His only hope was that Estella would tell Ray what had happened here in her tent. Francis hadn't bothered to let anyone know where he was going.

No longer struggling, Francis allowed himself to be taken out of the fairgrounds, through the back ways among the cars and trailers belonging to the carneys. No one disturbed them or even saw them go this way; obviously his captor did not want mortal witnesses. Francis was shoved into the back of a van. There were no windows and the doors had a solid iron bar that slid across the back. He could probably escape by kicking the doors open, but it would take a lot of time. As soon as he was down on the floor of the van, his captor bound him tightly with duct tape and rope; the rope looked like the type of hawsers used to secure ocean liners to the dock. His mouth was duct-taped, too.

It wasn't the first time this stranger had captured another vampire. That wasn't a reassuring thought. It would be nice if Francis had even the faintest idea what this was all about...

Estella found a phone and managed to get Ray's number from information. He was the only person she could think of to call, even though she nearly hated herself for it.

Typical female, she muttered to herself, *turning to the man to help in a crisis.* Yeah, right, so what else was she going to do? Take on a powerful vampire by herself, in order to rescue another vampire? She remembered the surge of magical power that had made her flinch when she'd first touched Ray Griffin's hand. She wasn't turning to just any man, after all, but one who conceivably could actually help.

Ray was almost at the phone, reaching for it, when it rang. Damn telemarketers, calling just when he needed to talk to Michael!

"Hello?" he asked breathlessly.

"Mr. Griffin?" asked a voice that sounded vaguely familiar.

"Yes, who's this?"

"Estella Smith, from the fair."

Ray stared blankly at the phone. Why on earth would she be calling him? "What can I do for you?"

"Your friend Francis is in trouble."

"Yes, I know...how did...never mind. Do you know what's happened to him?"

"I think so, yes. But I shouldn't really say over the phone. How quickly can you be here?"

"Extremely quickly," Ray answered grimly. "May I bring someone with me?"

"No vampires."

"Fine. I'll be there in no time."

"I'll meet you at the gate, so you don't have to pay admission."

"See you there."

He hung up and quickly dialled Fairlawn's number. "Hey, Galen, let me talk to your dad, it's an emergency. Michael, how fast can you get over here? Something's happened to Francis, and that fortune teller knows about it, she wants us to meet her. Okay, I'll wait."

It took Michael very little time to get down the road. The Archdruid merely honked his horn; Ray flew out of the house, admonishing Andrei to stay put, and jumped into Michael's car.

"Floor it!"

"This isn't a Ferrari," Michael said, but went as fast as the Cliff Road allowed.

They arrived at the fair in short order. Estella was waiting for them, having cancelled her remaining readings for the night. She suggested that a fair full of roustabouts looking for trouble at the drop of a "Hey, rube!" was not the best place to talk. Michael and

Ray agreed, and she joined them on the other side of the gates.

"Michael Fairlawn," said Michael, once they were clear of the crowd at the gates.

"Estella Smith," said Estella. She didn't take his extended hand.

Michael raised his eyebrows, but said nothing.

Estella turned to Ray. "We'd better go somewhere to talk, where people can't hear us."

"Michael's the driver," Ray said.

Estella got into Michael's car, not looking entirely certain that this was a good thing. Then she noticed that there were muddy footprints on the car floor, gum and candy wrappers strewn about, a deflated soccer ball, a three ring binder, and a torn mitten all abandoned to their fate.

"You have children! All right, I'll trust you. Drive on."

He ended up driving them to the Fletcherville Inn, a quiet retreat in the village where they could talk without worrying about anyone listening. They took a booth in the back. The waitress brought them drinks and finger food, then left them alone.

"You know what happened to Francis," Ray said, looking at Estella. "Tell us."

"He was taken," she replied, sipping her Coke. None of the three of them had ordered alcohol. "Taken by another vampire."

Neither of her two companions looked surprised, she noted. It would require incredible force to take a vampire against his will, after all, and only another vampire or some other preternatural being would have that kind of power.

Power. There were all kinds; physical, mental, metaphysical, psychic...both these men sharing her table had power, though it flowed differently in each. She found herself automatically trusting the one named Michael. Ray Griffin was still a question mark. A big one.

"Do you know this other vampire, Estella?" Michael asked.

"Yes, I know him."

The van stopped, finally. Francis had been shaken and banged around quite a bit in the back, for the mooring ropes hadn't been used to secure him to anything. He was fighting mad by the time they pulled off the road, but was completely unable to do anything about it. The doors opened and the tall, unknown vampire reached in, grabbed Francis by the handiest hunk of rope, and pulled him out.

They had driven for at least three hours, by Francis' best

reckoning, but he had no idea which direction they'd taken. In detective novels, kidnap victims could listen for tell-tale sounds as they were being abducted, but all Francis had heard was the van's engine and the bangs he made against the panels. Though he had excellent night vision, there wasn't much to see when he was taken out of the van. They were inside a building; possibly a warehouse or something of that nature because the size of the place dwarfed the van and there were some large crates and bits of machinery lying about.

He wasn't allowed a more leisurely look. His captor ripped the duct tape off his mouth, taking a bit of skin with it, and frog-marched him into what seemed to be an office. An office, Francis did have time to notice, with no phone, computer, or other outside means of communication. It did have at least one chair, into which he was thrust, still bound more tightly than Houdini.

"What the hell..." he began, but a blow to the side of his head stopped him.

"I ask the questions," said his abductor.

It was the first time Francis had seen the strange vampire face-to-face. He was a heavy-muscled, heavy-jawed man of nearly six and a half feet, with brown hair and deep-set brown eyes, and a nose that appeared to have been broken more than once. He was wearing ordinary clothing that wouldn't stand out in a crowd. Right at the moment, his fangs were showing and there was a red light behind his eyes.

"What were you doing in Estella's tent, boy?" asked this formidable vampire.

"Don't call me 'boy.'"

"You have not been one of us for even fifty years yet. You are a boy."

"How do you know how long I've been turned?"

"I can smell it on you," sneered the other. "And I said that I ask the questions. Or would you like another reminder?"

Francis flinched automatically, for his head still rang from the first blow. The other man laughed.

"I thought not. Now, what were you doing at Estella's tent?"

"I came for a reading, that's all." Francis wanted, very badly, to ask what business it was of this stranger's, but he kept quiet.

"You were there last night, too." The stranger leaned in more closely. "One reading, I would almost believe; except that I know Estella too well. She would not read for you even one time, let alone two."

"I came for a reading," Francis repeated.

"She will not read for vampires." The stranger drew back, looking down at Francis. It was a threatening pose. "And she would know what you are. She does, doesn't she?"

"Yes," Francis sighed. "She wouldn't even touch me."

"Estella hates the undead. Even a boy like you would upset her. Your companion must have been highly unusual, for her to admit you both to her tent."

Francis said nothing. He would not give Ray away. Not a word about the Brotherhood would escape him. This vampire was obviously inimical to his own kind; to mention the Brotherhood would be betrayal.

"Odd to see a vampire so loyal to a mortal," sneered the older man. "He must be someone special to you. A lover?"

It was baiting, pure and simple, nothing Francis couldn't handle. The kidnapper was expecting Francis to react angrily and deny a homosexual interest in his companion, possibly by giving away a name or more information. Besides, he'd known Gideon and Joshua too long and too well to think there was any particular shame in being gay.

Another unexpected blow to his head made Francis wince. He had no way to fight back or defend himself. He hated not being in control

"Why did you go to see Estella tonight?" asked his tormentor.

"I went for a reading."

The admonishing hand dropped. "Very well. You are stubborn, but so am I."

He lifted Francis bodily out of the chair and carried him out of the office as if he was a parcel. A long walk through the echoing warehouse, and they came to a small cage with a set of solid-looking steel doors. These had two half-foot-thick steel bars across them, which the stranger slid aside with ease. He pulled open one of the doors. Inside was a box, a windowless, bar-less cage not quite large enough for Francis to stand up or turn around in. It was just the right size, Francis couldn't help noticing, to fit into the back of the van he'd been transported in. He was tossed, still tied and duct-taped, into this and kicked until he lay still, groaning.

"Just in case you watch *Angel,"* said his captor, once again sneering, "this cage cannot be kicked open by using a repetitive action in the same spot."

The door was pushed shut. Francis heard the bolts being drawn back into place.

"You inherited him?" Michael repeated incredulously, a forgotten stick of celery dropping from his fingers.

"Some families get good jewelry, or the parlour table, or horrible watercolours by forgotten amateurs," Estella nodded. "My family has a vampire."

Ray looked at her to see if she was joking. She met his gaze calmly, no hint of laughter in her eyes. When it threatened to become a staring contest, Michael cleared his throat.

"A few details would be nice," he said gently.

"The vampire is my great, great, great Uncle Rigo," Estella said. "He was made a vampire by another, many years ago."

"Not by a gypsy curse?" Ray repeated, radiating sarcasm.

"Do not mock the ways of my ancestors, gadjo," Estella said, then laughed at herself. "I'm only half Rom, and don't really follow the ways of my people. You should hear the arguments about that!"

"I believe it," Michael said, giving Ray a stern look.

"It should be a gypsy curse," Ray objected, "or what's the point of Uncle Rigo being a gypsy?"

"Oh, hush, let her tell the story."

"We don't know why Uncle Rigo was changed," Estella continued. "He won't say. He claims he's forgotten the reason. Nothing anyone did could cure him or end his existence; and nobody wanted to stake a family member in the heart. We take family very seriously. Others who weren't family offered to destroy the wampyr, but nobody wanted to say 'yes, do it.'"

Michael nodded to show he understood. Ray still looked faintly incredulous, but he was hooked on the story in spite of himself.

"So Uncle Rigo outlived everyone in his generation, and there was no one in the next generation, either, who wanted to be responsible for staking the family vampire. Uncle Rigo chose one person in the family to...haunt is the only word I can think of."

"Haunt how?" Ray asked.

"That one person," Estella answered, then suddenly laughed, although it wasn't a humourous sound. "The 'Chosen One' of each generation," she snorted, "would be shadowed by Uncle Rigo, protected in a way, but actually used more like a sort of shield. If anything happened to Rigo, any unexpected stakes or exposures to sunlight, the family member would die in an unspecified horrible way. Somehow, he found a way to connect whatever animates him to the life of the person he chooses. I've tried to do some research on how he did that, but every time I get close, he finds out and stops me."

"So you are his choice for this generation?" Ray's voice had a trace of sympathy now. Uncle Rigo sounded like an unpleasant type.

She nodded. "I had hoped that by travelling around a lot, following the summer fairs and the psychic fair circuit in the winter, that I could at least lose him from time to time. He always finds me. At least he makes his own arrangements for food and accommodation, and we never stay in one place long enough for his eating habits to become a problem with the police."

"Why you?" Michael queried.

She shrugged. "The Sight also runs in my family, though it is seen as not much better an inheritance than Uncle Rigo. Fortune telling is not a highly-regarded trade among the Rom. It's just to fleece the gadje. But Rigo has usually chosen whichever family member has the strongest touch of the Sight to be his inheritor."

"Probably because they would be able to spot other vampires, and those with occult connections, and warn Rigo of their presence," Ray said, surprising himself and the other two. "Rigo was undoubtedly somewhere nearby last night; I could feel something menacing, out of place, about your tent. I just couldn't identify what it was. He must have seen Francis and I go in."

"Yes," Estella nodded. "He warned me long ago to stay away from other vampires. He's very curious about you." She spoke to Ray, since neither she nor Rigo had seen Michael before this meeting. "If he finds out that I have left the fair, and consulted two men with power, he is going to be furious with me."

"Will he hurt you?" Michael asked in concern.

She smiled at him, and for the first time, she looked rather pretty. "There is no one yet in the next generation to inherit him. He does not hurt family. But your friend Francis may be in serious danger."

"So Rigo has Francis?" Ray demanded. "Where?"

"I don't know," Estella sighed. "I never know where he finds to hide."

Francis was not a happy vampire. Bound with duct tape, tied with three-inch thick ropes, kicked and beaten, and thrust into a solid steel cage, all by a vampire whom he had never previously met. He knew that sometimes he upset other vampires with his insouciant attitude, but this was ridiculous.

After what seemed like hours and hours of uncomfortable captivity, he heard the bolts being drawn off the cage door. It was flung open and his captor entered. Francis was once more lifted by the handiest length of rope and carried back out of his prison.

He was taken back to the "office." The rope and duct tape were removed, not gently.

"We shall try this again," said the abductor. "In a more civilized fashion. There is no use in your attempting to escape. I am faster and stronger than you."

Francis did not doubt this, as he had experience to verify it. He massaged his abused legs. "No more hitting."

"I make no promises, boy."

"And don't call me boy!"

His captor raised a hand, then dropped it. "What is your name, then?"

"Francis Calvert. What's yours?"

"Rigo Smith." His captor looked at him. "There, we are civilized now."

"Rigo Smith," Francis repeated. He was feeling so disoriented that he decided it was best just to play whatever game this madman was directing. "What do you want of me, Rigo Smith?"

"You will tell me why you went to visit Estella a second time."

"She wouldn't read for me the first time I went," Francis answered truthfully. "So I went back tonight to talk to her, to find out why she hates vampires." That wasn't entirely the truth, but it could have been. Once he'd finished explaining the importance of not upsetting his friends to Estella, he might have steered the conversation in that direction.

"I don't believe you."

Francis dared a shrug. "She told me I have no future, because I'm dead. I thought that warranted a second visit."

Rigo was studying him very closely, and Francis was glad that he could no longer sweat. He was not precisely lying; it was sin by omission.

"The man you were with last night—he was not a vampire."

"No. He's just a friend. He has no part in this."

"You are protecting him."

"Because he's mortal, and I don't want a pissed-off vampire beating him up."

"Estella read for him." Rigo's dark eyes, with their hint of hellfire, burned into Francis' innocent blue orbs. "I could sense you both, in that tent last night. I was nearby, for I could smell another vampire and I had to protect Estella. Your friend puzzled me. He is not an ordinary mortal."

"He has no part in this," Francis repeated.

Ray Griffin pushed his empty glass aside and gave Estella a hard, swift look that she could not quite interpret. This strange, thin man in black with his multitude of scars and barely suppressed cynicism was a total mystery to her. There weren't many total mysteries to someone with the Sight. The glimpses she'd had from the reading she'd done for him had all been horrific. He had suffered much, paying for the power that radiated from him in ways she shuddered to think of.

She didn't have to touch Michael Fairlawn to know that he was a healer, had a touch of the Sight, and was completely in tune with the Earth and the Mother Goddess, no matter which name he used for her. She liked him already.

"Anything else?" The waitress appeared at the table, removing the empty glasses and the plate of appetizers.

"Nothing else for me," said Estella with a smile.

Ray just shook his head, and Michael also said he needed nothing else. The waitress returned with their bill.

"Take your time," she assured them.

Michael paid, ignoring objections. "Estella," he said, returning their attention to the matter of Francis and Uncle Rigo, "perhaps you do not know where your uncle hides out, but you must at least know how he travels."

"He has a van. Just a plain dark blue panel van that nobody would notice. He has a solid steel container that he carries in the back; it serves him both as a safe place during daylight and as a cage should he need to hold someone prisoner."

"Is he in the habit of taking prisoners?"

Her nod was not a happy one. "He is careful to never be seen, and to take those who will not be missed, or at least not immediately. Especially other vampires. He hates other vampires. That is why I called you," she nodded to Ray. "I don't like vampires, either, but I couldn't let Uncle Rigo hurt your friend."

"Do you think he's going to kill Francis?" Ray asked. So much time had already passed. Francis could already have met the true death. Somehow, Ray didn't think so, and he clung to that frail hope.

"I don't know," Estella replied. "If he thinks that Francis was going to hurt me, probably, yes."

"I need to go home and get my cards," Ray said, standing up. "I'll try to contact Francis. He might be able to tell me where he is, or perhaps I can get a feeling from the Trump."

"Cards?" Estella was looking at him. "Trump? You use the Tarot?"

"Not as you know it. I have cards with pictures of people I know on them; they are all called Trumps. I can use them to contact the person; although it doesn't always work."

"That's serious magic."

"Serious is the only kind of magic I know."

"What about Francis' Harley?" Michael asked. "It's parked at the fair, and someone will call the police about it if it's still there in the morning."

"Drop me off at the fair parking lot, and I'll drive the Harley home," Ray said. "Nobody will think twice about seeing me with it; they all know Francis and I are friends. If anyone does question me, I'll come up with some story."

Michael looked at Estella. "I'll follow Ray, so that I'm there if he locates Francis and we can get on the road right away. What did you want to do?"

She bit her lip, thinking it over. "I want to go with you when you find out where Francis is. I might be the only one who can control my uncle."

"All right," Michael said.

"You'd better clear this with Mary," Ray reminded his friend.

"Good point." Michael went off to use the inn's phone.

Estella and Ray were left alone together. They got up from the table and made their way to the door, waiting for Michael to get off the phone.

"He's very nice, Michael," Estella commented, for something to say.

"Salt of the earth," Ray agreed.

"Michael's not his real name, though."

"No, but he doesn't like his real name to be used."

Estella nodded. Real names had power. "Is his wife like him?"

Ray pondered how to answer that. "She's very nice," he finally answered, "if that's what you mean. If you mean does she have any magical abilities, then the answer is no."

"So, she's mortal, and he is not." Estella spoke this so softly that Ray barely heard it.

"You're too perceptive for your own good," Ray said.

"So I've been told."

Ray couldn't think of a good come-back for that, so he lapsed into silence. Michael returned to find them both studying the decor of the bar area, studiously avoiding looking at each other. He fought back a grin.

"Let's get going," he said.

They walked out to Michael's car. He sighed as he opened his door and a candy wrapper flew out. "It's Galen's job to clean out the car," he said, shaking his head. "I guess I need to remind him of that."

"How old is Galen?" Estella asked, glad to have something to say, and to not have to look at Ray.

"Thirteen," Michael grimaced. "We've hit the teen years once again. He has a twin sister, and I have a twenty-four year old daughter as well."

"Twins are lucky," Estella said.

"They'll be lucky to see fourteen," Michael said, but he laughed. "No, they're really good kids, actually. Mary says I'm too soft on them."

She didn't ask Ray if he had a wife or children. She had seen the answer already in his palm.

Rigo glared down at Francis, but the younger vampire stood his ground. He would not be beaten or intimidated into saying anything about Ray specifically or the Brotherhood in general.

"Estella is my niece," Rigo said. "I have made myself her protector. Those with the Sight are vulnerable. All sorts want to use them, prey on them, make them See things best left hidden. So all things that concern Estella concern me. Do you understand?"

"Yes."

"Then why do you not understand that I need to know why you went to see her tonight? It is a serious thing, for a vampire to visit my niece."

"I just wanted to talk to her, to see why she wouldn't give me a reading."

"That lie is growing old, boy."

"I told you not to call me boy."

Rigo swore at him in a language Francis didn't understand; then knocked him to the ground with a fist that moved so fast it was just a blur. He picked Francis up before the young man had time to recover, and carried him bodily back to the cage. Francis was thrown in and bars drawn across the doors.

"Stay and rot there until you decide to tell the truth!" he heard Rigo's voice taunt.

"Well, this sucks shit," Francis said.

Ray was growing heartily sick of the sight of the summer fair. Even from the parking lot, the view of the lights and attractions made him nauseous. His best friend had been forcibly removed from this fair by a hostile vampire. He'd met the world's most annoying woman here, and it looked like he was stuck with her company for the foreseeable future.

"Estella," he said as that thought crossed his mind.

She jumped. They were standing in the parking lot, looking for Francis' Harley.

"Yes?" She looked poised for flight.

"Did you see any of this happening, when you read my palm?"

"It doesn't work like that."

"There's the bike," Michael pointed. "I'll walk over with you to make sure it's okay." He gave Estella a pointed look.

She correctly interpreted it to mean that Michael wanted to talk to Ray privately. She nodded, and stayed by Michael's car.

"Don't you dare," Ray said before Michael could speak.

"Don't I dare what?"

"Tell me to give her a break, or take it easy on her, or anything along those lines."

"Wouldn't dream of it. I just was wondering if you've thought of what's next."

Ray looked puzzled, as well he might. The plan had already been discussed. "I use the Trump to contact Francis. We find out where he is, and go get him."

"Just like that?" Michael wasn't being confrontational. His posture remained relaxed. Only the lines around his eyes showed his own tension and worry. "You plan to go charging to the rescue without knowing your opponent, the situation, or the territory?"

"It's what Francis would do for me."

"Francis is a nineteen year-old hothead immortal," Michael replied, still quietly.

"Time is ticking away, Michael. Who knows what Estella's crazy uncle is doing to Francis?"

"I know." This time, Michael did give in to his impulse to offer comfort, and squeezed Ray's shoulder. "But even if time is against us, rushing into the unknown is never wise."

"So how do we turn the unknown into the known?"

Michael's eyes flickered to Estella. Ray sighed.

"All right," the mage said. "I'll be nice to her."

"I'm not asking for miracles," Michael nearly smiled, but stopped himself in time. "Just a cessation of open hostilities. I asked Mary to call the others, they'll meet us at your place."

"That will be a shock to Estella," Ray said, a rare smile appearing at the thought. "She hates vampires, and you're throwing Alex, Gideon, and Josh at her all at once."

"Francis is their friend, too," Michael answered. "Let's go."

"See you at my place." Ray straddled the Harley.

"Do you have the keys?"

"Oh, please." The bike started without any visible effort on Ray's part.

"Show-off," Michael muttered. Over the roar of the Harley's engine, he was certain Ray couldn't hear him, but the mage laughed at him.

Michael walked back to his car and the waiting Estella, looking thoughtful. He hadn't spoken to Ray of his deepest misgiving that Ray would be unable to contact Francis via the Trump.

"Are all your friends that tightly wound?" Estella asked when Michael rejoined her.

"His best friend has been abducted by an inherited vampire," Michael replied. "You'd be a little on edge, too."

"Are they just friends?" Estella asked, as delicately as possible.

"Yes, they are just friends. They are both straight. But Ray never had a good friend before he met Francis, so he takes this pretty seriously."

"I see." Estella watched the scenery go by with feigned interest. She hadn't ventured near the almost-mythical Cliff Road before, but she was too nervous to much care. Part of her unease was the fact that she was in a car with a man she barely knew, being taken to the house of another near-stranger. Her mother had warned her about this sort of thing. Yet Michael "felt" completely non-threatening, as if he was a favourite uncle. As opposed to her least favourite one...

"I assure you," Michael said, not taking his eyes off the road, "you are perfectly safe. I'm very married."

"Do you read minds?" Estella asked.

He smiled. "You were edging as far away from me as you could get. It wasn't difficult to guess what you were thinking."

"Can I ask you something?"

"Go ahead."

"Why did Francis make Ray come to see me?"

"Because Francis can be a little shit when he so desires."

She stared at him, mildly shocked at this response.

"I have teenagers," he reminded her. He was still carefully studying the road, but he must have caught a glimpse of her reaction.

A driver had to study this road, she quickly realized. It wound up the side of a dramatic cliff. There was no guard-rail. When they reached the top, she was rewarded with what would have been a breathtaking view of the Atlantic Ocean, in daylight. It being now somewhere around midnight, all she saw was lights: the town, the automated lighthouse, the handful of houses up here.

"Don't your kids find this isolated?" she managed to ask.

"Do you know how much mileage is on this car?"

They had long since lost sight of the Harley, Michael not possessing Ray's lead foot. But when they drew up at the small bungalow, the lights were all on and there were four other cars already parked in the driveway and on the road. Michael pulled up behind a gleaming black limo. Not, Estella was obscurely grateful to notice, a stretch limo; more like one of the kind you caught at the airport.

"Is he having a party?" Estella asked.

"Francis has other friends," Michael replied. "Come and meet them."

He didn't knock, simply walked in. Only very good friends could do that.

Estella followed him since there really was no other choice. She found herself being led into a living room packed with people who made her skin crawl. Three vampires! She spotted them immediately. The drop-dead-gorgeous man, classically tall, dark and handsome, the lean, friendly-looking one with the sandy hair, and the short, dark-haired one with the unreadable expression. As for the others, a long and lanky young man with unkempt brown hair made her palms itch. For some reason, his eyes made her think of a wolf. The stunning red-haired woman standing near Ray, teasing Andrei, was harder to read but seemed to fall into the same general category as Michael. There was no feeling at all that she could interpret from the burly, auburn-haired man who hovered near the shortest vampire.

"What the hell is this?" Estella demanded.

"Estella Smith," Ray broke away from Maggie to greet the new arrivals, "meet the Brotherhood of Darkness."

Once again, Francis heard his cage door open. He blinked in the sudden light. Rigo hauled him out, somewhat more gently than before.

This was growing tiresome. Francis scowled up at his captor and spat, "Now what?"

"You must be hungry," said Rigo. He offered a wine bottle. The scent that rose from it was not wine.

"Tha's human blood." Francis' voice was slurred because his fangs had descended. Pavlov would have been proud.

"Of course it is! You are a vampire!" Rigo thrust the bottle into Francis' unresisting hand. "Or are you one of those who only drinks from rats and other vermin?"

"Pig's quite tasty, you know," Francis murmured, but he raised the bottle to his lips. Ah, sweet human blood, how long had it been since he had last tasted it?

Last week, actually, said a tiny voice in a back corner of his mind.

"Why did you give me this?" he asked once he'd drained the bottle.

"You must eat, no?" Rigo draped his arm around Francis' shoulder. "And perhaps now that you have fed, you will feel more like telling me the truth."

"What did you do, spike the blood with sodium pentathol?"

"Pah." Rigo's arm slid away, to Francis' relief. "Fewer of these japes at your elders would serve you in better stead, boy."

"Japes?" Francis repeated incredulously. He had never heard anyone actually say that word out loud.

"Can you not see that I wish to protect my niece?" Rigo asked, ignoring the response to his previous statement.

"You have a strange idea of protection, Uncle Rigo," Francis told him. "Dragging me out of her tent like that. What if we'd been seen? Your niece would be answering some hard questions at police headquarters."

"I fear nothing from the human police."

"Maybe not, but Estella might."

"Pah. I took care that we were not seen." Rigo seized the empty wine bottle and threw it against the far wall, where it shattered. A few last drops of blood streaked down the wall. "I do not like having other vampires bother my niece."

Francis recalled the expression on Estella's face when she had seen her uncle seize him. Maybe, just maybe, she'd been upset enough to contact Ray. If so, Estella was going to be "bothered" by three vampires, a magic-user, a werewolf, two Druids, and whatever it was Evan was. He wisely kept this thought to himself.

"So," Rigo continued, "I protect her. And she protects me."

"How?"

"Our blood is tied. If I am destroyed, she will die."

"Some protection."

The Rom vampire bared his teeth. Perhaps it was meant as a smile. "It serves. She takes great care that no slayer," the word dripped sarcasm, "scents my trail."

Francis stared at him. "You old bastard!" he shouted. "You just let her believe it so that nobody will kill you; there's no such tie!"

Rigo's long, thick fingers wrapped themselves around Francis' neck, pressing on the throat.

"Your friend from last night," he snarled, "the one who stank of magic, will he be looking for you?"

Frightened beyond caution. Francis nodded.

"Then he had best act quickly, for you have just doomed yourself."

Predictably, Francis was thrust back into the steel cage. The bars were slammed across it with emphasis. He was left alone in the dark, wondering whether or not to hope that Ray was trying to find him.

Introductions finished, Estella studied the assembled Brotherhood. Whatever thoughts she had about the name she kept to herself. None of the three vampires had immediately pounced on her neck. In fact, the short one, Gideon Redoak, had insisted on surrendering his chair to her and was now standing beside the lean, sandy-haired Joshua. She pretended not to notice that they were holding hands.

The Brotherhood members were all, every one of them, worried about Francis. That was natural. But what disconcerted Estella was that they were all also concerned about her. Ray had disappeared into his workshop, and Estella understood that he was going to do whatever it was he did with the Trumps, whatever they were.

"Do you think he's having any luck down there?" Estella asked.

Everyone must have heard her, because they all turned to look at her, then look towards the back of the house, where the entrance to the mysterious workshop lay.

"We'll know soon enough." Michael said. "Let's keep our hopes up."

They waited; small talk occasionally breaking out but not living long in the tense atmosphere.

Finally, they heard footsteps coming from the back rooms. Andrei ruffled his wings and launched himself from his perch, forcing several people to duck as he flew out of the living room to find his master. A minute later, Ray appeared; the falcon on his shoulder pecking at his earring. He looked tired.

Nobody spoke. Ray smiled as he accepted a glass of something from the red-haired woman, draining it in one gulp. When he set the glass down, he looked at Michael, then Estella.

"I didn't have much luck," he said. "I managed a brief contact, but he couldn't tell me where he was. I got a vague impression of something like a warehouse, but that was all."

"I can find him," Estella said in the grim silence that followed this statement. Something about Ray's voice and posture had moved her to offer. He looked so sad.

Ray's head came up and his blue eyes nearly skewered her. "I thought you said you didn't know where your uncle's hideouts were."

"I don't. I can't find Uncle Rigo. But I can find Francis." Aware that they were all staring at her, she said defensively, "I didn't realise that it was so important to so many people to find him. I would have said something sooner "

"It's all right," Michael said. "What do you need?"

"Clothing would be best, something he wears often."

"Not a problem." Ray got up, still moving like a man who needed a nap, and disappeared towards the back rooms again. He returned quickly, carrying a black t-shirt. "He's always leaving the damn things over here. He seems to think I'm a laundry service."

Unwashed vampire, how nice, Estella thought. She ignored the scent, the grease stains, the defunct rock band logo. Francis wore this shirt. It certainly didn't look like something anyone else in the room would wear.

Andrei flew over to watch her from the back of Maggie's chair, but nobody else moved or spoke.

Estella took the shirt, feeling it with her fingers. "This isn't an exact science," she warned. "I'm not going to get a street address."

"We understand," Michael assured her.

Of course they did. This was a room full of people who understood how inexact the power was.

She closed her eyes, concentrating on the shirt. The smell of motorcycle rose around her. She ignored it, reaching beyond the feel of worn cotton, the scent of second-hand Harley.

"It's dark," she said, although without any of the theatrical overtones a movie psychic would give to the statement. "Dark and confined." She winced, as if feeling pain. "He's been kicked, hit knocked to the ground. I can feel my uncle's anger." She shivered, but kept her eyes closed, kept her hold on the shirt, kept the link to Francis. "There is steel all around him; the cage from the van is his prison. But they are not moving; the cage is in a big warehouse. North. Away from the ocean. There is water nearby, but no smell of salt or sound of breakers...a river? It feels like a larger town; industrial. Perhaps three hours drive; the van drove quickly." She opened her eyes. "There is nothing more. He saw nothing of the town, did not know which direction they drove."

"There's only one place like that within a three hour's drive that's not near the ocean," Evan spoke up for the first time since introducing himself. "Bangor."

"We're so short of time," Estella said, "I fear that if we do not find Francis before dawn that Uncle Rigo will kill him. In three hours, it will be nearly dawn."

"It won't take us three hours to drive to Bangor," Ray said flatly. "Will it, Evan?"

The muscular Evan glanced briefly at Gideon, the short gentleman vampire. He nodded. Evan turned back to Ray.

"Of course not. The limo and I are at your disposal."

"Michael, are you coming with us?" Ray asked, rising to his feet. Andrei flew to his shoulder.

"Of course. You may need an older and wiser friend along."

"Don't mind us," Josh grumbled. "We'll just walk home, shall we?"

"I'll drive you," the gorgeous Alex told him. "Such a fuss over a couple of miles."

"No offence to the rest of you," Ray said to the assembled Brotherhood, "but get out of my house."

The four who made up the rescue team waited until the others had filed out, then went out to the limousine that waited on the road.

"What about your car?" Estella asked Michael.

"It will be fine here. I'll pick it up on the way home."

They climbed into the black Cadillac, Evan sliding with ease behind the wheel.

"Fasten your seatbelts," he warned.

"It's going to be a bumpy ride?" Estella couldn't resist.

He looked scandalised. "In a Caddy?"

They started rolling down the Cliff Road. When they reached the main road heading out of Fletcherville, Evan punched some buttons on what looked like a computer attached to the dashboard. The scenery went blurry.

Dark. Cold steel all around. Cramped, confined, beginning to believe there would be no rescue. Knowing that Rigo, his captor, was a crafty old bastard who was toying with him. Francis had felt the cold magic of the mysterious Trumps that Ray used to contact his friends. But although contact of a sort was established through the bite of the magic card, Francis hadn't been able to give his friend much information. Dark and cold steel were all he knew.

Francis cut the contact short, afraid that Rigo could somehow detect the use of magic. He had said, tonight, that Ray had stunk of magic. He had not mentioned before that he could detect the power. Rigo was obviously not your average vampire.

Ray couldn't rescue him. Francis hadn't been able to name his location; he didn't know which way the van had driven or whether or not they were still on the coast. He was doomed. Rigo was going to kill him, because he knew Rigo's secret. And he was missing a broadcast Stones concert.

That really hurt.

The blur outside the windows of the black Cadillac limousine gradually became real scenery again. A city, taller buildings than in Fletcherville, wide streets, traffic. Bangor, the second largest city in Maine.

Estella saw that Ray Griffin was looking at her intently. More correctly, he was looking at the black garment she still held in her hands. He said nothing, but his eyes begged her to focus on the task at hand.

That steadied her. Her family was never going to believe this. She was in a car powered by magical sigils that enabled it to drive through time and space, she was with two powerful magic-users and a...a...and Evan, and she was trying to rescue a punk kid vampire from her Uncle Rigo. Her family would be furious. Rigo was to be protected, not exposed.

Too damn bad.

She closed her eyes and concentrated on what she could read from the shirt and its link to Francis.

"North," she said finally, her palms prickling as they touched the shirt. "It's an industrial area; no houses, not many cars. It's on a river, I can hear it and smell it."

"Right." His jaw set, Evan sought for a street headed in the right direction. Even though the Caddy had materialised from nowhere onto a road in Bangor, nobody seemed to notice. It was nearly one in the morning, which helped.

The streets of Bangor went past. The occasional light; the empty stores; the all-night garage where the attendant dozed behind the desk. Slowly the buildings became sparser, farther apart, and the industrial area lay before them. Several warehouses, most of them on the Penobscot River, loomed in the near distance.

"I can't tell," Estella said helplessly, holding the shirt in nerveless hands. "He's somewhere close by, but these places all look the same."

Ray stirred. From his jeans pocket, he removed a small box. It was covered in frost. Although the Caddy had air conditioning, it was not turned on that high.

"Francis closed the last contact," he said, opening the box and offering a tantalising glimpse of the hand-drawn cards inside. Estella caught quick impressions of various members of the Brotherhood before Ray removed a card with Francis' portrait on it and shut the box again. "I think he's afraid that Rigo can detect magic." Ray looked at Estella.

She sighed. "My uncle is sensitive to magic. He can feel the vibrations it makes. He says he can smell it on someone."

"Now you tell us." That was Evan.

Ray's cold blue eyes did not release Estella from their steady gaze. "Tell us about Rigo. Why does he abduct vampires?"

"I think he's actually afraid of other vampires," Estella said. "I don't really know Rigo that well. I just know that when my Aunt Danube died, I inherited her lace shawl and Uncle Rigo. Danube had the Sight, and Rigo used her for his protection. I was told that is how things have always been in the family, since Rigo became wampyr. He showed up at my parents' house and I was forced to learn to deal with him. Usually he isn't a problem. He looks after his own business and leaves me to mine; but he always follows me and prevents other vampires from speaking to me or questioning him too closely about our family ties. He does not share the secret of this tie, of how he insured that we could not betray him because we would die as well, and he makes certain that other vampires do not learn of this secret."

"And he never drinks your blood, or makes sexual advances on you?" Ray asked.

"No. I told you, we take family very seriously. If he raped me, in either way, the family would kill him, consequences or no. But one look at Uncle Rigo, and any potential lover for me has vanished. I don't blame them."

Ray, who hadn't had very many potential lovers himself, though not because he had an uncle who was a vampire, almost looked sympathetic.

Michael noticed the increasing chemistry and empathy between Ray and Estella, but wisely kept these observations to himself. Evan was paying attention only to the streets, alert for trouble.

"It will be a warehouse large enough to drive the van into completely," Estella said, aware that they were waiting for her to explain more about her uncle. "Rigo is not careless. He wishes no confrontations with police, because questions would lead back to me. It will have to be an empty facility, one with no night watchman or alarm system."

"When you first read the shirt," Ray said, "you said that you could feel Francis had been hit and kicked."

"Yes," Estella nodded sadly. "Uncle Rigo is no gentleman, not like your friend Gideon."

"Then they would have to be someplace where sound wouldn't carry, too. We're looking for a relatively isolated warehouse."

Evan made a gesture at the maze of places before them. But he said nothing, merely drove the limo around in wide sweeps of the area, hoping to pick up the trail.

Ray tapped the card in his hand. "I don't know if I dare use this or not," he sighed. "I may endanger Francis by contacting him, but he is endangered if I do not." He glared at the back of Evan's head. "And anyone saying anything about being damned will suddenly find themselves green and squelchy."

"Did I say a word?" Evan asked in mild protest.

"Can we link up?" Estella asked, a brave suggestion.

"What do you have in mind?" Ray asked.

"Touch the card to the shirt, and let's see what happens."

Ray looked at the card in his hands, then at Estella. He'd never tried doing this sort of thing before; but then, he reminded himself, neither had she. Their hands brushed as he lowered the Trump to the shirt, and she smiled at him. He found himself smiling back.

Maybe she wasn't the world's most annoying woman.

Frost crackled along the shirt, up both their hands, and their minds touched each other as well.

She saw into Ray's mind, saw the blaze of pain and unhappy memories, saw the gentle heart hidden behind the wall of cynicism to protect it against further hurt. He was not, as she had already seen in his palm, an evil man. She saw genuine love for his friends, and a deep concern for Francis that made her want to save the young vampire, too.

Ray saw Estella's mind opened to him with equal clarity; saw her deep loneliness, her fear that her uncle would drive away any chance she had of finding love. Her mannerisms were calculated to keep her from being too badly hurt by the life she'd been forced to lead.

Estella gasped and dropped the shirt, breaking the contact. Something of the link remained, though, a new-found mutual sympathy that made them both regret earlier harsh words.

"I wasn't expecting that," she said, shaken.

"Me, either."

"Are you both okay?" Michael asked, healing instincts aroused.

They nodded. Estella picked up the shirt again, and looked at Ray.

"I'm prepared this time," she said. "Let's try it again."

Bracing himself mentally, Ray touched the Trump to the shirt, willing the contact to work. Estella's mind opened to his, a touch more intimate than any physical one. He wasn't used to somebody else seeing his mind, either. There was a distinct taste of Francis in here, too; the shirt and the Trump both made the young vampire a presence in the limo.

Estella ignored the distractions created by her mental link with Ray, although the electric pulses of power made her almost giddy. She concentrated on the scent of Francis, the feel of his presence, the pull of the shirt and the card to him.

"Turn left here," she said in a voice that could not be disobeyed.

Evan turned left.

"Now right. There is a little side road beside the warehouse. Turn down it."

The car complied.

"This next warehouse. This is the place."

It looked like all the others, except that there were no lights on at all, not even over the doors. No hint of life, unless the overgrown bushes counted. A faded "for sale or lease" sign was half-hidden by a branch. The smell of the river overpowered any other scents.

"How did Rigo ever find this place?" Michael wondered as they emerged from the car. Andrei launched from Ray's shoulder, flying in circles above the warehouse.

"He checks the real estate listings online," Estella replied.

"Ah, of course. The internet; the vampire's new best friend."

"Uncle Rigo's pretty techno-savvy," Evan remarked.

"You think perhaps that because we are Rom, we still travel in caravans and steal horses?" Estella snapped at him.

"Easy," Evan laughed. "I know a vampire about Rigo's age who wouldn't know the internet from a fishing net. Some of the undead find it hard to keep up with the times, no matter their origins."

She blushed. "Sorry. Uncle Rigo enjoys technology. He loves television, especially American television. He adores Joss Whedon."

"Your uncle watches *Buffy?*"

She nodded, looking slightly embarrassed, but her three companions seemed to find it amusing. It distracted them from the fact that they were still outside the warehouse, facing the unknown. A friend of theirs was being held prisoner inside this warehouse. His captor was a strong, wily vampire who could smell magic. On their side, they had an Archdruid, a mage, a skilled warrior, and a psychic. Evan had brought his usual selection of assorted weapons. Ray had his knife and Andrei. Michael and Estella were both unarmed.

Both refused to allow Evan to give them a weapon of any kind. Michael didn't use steel. Estella knew how to fire a gun, but could not bring herself to bear a weapon against her uncle.

"You really do take family seriously," said Ray. He felt a bit envious, even in this ludicrous situation.

"Oh, yes. And remember, if Uncle Rigo dies, so do I."

"We remember," Evan assured her, but notched the string on his crossbow anyway.

"Does Andrei see a way in?" Michael asked Ray.

The mage looked up for his falcon. Seeing through Andrei's eyes, which he could do because of the link between them, always gave Ray vertigo. At his command, Andrei searched for an open window or an unlocked door.

"He doesn't see anything," Ray reported finally, "but he does have trouble telling if a door is locked or not. Rigo must have found a way in. Locks don't mean anything to me."

"We must hesitate to use magic," Michael warned him. "Remember what we know of Uncle Rigo."

Estella nodded, looking scared. "He will smell it, if you use it."

"I showered and everything this morning," Ray said.

"Locks don't mean anything to me, either," Evan growled. "And I don't use magic. Let's find a door."

Ray whistled for Andrei, who came down and landed on Estella's shoulder. She tried not to flinch from his close proximity, or sag under his unexpected weight. The falcon gave her earring a friendly nibble and shrieked his disconcerting laugh.

"He likes you," said Ray.

"I'm honoured," Estella responded, secretly hoping that the falcon didn't crap down her blouse. His claws pricked through the material, so it was probably ruined anyway. Ray must have all his clothes reinforced with leather patches under the shoulders, she thought. Amazingly, though, the grip of Andrei's talons didn't break her skin or draw blood.

Evan led the way to the nearest door. Just in case, he tried it. It was locked.

"At least there's not a deep pond with a ravenous beastie in it, ready to pounce on us should we fail to enter," Ray quipped..

"If there is a deep mine inside this door," Michael said, quite seriously, "you are the first volunteer to face any Balrogs."

"Duly noted."

Evan produced a set of lock picks and fiddled with the door. A minute later, he pushed it open.

"You don't need Gandalf," he said with a grin, "when you have Raffles."

"I absolutely refuse to be Bunny." Ray said.

Evan went in first, with a flashlight he'd produced from whatever mysterious place he kept his weaponry. A vast, echoing space swallowed the thin beam. Whoever had owned this warehouse hadn't cleaned up too well; bits of machinery, packing boxes, coils of wire and a thick layer of dust covered the floor.

"No footprints in the dust," Evan observed, shining the light downwards. "Even a vampire leaves footprints. Uncle Rigo doesn't use this part of the warehouse."

"This place must be about a block in size," Estella said, looking at the huge space.

"Let's see if we can find the original office," Michael suggested.

They stayed close together; all of them had seen too many horror movies where the search team that split up was picked off one by one. Besides, Evan had the only flashlight.

At first it looked like just one more forgotten piece of inventory left by the careless owners. Michael walked right past it, but he had no feel for cold steel. Ray and Estella both paused, their powers still linked through the now limp t-shirt that Estella held, sensing that here was their goal. Their hands sought each other, almost without either of them realizing. It felt natural. Evan realized that two of the party had stopped at what appeared to be a steel safe. He'd been looking at the prints on the floor. Someone had been dragged here, and the person doing the dragging was big.

The steel box was about the right size to fit in the back of a large panel van. Two solid steel bars had been locked in place over the door.

"There are no airholes," Estella said, then blushed because

she realized why. She noticed she was holding Ray's hand, but didn't release it.

"Francis is in there," said Ray. He did not sound happy. He didn't let go, either. It felt good to have someone there.

Andrei shrieked a warning just as the tall, well-muscled vampire came around the corner from the other side of the steel box. He crossed his arms and stared down at the rescue party. Only Evan came even close to Rigo's height; Michael looked like a dwarf.

"So," said the Rom vampire, looking at Estella, "this is how you honour your family, Estella. You bring strangers here, two of them stinking of magic."

"This has to stop, Uncle Rigo," Estella told him. Her words were defiant, but her lips were trembling. Only then did she step away from Ray.

"What has to stop, traitor?"

"You must let Francis go, Uncle. No more kidnapping vampires that just happen to meet me. No more bullying."

"I have to protect you."

"Is this your idea of protection?" Ray stepped forward. "My friend is in that box. How is that protecting Estella?"

"I do not parlay with witches. Begone!" Rigo turned his back on Ray, only to find Michael looking steadily up at him. "Pah, another one!"

"Actually, I'm not a witch," Michael said equitably. "I'm a Druid. Ray's not a witch either, are you?" He looked at Ray.

"I don't know what to call myself," Ray answered, as if this was a perfectly normal conversation. "I generally prefer 'mage' because it's neutral."

"I hate the smell of magic!" Rigo backed away from the supposed stink of a mage and a Druid. He found himself almost backing into Evan, crossbow and all.

"I think that's far enough," said Evan, finger on the trigger. "Don't you?"

Rigo studied him. "You," he finally said, heavy-voiced. "You are one of those I have heard of, the so-called protectors. You must understand why I wish to protect my niece."

"If I thought you were actually protecting her by your actions, I would understand," Evan replied. His finger did not relax; he was too aware of the close proximity of a large, potentially dangerous vampire. "But I fail to see how holding Francis in that box is protecting Estella."

"He was bothering her!" Rigo shouted. "He came to ask her

questions! He wanted to know why she hates vampires! She might have betrayed me! As you can see, she is quite capable of doing so." He glowered at his "niece."

"So you weren't protecting her," Michael said. "You were ultimately protecting yourself."

"Shame on you, Uncle Rigo," Estella told him. "For shame. Is this how you repay the family trust, the protection we have given you all these years?" She gestured at the box. "Francis is no threat to me. Let him out! You are already revealed to these people, but they will not betray you."

"How can you be so certain?" Rigo made no move towards the box.

"You would already have embraced the true death should we mean you harm," Evan said, and his voice was as cold and solid as the steel cage that held Francis. "Now open that damn box and let Francis out."

Rigo looked for some sign of support, but even Estella was glowering at him. Evan's stance and tone were convincing. Who knew what the two witches were planning, and that damn falcon kept swooping at him. Outnumbered, he shrugged and moved towards the box. His steps put him within reach of Estella. As if guessing Rigo's half-formed intention, Ray Griffin stepped smoothly in front of Estella. Rigo stopped, held in place by the force of Ray's will.

"Open the door," Ray said calmly. "Or I will." He barely glanced at the cage, but the steel bolts slid out of their holders and clattered to the floor.

Damn that stinking witch! Rigo snarled, but found he could move now. He wrenched open the cage door. A pale, angelic face, framed with dirty platinum hair, blinked out at them in the sudden light.

"Hullo," said Francis, falling out of his prison, "is it tea time already?"

A war council was held in the office of the warehouse. Francis, wrapped in Evan's jacket, kept fending off Michael, who wanted to examine his various bruises and hurts. Rigo was being firmly kept in a corner by Evan. Ray and Estella, still psychically linked though not as strongly, were looking at each other awkwardly. Their hand-holding had made them realize their mutual attraction, and neither knew what to do about it. Andrei sat on the top of a dusty filing cabinet, devouring a mouse he'd managed to find.

"I still don't believe you lied, Uncle Rigo," Estella said, breaking off wondering what to say to Ray in order to berate her uncle. "The family still would have protected you! How could you not believe that of us?"

"I am a vampire. I had to have insurance."

"Wait until I tell Mother."

Somehow, Rigo managed to go paler than he already was. Ray found himself wondering about Estella's family, especially her mother.

"She will kill me, Estella!"

"Serves you right."

"Please. Have I not been a good uncle to you, other than that little lie? Have I not served well as your protector?"

"No more lies, Uncle Rigo. No more kidnapping of anybody, human, witch, vampire, whatever. No more stalking me and following me everywhere."

"I swear, by the family honour."

A mouse foot dropped down the back of Rigo's shirt. He didn't even squirm. Andrei laughed.

Estella looked her uncle in the eyes. He met her look. "I swear," he repeated.

"Very well; but if I hear of any misbehaviour, even one step towards me when I don't want you there, I go straight to Mother."

Vampires don't sweat, but Rigo's forehead looked like it should have been shiny. "No more kidnappings," he promised. "No more following you. No more lies."

She looked at Ray and Michael, wondering if they could detect honesty. They both nodded. Rigo was telling the truth.

"Apologise to Francis," she said.

"It's okay, really," Francis insisted, not wanting Rigo anywhere near him.

A futile protest, since Rigo seized him, lifted him up, and kissed him on both cheeks. "You will be as a son to me!"

"Oh, boy," said Francis.

"We really need to get going," Evan checked his watch. "Even the Caddy can't beat the dawn. Rigo, all promises aside, my people will be keeping an eye on you. One misstep and Estella's mother won't have anything to chew out. Catch my drift?"

The big vampire nodded. "We're five by five."

Evan rolled his eyes. "Let's get going," he said. He put an arm under Francis's shoulders to help the young vampire out. Michael followed, frowning at the fact that Francis didn't protest against this help.

"Be good, Uncle Rigo," Estella warned.

"You be good, too," he told her. He looked at Ray. "You treat her properly, magic man, or promise or no, I take you apart at the seams. Hey?"

"What are you talking about?" Ray and Estella chorused, then looked at each other again.

"I see the way you look at each other! I see you holding hands!" He could detect the mental link between them, too, but he didn't mention that.

"She isn't...I'm not...we're not..."

"You like each other, no?"

"We just met, Uncle Rigo!" Estella protested.

"So? You like him. He likes you. I see it in your eyes."

Andrei laughed.

"Oh, shut up," Ray told his falcon.

"Kiss her, magic man," Rigo ordered. "Kiss her, and you will see that you like each other."

"Ummm..." Ray looked at Estella.

"We'd better do what he says," Estella said, smiling, suddenly shy. "He *is* my uncle, after all."

Feeling stupid, Ray took her hands in his. She didn't flinch. "You really want to try this?"

"Very much," she replied, not looking at her uncle.

Ray sighed. Kissing a woman wasn't something he was too accomplished at doing in the first place, let alone with an audience of a half-hostile vampire and Andrei. His arms hung at a stiff, awkward angle as he closed in on Estella and offered her a chaste kiss.

But then her arms went around him, and he held her more naturally, and the kiss deepened into something interesting that held a promise.

The office door banged open and Evan stormed in, furious with the delay. "Are you two coming, or...oh."

Laughing, Ray and Estella broke apart.

"Sorry," Ray said. "We're ready to go now."

"Uncle Rigo made us do it," Estella grinned.

Evan looked at Rigo, who nodded. "They like each other," the Rom vampire grunted. "What can I do? Young people these days."

"All right," Evan sighed, "but we have to get moving if we're going to get back to Fletcherville before dawn. Let's go."

They trailed the protector out to the limo, once again holding hands.

"Do you have any more little family secrets like Rigo that I should know about?" Ray asked as he held the door open for Estella to climb in next to Francis.

"Just wait," she replied, settling herself on the seat, "until you meet Mother."

Follow That Falcon!
(2004)

The carnival had moved on. After one last day of spinning rides, wheels of fortune and cotton candy the great packing-up and moving-on had begun. The Ferris wheel had been taken apart, piece by piece, and laid in its flatbed truck. The circular bases of the kiddie rides folded up, the various cars, boats or horses stowed in special compartments. The tire ruts in the field were two feet deep in places from the big trucks heading out with their loads of mirth and nausea. Soon all that remained were the ruts, a few peg holes where tents had been erected, and a lingering smell of popcorn and excitement.

Then there was not even that. Work crews came in to smooth out the tire marks, replace divots, and clean up the garbage. The local children once again played soccer in the field, only occasionally pausing to remark on how much fun the fair had been.

The carnival had moved on, but one trailer had not followed them to the next town, the next field, the next gig. Mistress Estella, the wicked good fortune teller, had stayed behind in Fletcherville. She had seen the future—her own future. Oddly enough, it came in the shape of a thin, craggy-featured man with curly brown hair, an earring, a truly astonishing collection of scars, and a rarely seen smile that made her knees feel like rubber. So although the carnival had moved on, she had stayed, because she loved Ray Griffin.

Estella wasn't quite certain when she had realized that. When he had first come into her fortune-teller's tent, followed by a vampire, she'd been slightly afraid of him. To those with the eyes to see, Ray gave off an aura of occult power that was almost overwhelming. There was also his staggering collection of scars to consider, not all of them visible. He had enough emotional baggage for an entire around the world trip, including carry-ons. He had a falcon, made of a magic that Estella didn't understand, who thought that earrings were appetizers. Reading his palm had been one of the hardest things she had ever done, because the future she had seen there had been...well, no future. Not that he was going to die, but that his life was stalled.

He was a witch. He preferred the word "mage," but power was power. He was a killer, and a witch, and had once tried to commit suicide. His best friend was a smart-ass punk vampire, and almost all his friends were immortal, undead, or had the power to some extent. He worked part-time as a mechanic in town when they needed him, and was always broke. Not exactly the man she had dreamed of catching.

But then, she was a half-gypsy telling carnival fortunes to the gadje, a profession that her own people looked upon as virtual treason. It wasn't her fault that she'd inherited the Second Sight. Her other unwelcome inheritance had been a vampire. Really, she and Ray had been practically destined for each other, if you wanted to look at things that way.

But love? When had she fallen in love? When he'd kissed her the first time, in that dusty warehouse in north Bangor, the Penobscot River flowing just outside, with two amused vampires, a whatever Evan was, and a slightly bewildered Archdruid as an audience? It had been an awkward kiss, at best, and both of them had blushed, but it had definitely not been love.

She hadn't, she realized, precisely *fallen* in love. She hadn't woken up one morning with little pink cherubs fluttering over her bed, firing arrows into her heart. It was more like going swimming in a strange lake of chilly water. First you get your toes wet, then your knees, then the edge of your suit so that the water creeps up it and it clings to you and you get goosebumps.

She had the distinct feeling that Ray was still at the knees stage. It would take him a long time to get up the nerve to dive under the surface of the lake.

Meanwhile, she had to keep her head above water. Fletcherville was a very small town and jobs were scarce, especially off-season, but she had managed to find a part-time niche serving drinks in the nightclub (she highly suspected that the fact the nightclub owner was a member of the Brotherhood of Darkness had something to do with her finding employment) and did readings for the townspeople in her off hours. As most of them had already come to her at the fair, or were highly suspicious of fortune tellers, this wasn't a particularly lucrative pastime. She lived in the trailer, which was now in the mostly deserted trailer park.

Dating a mage was an experience, especially considering he'd never really dated anyone before. Neither had Estella, when it came to that. Rigo had always scared off anybody who'd started to get serious. She and Ray were a bit old for the movies and pizza routine, but Fletcherville didn't offer much in the way of activities, especially in the fall. Still, they'd managed to have something resembling a relationship.

She was meeting him tonight, in fact, for dinner. He didn't cook much, so he'd offered to take her out. Off-season, it was either the club or the Fletcherville Inn, or the Lobster Trap if you wanted to go upscale. They were going to the Inn...and if she didn't stop staring at the field, gathering moonbeams, she was going to be late.

It would be nice, Estella thought a bit wistfully, to see Ray in something besides black. He'd dressed up tonight, though he'd worn a black jacket, and black pants that weren't jeans, and a button-down shirt—black, of course. Other than the omnipresent gold earring and his watch, he never wore jewelry, not even a ring. He would look nice in blue, she thought, to match his eyes. Or red. Or even brown.

She'd asked him why he only wore black. He'd shrugged.

"It goes with everything," he answered, and that was that.

He kissed her, though, without any prompting. He was learning; it wasn't awkward at all.

Conversation at dinner was the usual; work, the town hall meeting, the various ups and downs of life in a small town, the doings of the Brotherhood. Estella was making a few friends in town, and talked about them. They ate and shared half a bottle of wine (Ray was driving) and talked and laughed. It was good to hear Ray laugh.

"Coffee and dessert?"

Where had that waiter come from? Estella blinked at him. Surely dinner couldn't already be over? She opened her mouth to ask for coffee, but Ray squeezed her hand.

"We can have coffee at my place," he said. "Mary dropped me off some cookies and date squares today, too."

It was a long haul out to the Cliff Road just for coffee and cookies. Then Estella mentally kicked herself. This wasn't an invitation for coffee.

"Sounds good to me," she smiled.

"Just the check then, please," Ray told the waiter.

There were coffee and date squares. Andrei had been firmly put to bed on his perch, hooded and jessed to keep him quiet. The house was peaceful; the radio was tuned to soft jazz that barely intruded on their senses. Suddenly shy, Ray turned to look out the window of the kitchen towards the ocean, simply a dark blot below the cliff's edge at this time of night.

Estella came up behind Ray and draped her arms around his shoulders. She could feel him fighting his automatic reaction, which was to flinch away from the contact. At least he was fighting it. Maybe in another twenty years, he wouldn't have to.

"You should let me give you a massage," she said, running her hands over the sharp lines of his shoulder bones.

He turned his head to look at her. She returned the look calmly.

"I'd have to take my shirt off."

"Ray, sooner or later, I'm going to see what's under your shirt."

He snorted, trying not to laugh. "I know," he admitted, sheepishly. "I just wish..." He shrugged, unable to finish the thought.

She put a hand on one side of his face, gently. "Don't. There is nothing to be gained by wishing."

Ray's lips twitched as he recalled a certain fairy godmother problem experienced by a friend, but he didn't say anything about it.

Estella took his unresisting hand, ignoring the flush of psychic insight the contact gave her, and led Ray into his bedroom.

There was an awkward moment when they stood there, looking at each other. Then, with another shrug, Ray unbuttoned his shirt.

It was all Estella could do not to gasp at the random patterning of scar tissue thus revealed. She had known it would be bad. His hands, wrists, neck and face all had their souvenirs of violence, but they were minor compared to his back. There were the unmistakable scars left by a whip. There were cigarette burns, welts, and harder-to-read marks that might have been left by a belt buckle or some other hard metal object. Worst of all was the shiny, melted mess across his left shoulder-blade, as if he had been caught in a very localized, very hot fire.

Her hand shaking, Estella touched this ugliest scar. Searing pain...a concentrated jet of fire...a man screaming that all witches must burn...Her hand dropped.

"Someone really hated you," she said.

"My father," Ray answered. There was no bitterness in his

tone. There was nothing at all. "He hated both me and my mother for having the power when he didn't."

"What happened to your mother?" Estella asked, although she had a fairly good idea what the answer was.

"He killed her," Ray said, still in that awful emotionless voice. "He pushed her down the stairs, and she broke her neck. He said it was an accident. Just like turning the blow torch on me was an accident. I must have had the highest number of 'accidents' of any kid in Chicago, but nobody ever caught on or investigated. My father was a very plausible liar."

"And the whip marks?" Estella wondered, not quite touching those, not wanting to feel that pain. "Surely even your father wouldn't explain those as accidents."

"Ah, well," Ray said, some emotion that she couldn't identify creeping into his voice, "Those aren't from my father. Those are from Matthew."

"Matthew?" The name was unfamiliar, at least in this context. She had at least two cousins named Matthew, but something in the way Ray pronounced the name made her think that this Matthew was not a cousin.

Ray sat down on the bed, and patted the space beside him. She joined him, wondering what she'd let herself in for.

"I ran away from home when I was thirteen," Ray said. "All I took with me were my clothes and my grandfather's pocket knife. Somehow, I had managed to save that from all of my father's raids on my room. I had no idea where to go or who to turn to. My father had estranged himself from everyone else in his own family, and I didn't know any of my mother's family. So I wandered the streets, just another runaway kid, and fell in with a gang. The power was growing steadily, and I think I scared the rest of the gang, because even though I was pretty bad at being a street kid, they let me hang with them. I learned fast, though. But when I was fourteen, they had a purge of the streets, rounded up the gangs, and sent those of us under eighteen to Juvenile Hall.

"I wasn't there very long when I was taken out. Not by my father, who reportedly had told them to let me rot when he found out where I was. A smooth- talking lawyer representing a philanthropic gentleman who wanted to make me his legal ward got me out. I doubt if they'd get away with that these days, but this was almost thirty years ago; child protection laws and so forth were much less strict than they are now. I was released into the lawyer's custody."

"Were you excited?" Estella asked, hoping that asking

questions wouldn't interrupt the flow. He'd never really talked about his past before.

"I didn't know what to think. The only truly happy moments I'd ever had in my life had been with my mother, and they were marred by memories of my father beating the crap out of both of us for being happy. I was a pretty cynical fourteen year old. I wondered what this philanthropic gentleman really wanted. I wasn't worried about rape or anything; first of all, it didn't even occur to me, and even if it had, I was no great beauty even then. There are easier ways to procure young boys than taking them out of Juvie Hall, after all. I just figured that he wanted me for something else, maybe because I was a witch.

"And I was right. The lawyer worked for Matthew. I never knew Matthew's last name, he hid it to keep himself safe. Probably Matthew wasn't even his real first name. He was a master sorcerer, what in some circles is called a ceremonial magician; a powerful magic worker on the Left Hand Path."

"Not a Satanist?" Estella asked.

Ray shook his head, not impatiently, just resignedly. "Most definitely not," he replied. "First, true Satanism is a lot rarer than people think it is; a lot of Pagans get tarred with the Satanism label but they aren't Satanists. People just don't understand witchcraft...call it what you will. Words are so misleading when it comes to the power. Satanists are just the obverse of Christians. Satanism is a Judeo-Christian religion, like it or not. No witch of any path or craft or colour or what have you would have anything to do with Satanism. Matthew was a lot of things, but he did not worship the Father of Lies. No, he just wanted the power that comes with darkness and followed the appropriate path."

"And he wanted you," Estella put her arm around him. She could feel his heart beating inside his chest.

"Power calls to power," Ray said simply. "When I walked into your tent, I knew you had the Sight. I could sense Matthew myself, dimly, without knowing what it was I sensed. It was like the echo of a toothache. But I must have been like a whole mouth full of rotten teeth, to extend the metaphor, to anyone with the power. He got to me first."

"And he was evil." Estella hugged him to her.

He briefly put his head on her shoulder. "Evil seems such a trite word. It's overused and has lost its true meaning. I can't really think of a better one, though. Matthew was ambitious and self-centered and didn't give a damn about the consequences to anyone or anything as long as he got the results he wanted. He wanted to make me his star pupil, to groom me to be his successor. Ultimately, I think he wanted to steal my power from me to make it his own, but he wasn't strong enough to do that. He couldn't find the key that would make the transfer without killing him. Killing me, he didn't care about as long as my power went to him. But he couldn't figure out how to do it. He sure tried hard enough."

"Would there have been a way?"

"Oh, certainly. I've known of at least two ways for years. Both unfortunately leave the original possessor of the power quite dead. But Matthew, luckily, never found them out. So he tried, instead, to make me be what he wanted me to be...as evil as he was."

"And when you wouldn't, he beat you."

"As you can see," he nodded. "And that's just the physical beatings. Magic leaves no marks, but trust me, it still hurts."

"When did he whip you?"

"When I got this," he touched the gold earring in his left ear. "Oh, that made him furious."

"I'm amazed he let you keep it."

"The earring, or the ear?" Ray smiled. "He calmed down after I'd bled enough, and said it would damn well serve me right if it got infected. It never did."

"How did you finally get free of him?"

"I killed him."

Estella remembered when he and Francis had come into her tent, and she had read his palm. "There is blood on these hands," she murmured, taking his scarred right hand and kissing it in the exact centre.

"These hands have done evil," he nodded solemnly, shuddering slightly as she kissed him. Even he could not tell if it was from pain or pleasure.

Her dark eyes raised from his hand to his face. "But their owner is not evil. He died hard, Matthew."

"Can you See that?"

"Flashes," she answered, not letting go of his hand. "But I know it, because I know you, and it would not have been easy."

"We duelled," Ray said, aware of her lips, now nuzzling the sensitive spot on the inside of his wrist. "He wasn't the first person I killed, Matthew. Or the last."

She stopped what she was doing, to Ray's inner regret, and put her arms around his too-thin body. "Don't live in the past, Ray," she said, smiling a little, because she'd told him that at their first meeting, too. "I won't say it doesn't matter, because of course it does, but the present matters, too."

"But I'm a..." he started to protest.

Her lips closed over his, preventing him from finishing the sentence. He admittedly didn't try very hard. His arms went around her, and then suddenly they were both on the bed and the kissing had an added dimension of urgency to it. Ray looked down into Estella's eyes, and knew that he wanted her very much, wanted to lose his pain inside her.

With a slow, shy smile, she took his hands and guided them to the zipper of her dress.

He started to speak, but she put a finger on his lips.

Clothing was always the most awkward part. There's just something inherently ridiculous about getting undressed in front of another person, especially when it's for the first time.

It really was the first time, for them both. Ray had seen naked women before, but he had never been permitted to *do* anything about it, not even to touch them except in a very impersonal way. Matthew, while he had controlled Ray's life, had wanted his protégé kept virginal. He had believed it would increase Ray's magical aura; and while Ray had noted bitterly that Matthew himself screwed whatever woman would lie still long enough, he had held to the prohibition about sex. After he had killed Matthew and fled to the protection of the Brotherhood, he simply hadn't felt the desire. There was not a huge supply of available women in Fletcherville to begin with, and most of them were slightly afraid of him. In the Brotherhood itself, there was only Maggie, and while she wasn't uninteresting, there'd never been any particular spark between the two of them.

There'd been sparks almost the moment he'd set eyes on Estella; they'd both just been too preoccupied to see them.

He had more scars, revealed when he took off his jeans and underwear. Estella had almost none at all, except for a small knobbly one on her left knee that she said was a souvenir of falling off her bicycle at eight.

"You're beautiful," Ray said.

"So are you," she smiled.

For once, he didn't argue. They fell back on the bed, and explored each other's bodies, hands and lips discovering the ticklish spots, the tender areas, the little secret hollows and places that made the other one gasp.

There was very little speaking. Eye movements, gestures, nods...these were enough. Neither of them had ever done this before, but some things are instinctual. When she felt she was ready, Estella cupped his erection and guided him in.

Out in the kitchen, Andrei, hooded and jessed on his perch, shrieked.

Estella was on the phone with her mother. She made frantic hand signals to Ray, who was wandering aimlessly around the trailer while waiting for her to finish the conversation so that they could go to a movie. He took the hint and sat down quietly and pretended he wasn't there.

"I think it's about time I met this boyfriend of yours," Estella's mother was saying.

"We aren't in high school, Mother," Estella rolled her eyes for Ray's benefit. "He's not my 'boyfriend.'"

"Would you prefer that I called him that gadjo?" her mother demanded, with some asperity. "Or would 'lover' be a better term, now that you've slept with him?"

Estella didn't ask how her mother knew that. Mothers have a Second Sight all their own. "Boyfriend is fine," she sighed.

"You will come and visit me this weekend," her mother said. It was not a request.

"Yes, Mother."

After a few more "Yes, Mothers," Estella told her mother she loved her and ended the conversation. She sat staring at the phone for a minute.

"Estella?" Ray asked.

"Do you have any armour?" Estella asked him. "Full plate, for a preference, but chain mail will do."

He blinked. "I have a sword."

She shook her head. "Never mind. I hope you didn't have any plans for this weekend."

"No. Why?"

"You're going to meet my mother."

"Oh."

She went over and kissed him. "You poor unsuspecting man."

Ray thought about this. Estella's uncle Rigo, a strong, tough vampire of the old school, was terrified of Estella's mother. "I guess we're not taking Francis with us."

"The only member of the Brotherhood, besides you, that I'd introduce to my mother is Michael."

"Because he's a powerful magic user?"

"No. Because he's small and cute, and Mother wouldn't pick on him."

Francis laughed like hell when Ray repeated those words to him. "You'd better not tell Michael that she said that," the vampire snorted.

"Believe me, I don't intend to."

"Though really," Francis said, when he could stop snickering, "I can't see that Estella's mother is really all *that* bad."

"You haven't met her," Ray said. "Of course, neither have I. So how do you know what she's like?"

"Women take after their mothers. Estella's not that bad, so her mother can't be that bad."

Ray thought about Estella. Their first few meetings had been pretty rocky. When Estella set her mind to something, it took a cataclysmic event to divert her from it. That strength of purpose, magnified, could be daunting.

He also noted, with a private smile, how Francis' opinion of Estella had changed. "I'll let you know for sure if I survive the weekend. Anyway, we're off first thing in the morning, so I should get back."

"Lot of packing to do, I expect." Francis winked at him.

"That, too," Ray nodded, allowing a grin to escape.

"I'm happy for you, man."

He really was, Ray realized. He'd been worried that Francis would be jealous that Ray now spent so much time with Estella. But Francis had accepted it with a grace that surprised everyone.

"You need to find a steady girl," Ray said. Looking around the untidy shack in which his best friend lived, for lack of a better word, he added mentally, *One who would burn this place down, for a start...*

Francis dug under an unidentifiable pile of junk and produced a little black book. "Got seventeen of them," he replied with some satisfaction.

"You're hopeless."

"Ah, well," Francis smiled, with more than a suggestion of smugness. "After all, I have no future."

"Estella said she was sorry about that," Ray sighed, then shook his head. Francis was baiting him. "Never mind. I'll see you when we get back."

"If you get back. Good luck with Estella's mother."

"Thanks."

Estella's mother lived in New Hampshire, a longish drive from Fletcherville. Ray and Estella left while it was still thinking about being dawn. Andrei had been left in the care of the Fairlawn family. He wasn't happy about this, but meeting Estella's mother was complicated enough for Ray without having his magical falcon along for the ride. Anyway, Galen and Vivain got a kick out of the bird, so he'd be well looked-after.

The fall colours were in full display as the car travelled south and west. The two of them talked to pass the time; though very little of any lasting consequence was said. Neither of them was inclined to discuss their future together, their relationship, or the upcoming visit. Everything was still too new and too wonderful for words.

It seemed a good time for a meal break when they reached the border of Maine and New Hampshire. Estella would take over the driving once they'd eaten. They were taking their time, going at their leisure and enjoying the scenery. Estella's mother wasn't expecting them until supper time.

Neither of them noticed the car that followed them out of the parking lot of the restaurant where they'd stopped for lunch.

Ray opened his eyes, and knew he was in deep trouble. The magic had always been there, his whole life, even before he had known what it was. Now it was gone. No, not gone, not precisely, but unavailable. It was a bizarre feeling. He knew he had the power, but he could not access it.

What the hell had happened? He and Estella had been forced off the road, just like it happened in the movies and then...then blankness, and this terrible awakening to being powerless.

He was lying down, on a floor. Nothing *hurt*, physically, though he felt a bit sick and disoriented. Whoever had ambushed them must have used some sort of gas, or possibly magic, to disable them.

Them. Where was Estella?

It was dark in here, wherever here was. Ray groped around, found floor, walls, something that might have been a door, but no amount of frantic searching yielded the touch of another body.

He hadn't been tied up, at any rate. But he was alone, in the dark, unaware of what had happened to bring him here, and cut off from his power and his lover. He felt around the walls until he came to the door again, searching for a latch or knob. It was locked, which didn't surprise him. He was obviously a prisoner. Of whom, and for what reason, he had no idea.

Whoever it was, though, had to be powerful magically. That narrowed the field somewhat.

His bladder made an urgent request. In his groping around he'd discovered a bucket in one corner. Chances were whoever had locked him in here wasn't going to let him out to go to the bathroom.

Somebody—and the options were limited—had already vomited into the bucket at least once. Still, there wasn't much choice except a wall, and he was too civilized for that.

He moved to the opposite corner to be as far away from the smell as possible. Things were going to get unpleasant if he was in here for any length of time.

Where was Estella?

He checked his pockets, without any hope of finding anything. Empty. No cell phone, no wallet, nothing. They—whoever They might be—had taken his Trumps, the deck of hand-drawn cards that enabled him to contact his friends. Without access to his power, he doubted if he could have used the Trumps anyway, but they were a part of him. The lack of them ached. His watch was gone, too, not that he could have read it in total darkness.

Thirst, he realized after awhile, was also going to be a problem. Whoever had thrown him into this room wanted him kept alive, so chances were they wouldn't allow him to die of dehydration, but they would let him suffer.

Just when he was considering throwing up again, but trying to choke it back down because the room was already foul enough, the door opened. Before he could react, he was hit with a taser. His vision blurred and he collapsed instantly, with total loss of muscle control. It left him shaken for a minute.

A hand reached down, grasped his arm, and hauled him to his feet. By then the effect had passed, but he was not anxious to repeat the experience.

"Amazing," drawled a voice that Ray had not thought he would ever hear again, a voice from almost thirty years in his past. "There are people afraid of this pathetic wreck."

Someone snickered, in the background. Ray's guts heaved, but there was nothing left in them to throw up. That wasn't from the taser, he knew. Whatever they'd used to knock him out in the first place had made him nauseous. He tried to focus, but the light coming in from the hallway only blinded him after his long stay in the dark. There were at least three, possibly four people there, including the one holding him up—the one with the familiar voice.

"Eric Bates," he said, managing to make it a sneer.

"So, you remember me," said the man gripping him. "How touching."

"What did you do to Estella?"

"Is that her name? Nothing."

"Where is she?"

"Safe. For the moment. And as long as you cooperate with us, she'll stay safe."

"Let her go. She's nothing to you; she's got no connection with my past."

"Perhaps not," the shadowy Eric Bates conceded, "but she does mean something to you, so we'll keep her for insurance." He gestured to the figures in the doorway. "Clean him up; he's no danger at the moment."

Not as long as they had the taser, Ray thought sourly. They took him to a bathroom and sluiced him down in the shower, then, blessedly, let him drink some water. His stomach threatened to rebel against it, but he managed to keep it down. Water was important. He had no idea when he'd be allowed more. Clothes were thrown at him. They were his, from the duffle bag he'd packed for the weekend. He put them on and waited to see what would happen next.

So, Eric Bates. The past had finally caught up with Ray. He'd been expecting this particular shoe to drop for over twelve years now. Eric had been Matthew's toady; and a far nastier piece of goods than even the master.

What had the son of a bitch done with Estella?

Twelve years was a long time to wait for revenge, but Bates had always been cautious. No doubt he'd just been biding his time, waiting until Ray dropped his guard and was vulnerable. Had the bastard actually waited until Ray found a girlfriend, so that he'd have that extra leverage? Nothing would be too surprising, where Bates was concerned.

Ray was amazed he was still alive, but probably he was meant to suffer. There'd undoubtedly be torture. He knew the way the other man's mind worked. He shuddered, knowing that Estella was the one in real danger, that Bates would think it amusing to make Ray watch while Estella was hurt, even killed.

He should have taken Bates down at the same time he'd killed Matthew. Of course, he'd barely been alive himself at the time.

The other men herded him out of the bathroom again. They weren't witches. Their only power was in their muscles, but it was enough to make him comply. And they had the damn taser. Oh, yes, very magical, that.

He was taken into a different room than the one he'd woken up in. This one had furniture, and a window. The window was barred, and the furniture all either incredibly heavy wood or metal, nothing easily breakable. Eric Bates was sitting in a big leather chair, smiling at him.

"Where is Estella?" Ray asked.

"You're in love," Bates said, the smile not wavering. "How sweet. I suppose you've already screwed her. You know Matthew wouldn't have approved."

"Matthew's dead. Where is she, Eric?"

"Yes, I know Matthew's dead. That's why you're here, really."

Ray sagged against the nearest wall. He still felt sick and weak, and the loss of his magic had him seriously off-balance. It was frustrating as hell to know that the magic was still there, but as unreachable as if locked in a vault. He knew at least a couple of spells that could do that; but they were very advanced. Eric hadn't used to be that talented. His skills had lain in other directions than magic.

There was another witch here, then. Someone very, very good.

"So, this is about Matthew," Ray sighed. "Look, Estella's no part of it. She never even met him. Let her go."

Eric quirked an eyebrow. Twelve years had left him looking twenty years older; his hair was thinning and grey and there were lines on his face, but he still looked like a smart, dangerous weasel.

"Let her go," he repeated, as if considering it. Then he shook his head. "So that she could go running straight back to that idiotic bunch of do-gooders you call friends? I think not. We'll have no dramatic rescues by the Brotherhood of Darkness."

"They'll still come looking. We were going for a weekend visit. We'll be missed. There will be an alarm, and searchers."

Eric dismissed this with a wave. "They'll have some trouble finding you without your precious pack of cards, and you have no magic to be traced at the moment. Not to mention that we seem to currently have the best psychic in the area under lock and key. Vampires are clever, Griffin, but they aren't good trackers, and the damned Druid can't find you without the trail of magic to sniff." He stood up. "And we made sure there was no scent trail, just in case they get clever with the werewolf. No, I'm afraid that they will look, but quite in vain."

"You waited a long time before coming to get me," Ray said. "Why?"

"Several reasons; most of them are vampires."

"You're afraid of the Brotherhood. But I've left the valley several times before this."

"Yes, but you never had a woman with you before."

"You were waiting for me to get a girlfriend?" Ray blinked. "How did you know I would?"

"I didn't, of course," Bates replied. "But I reasoned that, sooner or later, you would be vulnerable somehow. Let your guard down. The woman was a surprise, but a handy one."

"So as soon as you saw me with a girl, you pounced." Ray shook his head. "Even for you, that's devious. And a lot of effort to go to just to kill me."

Bates raised an eyebrow. "Who said anything about killing you?"

"Isn't that what this is all about?" Ray stared at him. "Revenge? Killing me to avenge Matthew?"

"Why would I want to avenge Matthew?" Bates stood up and walked to the barred window. "I have no intention of killing you, Ray."

"Then why did you go to all this trouble?"

"If I'd wanted to kill you, would I have gone to all this trouble? A simple car accident would have been far easier to arrange, don't you think? Oh, no, I don't want to avenge Matthew. I want to replace him."

Ray's head and stomach were still deeply troubled by previous events. He didn't quite follow. "All you'd have to do is take over the coven. You don't need me for that."

"I don't mean replace him personally," Bates scoffed. "I get much more done as the power behind the throne, so to speak. We have had a certain amount of...difficulty finding a suitable candidate to replace Matthew as coven leader. Things have been in chaos for the last twelve years. So I thought that it would be most suitable to replace Matthew with someone he trained for the job."

"What are you talking about?" Ray asked, although he had a feeling he knew.

"You."

"You're insane."

"You were very thoroughly trained, I believe."

"I would have thought that my killing Matthew indicated my opinion of following him."

Eric shrugged. "It's not unprecedented for the apprentice to kill the master in order to take his place."

"I killed him because he was an animal," Ray said, anger tightening his voice. "I am not replacing him. I changed paths."

"You may have thought you did, but the dark never really leaves. Not truly. Does it?"

"You know nothing about it. You are too firmly on the Left

Hand to know."

Eric sat down again, regarding Ray calmly. "Tell me truthfully that you have never had doubts. Never had nightmares. That you have never questioned your commitment to the light. Tell me that you have never looked at your hands and known what they did, seen and smelt the blood on them. That you have never tried to end your own life because you could not live with the knowledge of what you are."

"You son of a bitch." It was said quietly, not shouted.

The other man leaned back in the chair, his gaze never wavering. "Matthew trained you too well for you not to take his place. You will be coven leader."

"I will not."

"Then I'm rather afraid that we will have to kill your girlfriend."

"You'll kill her anyway," Ray said. *Estella,* he thought, cold seeping into his bones. *Oh, Estella.*

"No. After all, we must have some insurance that you will do what you're told."

"I won't play your games, Eric."

A flicker, then, in those brown eyes. "I see that even a girlfriend isn't enough to bring you to heel. You always were too stubborn and disobedient. Perhaps what you really need is to be reminded of what you were...a talented but undisciplined brat. I wonder...where do you think we can procure a magically inclined thirteen year-old or two?"

Ray froze. "You wouldn't *dare* touch those twins," he hissed.

"Twins? Did I mention any twins? Oh, dear, what can you be thinking?"

"You know perfectly well who I mean."

"It's really quite tempting, considering how often they leave the protection of the wards you so carefully constructed. Something of an oversight on their father's part, signing them up for soccer. Pity the older girl hasn't an ounce of talent; she'd be extremely useful, too."

"Stay away from the Fairlawns," Ray growled.

"If you do what you're told."

So that was it. Estella was a literal hostage, and the Fairlawn children potential ones, in exchange for Ray himself switching back to black magic.

"Aren't you going to tell me how much more alluring and rewarding the dark side of the force is?"

Eric raised an eyebrow. "You watch too many movies. I don't have to tell you anything about the Left Hand Path, Ray. You walked it long enough to know the power it gives."

"Tainted power. Blood magic."

A shrug. "Whatever it takes."

Ray sagged down onto a hard metal chair. "You have someone binding my magic. That's a powerful spell. I don't brag about my power, but I am one of the best. It would take a lot to cut me off from it. Whoever is doing that should be your coven leader."

"Ah." Eric smiled, but there was no humour in it, no warmth. "You have hit on a little problem."

"What do you mean?"

"Come and see." He nodded to the shadowy tough guys. "Give him another jolt, just to make sure he behaves."

Again the blurred vision, the instant loss of muscle power, the moment of weakness. The bastard had shoved the prongs in hard, too.

"Such magic," Ray said when he could talk and move again.

"I use whatever resources are necessary."

Ray was hustled out of the room and into yet another room down the hall. This one was better furnished, and there were no bars on the window. The way that one of the husky guards went and stood in front of the window told Ray that there would be no escape that way. This room was already occupied. A small form sat huddled on the bed, knees drawn up to its chest. Milky white eyes stared at nothing, but the head had turned when they had entered.

"Matthew's biggest secret," Eric said, smiling again at Ray's shocked expression. "You never knew, did you?"

"Who is this child?" Ray asked.

The sightless eyes turned towards him. "I am Deirdre." It was a whisper, a breath. "You are Ray Griffin."

"Yes, I am. Are you Matthew's daughter?" It was hard to be sure. The child had wispy blond hair, but seemed far too fragile to be an offshoot of the robust Matthew. Not to mention that, logically, she had to be at least thirteen or fourteen. She looked much younger.

"I hold your power," said Deirdre, ignoring this question. "Eric told me to. Since my mother and father are dead, Eric looks after me. He is very kind."

Ray shot the weasel a hard look, which was met with another bland smile. "I'm sure he is," he replied. "Who was your mother?"

"She died," the girl replied, in that wisp of a voice. "Falling, falling, falling."

"Your mother was Gemma?" Ray's voice almost strangled in

his throat.

"She fell, and the sea took her away. It was dark, and the cliffs were like teeth."

"And your father?"

"The things in the woods ate him, after you slew him. They are always hungry. They will eat you one day."

"How are you holding my magic?"

The guard hit him with the taser for asking, and he collapsed to the floor.

"Falling, falling, falling," said Deirdre.

"I won't let him bother you again, Deirdre," said Eric, kicking Ray back up to his feet. "You get some sleep now."

Ray was herded back out and back into the room with the bars.

"Jesus!" Ray said, ignoring the distress this caused. "Matthew and Gemma had a daughter? How did they ever keep that a secret?"

"Easily enough," Eric replied. "Gemma liked those flowing robes, you may recall, and she wasn't much interested in motherhood. The baby was given to me to raise. You were deliberately not told about her."

"She has a remarkable talent," Ray said.

"And it has been very well trained."

"Funny, I didn't notice any scars."

"Deirdre is more...tractable than you were. Also, I've had her since she was a baby. She thinks of me more as her father than Matthew, whom she barely knew."

"So you want me to be coven leader just until Deirdre is old enough, is that it?"

"Deirdre will never be coven leader. Yes, the talent is there, but she is otherwise unsuitable. She's far too fragile."

"She's blind, you mean."

"Fragile. She wouldn't last ten minutes in the coven."

"You'll have to make her give me back access to the power."

"That won't be a problem, once we have your pledge of cooperation."

"What do the other members think of this?"

"They do what I tell them."

Ray nodded. That didn't surprise him. Unless the membership had changed radically in twelve years, the coven members were all cowed by the combination of Matthew and Eric. They had, he remembered bitterly, been cowed by *him*, as well.

"So, do I have it?" Eric asked.

"What?" Ray's thoughts had been miles and years away.

"Your pledge."

"Go to hell."

Eric nodded. "I thought you might say that." He gestured to the bully boys. "Hurt him, but no permanent damage. I will go have a little chat with the girlfriend."

Bates walked out and shut the door after him.

Pain happened.

Estella looked up as the door was unlocked. This...house or whatever it was seemed to have an infinite number of rooms. She didn't know it had been deliberately built by Matthew and Eric to house the unwilling. It was an elaborate prison. The room she was held in was very similar to the second one Ray had been taken to: heavy furniture, barred windows, no breakable knick-knacks or things that could be thrown.

She'd been allowed bathroom trips and food and drink. The food hadn't interested her very much, because she'd been just as nauseous as Ray upon waking. Her stomach had settled a bit, but all she'd allowed it was some water.

"You again?" she sighed as Eric Bates came in. "Where's Ray?"

"Your concern for each other is truly touching," Eric replied. "He asked frequently about you, as well."

"If you've hurt him..."

He laughed. "There is precisely nothing you can do about it. What should be worrying you, my dear Estella, is what we are going to do to you."

"I'm no longer qualified to be a sacrifice."

His infuriating smile tweaked his lips. "That's Satanists, I'm afraid."

"Are you saying you don't sacrifice people?" Estella glared. "Because Ray told me..."

"We don't sacrifice people," Eric replied. "We just kill them."

There was something in his voice and manner, in the cold hardness of his utterly sane eyes, that said he was telling the truth. She had *Seen* things Ray had done. There wasn't enough money in the world to persuade her to touch Eric Bates.

"Then kill me and get it over with. Or haven't you ever read any of the Evil Overlord website?"

Eric's lips actually twitched before he controlled himself. "You and Griffin are certainly made for each other. We don't kill hostages. Not as long as they're potentially useful."

"I'm a hostage? No one will pay ransom for me. My mother

has no money."

"I'm not interested in money. That isn't the ransom I'm demanding."

"What do you want, then?"

"Your boyfriend."

Estella's own eyes narrowed. "Really? You're going to be disappointed, then. Ray's not interested in other men."

He didn't react, just looked at her. "You're trying to make me angry. It's quite a stupid thing to do. I won't just slap you, Estella, if you make me angry. I am not interested in Griffin sexually. If I was, I could have had him twenty years ago. I need him for other purposes."

"Like what?"

"We need someone to replace Matthew. Ray happens to be the most qualified person available."

Estella stared at him. "Are you kidding?"

"I assure you, I never kid."

No, of course he wouldn't. Not this weaselly man with the cold brown eyes—and she'd never thought that brown eyes could be cold—in the tailored grey suit. Matthew had been a monster, but Eric Bates was the man behind the monster. Ray hadn't mentioned Eric to her. Some things are worse than nightmares.

"And me?" she asked.

"Insurance," Bates replied.

"People will be looking for us."

"Yes, so Ray mentioned, as well. They can look in vain. Vampires and Druids don't worry us much."

"My *mother* will be looking for us."

"Am I supposed to be frightened?" Eric almost chuckled. "What can she do, little fortune teller? A gypsy curse, perhaps?"

Estella just shook her head. She couldn't begin to explain her mother to this man, who wouldn't believe her, anyway.

"So you just keep me here as a prisoner forever? To make Ray do want you want?"

"For the moment," Bates nodded. "That is what one does with insurance, after all." He rose, but seemed to be waiting for something. "Isn't this where you're supposed to say something like 'You'll never get away with this?'"

She just looked at him. He almost smiled, that tight little weasel smile, and walked out, locking the door again.

Estella lay back on the bed, staring up at the ceiling. "Come *on*, mother!" she said out loud. "*Do* something!"

Francis was just leaving the bar he'd been visiting in order to catch the football game and heading for his Harley when a heavy arm fell on his shoulder.

A normal human would have made some exclamation of surprise or alarm, and tried to get away. Francis wasn't a normal human being. Although he hadn't sensed anyone around him, he wasn't that terribly surprised by the arm. He knew whose arm it was even before its owner spoke.

"Ah, my son!" exclaimed a hearty, slightly accented voice, "You are a very neglectful son! You have not been to see me!"

Francis sighed and turned to face the heavy features of Rigo Smith. "I'm not your son."

Rigo thumped him across the shoulders, making the slender young vampire stagger. "I told you," he boomed, ignoring the curious stares from the other patrons of the sports bar, "that you shall be as a son to me. And a son should visit his Papa, no?"

"No," Francis replied firmly.

Earlier in the year, Rigo had kidnapped Francis, bound him, locked him in a steel cage, kicked and beaten him, and tried to force information about the Brotherhood out of him. None of this had been calculated to produce any sort of filial affection.

Rigo sniffed, but made no further reaction to Francis' reply. Instead, he draped his arm around the younger man's shoulders again. "Come. We must talk where these..." he hesitated, looking for a word that would not draw attention, "...strangers cannot hear."

He drew Francis aside into a little clump of trees.

"What do you want, Rigo?" Francis asked, with little grace. "You were told to behave yourself."

Actually, Rigo had been threatened with annihilation from the Nameless Ones should he step out of line again.

"My niece is in trouble," Rigo said, dropping his voice and letting his worry show. "And your friend the magic man."

"Ray and Estella are in trouble?" Francis stared at him. "Why didn't you just say so?"

"In front of the cattle?" Rigo didn't bother to hide his contempt for humans now.

"Where are they? What kind of trouble?"

"More than just you and I can help with. We need others. The protector. That little magic man. The other vampires."

"What kind of trouble?" Francis repeated. "The Brotherhood will want to know."

"We are wasting time! Take me to them!"

If Ray and Estella really were in trouble, Francis thought, then the Brotherhood needed to know. He took his cell phone—a present from Michael after the kidnapping in the summer—and called Fairlawn.

"Michael, get everyone together. I'm bringing in Uncle Rigo. He says Ray and Estella are in trouble. Call a meeting." Francis ended the call and looked at Rigo. "Is your van here?"

"Nearby."

"Then follow me."

Francis didn't really want to introduce Rigo to the whole Brotherhood, after spending an entire night protecting his friends from this intimidating vampire. But he felt he had no choice. Ray was his best friend; and, after some initial misunderstanding, Francis and Estella had come to cautiously like each other.

However, when the current crisis was over, Francis was really looking forward to telling Michael that Rigo had described him as "that little magic-man."

Thus it was that Rigo's van followed Francis' Harley onto the Cliff Road, up past all the houses to Fairlawn.

Francis counted cars. Everyone was there, with the notable exception of Ray. But then, he and Estella were off visiting her mother, right?

The meeting-room of the Brotherhood of Darkness had its own private entrance, so that members would not disturb the household. Francis guided Rigo to this door.

Michael met them there. "Come in," he invited Rigo. "You are welcome in this room."

The careful wording was noted. Rigo nodded, and entered the room.

Everyone was looking at Rigo; it was the first time most of the Brotherhood had seen him. Rigo scanned the room, looking mostly at the vampires. They looked back at him, not with any great enthusiasm. They all knew what he'd done to Francis.

Rigo surprised everyone, possibly even himself, by going to stand in front of Gideon and dropping to one knee.

"Forgive me, my lord. I erred when I took this boy." He indicated the thunderstruck Francis.

Gideon was aware that now everybody was looking at *him*. He felt slightly bewildered, but was careful not to show it. He'd had a lot of experience in not showing his emotions. He nodded regally and gestured that Rigo should rise.

"It is not my place to forgive you. Francis is not of my line."

"But you are the senior most vampire," Rigo said. Gideon

looked at Francis. The younger vampire shrugged. He didn't know what was going on here, either.

"Let us say no more of it for the time being," Gideon said. "Tell us your news."

"My niece, Estella, and the magic man were going to visit Estella's mother," Rigo said, just suppressing a slight tremor. "I was to join them for dinner when they arrived. They did not arrive."

"Could they have met with some accident?" Michael asked. It was a hopeless question. They would have heard about an accident by now.

Rigo shook his head. "Estella's mother called the highway patrol, the hospitals, everywhere. Nothing. Their car has not been found."

Michael nodded resignedly. He had not really expected any other answer. "I tried raising Ray through the Trumps as soon as Francis called me. Nothing."

"Someone's got them," Francis said angrily. "Kidnapping seems to be a real sport around these parts." He glared at Rigo.

"I had nothing to do with this," Rigo protested. "I would not hurt Estella."

"What can we do?" Mitch asked, leaning forward. "Could we trace their route? Do you know which way they went?"

"I know which would be the most direct way," Rigo said. "But that is the way I came, to find you. There was no sign of them."

"There's got to be *something* we can do," Francis said.

"It's been at least twelve hours since they disappeared," Michael sighed. "They could be anywhere."

"Estella's mother has received no ransom demand, I take it?" Josh asked Rigo.

He shook his head. "This is not a normal kidnapping."

"Well, it was worth a shot," Josh said defensively.

Gideon patted his hand. "If they took Raymond's cards, then they know they are dealing with a magic-user. Obviously, there is witchcraft at work."

"Can you do anything?" Francis looked at the two other magic-users in the room.

The Druids exchanged glances. Neither of them looked very hopeful.

"This isn't our kind of magic," Maggie said. "We'll try, of course."

"Ironically, this is a situation where Estella would be useful," Michael said. "She found you, after all." He nodded at Francis.

"Still, we will try."

"If we only knew *where*, exactly, on the route they were taken," Mitch growled, his normally blue eyes glowing amber, "I could probably find the trail."

"I imagine that whoever took them thought of that," said Michael. "They seem to have been very thorough. Whoever has them knows about the Brotherhood, you may depend on it, and they'll have taken measures to block us from a rescue."

"We're all thinking the same thing, aren't we," spoke up Alex gloomily. "This is the work of Matthew's old coven."

"Who is Matthew?" Rigo asked.

The four who had been in Boston, fourteen or so years earlier, and encountered the coven master first-hand, all nodded. Alex, Michael, Gideon and Francis knew Matthew.

"Matthew's dead," Francis said. "So's Gemma," he added with a certain amount of relish. Gemma, who had been a very intimate follower of Matthew's, had done her best to kill Francis. She had ended up falling off the edge of the cliff.

"That leaves ten people unaccounted for, assuming the coven had the traditional number of members," Gideon pointed out.

"Please, who is Matthew?" Rigo asked again.

"Ray's master," Michael replied. "And as vicious a snake as you would never want to meet. The type who gives wicked witches a bad name." He raised a hand in anticipation of objections. "I was just making a point."

"Mitch and I will follow their route," Evan said. "We might pick up something, after all."

Evan was a man of action. Sitting around doing nothing was against his nature. He did remember to look at Gideon for approval. The Baron, still slightly stunned by Rigo's apology, nodded.

"But stay in touch," he warned his employees.

Michael stood up, as did the other Druids. "We will see what we can do. Meanwhile, the rest of you might as well go home."

Rigo looked around. "I cannot. It is too far and the night is already nearly over. I beg your protection."

Everybody looked at each other, knowing there was no way Michael would invite a strange vampire to stay in Fairlawn. Not with Mary and the kids there.

"You may stay at Oakwoods," Gideon sighed. "Under your word of oath that you shall not raise a hand to anyone in my household or the Brotherhood."

"You have my word," Rigo said. "And my gratitude."

"I'll wait until morning to go out then, with Mitch," said Evan, firmly. “We couldn’t find a trail in the dark, anyway.”

Evan could have found a trail, had one existed, in the ocean in pitch black. Gideon wasn’t fooled. But he nodded.

The meeting broke up. Francis looked particularly disconsolate.

“Chin up,” Evan told him. “We’ll find them.”

“Why did those bastards wait so long?” Francis asked, not comforted. “Ray thought he was safe, damn it.”

“Perhaps that’s why,” Evan said.

“Why don’t you come along to Oakwoods, too?” Josh asked. “Then you won’t have to wait alone for news.”

The platinum blond head came up, contemplating this. Then Francis looked at Rigo, and scowled. “Not as long as he’s there. Thanks all the same.”

Rigo watched the young vampire stalk out. “I apologized,” he said, in a hurt voice. “And still he does not forgive me. I told him he shall be as a son to me, and he does not treat me as his Papa. What more can I do?”

“Just leave him alone,” Josh suggested. “I don’t think he’s ready to forgive you, let alone be your son.”

“That’s a relationship that has to be earned,” Mitch added, with a wink and a grin at Josh.

“And tying someone up and beating them is not a good way to earn it,” Gideon contributed, with a certain amount of feeling.

Rigo sighed, and followed the Oakwoods residents back to the mansion.

Back in Fairlawn, Mary looked up as Michael and Maggie came into the living room. One look at their faces told her how the meeting had gone.

“Is there anything I can do?” she asked.

Michael shook his head and kissed his wife. “Not that I can think of,” he replied. “I’m going to scry, to see if I can locate either Ray or Estella. I doubt it will work, but it must be tried.”

The two Druids left the living room and went down to the basement of Fairlawn. This held the usual debris of a household with children—Bess’ old rocking horse, a smashed bicycle, the soccer equipment that seemed to be everywhere, tools, old furniture, and boxes piled treacherously. But through a locked door there was a different basement. Michael kept his goldsmithing equipment in the locked room; but mostly it was given over to his other vocation.

They changed into the long, plain white woolen robes that hung on hooks in this room. There wasn’t any embarrassment about changing in front of each other. They'd been doing this together for far too long. Maggie lit candles and set them around the room, then retrieved a large, plain ceramic bowl from its shelf and filled it with clear water. Michael stood in the middle of the room and chanted, raising the power.

Maggie set the bowl carefully down on the floor. The Archdruid sat on the floor and gazed into the bowl, still chanting to focus the scrying.

It wasn't like a television screen, where pictures came with clarity. The most he could hope for was impressions, clues. The water remained still and clear, yielding not even a hint of the fate of his friends.

Finally he stopped chanting and stood up. He felt every one of his two thousand plus years. Something—some*one*—was blocking his vision. They were very good.

"It's no use," he sighed as Maggie looked at him in concern. "There's someone keeping me out." What he didn't say was that he'd felt brief contact with that someone, and it was disturbing him to the marrow of his bones. The contact hadn't felt strong enough, *adult* enough, for the amount of magic involved. He needed to think about that.

"Now what do we do?" Maggie asked.

"Hope that Evan and Mitch find something," Michael saidd. "And pray."

"Go and get some rest," Maggie advised her old friend. "You look done in."

Michael nodded, too dispirited and contemplative to argue. They changed back into street clothes, and Maggie left without a word. The Archdruid climbed the stairs up to the kitchen, noting that Andrei was restless on his perch. The kitchen had been selected as the best place for falcon sitting because of its easy to clean tile floors. The falcon's hooded head turned towards Michael.

"You know something's wrong, don't you?" Michael asked, feeling stupid for talking to a bird.

He kept walking, though, on his way to the main stairs up to the bedrooms. So he didn't see Andrei flap his wings in agitation, or hear the falcon's annoyed screech.

"This is a very nice house," said Rigo, upon his first view of the interior of Oakwoods.

Gideon just nodded. He wasn't all that certain that inviting this strange vampire to spend the day was a good idea, but there'd been nowhere else for Rigo to go. Fairlawn hadn't been an option, and Francis's shack was completely out of the question. There was Valley Mansion, of course, but Alex hadn't looked very eager to play host, either.

"Remember that we have his word that he will behave," said Evan, as usual reading his employer's mind, or at least interpreting Gideon's posture. "Plus, I'll stake him and cut his head off with a dull paper knife if he steps out of line."

"I will behave," Rigo promised. "You are the vampire lord here, your word is law."

"There you go again," said Joshua amiably, noticing that Gideon still looked astounded at the title. "What's with this vampire lord business?"

Rigo turned to Joshua. "You are very young," he said kindly. "You would not understand. In the old country, we have a...I do not know the English word. Many levels of power, with one lord or lady in command."

"Hierarchy," Gideon supplied, suddenly understanding. "Yes, I've heard of that. We don't practice that over here."

Evan and Mitch exchanged looks, smirking. That wasn't precisely true. The other vampires in the Brotherhood quite often deferred to Gideon as the senior most. They wouldn't call it a hierarchy, of course, they'd just say it was seniority or good manners. When Genevieve visited, generally anything she wanted got done and Gideon deferred to *her.* He would say it was because she was a lady and his mentor.

Josh caught the smirk. Gideon, fortunately, didn't. Rigo was too worried to notice.

"All the same," Rigo said. "To me, you are the vampire lord. I am in your command while I am in your house, and in this valley." He carefully didn't mention that this was precisely the reason he had not previously entered Fletcher's Valley. He'd known the vampire lord was bound not to have approved of what he'd done to Francis.

"Estella's mother," said Josh, changing the subject and noticing Rigo wince. "She scares you?"

"You have not met her," the gypsy replied with a shudder. "Or you would understand. She is a most formidable woman."

"But only human, I gather."

"I think I understand," Evan said. "Gypsies are matriarchal, for one thing."

"Even if we were not, Estella's mother would be formidable." Something in Rigo's voice conveyed his utter conviction.

"She must be very worried about her daughter," said Mitch.

"Has she called the police?"

Rigo shook his head. "She knows that whatever happened, it is not for human police to help. She did call them to ask if there had been any accidents, but that is all. She believes that I and you can save her daughter and the magic man."

"Not if we can't find them." Gideon sighed with worry and frustration. "Someone has covered their tracks very well."

"Not well enough, maybe, for a werewolf," Mitch growled. "Evan and I will leave at first light."

"I have the horrible feeling that whoever took Ray and Estella thought of that," Evan said. "All the same, little thief, we shall try. Go get some sleep so you'll be fresh."

Mitch opened his mouth to argue, realized this would be stupid, and got up off the couch he'd flopped on. "Night, everybody."

"Why did you call him 'little thief?'" Rigo asked when the werewolf had gone.

"Caught him breaking into the house, years ago," Evan replied. "The idiot."

"He robbed you and you hired him?" Rigo stared at Gideon in amazement. "Truly, you are a great vampire lord."

Gideon shrugged in embarrassment. "I couldn't really send a werewolf to jail. He didn't actually steal anything."

"Because I was there," said Evan smugly.

"Why don't you go on up to bed, Evan?" asked Gideon, a very slight edge to his voice. "Early start, after all."

Evan's expression conveyed his extreme reluctance to leave his employer, whose safety was paramount, unprotected with Rigo in the house.

"I have his word," said Gideon quietly.

"Right you are." Evan rose up. He coincidentally brushed past Rigo on his way upstairs. "There isn't any place on this *planet* you could hide if you do anything to harm Gideon or Josh," he whispered, in the friendliest possible way.

The gypsy nodded. Evan left the room.

"He is very fierce, your protector," Rigo commented.

"He sometimes leans to the overprotective," Gideon said, allowing himself a smile. "Would you care for a drink? My special stock?"

Rigo looked from Gideon to Joshua. Josh's normally open expression was guarded. It was a test, then.

"Thank you, my lord," Rigo said. "I would very much like one."

A bottle was opened and poured. The liquid that came out was thick and had a smell that had nothing to do with fermentation.

“Animal blood,” said Rigo, working very hard on not allowing any disdain into the words.

“We have an…arrangement,” said Gideon. “The Brotherhood, and other like-minded vampires. We hunt very seldom, and never kill.” He saw Joshua’s grin. “Almost never,” he amended. “And only when it’s completely necessary. We drink animal blood, which is obtained for us by the Nameless Ones, many of whom work in the meat packing industry. This way, we can stay in one place longer, without worrying about discovery.”

“People no longer believe in vampires,” Rigo snorted. “There is less fear of discovery now.”

“Stay in one place for a hundred years, never age, and have people die or mysteriously disappear in noticeable numbers, and the humans will believe,” said Gideon.

“That is why it is wise to move around.” Rigo shrugged. Then he took in his surroundings—the comfortable wing chairs, the deep, expensive carpet, the animals lolling around underfoot. “You do not wish to move around.”

“I enjoy my comforts,” Gideon said. “I’ve earned them.”

“There are vampires who would call you traitor.”

An elegant shrug. “Words do not concern me.”

Rigo looked at Joshua. “And you? You are still so new to the blood that I hear it sing in your veins. Does the blood not tell you that this way, your lord’s way, is wrong for us? That the blood calls out for more blood, for the joy of feeding?”

Joshua thought about it. “A very small part of me might admit that you have a point,” he confessed, ignoring the astonished look on his lover’s face. “But that part is overruled by the knowledge that this way is better, safer and more civilized.”

“Civilized!” Rigo snorted. “We are wampyr!”

“That’s no reason to act like monsters.”

Rigo threw up his hands and subsided. “Of course,” he said, a bit sadly, “you follow your lord’s dictates. A good fledgling, to obey his sire so.”

“I’m not Gideon’s fledgling. I certainly don’t consider him my vampire lord.”

The gypsy opened his mouth. “You are not?”

“I agreed to be turned, in order that I could stay with Gideon, because I love him. And because I love him, I wouldn’t let him turn me. Someone else did it.”

Rigo couldn’t think of anything to say to this. They sat in silence, wine glasses in hand, watching Smoke, Pumpkin and Warg vie for the most comfortable spot in front of the fireplace.

"Would you like to see your room?" Gideon asked eventually, when the silence had stretched beyond comfort.

"Yes, my lord," Rigo nodded gratefully.

"You don't have to call me that," sighed the Baron. Nobody had called him that for many long years. His title was less than meaningless, here in America, especially since he was dead and somebody else was the Baron of Redoak.

Rigo bowed. "I must," he replied. "My lord."

"You don't seem to be much with names anyway," Josh noted.

"Names have power, fledgling."

"This way," Gideon said.

They put Rigo in the Willow Room, one of the interior guest rooms with no windows, and which incidentally was several twists and turns and two corridors away from the master bedroom. The interior of Oakwoods was a maze. "I'm afraid we don't have any pajamas that would fit you," Gideon said. Rigo topped him by nearly a foot.

"Is okay," the other vampire grinned. "I sleep in my skin."

"Well, good morning, then."

"My lord," Rigo bowed again. "Fledgling."

They left him to his own devices and made their way to the master bedroom, full of doubts and worries.

Mitch and Evan left at dawn. Not without some misgivings on Evan's part, but as Mitch pointed out, Rigo would be inoperative during the day. They followed the most likely route that Ray and Estella would have taken to get to her mother's place.

But the trail was cold, and not even Evan could follow one on a paved highway. Not even Mitch's nose could scent their quarry, or differentiate from among the smells of gas, rubber, hot engines, antifreeze, cigarettes, coffee, garbage, urine and dog faeces that permeated the highways and shoulders.

"Sometimes I wonder if progress was such a good thing," Evan remarked, noting yet another spot where a car had pulled over in order to dump garbage or allow the driver to relieve his bladder.

Mitch was twitchy, impatient. His eyes still burned amber, and his hair was even shaggier than normal. There'd been a very strong smell of dog last time they'd investigated a spot. "We're not going to find them," the werewolf growled.

"We will," Evan countered. "Or if we don't, somebody will. That's what the Brotherhood does. We rescue people."

"Help the hopeless?" Mitch laughed. It sounded like a bark.

"We were doing it first," said Evan calmly, refusing to rise to the bait. "Besides, we dress better."

There were too many skid marks on the highway, too many spots where a car had gone off the road. Investigating all of them would take a lifetime. While both Mitch and Evan had lifetimes to spare, Ray and Estella most likely did not.

Still, they kept trying. It was what the Brotherhood did.

The Fairlawn household was also up early, but this was because there were two teenagers to get off to school. Toast and homework, sneakers and textbooks, orange juice and calculators; a typical morning's panic.

"I'll drive them in," Mary offered, seeing that her husband looked preoccupied.

Andrei, freed from his hood and jesses, flew to the back of Galen's chair and snatched toast from the boy's hand.

"Three more years, and we can drive," said Vivain, paying no attention whatsoever to her brother's outraged flapping at the falcon.

"You can get more toast, Galen," his father pointed out. "Leave Andrei alone, he's distressed."

The falcon took off back for his perch with his prize. He knew, in his own way, that pecking either of the twins or Mary would be a really stupid thing to do. Michael was fair game, though, and had already felt the falcon's beak. What did it take to get a message *through* to humans?

"Yeah, poor Andrei," said Vivain. "He must know something's wrong with Ray."

"Well, of course he knows," Galen scoffed, taking another piece of toast and wolfing it down before anything could happen to it. "Otherwise, why would he be stuck in this house?"

"Maybe we should take him out," Vivain said. "I'm pretty sure I can swing the lure."

"That's not a good idea, honey," her mother told her. "What if Andrei didn't come back to the lure?"

"He could take us to wherever Ray is, I bet!" Vivain exclaimed.

Her brother stared at her, then burst out laughing. "You dummy! Andrei's a falcon, not a collie!"

Vivain glared at him. Mary decided it was a good time to change the subject.

"Do you have your permission slips for that field trip to the museum?" she asked.

"Yep," Vivain nodded.

"I don't see why we have to go," Galen complained. "We don't need to visit a museum to find out about old stuff. We can just ask Dad."

"Oh, go to school," his father snorted.

A few minutes later, still bickering, the twins were ushered out to the family car.

Michael looked thoughtfully at Andrei. The falcon had finished the toast and was eyeing the remains of breakfast, wondering what else he could steal.

"What *do* you know, I wonder?" the Archdruid mused.

Andrei shrieked and flapped his wings. He launched himself off the perch and flew around the kitchen, making Michael duck.

The trouble was, the ancient Druid realized as the bird tried its damnedest to eat his right ear, that everybody forgot that Andrei was not a real falcon. He behaved like a real falcon—he flew, ate, crapped, had to be hooded and jessed, was trained to the lure and the whistle—but he had not been hatched from a falcon egg.

Magic. Andrei was a magical construct. There was far too much magic involved in this disappearance already; as much as Michael hated to categorize the craft, it mostly felt like evil magic. Rather, magic used for evil purposes. The mind he had felt last night, that odd, child-like mind with the power like singing wind, was blocking all magical attempts to find Ray and Estella. So probably Andrei wouldn't be able to find his...owner, for lack of a better word. The falcon wasn't precisely a familiar, but Michael was hard put to find another term for what he was.

No, it had been a good thought, but yet another blind alley. He'd have to tell Vivain, though, that she'd had a really good idea—preferably in front of Galen.

It wasn't until much later in the day, when Michael was down in his workshop designing a bracelet as a surprise gift for Mary, that it hit him.

Andrei wasn't just a magical construct.

Blood. Blood and pain. Blood and pain, and magic.

Blood called to blood. Trite, but there you had it.

The relationship between Ray and his falcon was complex. It was more than master and pet or mage and familiar. Andrei had been made from Ray's blood and pain. In a way, he literally was a dissociated part of Ray.

Michael dropped the bracelet (it could always be recast) and raced up the stairs to the kitchen, to find Andrei plaguing the ancient family dog Ruddigore.

"Can you find him?" the Archdruid asked excitedly.

The falcon screamed and leapt into the air, narrowly avoiding cracking a wing against the kitchen ceiling. Andrei was clearly saying, "It's about bloody damn time someone asked!"

Ruddigore barked.

"I guess we'd better just go home," Mitch sighed. "If I smell one more pile of dog shit, I'm going to puke."

"I've smelled enough of that, too," Evan agreed. "We tried, though, partner."

"Someone covered the trail."

"We aren't dealing with amateurs. Come on, I'm hungry."

They arrived back at Oakwoods before sunset. There was a message on the answering machine, asking someone in the household to contact Fairlawn ASAP.

"I think we can find them," Michael said without preamble when he heard Evan's voice.

"How?"

"Andrei."

"That's great! Let's go!"

"No, I think we'll need the vampires. Get everybody over here as soon as they're ready, even Rigo. We'll need the limo."

It had not been a good day. The thugs knew their stuff. Not a bone was broken, but Ray hurt all over and his lip kept bleeding. Since they'd beaten him, they'd left him locked in the room. Nobody had brought him food, though he'd been allowed some water and a bathroom trip with the inevitable jolt from the damned taser to remind him to behave.

He remembered this house. A dozen rooms, all of them cells of one description or another. Magical and mundane locks on the doors leading outside, the windows barred and magically sealed. It had been built with the very clear idea of holding prisoners. It was not a house in which a delicate, blind child should have been raised, but he supposed that Deirdre was as much a prisoner as he was.

Was Estella still alive, or had Eric killed her? Ray had no way of knowing. He hoped the twins were taking care of Andrei for him. He wasn't sure what would happen to the falcon if he died.

After Ray had been left alone for most of the day, Eric came in. Of course he was backed by the thugs, but Ray hurt too much to try anything, anyway. He hadn't seen any of the other coven members yet, but of course he wouldn't, not until he'd promised to be their leader.

"Enjoying yourself?" Eric asked.

"I can't be your coven leader if you beat the hell out of me and starve me to death." Ray was having trouble mustering defiance.

"Oh, I won't let you starve." Eric nodded, and one of the thugs left the room. He returned shortly with a tray.

"You think I'm going to touch food you prepared?"

Naturally, he ended up being forced to at least drink the soup. It was swallow or drown.

"I wouldn't use drugs," Eric said. "They're too easy. No, you must eat, or I won't let you see your girlfriend."

"Estella's okay?" Ray croaked. The soup had been, apparently, drug free. He tried some bread, wincing as it hurt to chew.

"Of course. I told you, she's insurance. I don't waste insurance unnecessarily."

"And you'll let me see her?"

"I'm not a cruel man," Eric lied. "Of course I will."

Estella, too, had not passed an easy day, but most of her worries were about Ray. She'd been fed and treated fairly well; nobody had beaten her or tortured her although nobody had spoken to her, either. Then, sometime in the afternoon, one of the strong-arms had come for her.

"You're to follow me," he said. "And don't try anything smart, or I'll use the taser on you."

Here it comes, Estella thought, *the torture.* She remembered some of Ray's scars, and shuddered.

But she was not led into a room with chains and branding irons. Rather she was taken into a nice little bedroom, somewhat sparely furnished, where a child sat on a bed.

The thug warned her again not to try anything smart, and left her there, closing the door.

The sightless eyes turned to Estella, and her heart went out to this too-thin waif.

"You can See," said the child, and Estella heard the capital letter.

"Yes."

"Can you See my name?"

"No. Names are not something I can tell. Not usually, at any rate," she amended, because sometimes she could. It was rare, though.

"I am Deirdre."

"Hello, Deirdre. I'm Estella."

"Yes. I know. You are the Seer. You came with the murderer of my father."

"Your...father?" More information Ray hadn't given her. Imagine Matthew for a father!

"My mother died, too. The vampire killed her. The blond one."

"Francis? Francis killed your mother?"

"She was cast from the cliff, into the sea. Falling, falling, falling."

"Who takes care of you, then?"

"Eric. He has been my father and mother. I cannot go out, so Eric tells me of the world and the wickedness in it."

I just bet he does, Estella thought. "Don't you want to go out?"

"I cannot. I must stay here, and be the keeper."

"The keeper of what?"

"Secrets."

"You can keep secrets and still go outside! Haven't you ever been outside? Don't you go to school?"

The girl shuddered. Estella was getting a better and longer look at her than Ray, and realized that Deirdre was older than she at first seemed. The thinness, blindness and general delicacy made her seem very young, but that was not a little girl's body. She had to be at least Vivain's age, if not a year or two older. The comparison was devastating for poor Deirdre. Vivain was a healthy, active, fairly normal thirteen year old girl.

"I do not go to school," Deirdre said. "I am too different."

"There are schools for blind children!" Estella would have smacked Eric, regardless of the consequences, had he walked into the room at that moment. He had kept this child a prisoner, never even allowed her outside, let alone to school! No wonder she was so strange.

"No, not because I am blind, but because I have magic," Deirdre said simply. "I helped Eric bring you here. I hold your boyfriend's magic."

"How…?" Estella began.

But Deirdre had turned her face away. "I'm tired. Please go away now."

Estella didn't have the heart to press this delicate child any further. She went to the door and opened it, and was escorted back to her cell by the silent thug.

She was brought a meal, of sorts, a while later. "Let me talk to Eric," she asked the guard.

"Oh, he'll be coming to see you. So just shut up and eat."

She shut up and ate.

Time passed, and her door was unlocked again.

"I've brought you a visitor," Eric said. He stepped aside, and two of the thugs entered, dragging someone between them. It was Ray. Bruised, swollen-lipped, but alive.

Estella didn't waste time asking dumb questions, like "Are you okay?" because he wasn't, or "What did they do to you?" because it was painfully obvious what they had done. She glared at Eric, who merely looked amused, and sat Ray down in the one chair.

"Have you had anything to eat?" Estella asked, wishing she hadn't eaten all of the food that had been brought to her.

He nodded. "Looks worse than it is," he whispered.

"Don't bullshit me, Ray."

"Nothing's broken. I've had worse."

"But this time," said Eric conversationally, "if you refuse me, then my assistants will do the same thing to your girlfriend."

"My mother is going to take you to pieces," Estella said.

When full darkness had settled in for the night, the members of the Brotherhood of Darkness, plus Rigo, once more gathered in the meeting room at Fairlawn. There were signs that they had come in some haste—uncombed hair, missed buttonholes, a smudge of dirt. Several eyebrows were raised at the sight of the thirteen year old twins seated on chairs next to their father.

"They've earned the right," Michael said, anticipating questions. "It was Vivain's idea that led me to believe we could use Andrei." The girl grinned, enjoying the attention, while Galen scowled. Andrei, perched on Michael's desk, stretched his wings and managed to smirk, which isn't easy when you have a beak.

Maggie nodded to the other two redheads. "Aye, they're old enough," she conceded. "About time they started learning the ways of the Brotherhood." She winked at Vivain.

"So how do we do this?" Gideon asked, taking a moment to tuck his shirt in. Even he looked slightly rumpled. "We won't all fit in the limo."

"And I don't see how we can follow Andrei from an alternate dimension," Evan put in.

"Not Andrei, perhaps," Michael smiled, "but a magical tracking device, put on Andrei and attuned to the computer in the limo...?"

"Can you do that?"

The Archdruid nodded. "We are only blocked magically from contacting Ray, or finding out where he is. Nothing is blocking any other magic."

"Whoever has Ray and Estella seems to have overlooked a few

things," Joshua commented.

"I suspect that whoever it is doesn't have a very high opinion of the Brotherhood," Michael replied. "If it is Matthew's old coven, then they likely don't think that any magic other than their own is effective. They've taken our ace, I admit. But that doesn't leave us powerless."

"We still won't all fit in the limo," Gideon said.

"No, but those who can't go in the limo can fit in my minivan," Michael said. "I can travel magically without a computer."

"Can we go, Dad?" Galen asked, almost wild with excitement.

"Please?" Vivain said.

"Not this time," Michael said. Looking at their crushed faces, he added, "And not just because you're too young, or it would be too dangerous, or that your mother would kill me. But we don't know the situation we're going into or what we're facing, and if we have to protect you, we won't function properly. Besides, there isn't enough room in the van."

"Your day will come," Maggie smiled at the twins.

"Let us go!" Rigo exclaimed. "Enough talk!"

"For once, I agree with him," Francis said, from the opposite side of the room. "Let's go."

Michael looked around the room. Apart from the disappointed expressions his offspring were wearing, everyone else looked determined. "Let's go."

He put on a falconer's glove and Andrei hopped onto it. A brief green glow flickered around the falcon.

"I still do not understand," Rigo said, staring at the falcon as Andrei shrieked. "How is it that we can follow a bird? It is night. Hawks do not fly at night."

"Andrei's not an ordinary bird," Josh explained as they all made their way out to where the vehicles were parked. The twins, looking mutinous, trailed them. "He's magical, and he was made from Ray's blood. It's a bit complicated, from what I understand. Gideon was there; he might be able to explain it better."

"I was inside the church at the time of Ray's wounding," Gideon said, before Rigo could ask. "I did not see Andrei's creation. But from what I learned later, that is essentially what happened. Andrei was magicked out of blood and pain."

"But Ray's magic's being blocked," Francis spoke up, having drifted close enough to hear this conversation. "Nobody can reach him, and he can't reach us. They've probably taken his cards, he's cut off from his magic. Doesn't that mean that Andrei can't use magic, too, since he's Ray's?"

"That's what I originally thought, too," Michael said. He smiled at his youngest daughter. "Until what Vivain said made me start thinking along another line. Andrei is made from Ray's wound, yes, but not from Ray's *magic*. It was another who made him, not Ray."

Light dawned in a few eyes, though others still looked puzzled.

"What if the magic man and my niece are very far away?" Rigo asked. "How will one small bird fly so far?"

"More magic," Michael answered simply. "Andrei can travel in the same way as the limo and the van."

"Ah, magic." Rigo didn't understand, but knew better than to meddle in the affairs of wizards. "Galen, Vivain, get back inside, please," Michael said to the twins. "Everyone else, choose a vehicle; the van or the limo."

"Aw, come on, Dad, can't we please go?" Galen gave it one last try.

"No. It's a school night." That was that. The limo could seat six; besides the Oakwoods residents and Rigo, Alex came along for the ride. The Druids and Francis piled into the minivan.

"You are Romanian," Rigo nodded to Alex.

"But not Romany," Alex replied, with a slight smile. "I am a Magyar."

Rigo chuckled. "A Romanian vampire."

"I was a Count, in my lifetime," Alex sighed. "Go ahead and say it, everybody else has."

But Rigo just laughed again. "Count is not Romanian title."

"I told you, my family were Magyar—Hungarian. Count *is* a Hungarian title."

"Do you miss the old country?"

Alex stared out the window of the limo. "I have never been back," he replied, in a tone of voice not calculated to encourage further conversation.

Evan made sure everyone was buckled in, and turned the key in the ignition. He awaited Michael's signal.

Michael ushered everyone into the van, kissed his children (not without Galen making a face), made sure they went back into the house, and then unwound Andrei's jesses from the grip of the falconer's glove.

"Go find Ray and Estella for us," he said to the falcon. "If you do that, I'll personally catch a rabbit for you."

Andrei spread his wings, shook them, and leapt into the air. He circled around the van and the limo, shrieking. When he was certain he had everyone's full attention, he took off, winging frantically south along the Cliff Road.

"Follow that falcon!" Michael cried, and leapt into the van. He fastened his seatbelt as Nicholas, behind the wheel, gunned the motor.

Both vehicles peeled out of the driveway of Fairlawn, in hot pursuit.

Watching from the living room windows, the twins sighed.

"It's not *fair,"* Vivain moaned.

"It *sucks,"* her brother added.

Mary put an arm around each offspring. At times like this, she really missed Bess, who'd never expected to be a member of the Brotherhood. But her eldest daughter was studying hard at MIT.

"Come on," she said. "We'll make some popcorn and watch a DVD, okay?"

"We can go next time, right, Mom?" Vivain asked.

"That's up to your father. How about *Lord of the Rings?"*

"Okay," they chorused, hearts not in Middle-Earth.

Far down the road, first Andrei, then the mini-van, then the limousine, glowed suddenly and vanished.

Estella's head reeled from the blow Eric dealt her. A bruise was already forming—it hadn't been a polite slap. Despite herself, she felt tears welling.

"Stop it," Ray coughed, raising his head wearily. "Don't hit her again."

"That was just to get your attention," Eric said. "Do I have it?"

"Fully."

"Then you do believe me, when I say that I will have her beaten?"

"Eric, there is nothing shitty I don't believe you capable of."

"Then you admit I hold all the cards?"

"All the..." Ray stared. He hadn't even thought about the Trumps. "Where are my cards, you bastard?"

"Those things? A bit too New Age, aren't they? Nice artwork, though, I didn't know you had talent."

Ray bit his lip to keep from cursing. He didn't want to say too much about the cards. "They're mine."

"Ah, no, they're mine now, along with the keys to your car, your cell phone, and the contents of your wallet. Obviously, being on the Right Hand Path doesn't pay well."

"I don't do it for money."

"That's good, because I'm not going to offer you any. You will be coven leader for nothing, because otherwise she dies." Bates moved so quickly that even Ray had trouble following him, and suddenly there was a knife at Estella's throat.

"What happened to not killing your insurance?" Ray asked.

"I'm getting impatient."

"All right, Eric. You win." Ray spread out his hands. "Put the knife away, and we'll talk."

Knife, that was another thing Eric had taken—Ray's knife, the knife that had been his mother's and his grandfather's. Even more than the cards, it was a terrible personal loss.

Then he knew how his magic was being held. The Trumps and the knife, two things imbued with his personality and magic, could be used to lock his magic away from him.

"That's a terrible thing to teach a child," he said, when he saw that the knife was no longer near Estella's throat.

"What?" Eric asked.

"To use someone's personal belongings against them."

"Deirdre is not an ordinary child," Eric said.

"Ray, he's never let that girl outside," Estella said. "Or let her go to school."

Bates looked at her. "Technically, Deirdre does not exist. Her birth was never registered. It's difficult to send a child to school when she doesn't exist, wouldn't you agree?" He nodded towards Ray, who was still slumped in the chair, hurting too much to move. "Besides, your boyfriend can tell you what an excellent teacher I am."

Ray's eyes narrowed. "You know, I wondered why you had the strong-arms, and why there are no coven members around. It's something to do with Deirdre, isn't it?"

"You'll find out, if you do what you're told," Eric replied, though he was obviously not happy with Ray's question.

"Don't do what he says, Ray," Estella urged him. "Not even to save my life."

"Too late," Eric said. He motioned to the thugs. "Take him back to his room."

They hauled Ray to his feet, but even as he groaned, another sound came from the front of the house. Incredibly, someone knocked at the door. Ray was unceremoniously shoved back into the room with Estella, one of the thugs was left there to guard, and the door was locked.

"I hope it's kids selling Girl Scout cookies," Ray managed to quip.

Estella helped him up, glaring at the unmoving strong-arm

guard, and cleaned up his bruises and abrasions the best she could. She, too, wondered who had knocked at the door. It was too much to hope for rescue.

Cautioning his guards to stay within easy reach, Eric went to the door. Whoever it was knocked again. From the outside, this looked like a large, but ordinary, house. Probably a political campaigner or someone collecting for some charity.

He opened the door to a staggeringly lovely women, with flaming red hair, green eyes, a skirt slit to the neck, and stiletto heels.

"Hi," Maggie breathed at him, beaming from ear to ear. "I'm your local Avon representative." She stepped gracefully to one side.

Five pounds of furious feathers, beak and talons hit Eric in the face before the thugs behind him could react.

"Oh, yeah, I forgot, watch out for the falcon." Maggie laughed, then turned to the nearest muscle boy. "Let's go out to dinner and a movie."

"What?" The confused thug was watching his employer struggle with an enraged falcon; he still didn't think that one beautiful woman was much of a threat.

Maggie sighed and kicked him, hard and very accurately, in the groin. By this time, the other muscle man was moving. She stepped across the threshold and turned towards the outside.

"Come on in," she called out merrily. "It seems the owner of the house is a bit occupied, so my invitation will have to do."

Eric managed to fling off Andrei; the falcon slid, stunned, down the wall and lay in a sad little heap of brown feathers.

"Stop!" he cried out. "I do not invite you!"

"Too late, I'm afraid," said a voice at his ear.

He turned and saw fangs.

The other muscle man, stepping around his gasping, green-tinged colleague, encountered Evan. He was rapped neatly over the head with a cosh and left to lie. Evan whacked the other one, too, out of mercy.

Eric lashed out wildly at Alex, catching the vampire in the stomach, and then raced into the house.

"They'll both be dead before you can rescue them!" he called out from the top of the stairs.

Four vampires, who could move faster than thought, gave chase. Gideon turned around and headed back downstairs. He collared Mitch, who was bounding up on all fours, and said, "Let's check the windows, from the outside."

The werewolf followed his employer. Evan starting checking

rooms for more muscle, this time with a gun in hand. Michael had knelt by Andrei and was tenderly holding the falcon, his eyes closed. They let him be. Maggie was braced to meet any magical attack. Evan kicked open a door, gun drawn, then stopped in surprise. He hadn't expected to find a little girl.

"Who are you?" he asked.

The girl drew back on her bed, and turned her blind eyes to him. "Please don't hurt me," she said.

"Of course I won't hurt you," said Evan, who was the father of a girl somewhat younger than this. "I'm Evan Jones, a friend of Ray Griffin's. Is he here?"

"He killed my father. I don't want him here, but Eric does."

"Then I'll take him away with me. Estella, too. If you'll tell me where they are."

"She's nice. I like her. Eric brought them both here. Eric looks after me."

"That would be Eric Bates, right?" Ray had told Evan about Eric...but not about this strange child.

"He looks after me."

This conversation was getting nowhere, and there were bangs, yells and thuds coming from upstairs. Evan needed to be where the action was, not here.

"Listen, I'm going upstairs to see what's going on. You sit tight in here, so you don't get hurt."

"Please don't hurt Eric," the girl begged.

"I can't make any promises, honey. But don't you leave this room!"

Upstairs, indeed, Eric was in serious trouble. He had locked himself in one of the stouter cells, but it hadn't been designed to keep out vampires. The hinges were even now pulling away from the frame as Rigo and Alex hurled themselves against the door.

Francis and Josh were concentrating on finding Ray and Estella. The thug guarding them had heard all the noise and concluded that a rescue was underway. He had dragged a heavy desk in front of the door and was threatening Ray and Estella with a gun.

"If they come in here, you die," he said.

He didn't think about the window—after all, it was barred, and on the second floor.

There was a grinding noise of metal in pain, and the bars were wrenched away from the window. Less than a minute later, a vampire and a werewolf leaped through the shattering glass, shards spraying everywhere. The thug aimed wildly and fired;

there was a yelp.

"Sorry, cove, got to be silver bullets," growled a voice just before fangs descended into his throat.

Baron Gideon Redoak shook slivers of glass off of his ruined jacket and bowed to the other two occupants of the room. They were both staring at him.

"What?" he asked.

"Gideon?" Ray tried to stand up. "I don't believe you just did that."

For a brief second, Gideon winked at him. "It's not all roses and brandy, you know." He extended a hand, the manicure on which was now beyond repair, to Estella. "Shall we?"

"Is that Mitch?" Estella asked, horror and fascination mixed equally.

The werewolf raised a blood-stained muzzle. He was somewhere between both states, and having a hell of a good time. "Woof?" he said.

"I think that's about enough, Gaylord," his employer told him.

"Bum." There was a cracking noise, a blur of fur and skin, and Mitch stood up in human form. "My god, I kept my trousers on," he said in surprise. He and Gideon moved the desk away from the doorway, after kicking aside the body of the guard.

The door was opened from the outside by Francis. "Oh, hey, you look terrible," he greeted his best friend.

"Yeah, well, you didn't look so great when I rescued you, either."

"So, whose turn is it next?"

Ray just shook his head, and gratefully accepted Francis as a leaning post. Estella, looking dazed, had her hand tucked into the crook of Gideon's arm. Alex and Rigo, with Josh giving them advice, were doing their damnedest to break down a door further down the hall. Evan was just coming upstairs; he stopped and spoke to Maggie. She cast a concerned look at Ray, but went downstairs.

"The bastard is in here," Rigo grunted when everyone had reached the doorway he and Alex were demolishing. The door crashed open, the hinges weakened beyond all hope. Almost without thinking about it, Alex reached in and grabbed the man cowering inside the room.

"Who is this worm?" he asked.

"Eric Bates," Ray answered. "Matthew's right hand man. Not really much of a witch, but a power broker, the real brains of the outfit. He wanted me to replace Matthew so he could have a coven leader he could control."

"Kill him," Rigo said. "He kidnapped my niece."

"No!" cried out a voice from the steps.

Maggie had reappeared, helping Deirdre up the stairs.

"Don't release him, Alex, no matter what you hear," Ray cautioned.

"No problem," said Alex. Vampires don't tire easily.

"Who is this girl?" asked several people.

"Matthew and Gemma's daughter, Deirdre," Ray said, shifting his weight on Francis. "How'd you find us, anyway?"

"Andrei," said Michael, bringing the healed falcon upstairs.

"The gang's all here," Francis cracked.

"Deirdre," Eric said. "I want you to listen to me carefully. These people are evil. The vampire who killed your mother is here, and the man who murdered your father. Destroy them all!"

Deirdre shook herself free of Maggie's grasp. "How, Eric?"

"You know how. Remember what I taught you?"

"Getting a child to do your dirty work for you?" asked Ray. "That's beneath even you, Eric."

"She holds your magic, Griffin, she can at least destroy *you!*"

The girl held up a leather bag that she'd brought out of her bedroom. "I can use this," she said. Her sightless eyes glowed, and the hair raised on everyone present. Nobody knew how to stop her, or wanted to—she seemed so innocent and so...fragile. Yet her power was undeniable; they all felt it.

She screamed and dropped the bag, though nobody had touched her. "It hurts!" she cried out.

"Keep trying!" Eric urged her. He flung what little power he had to her, wrapping her in a cone of magic.

Unnoticed, Michael reached down and picked up the leather bag. His heart bled for the screaming girl, but there was nothing he could do for her. She gasped and dropped to the floor, still wrapped in the power. Suddenly it was Eric who screamed and sagged, unconscious, in Alex's grip.

The power around the girl crackled and went out. Michael at once went to her side, feeling for a pulse.

"She's dead."

Michael went to work on Deirdre, ignoring Eric, but it was no use. The girl was burnt out. Silence fell over the assembled Brotherhood. They all stared at the girl's slight body, unable to summon any emotion.

"She was too warped by this bastard," Ray finally said, indicating Eric's limp figure. Alex had finally dropped the witch on the floor. "She could never have been trusted. It might actually be better this way."

"What do we do about this son of a bitch?" Francis prodded Eric with his boot.

"All his power was in the girl. Let him live with the knowledge that he killed her."

Michael opened the leather bag and checked the contents. "This is yours, I believe," he said, handing it to Ray.

A jackknife. A cell phone. A wallet. Car keys. A deck of cards, cold to the touch.

At the feel of each item, power came flooding back, the locks opening in Ray's mind. "What a terrible thing to teach a child."

"She said he was kind to her," Estella sighed.

"Yes, but what other kindness did she ever know?" Ray shook his head. "No, it sounds tough, but I think I'm right. It's better this way."

"What should we do about...her?" Michael asked.

In the end, they buried the sad little body out behind the building. It was a deserted area; chances were nobody would ever find the lonely grave.

"A whole family, wiped out by the Brotherhood," Gideon said.

"Do you know how many families Matthew and Gemma destroyed?" Ray retorted.

"Come on," Michael sighed. "Let's get home, so we can look after those bruises."

"What am I going to tell my mother?" Estella groaned.

"You still owe me a weekend visit!" her mother sniffed from the telephone, once Estella had done her best to explain.

"Is now really the time, mother?" Estella sighed, looking at Ray for help.

"Of course," her mother said. "After all, we must discuss wedding plans."

"Wedding plans?"

"Wedding?" Ray repeated.

Andrei shrieked.

But I Didn't Shoot the Deputy
(2007)

"Are you okay?" Evan peered down at the young man sitting at a table in the library at Oakwoods.

The young man looked up, blue eyes widening innocently. "Fine. Why?"

"This isn't where I normally find you," Evan said. "Why have you been hanging out in the library lately?"

"Free country," Francis said. "I'm reading. That's okay, isn't it?"

"I didn't know you could read."

"Hah hah."

"What are you reading, anyway?" Evan reached for one of the books piled in front of Francis, but the young vampire snatched it out of reach.

"None of your business."

"Okay. As long as you're staying out of trouble..."

"Come on, give me a break, I haven't done anything stupid for ages."

"I know, that's what worries me. You're overdue."

Evan walked away, still wondering. Francis had been very quiet lately. Come to think of it, he had been studying last year, too, before Christmas, and had been spending a lot of time online. He'd gotten something in the mail which had seemed to please him, but he hadn't shared it with the rest of the household. This was all very odd behaviour from the boy. Should he, Evan, be worried? Speak to Gideon?

He shook his head. Gideon had enough problems, and Francis wasn't causing trouble or in trouble. Evan wanted to know what he was up to, but he had no right to probe as long as whatever it was wouldn't upset the household.

Francis waited until Evan's footsteps had faded down the stairs before cracking open the books again. That had been close.

His tongue protruded slightly from between his lips as he concentrated on the next chapter he had to read.

Thank God Evan hadn't seen the title.

He'd been quite serious, back when he'd told people he wanted to get a job. He was tired of mucking out stalls in Oakwoods and having Evan watch his every move—though that had eased off considerably lately since he'd started behaving himself.

What Francis had found out quite quickly was that nobody wanted to employ a high school dropout. What had seemed cool and rebellious in 1965 now looked stupid and pointless. Of course, he didn't tell people he'd dropped out in 1965, since he didn't look any older than 20 or so. Vampires could get a lot of fake IDs through "connections," but those connections refused to fake a high school diploma for Francis. So he had gritted his teeth, talked very privately to a surprisingly sympathetic Gideon, and knuckled down. He had taken internet courses and achieved his GED. He'd been proud of himself, but hadn't told anyone except Gideon, who'd supported him quietly. He couldn't bear the thought of being teased about it.

And now...well, he hadn't even told Gideon. White-hot embarrassment flooded over him at the mere thought of sharing this secret with anyone. The one person who did know was the one who had encouraged him to go for it—and nobody in the Brotherhood would ever believe who that one person was.

He'd gone into town for the evening. Everyone at Oakwoods assumed that their wild child was out joyriding or drinking or toking up or otherwise occupied, but Francis was pursuing his goals. The town hall, that bastion of Fletcherville, was open after dark on Thursdays, the only night it stayed open unless there was a town meeting. One of the things that could be found inside its stale-coffee-scented corridors was a board with job postings. There were never very many. Fletcherville was a town with an unemployment problem, especially in the off season.

Francis checked the board every couple of weeks or so, just in case. So far the only night job had been pumping gas, and that had lacked any appeal at all. This particular trip didn't yield anything new. Even the gas-pumping job was gone. He turned away, sighing.

"Francis?" asked a voice he knew—and dreaded.

He looked up into the sheriff's eyes. "Um. Hi, Sheriff," he said lamely.

"Never thought to see you here," said Gains.

"Just um...came to renew my motorcycle license."

Gains raised an eyebrow. "The license office is on the next floor. And besides, your license doesn't expire for another two months or so."

"Always pays to be early..."

The sheriff leaned against a door jamb and watched him closely. "You aren't in any trouble. So why are you lying to me?"

"Um."

"There's no shame in wanting a job, Francis."

"There is if you've got my reputation," Francis muttered.

"Hm." Gains studied him from head to foot. "You've been toeing the line lately, though."

Francis shrugged. "Hard not to, with Evan breathing down my neck. And I don't want to cause Gideon any more trouble than he's already got."

"That's commendable. You know, I could use a new deputy."

Francis stared at him. Surely Gains wasn't serious? "What?"

"Someone who could work nights," Gains went on, as if Francis hadn't spoken. Indeed, he didn't appear to be talking to Francis at all, just sort of thinking out loud. "Someone who knows the...special problems of the Cliff Road Crowd and their friends, who would be able to provide an...extra layer of law enforcement. Someone who could handle situations like the one we had awhile back, with Mrs. Griffin's uncle. Ayeh, could sure use a deputy like that."

"But I have a record..." Francis began.

Gains examined his fingernails. "Deputy like that...I might be willing to pull a few strings to get him on the force. Or her, of course, if there was anyone willing. A few traffic misdemeanours...no problem. Long as there's no felony charges. Course, there's a few tests. I could steer them to the right books to bone up on. Physical wouldn't be a problem, the problem would be not looking like a superhero. And the background check...well, could be made to be not a problem. For the right person."

Francis rocked on his engineer boots. A deputy? Him? It was a staggering thought.

"Course," Gains continued, still talking to himself, "whoever it was would have to keep their nose clean. No more speeding tickets. No more pot or pills."

"Um, Sheriff, looks like they want to close up the Hall," Francis said. "It was great running into you."

"Right," Gains nodded. "Behave yourself, young Francis."

Francis nodded and all but fled.

So that was why Francis was now sitting in the library at Oakwoods with *Police Officer Exam 2nd Edition—The Complete Preparation Guide* open in front of him, making study notes and hoping like hell Mitch wouldn't come in.

He'd thought about it a lot, since that conversation with Gains. Working for the police was the last thing on earth Francis had ever expected to find himself contemplating, but the 60s had been a long time ago. He wanted some self-respect, and despite his comfy quarters there, he wanted to get the hell out of Oakwoods. He was not treated badly. He had everything he could possibly want—except independence.

Also at the back of his mind, where he wouldn't admit it lurked, there was the thought that "deputy" had a certain cachet to it; and that young ladies who spurned a feckless biker boy in torn jeans might look with favour upon a man in uniform.

He just wasn't sure how he was going to keep this a secret from everybody he knew. They'd all think he'd...sold out. Or they'd laugh. Nobody would understand.

Blinking back sudden tears, Francis bowed his head over the book. Keep the mind busy, keep the loneliness at bay.

Passing the physical was pretty easy. The hard part was, as Gains had said, not looking *too* good for it. It was a snap. Francis grinned as he finished the final run, letting himself pant just a little for verisimilitude.

It had been a little harder passing the initial written test, for general knowledge of spelling, grammar, and so forth, but he had done it. Just like getting his GED.

The next written test, the one he needed the text book for, worried him a lot. He would be writing it with an impartial proctor watching him, not Gains or Ghir or a helpful Fletcher.

"It'll be okay," Gains reassured him. "There won't be any mirrors in the room, and you know how to fool a person. You'll be fine."

"Sheriff," Francis said suddenly, not sure why he was confessing, "I haven't told anybody what I'm doing. They know I'm studying but not for what."

Gains' eyebrow predictably went up. "Are you lying to

everyone? That ain't a desirable trait in a deputy."

"No, I'm not lying," Francis protested. "I'm just not...telling people."

The sheriff chuckled. "That's called lying by omission. Out of curiosity, why aren't you telling them?"

Francis mumbled something to his shoes.

"Sorry, didn't catch that."

"They'll laugh at me."

Gains shook his head. "You're a bit old to be worrying about that, ain't you?"

"They think I'm just a useless pretty boy. A leftover hippie no good for anything but shovelling shit."

"Who said that? Evan?"

'Well...nobody actually said it, but it's what they think."

The sheriff tilted back his Stetson. "Are you sure it's not what you think, Francis? Seems to me you're selling your friends a bit short. Not to mention yourself."

"Um..."

"You need the support of your friends, Francis," Gains went on, not letting him off the hook. "Promise me you'll tell someone. Ray's supposed to be your best friend. And don't you dare pull the 'but now he's married and got a kid so he's got no time for me' line. You go talk to him. Or Baron Redoak. I bet you'll feel better and they won't laugh."

"Evan will laugh. So will Mitch."

"So? You do the laughing when you're wearing the uniform and you pull Evan over for littering out his car window."

A twitch started at the corner of Francis' mouth. Suddenly, both he and Gains were laughing.

"Go on," Gains said, "go talk to your friends. I'll be very surprised if any of them laugh, except maybe Evan or Mitch. Or if they do laugh, it will be with surprise and pleasure. Get on home with you now, and study hard for that test."

"Yes, sir. Good night." Francis headed for his bike, and stopped halfway. "Oh, when I'm deputy, can I call you Gains?"

"Not if you want to sit that bike. Now go home."

"Why didn't you tell me this sooner?" Ray Griffin asked.

Francis shrugged. He and Ray were dissecting the engine of yet another vintage motorcycle. Ray had found he could make some money by buying neglected old machines cheap and restoring them, then selling them to collectors and enthusiasts for considerably more than he'd paid. It was definitely helping out the household finances; Francis had noticed a new living room couch and new kitchen curtains.

Ray was turning domestic. Francis sighed.

"What's the sigh for?" Ray asked.

"Everyone is settling down. You're married and have a kid, and now you're working..."

"It's not like a real job," Ray objected, trying to wipe oil off his face. "I don't have a boss, or a regular salary, but it's something I can do. I wasn't very happy with Estella having to be the only earner."

"You could send Eleanor out to work."

Ray snorted. "So, you got your GED. Congrats. And what are you going to do with it?"

Francis had been getting to that part. "I've been job-hunting."

The scarred mage straightened up. He looked startled. "You have?"

Andrei shrieked from his perch near the garage door. Both men ignored the falcon.

"Um, yeah. I mean, I'm really grateful to Gideon and everyone, and I like living in Oakwoods, but..."

Ray nodded. "You hate feeling like the poor cousin, and having to *be* grateful. Yeah, I understand, believe me."

"But even with my GED, there aren't very many jobs out there," Francis went on. "But when I went into town the other night to check the board...someone offered me a job, if I'd study for it."

Ray's blue eyes met Francis'. Ray was not laughing. "But that's good, isn't it? If you could study for and earn your high school diploma equivalent, surely you can study for this job. What is it?"

"Um." Francis looked at Andrei, who spread his wings but didn't shriek. The bird had an expression remarkably similar to his master. "Well, deputy."

"Deputy? Deputy sheriff?" Ray blinked. "You'd be working for Gains?"

"Yeah." Francis let out an unnecessary breath. "He seems to think I'd be useful, like if Uncle Rigo comes back to town or something, and I can work all night shifts and not complain, and..."

"But that's great."

"It is?"

"Of course it is. Good for Gains, recognizing you've got what it takes. And good for you, trying for it. Why haven't you told anybody?"

"I thought you'd laugh." Francis was glad he couldn't turn red.

Ray shook his head. "Only an asshole would laugh at you for this, Francis."

Evan laughed. "Deputy?"

Joshua glared at him. "Shut up, Ev. Francis, that's wonderful. Congratulations."

"I haven't passed the test yet," Francis said.

"You will," Mary told him, giving him a beaming smile. "Gains thinks you can, and so do I."

"Thanks, Mary." Francis beamed back at her.

Everyone had been called together for an informal social night—not an official meeting of the Brotherhood, just a gathering to be told Francis' news and so they could all see that Gideon was doing just fine as a mortal.

"We'll all have to watch our step when we're in town," Maggie grinned. "Got a new deputy who will run us in."

Galen walked over to stand in front of Francis. The young Druid was now taller and much more muscular than the blond vampire. "If you ever try and give me an unofficial, off-the-record talk, I'll pound you," Galen said conversationally.

"Wouldn't dream of it," Francis said.

"No wonder you've been holed up in the library so often," Mitch said. "I was wondering if maybe you'd found a secret stash of porn."

Gideon snorted, in a very genteel fashion. "Not in my library."

"Um..." said Evan, not looking at his boss.

"So, everybody's okay with this?" asked Francis, looking from face to face.

"Of course we are, Francis," Michael said. "It's a really good thing. We're all behind you, and if you need any help or encouragement, you can come to any of us. Can't he, Evan?"

"Uh, yes, of course." The Nameless One looked a little guilty. "Sorry I laughed, but you took me by surprise. I think you'll be a great deputy."

"And you're not shitting me?" Francis looked directly at Evan.

"No, I'm not. Scout's honour."

"I still have to pass the test," Francis said. "And the background check and all that."

"Gains as good as said Ghir will fake the background check for you," said Mitch dismissively.

"And you will pass that test if we have to chain you to the library table," Josh put in.

"We'll grill you every night," Gideon promised—or threatened.

"Um, thanks, guys," Francis said, choking a bit. He hadn't expected this much support. "This means a lot to me."

"Just pass that test," said Michael.

"Passed," Francis said quietly.

"With flying colours," added Gains.

Francis cringed slightly. The sheriff had insisted on coming with him when he made the announcement to his housemates at Oakwoods. This was in order to insure that Francis did make the announcement.

Josh jumped up and hugged Francis, who looked dreadfully embarrassed. Gideon and Evan shook his hand; Mitch punched him on the arm and said, "Wicked!"

"Of course," said Gains, eyes twinkling, "he has yet to meet the stringent hiring requirements of the sheriff's office. Just passing the test doesn't mean he gets a job."

"What?" Francis said, startled.

"I don't hire long-haired freaky hippies," Gains said, straight-faced. "You want to join the force, you're going to have to get a haircut."

Francis's jaw dropped. He'd done the studying. He'd done the tests. He'd passed the physical. He'd even given up his precious pills and pot. But...a haircut? Lose his beautiful long blond tresses?

"Forget it."

"Departmental regulations," said Gains, running a hand through his own short hair. "Can't give the bad guys something to grab."

Francis folded his arms. "They won't get that close," he said quietly.

"Francis," Joshua began, but Gains shook his head.

"This is between me and my deputy," he said politely, but firmly.

Josh opened his mouth again, met Gains' eyes, and shut it. He had to fight a grin.

"You wanted to hire me for my special qualities," Francis told Gains stubbornly. "That includes the hair. Anyone grabbing my hair will definitely be sorry."

The eyebrow went up. "Insubordination already," Gains sighed.

"Fine," said Francis. "I've proven myself, that I can do tests, and pass as a normal, I can find some other job. One where they don't give a damn about my hair..."

Gideon couldn't take it anymore. He got up out of his chair, and walked over to Francis's side. He leaned in close, putting a hand on the blond boy's arm.

"Francis," he whispered, "you've already got the job, that's what he's telling you."

"It does grow back, you know," Joshua commented.

snip

Francis choked back a sob.

snip

"As long as you're in uniform, you have to abide by the regulations, Francis," said Evan, brandishing the shears just a little too close to Francis's ears.

snip

"Yeah, okay, I know that," Francis whined. "But why did it have to be you giving me the haircut?"

"Because I'm the only one besides Mary who's ever cut hair, and she hasn't done it since the twins sported identical pudding bowl cuts at five," Evan replied calmly. "And I am the only one who knows the military regulations for hair."

"I'm not joining the military!"

"Same difference," Evan said.

snip

"Look at it," Francis said sadly, indicating the mass of blond curls on the floor. "It took me forever to get it just right."

"Think of this as the total new you makeover," Joshua suggested.

"We should have done one of those shows for television," Gideon laughed.

"What?" Mitch asked, looking up from his video game. "Pimp My Hair? Flip This Vampire? Total Makeover: Francis?"

snip

"I was thinking more along the lines of *Fear Factor,* actually," said Gideon, grinning.

snip

Evan put the scissors down and got out the razor. Francis put his hands over his head in self-protection.

"No, no, not the razor!"

"Do you want me to get the razor strop instead?" Evan breathed in his ear.

bzzt

"There," said Evan, stepping away and surveying his handiwork.

"Come on, Francis, let us see," Josh coaxed him.

Nearly in tears, Francis stood up. With his hair almost buzz-cut short, he looked odd—older.

"Now you can go and put the uniform on," said Gideon, smiling at him.

"I look like a freak!"

"No," said Joshua seriously. "You look like a man."

Twenty minutes later, when Francis came downstairs again, he was in crisp navy blue, carrying a holstered gun, a black Stetson hiding most of the new 'do. There was a badge pinned to his chest.

"Go ahead," he said morosely. "Laugh."

Nobody did. "You look great," said Joshua.

"You really do," Gideon nodded. "Congratulations, Deputy."

Francis had to sit down, he was so surprised. "You guys really mean it. You don't think I'm an idiot or a prat, and you think I can really do this."

"Of course we do," said Evan, clapping his shoulder.

"We mean it," Mitch gave him the thumbs up.

"Now get out there," Joshua pointed to the door, "and fight crime."

www.ingramcontent.com/pod-product-compliance
Lightning Source LLC
Chambersburg PA
CBHW030422310726
48979CB00009B/1571/J

* 9 7 8 1 9 3 5 3 0 3 2 6 8 *